MAGGIE NEEDS AN ALIBI

"Deliciously funny . . . Michaels handles it all with aplomb, gaily satirizing the current state of publishing, slowly building the romantic tension between Maggie and her frustratingly real hero, and providing plenty of laughs for the reader."—*Publisher's Weekly*

"Readers will relish Michaels's clever and highly amusing mystery."
—*Booklist*

"The innovative Kasey Michaels comes up with a bewitching story that will have you laughing out loud. The plot is fresh, Maggie appealing, Detective Wendell charming, and Saint Just—well, meet him and decide!"—*Romantic Times*

"A great read . . . funny and well-written."—*Mystery News*

MAGGIE BY THE BOOK

"Colorful characters and humorous dialogue populate this wonderful sequel to *Maggie Needs an Alibi* and leave the reader waiting for more."
—*Booklist*

"Romance and cozy fans will welcome this cross-genre sequel to Michaels's *Maggie Needs an Alibi*, with its original premise, sympathetic if reluctant heroine, and lively supporting cast."—*Publishers Weekly*

"Once again, we're thrown into mayhem and enjoy every moment. Kasey Michaels's unique voice has developed another song—a true joy. Oh, what fun! More please."—*Rendezvous*

MAGGIE WITHOUT A CLUE

"Michaels delivers more fantasy and fun in her third witty, well-plotted cozy . . . a surprising conclusion will leave readers wanting more."
—*Publishers Weekly*

"Pure magic—if you love a good mystery, lots of laughter and a touch of romance, Maggie's your girl. As always, Kasey Michaels tickles the funny bone and touches the heart. If you haven't met Maggie yet, what are you waiting for?"—Mariah Stewart, *New York Times* bestselling author

HIGH HEELS AND HOMICIDE

"Michaels has a true flair for observant characterizations, witty dialogue and high crime, and Saint Just is simply delicious. Really good fun."
—*Romantic Times*

"A wonderful send-up of the British country house murders and the movies thereof. A colorful delight."—*Mystery Lovers Bookshop News*

Books by Kasey Michaels

Can't Take My Eyes off of You

Too Good to Be True

Love to Love You, Baby

Be My Baby Tonight

This Must Be Love

This Can't Be Love

Maggie Needs an Alibi

Maggie By the Book

Maggie Without a Clue

High Heels and Homicide

High Heels and Holidays

Bowled Over

Published by Kensington Publishing Corporation

Bowled Over

KASEY MICHAELS

KENSINGTON BOOKS
http://www.kensingtonbooks.com

KENSINGTON BOOKS are published by

Kensington Publishing Corp.
850 Third Avenue
New York, NY 10022

All Kensington titles, imprints and distributed lines are available at special quantity discounts for bulk purchases for sales promotion, premiums, fund-raising, educational or institutional use.

Special book excerpts or customized printings can also be created to fit specific needs. For details, write or phone the office of the Kensington Special Sales Manager: Kensington Publishing Corp., 850 Third Avenue, New York, NY 10022. Attn. Special Sales Department. Phone: 1-800-221-2647.

Kensington and the K logo Reg. U.S. Pat. & TM Off.

ISBN-13: 978-0-7582-0884-2
ISBN-10: 0-7582-0884-7

First Kensington Trade Paperback Printing: November 2007
10 9 8 7 6 5 4 3 2 1

Printed in the United States of America

To Elsie Hogarth, with many thanks!

"Ay me! For aught that ever I could read,
Could ever hear by tale or history,
The course of true love never did run smoothe."

—William Shakespeare,
A Midsummer Night's Dream

"If I had as many affairs as you fellows claim,
I'd be speaking to you today
from a jar in the Harvard Medical School."

—Frank Sinatra,
Life magazine, 1965

Once upon a time . . .

. . . there was a girl named Margaret Kelly, who longed to grow up, leave her New Jersey home, and become a Famous Author in New York.

Of the three hopes, the *leaving home* part often ranked right up there at Number One.

Very often. Exceedingly often. Depressingly often.

And one day Maggie—now known only to her mother and her shrink, Doctor Bob, as Margaret—achieved two of the big three.

She grew up.

She left home.

The Famous Author part didn't naturally follow.

Maggie began her fiction-writing career in Manhattan as Alicia Tate Evans, employing her mother's first name, her brother's first name, and her father's first name, all to make up what she thought would be a whiz-bang, romantic-sounding pseudonym. Maybe even an important name, one with the power to impress the hell out of publishers and hint that maybe she'd majored in English Literature or Quantum Physics, or something, and would thus be Taken Seriously and given promotion and her own twenty-four copy dump in the front of the chain stores.

After all, publishers, by and large, have to be told you're marketable, and worthy, and all that good stuff—they can't seem to figure that out on their own just by looking at your work. If you'd slept with Brad Pitt, you were in. If you'd murdered your lover, you were in. If you'd scaled Everest in your skivvies, you were in.

But if you were just an average person from an average background, had average looks, an average bust size, an average head of brown hair, and you sat down and wrote a good book? Even a bordering-on-great book? Well, that was iffy . . .

Maggie knew all of this. She'd joined a writers group, We Are Romance (WAR—something nobody considered when christening the group), and she'd heard the horror stories. The quality of the work was important. Sort of. But, hey, can you sing, dance, or conjugate verbs in Ancient Greek? Give us something we can promote.

So Maggie gave them Alicia Tate Evans.

The idea that her parents and brother would be grateful, even proud, might possibly have entered into this decision just a tad, but it wasn't as if Maggie was sucking up to the family that never really understood her.

Much.

Anyway, the name was just perfect for Maggie's historical romance novels that would soon top the *New York Times* bestseller list on a regular basis.

Six published novels later, the *NYT* wasn't even in sight, and her mother and brother, less than flattered to have their names on "those trashy books" had not become Maggie's biggest fans.

Her dad was okay with it, but Evan Kelly was okay with most everything . . . nobody yelled at him if he just nodded, agreed with every word his wife said, and otherwise kept his mouth shut. Evan Kelly had earned his master's degree in Wimp, probably by the first anniversary of his marriage to Alicia Tate.

Maggie worried, a lot, that she was the female Evan Kelly, especially when her mother continually asked her why she didn't write a *real book* and she couldn't figure out a snappy answer. Hence Doctor Bob's presence in her life.

But back to Maggie and her great critical reviews, lame titles picked by committee (and maybe by the UPS guy who'd wandered through the office in his spiffy brown shorts and was asked for input), on the cheap cover art, lousy print runs, nonexistent publisher support, mediocre sell-throughs and—my, what a shock!— serious lack of name recognition after those half-dozen novels.

It came to pass after those half-dozen historical romances, with her career not exactly taking off like the proverbial rocket, that

Maggie found herself cut loose from her publishing house, Toland Books.

Alicia Tate Evans was dead in the water. Good-bye, good luck, don't let the door hit you in the fanny on the way out.

This left Maggie depressed. And broke. With no prospects.

All things being equal, and Maggie prepared to garbage can surf rather than crawl back to New Jersey and the "I told you so, Margaret" marathon bound to follow, she had herself a major pity party that included two half gallons of chocolate ice cream and three, yes, three, jars of real chocolate fudge topping.

She then sat down (first opening the button on her suddenly too-tight jeans), to reinvent herself.

She gave a moment's thought to renaming herself Erin Maureen, for her two sisters, but Erin, at the least, would probably sue.

And then, inspiration struck. Near the end of the third day of fierce concentration, Maggie Kelly became Cleo Dooley. She became Cleo Dooley instead of, say, Maggie Kelly, because she'd done some market research online while riding her chocolate high, and she'd concluded that a remarkable number of *NYT* authors had Os in their names.

Os also looked good on a book cover.

And think of chocolate, for pity's sake. Popular? Definitely. So notice the Os: Ch-O-c-O-late. Two of them, in that one wonderful word and three in the phrase "O-ne w-O-nderful w-O-rd," but that was probably pushing it.

In any case, enough said. Os, obviously, were the way to go.

All that was left to do now was to write the perfect book, and she'd be back in the game she'd been, even though published, mostly watching from the sidelines in the low-rent district, the dreaded midlist.

She needed a foolproof hook, something that would grab the readers right out of the box.

Historicals. Historicals worked. But sex also worked—her online market research told her that sex worked even better than historicals.

Not to mention that you didn't have to figure out new ways to say, "He reached for the foil packet," every time you put an

English Regency Era hero and heroine in bed. There were many perks in writing historical romance, but to Maggie, this one pretty well topped the list: the lack of the "oh, yuck, again?" factor.

And series books. Man, create a popular series, and you're home free.

A mystery series? Yes! But an historical mystery series, because Maggie knew more about Regency Era England than most sane people would think useful.

A sexy historical mystery series?

Whacka-whacka! Eureka! Don't you love it when a plan comes together! Pass the ch-O-c-O-late, Cle-O!

This was good. This was workable. Even d-O-able . . . um, *doable*. She was soon going to have to stop counting Os, or she might need professional help—more professional help than she was already getting with Doctor Bob (more Os!), or would, until she depleted her savings.

Ah, but the perfect series needs the perfect hero.

God. Doesn't everyone?

There was, luckily, another jar of chocolate fudge topping inspiration in the fridge.

With a teaspoon loaded with cold chocolate fudge firmly upside down in her mouth, Maggie sat down and went about creating Alexandre Blake, the Viscount Saint Just.

The perfect hero.

Everything she'd ever longed-for, lusted after in her daydreams, sighed over since hitting puberty, all wrapped up in one gorgeous hunk of man.

So where had all the heroes gone?

To the movies?

Maggie had a thing for old movies. She also had a pitiful social life, which explained why she had so much Saturday night time for old movies on cable. There definitely was no dearth of heroes in those old movies.

A little lean, flinty Clint Eastwood as he looked way-back-when in those spaghetti westerns. A little suave, sophisticated Sean Connery as James Bond, the only James Bond who really counted, except for Pierce Brosnan. So she threw some Pierce into the mix—everybody needs a little Pierce.

Maggie giggled at that. Who said she couldn't write sexy books?

She tossed in some veddy-veddy-English upper crust Peter O'Toole as he'd looked in *Lawrence of Arabia*. A bit of this guy, the meltingly sexy voice of that one, the mouth from this one, the eyebrows from another, the brooding indigo blue eyes of another one. On and on, slowly, as the level of fudge in the jar went down, she mentally constructed The Man in Every Woman's Heart.

And every woman's libido. That, too. Definitely.

She tossed in a few more physical attributes that, well, rang her bells, and finally had a mental picture of the perfect hero. Her perfect hero.

Handsome. Oh-God-Yes!

And smart. Leave the good-looking boy-toys for someone else—Maggie believed the perfect hero ought to have an IQ larger than his collar size.

Rich. Rich was good. As someone very wise once said, it's as easy to love a rich man as it is a poor man.

Witty. Sophisticated. A little bit arrogant, because the best heroes always were arrogant. In a nice way, of course.

Confident, something she wasn't, but Saint Just would be an absolute whiz at confident.

Brave, honest, steadfast—wait, that was the Boy Scouts, right? Unless a person had a square knot that needed tying or a pup tent to raise, who needed a Boy Scout? Not a perfect-hero-hungry woman! Let there be a little bit of larceny in the man's soul.

Maggie was on a roll. Knock her down, would they! Try to send her home to New Jersey, would they!

Heh-heh-heh. *Heh!*

Six weeks later, the Viscount Saint Just had become the hero of his very first book, *The Case of the Misplaced Earl.*

He was tall, lean, muscular, to-die-for handsome. He flattered his tailor just by wearing his clothes with the sort of elegant panache of a true gentleman. He carried a cane that concealed a thin rapier inside it. He favored a quizzing glass hung from his neck by a black grosgrain ribbon, and employed it to great effect when he stared down a villain. His coal black hair was done in the windswept style favored by Beau Brummell. He could ride, drive, shoot, fence, box, and recite Shakespeare.

He was a near god. He was Alexandre Blake, the sophisticated, wealthy, handsome Viscount Saint Just.

He was the perfect Regency gentleman. He was the perfect hero.

With the help of her friend and former editor, Bernice Toland-James, Maggie sneaked in the back door of Toland Books once more, this time as Cleo Dooley, bringing Saint Just and his sexy mind and body with her.

A few *The Case of . . .* Saint Just mysteries later, hello, *NYT!*

And that's how it stayed for several years—Maggie and her imaginary perfect hero. Cleo Dooley wrote the books, the to-die-for sexy Viscount Saint Just solved the crimes and bedded all the lucky ladies, and Maggie Kelly giggled all the way to the bank.

Never mind that she smoked too much, talked to her two cats too much, whined to Doctor Bob every Monday morning at nine, got out socially entirely too little, and had developed this unnerving habit of comparing every man she met to her perfect hero and finding those men lacking. Hey, she wasn't in New Jersey!

So where was she, exactly? This was a question she tried not to ask herself too often as she edged toward her thirty-first birthday, because she didn't much like the answer.

But then something strange happened.

The Viscount Saint Just happened. Alexandre Blake *happened.* Really.

One day Maggie turned around in her solitary Manhattan apartment, and there he was, in all his Regency Era glory.

She recognized him immediately. Why not? She'd *built* him.

And there was his sidekick, the lovable Sterling Balder, the darling, naïve, perfectly adorable comic relief, the sweetheart of a guy she'd created because even perfect heroes need someone to talk to or else they'd be talking to themselves, and folks tend to look at such people a little strangely.

Saint Just explained to Maggie—after she'd recovered from her faint—that she'd made him and Sterling so real, so complete, that they were able to "move onto her plane of existence."

Mostly he, Saint Just, after living inside Maggie's head for several years, observing her, was here, so he said, because she needed him.

Of course she did . . .

For the past several months Saint Just, known to Maggie's friends as her very distant English cousin, Alex Blakely, and his friend Sterling Balder, known as Sterling Balder because the fellow couldn't possibly carry off an alias without tripping over it, have lived in Maggie's world. They had been, she told her friends, the inspiration for her now famous characters.

Her friends believed her.

Some people will believe anything.

Maggie had stopped smoking, although she still saw Doctor Bob every Monday morning at nine. She talked about her childhood years, her fears, her hang-ups . . . even her inability to say good-bye to Doctor Bob and make it stick.

But she'd yet to tell him about Saint Just.

After all—she wasn't crazy. Even if she, after a terrible inner battle wherein she weighed common sense against the allure of the perfect hero—common sense losing in twenty-two seconds of the fifth round—was now romantically involved with a figment of her imagination.

Definitely a *once upon a time* sort of fairy tale, even if you couldn't exactly count on a slam dunk happily-ever-after when one was dealing with an imaginary hero come to life who could, you know, *poof* back out of your life as quickly as he'd poofed in.

This was, as Sterling would have said, "a worriment."

And then there's that other problem. Ever since the sexy, crime-solving Saint Just did his poof thing into Maggie's life, people around her seem to keep turning up murdered.

Chapter 1

Maggie sat with her back to her computer, looking around her living room, which also served as her office, her dining room, her den, her library, her—how had she ever thought this arrangement worked for her?

Claustrophobics-R-Us.

Figuratively choking herself with both hands as she stuck out her tongue and gurgled, she decided, once and for all, that she had to relocate. Expand. Grow.

Leave Alex.

Whoa.

Leave Alex?

This time the gurgle was audible, closely resembling a whimper.

Not that Alex lived with her anymore, showing up in her kitchen early in the morning, looking put together while she leaned against the sink in her ratty pajamas, just trying to stand up straight until her morning caffeine kicked in.

He wasn't sleeping just down the hall anymore, leaving the top off her toothpaste, beating every password protection she put on her computer, and generally driving her insane.

No. He was now gainfully employed as a perfume company's photo model, financially self-sufficient, and happy, living in his own condo directly across the hall. He and Sterling both were happy.

She was happy, having them live directly across the hall.

She could watch out for him, keep an eye on him, make sure he didn't do anything too herolike.

And then there was the fact that, once Sterling was tucked up in bed, Alex could tiptoe across the hall to her for a few hours and they could . . . well, how could she possibly leave Alex?

And the idea of moving had nothing—nothing!—to do with the fact that her onetime friend and now archnemesis, fellow author Felicity Boothe Simmons (once Faith Simmons, back before she went *NYT* and figuratively left the planet), had just bought herself a two-level condo soon to be featured in *Architectural Digest*.

Nothing to do with that. Absolutely nothing.

Okay, maybe a little bit.

But there were better reasons.

Maggie's accountant had told her she needed the interest deduction. Her bathroom was too small; she didn't even have a bathtub, for crying out loud.

She had to keep her new treadmill in the living room (the treadmill a gift from Faith no less, given just so that Faith could comment without commenting that Maggie still hadn't lost the weight she'd gained after she quit smoking), and Sterling had this way of walking in without knocking, to see her sweating bullets as she ran her tail off in the hopes of running her tail off.

There were a lot of reasons for her to move, sell the condo, buy a bigger one. Good reasons.

And one very big drawback. Leaving Alex.

But she'd just signed a new contract with Toland Books. An obscene contract. It wasn't as if she didn't have the money, plus most of the money she'd earned in the past six years. When success hit in the publishing arena, it hit. Big. Even her earlier Alicia Tate Evans novels had been re-released, and were in their sixteenth printing, for crying out loud.

So she had buckets of money, and it wasn't because, as Alex had teased on more than one occasion, she squeezed every penny until it squealed.

Okay, maybe a little bit.

For crying out loud.

"*For crying out loud*, I'm becoming *a little bit* redundant," she said, looking over at her Christmas tree, which had been shoved into the corner of the small room. Faith's tree had been a good twenty-feet high in her two-story living room. It was pink, with real crystal ornaments, and probably snowed on itself. Not that it mattered, for crying out loud, even a little bit.

Maggie swiveled back to face her desk and looked once more at the real estate page she'd brought up on the computer screen.

The building pictured on the screen was big. Extremely big. And it had character.

If you could call vaguely resembling a wedding cake having character.

Constructed of light gray stone, the ground floor had its own straight lines and straight roof, but then the next three floors rose in half-rounded tiers. Like a wedding cake.

Built in 1897, it had seven huge bedrooms, nine fireplaces, seven full bathrooms, two kitchens, a couple of balconies, a pair of staircases, a rooftop garden, and an enclosed backyard fashioned of marble, or something. At any rate, there were two huge stone greyhounds guarding the entrance to the patio like twin sphinxes.

If stone greyhound sentries didn't say class, what did?

And the house—not a floor, not a condo, an entire house!—was on West Seventy-sixth Street, just off Broadway. Close to Central Park, not too far away from Riverside Park, and not within easy walking distance of Faith's pink and white penthouse on the Upper East Side.

The interior had original woodwork to die for, kitchens that would be any gourmet's dream—Maggie didn't really care about the kitchens, but Sterling would—and the main room on the top floor had a twenty-by-forty-foot glass ceiling. A domed, many-paned glass ceiling! Jeez.

The house called to her.

Alex called to her.

She needed both of them.

She looked at the page again.

Much too large a place for one person, definitely, but not at all too large for three people. Alex and Sterling could move in, maybe even share expenses, and they could all be together and yet private from one another, even while they were all under the same glass roof.

Maggie loved it when a plan came together.

And all for only six million nine hundred and fifty dollars. For Manhattan, for a house like that, six million nine hundred and fifty dollars was pretty much chump change. Right?

"Meanwhile, back in the land of reality," Maggie muttered to herself, closing the window on a photograph of the roof garden. "Besides, when you get to nearly seven million, why bother with the fifty bucks on the end? That's so tacky."

Wellington, the black male Persian, stood up, stretched, and waddled over to rub himself against Maggie's ankles.

"I wasn't talking to you, fish-breath. I was talking to myself," Maggie told him, reaching down to scratch behind his ears. "But, as long as you're here—would you like a new house, hmm? It's got a walled garden out back. I could open the door, and you and Nappy could go outside, sprawl belly-up in the sun. You'd like that, wouldn't you?"

Wellington purred, rubbed his head against her hand.

"Sure, that's it," Maggie said, inspired. "I'm the old maid cat lady, thinking about buying a nearly seven-million-dollar house so her cats can lie in the sun. Is that as bad as Faith enrolling that pee-machine mutt of hers in doggy day care? No, it's probably worse. Cripes. Worse than Faith. You got to go some to be worse than Faith, Welly, trust me."

Wellington looked up at Maggie, meowed something probably Persian-speak for "I'm going to assume we're through here," and headed back to the still-warm spot on the carpet.

Maggie swiveled back to face the screen and called up the Realtor listing again. There it was; bottom right corner of the page: Rodgers Regency Realty. Regency? Like the English Regency, the one in which her perfect hero cavorted? Was that an omen, or what?

Especially the cavorting part.

It could work.

But did she have the guts to actually *do* this?

She and Alex and Sterling were leaving for New Jersey in a few days for the Annual Kelly Dysfunctional Christmas. By the time she got back, the house could be sold. An opportunity, gone.

Then she'd spend the next year or so kicking herself around the apartment, bemoaning her missed opportunity. And, with the size of this place, she'd be dizzy in a week, just from booting herself in circles.

She looked toward the bookcase, saw the Dan Mittman book Doctor Bob had given her for Christmas. Remembered a quote from the book: *The time is now, the place is here. Stay in the present. You can do nothing to change the past, and the future will never come exactly as you plan or hope for.*

Not so shabby, Danny boy, even if you ended with a preposition.

Maybe even prophetic.

Maggie picked up her nicotine inhaler—minus its medicinal cartridge now, so that it was, in reality, a pacifier—sucked on it like the pitiful ninny she was, and then reached for the phone.

And now for a little author intrusion

As Maggie knows, one of the time-honored (or timeworn) ways to heighten anticipation and keep readers turning the pages while the author is busily filling in the background information several books into an on-going series, is to introduce some shadowy figure at about this point.

Put him in italics at the end of a chapter, make him sort of deep, sort of ambiguous, sort of scary.

Foreshadowing. Foreboding. Dropping an oblique hint or two. Maybe a red herring to throw off the armchair crime-solver. Setting the hook in the reader's mouth.

Or, if feeling less literarily inclined—flipping the reader a fish.

One way or another, fish always seem to be involved . . .

Anyway.

The object of the exercise is that the reader hears the footsteps, knows Something Wicked This Way Comes a few chapters down the road.

So what the hell, why not.

Introducing, ta-da, the Shadowy Figure.

Just don't count on the baddie being *deep*. Not in Maggie's world . . .

Sometimes you just have to do what you have to do. Circumstances demanded as much.

And it wasn't like, hey, there were a million different ideas out there. Just this one. A good idea. Good ideas didn't come along that often. There had been Dad and the hula hoop, but somebody else got there first.

Somebody else was always getting there first.
Now. What about the weapon . . . ?
A gun?
God, no. Too loud.
A knife?
Ix-nay on the knife. Too messy.
Strangulation? No way. Much too up close and personal.
Okay, okay. So the idea still needed some work . . .

See? That's how it's done. Fun, huh? And not just senseless banter, either, because that wouldn't be fair to the reader. There's a clue in there, honest!

We'll do it again in a little bit. Stay tuned.

Chapter 2

Saint Just pushed open the heavy wooden door with the tip of his sword cane and peered into the darkness. "And this would be . . . ?" he asked Kiki Rodgers, daughter of the owner of Rodgers Regency Realty. Or, as Kiki had explained, pointing to the three gold Rs circled in gold thread on the pocket of her navy blazer, "That's our brand, sugar. The Triple R. Daddy's originally from Texas."

Saint Just wasn't as familiar with Texas as he probably should be, because he'd only been able to look at Maggie in confusion as they'd both stared at Kiki's remarkable bosom when they'd first met, without trying to look as if they were staring, and Maggie had whispered, "They like everything big in Texas, sugar."

In truth, he was still trying to sort out what was happening, as Maggie's request that he and Sterling accompany her to view a house she was considering purchasing was so completely out of character for the woman, who never did anything spontaneously, never acted on a whim—at least when it came to parting with a penny of her hard-earned money.

She studied every advertisement in the newspapers before she went shopping, planning her route, laying out her itinerary, and even then only purchased something new when he would finally put his foot down, insisting that she make a choice. He doubted she bought a packet of gum without first considering the thing.

And she was a creature of habit. The ornaments on her Christmas tree had to be placed in the same positions they'd been hung the previous years.

She always hesitated for a moment—five seconds, he'd decided, after keeping a mental count on several occasions—before putting out her foot (left foot first), and descending any staircase.

Her bacon went on the left side of her plate, her scrambled eggs always to the right. Even if she had to turn the plate around after it was placed in front of her.

She sat in the same chair, at the same table at Mario's, at Bellini's.

She always laid her napkin in her lap immediately, and then carefully rearranged the cutlery, moving the knife and spoon from the left and putting them to her right.

He could go on. Indefinitely.

Maggie was a creature of habit. A traditional person, one with routines, even rituals. Compulsive, in a nice way, he'd have to say. Reliable. Dependable.

Never spontaneous.

He didn't like feeling off balance, not the one in control. But Maggie seemed to have taken the bit between her teeth on this business of purchasing a new domicile, and what were women created for, if not to indulge them?

"Why, sugar," Kiki told him, suddenly not more than an inch away, her lush body brushing his as she leaned in beside him, "that there's the steps down to the wine cellar."

Behind them, Maggie chirped, "A real, honest-to-God wine cellar? I don't remember seeing that on the listing. Oh, *wow*."

Kiki turned to smile at her client. "Yes, it is exciting, isn't it? Here, let me show you," she said, reaching past Saint Just to turn on the light.

Saint Just stood back to allow her to precede them down the stairs, and then ushered Maggie and Sterling ahead of him before following the small troop to the cool, stone-walled room the size of Maggie's living room.

By the time he'd reached the bottom of the stairs, Maggie was poking about the floor-to-ceiling, freestanding shelves, gushing excitedly that she felt as if she was in "a library for wine."

"Yes, although depressingly small, don't you think?" he said, lifting his quizzing glass to his eye as he peered at the dusty label of one of the half dozen or more wine bottles still lying in holders on the shelves. Those few bottles had probably gone to vinegar and had therefore been left behind at the time of the previous owner's departure. "I do very much fear that my own cellars—plural, Miss Rodgers—at Blake Manor would dwarf this paltry attempt."

"Oh, for God's sake, Alex," Maggie muttered quietly, "you don't have a wine cellar. Cellars. You don't have a Blake Manor. I made all that up, just like I made you up. Remember?"

"I *remember*, my dear, that the more interest one shows in a purchase, the higher the price and the less reason to negotiate toward a lower one," he responded just as quietly. "You take my point?"

Maggie shot a quick look toward Kiki, who was deep in conversation with Sterling about the joys of the kitchen they'd just viewed. "Oh, okay, I get it. Sterling's going a little overboard, right? Should we call him off?"

"Possibly," Saint Just responded, tamping down a smile. "Although I believe I was referring mostly to you, and this distressing tendency to gush '*oh, wow*' every time a new door is opened."

"Oh." But then she grabbed his arm and pulled him behind the last rack, obviously not quite understanding the acoustics of a fifteen-by-fifteen foot cube constructed entirely of stone. "I want this house, Alex. It's perfect. We can be private, we can be together, we can—you know damn full well Faith doesn't have a wine cellar. A cooler, maybe. One of those under-the-kitchen-counter deals, but not a cellar. I mean, she lives on what, the twenty-sixth floor, or something? No way can she have an authentic wine cellar. Is that petty? Don't answer that."

"As I quite value my neck, yes, I do believe I will refrain from comment. I will, however, take my life into my own hands and ask if you're seriously considering purchasing a house in order to upset Miss Simmons, as it seems out of character for you, my dear."

"I know. My bad, right? But that's not why, okay? It's just that Faith got me thinking, you know? If she can buy a monstrosity like she bought, then I should be able to take a chance, a leap of faith—no pun intended—and believe in myself and my future enough to make a purchase of this size. You know what a purchase like this says, Alex? This house? This house says I've made it. I'm not going to get tossed out on my ear again, because I've got a real career. A real future. I'm secure. I mean, you can't owe as much money as mortgaging this place would cost, not if you weren't confident about your future. Right? This house, the mortgage—they'd be like affirming statements."

"Are you insinuating that you'd purchase this house in order to convince yourself of your own worth?"

Maggie frowned. "Don't be logical, Alex. And stop playing Doctor Bob, okay? I want this house. I want . . . I want *us* to have this house."

"Ah, now that's comforting. You've decided that I'm . . . staying?"

"It's been months, Alex, and you haven't poofed yet. So, yes, I've decided you're probably here to stay, that you're evolving, like you keep saying, becoming more your own person and not just my creation. Making your own place in . . . well, in the real world. It's goofy, but I'm beginning to believe it. Is that all right with you? That I'm thinking about making . . . plans?"

"I can say with all truthfulness, yes, I'm delighted. But you do pick your moments, my dear. We could hardly be less private, if you've taken it into your head to propose."

"I'm *proposing* us living in sin, not getting married," Maggie said, blushing delightfully to the roots of her thick, artfully sun-streaked brown hair.

"But you have been sadly compromised," he pointed out to her.

"Not exactly sadly," Maggie said, grinning at him.

"It is my duty as a gentleman to protect your reputation by offering my hand in—shall I go on?"

"No, I know the drill. But forget the drill. Are you with me on this house thing, or not?"

Saint Just peeked out from behind the rack as Kiki informed them that she and Sterling were going back upstairs for another look at the six-burner gas stove Sterling had been loathe to leave in the first place.

"You just follow when you want, sugar."

Maggie opened her mouth to answer—or to ask just who Kiki

thought she was calling *sugar*—but Saint Just put a fingertip to her lips, keeping her silent.

"We'll join you in a few moments, Miss Rodgers," he told her as Maggie glared at him.

Maggie pushed his finger away once Kiki and Sterling's footsteps could be heard on the wood floor of the kitchen above. "So what's your problem, Alex, because you obviously have one. You say you don't have a problem, but you do, don't you? Is it this house? Or me? Is it me? You don't want to live here with me?"

" 'There is a Spanish proverb, which says very justly, Tell me whom you live with, and I will tell you who you are.' "

"The Earl of Chesterfield," Maggie said, nodding. "So what do you think the earl would say about you, living with me?"

Saint Just thought on this for a moment. "That I, an esteemed member of the peerage and thus a person who should know better, should be horsewhipped? That, or that I, too, should be visiting weekly with Doctor Bob."

"Ha-ha. Nobody said ours was a . . . a normal association. Well, somebody might, if they knew what was going on, how you got here, but then that person probably wouldn't be normal. But it's normal for us, right? So that can't be the reason. Maybe you don't want to share expenses? Maybe you want to stay where you are, not live with me again? Because I'm not staying where I am. It's time I owned my own house, put down . . . put down roots."

"A commendable aspiration, I'm sure. I also thank you very much for your kind invitation to include Sterling and myself. I have absolutely no problems with the move, the purchase. However, I do feel somewhat unhappy over *your* motives, Maggie. You do have worth as a person, you have roots, as you say. And, if we're looking at facts, you already own the condo, Maggie."

She narrowed her eyes. "Don't confuse me with facts. I want this house. I mean, I really, *really* want it. The moment the page came up on the computer, I knew this would be the place. Kismet, fate. Something."

He relaxed somewhat, and teased, "No matter the price?"

Maggie opened her mouth, undoubtedly to say *yes, no matter the price*, but then the frugal part of her rendered a figurative slap to the side of her head and she coughed, probably choking on her admirable financial restraint, before bleating—oh, yes, the girl was bleating—"You'll talk to her? I can't talk price, Alex. I'd fold like an umbrella the first time she said the price is firm."

"Because, as you're so fond of saying, you're a wimp when it comes to confrontation?"

"And people with boobs the size of the greater Dallas-Fort Worth area, yes," Maggie admitted, flushing. "Confident people make me nervous. They're always so damn sure of themselves."

"I'm a confident person, Maggie," Saint Just pointed out, slipping his arms around her waist. "Do I make you nervous?"

She rolled her eyes. "Don't be ridiculous."

He moved his hands higher.

"Okay, that's making me nervous. But only because of where we are . . . the way you're looking at me—stop looking at me that way. Those baby blues might do it for Lady Prestwick, but they cut no mustard with me."

"I beg your pardon. Lady Prestwick?"

"Your next love interest. I was picking out names for the new book this morning, before I called you to come look at the house with me. Lady Jane Prestwick. You're going to clear her name even though she was discovered standing over her husband's body, a bloody letter opener in her hand."

"How heroic of me, and how wonderfully predictable, although I'm confident you'll handle the entire situation in a way unique to my tremendous powers of deduction."

"Bite me," Maggie told him, then shook her head. "One of these days I'm going to write a scene where you lose, if only for the moment. It would probably be good for you, build your character."

"And anger our readers. Saint Just never loses, you know that. So, what does Lady Jane look like, hmm? I believe my last amorous encounter was with a particularly fiery redhead."

Maggie pushed his hands back down to her waist. "I don't know. I didn't get that far yet. Why?"

"Well, if I might be so bold," Saint Just said, his mission one of hardening Maggie's resolve when it came to their *confident* Realtor. "I believe I might suggest a tallish, confident young woman. Blonde. Slim, but with a remarkably extraordinary bosom."

"Kiki," Maggie ground out, pushing herself free of him. "You want Kiki? You want that plastic, bleached former Miss Kudzu queen? Right. That's going to happen. Now come on, let's go low-ball the woman and see how she comes back at us. Well, at you. I'm planning on just standing there, looking bored."

Saint Just retrieved his cane, which he'd leaned against the wall. "Lowball? I'm not familiar with the term."

"Neither am I, but it sounds good," Maggie said, climbing the stairs ahead of him. She didn't hesitate when mounting stairs, but only when descending them. "We'll ask her to take us through the whole house again, and you point out all that's wrong with it, okay? Then we'll hit her with a figure. What do you think of five and a half? I think that's reasonable."

"Five and a half what, my dear?" Saint Just asked, following her up and into the main kitchen.

"Million dollars," Maggie whispered, although they were alone in the kitchen, Kiki and Sterling obviously having moved on to another part of the house. "I could go to six, but I want to start lower."

"So you'll pitch her a *low*ball and hope she *swings* at it? Yes, I begin to understand the concept, perhaps. We'll think of this in terms of baseball. What flaws, in particular, do you suggest I point out to the woman?"

"Hell, Alex, I don't know. I love every inch of this house. Just make it work, okay? It's vacant, it's ready to go. We could proba-bly move here right after the first of the year. If . . . if you want to, of course. Things are moving so fast, aren't they? Maybe you'd rather stay where you are?"

"I thought we were settled on that point. I am where I want to be, Maggie. I'm with you."

She rolled her eyes. "*The Case of the Pilfered Pearls*. Chapter six, I think. You're feeding me the come-on line I fed you to feed to whatever-the-hell the woman's name was that I put you to bed with in that book. That's disgusting."

"Ah, but a good line is a good line, yes?" Saint Just teased as Maggie turned on her heels and headed out of the kitchen.

Saint Just tarried for a few moments at the immense, granite-topped island, considering all that had happened since Maggie had summoned him to her condo shortly before luncheon and shown him the Internet listing of this house.

He'd admired the way she'd convinced Miss Rodgers to meet with them that same afternoon although, of course, that was before Maggie had seen the confident young woman's imposing bosom. He admired her taste in having chosen a building such as this in the first place. The tall, white-stuccoed structure would look quite at home in Brighton.

And he was amazed to think that Maggie was finally coming out of her shell enough to realize that there was more to life than sitting at her computer tucked into a corner of her living room, creating a fantasy world that in no way resembled her own rather circumspect lifestyle.

He'd like to think that he had played a part, a rather large part, in this metamorphosis, this digging Maggie out of the figurative cave she'd resided in much too long. Alone, not realizing she was lonely. Needing some life in her life . . . needing him in her life.

After all, she'd created him; her perfect hero. And now he would go out and slay a dragon for her. It was what he did.

He swung his sword cane up and onto his shoulder as he prepared to follow Maggie at his leisure. "I am, by and large, quite a remarkable fellow," he congratulated himself, smiling at his own smugness . . . and then quickly broke into a run when he heard a crash some distance away, followed by a pithy, feminine curse.

Chapter 3

Maggie sat on the litter of the Emergency Department of Lenox Hill Hospital—Saint Just's hospital of choice—her left leg straight out in front of her, glaring at the spot just below her ankle bone. The spot, area, whatever, on the outside of her foot that was turning a deep, suspicious blue, as opposed to the rest of her foot, which had puffed up like an angry blowfish.

"It's broken, right?"

"Fractured is the medical term we prefer. But, oh yeah, it's most certainly broken. You want to see? Most people want to see for themselves. It's the curse of too many medical reality shows on TV. Everyone's an expert," the young doctor said as he slammed two X-ray films up into the front of a light box.

"Cute," Maggie said, not feeling at all cute as she glared at the films. "Two left feet. Scratch any chance of appearing on *Dancing with the Stars.*"

The doctor obviously didn't get the joke, but that was okay. It was, as jokes go, pretty lame. Then again, Maggie was feeling pretty lame. Whoops, that made two bad jokes. It was a good thing she had her mystery series; she wasn't about to knock 'em dead as a writer on *Saturday Night Live*, either.

And, obviously, she was a little hyper, her mind racing along, barely under her control. She took a slow, deep breath, trying to pull herself together.

It wasn't working.

"You can see, Margaret, right here, where you pulled off the tip of the bone. This little one, here, fifth meta—well, let's not be all technical, okay? You want to know what's next?"

Maggie was still squinting at the backlit X-rays. "Actually, I want pain meds. Heavy duty pain meds. Idiot that I am, I insisted it wasn't broken, and walked in here on that thing. I'm not proud, anymore. I'm even open to begging."

"I think we can arrange pain medication once we get the cast on. Now, about this fracture. It's a tricky one."

"I thought you said it was a little one," Maggie said, turning to look at the doctor, who probably got his medical degree at fourteen. It was scary, getting to an age where the doctors are younger than you.

She'd always liked Doctor Helsing, who'd taken care of her while she was growing up in Ocean City. Gray, a little paunch, smelled of peppermints. You could trust a man like Doctor Helsing.

Of course, the guy was probably either dead or drooling in some retirement villa in Boca—but when he said you were going to be all right, you believed him. This guy looked like he still lived with his mom—and she still cut the crusts off his peanut butter and jelly sandwiches.

"Yes, Margaret, it is a small bone. But it's an important bone."

"Aren't they all important?"

"True. But some more than others. You rolled your foot over something, didn't you?"

Maggie was impressed. "Yes, I did. I was touring a house I plan to buy. An older house, and there was a metal doorstop nailed into the floor. A sort of round, metal thing. I didn't see it, stepped on it—just with the outside edge of my foot—and my foot sort of rolled over it as I tried to keep my balance. I didn't fall, either, which I thought was pretty spectacular. But the bone just hit the doorstop and broke, right? Well, the doorstop hit the bone. One of those two."

The doctor shook his head. "I don't think so. It was the *torque*, the rolling over, the attempt to regain your balance, actually, which did the damage. You see, you pulled the ligament away from the bone—the ligament taking part of the bone with it. I'm telling you this because I'm going to have to confine you to a non-weight-bearing cast, at least until you see me again. Let's say ten days, all right?"

"No," Maggie told him, her heart pounding, "let's not say. We're . . . I'm leaving for Ocean City, New Jersey, sooner than that. For Christmas."

"But you'll come back to the city to see me," the doctor said confidently. "If you've been good, if you stay completely off that foot, I might be able to promote you to a walking cast—not full weight-bearing, but at least you'll be able to get around better. But if you don't behave?"

She waited, but he didn't say anything else.

"You could probably drag this out more, Doctor, if you really tried, turn it into a miniseries. Maybe if I faked a drumroll, we could get on with it?" Maggie said, her nerves fraying badly. She was always her snarkiest when she was scared; snarkiness was her single weapon of self-defense.

"I'm making a point, Margaret. I was pausing for effect. But I can sense that it isn't working for you."

"Maggie. Don't call me Margaret, please. I already feel like I'm back in second grade."

The doctor laughed. "That's it, keep your sense of humor. You're going to need it. Now, as I was saying? If you're good, if you listen, we'll X-ray again and possibly put you in that walking cast. And if you're not—well, I operate on Tuesdays and Fridays."

Maggie finally decided it was time to pay attention and stop wishing for Doctor Helsing—who would have given her a nice cherry-flavored lollipop by now. "Operate?"

The word came out as more of a bleat.

"Ah, the magic word. Works every time," the doctor said to a nurse who'd entered the cubicle. "Swing your legs over the side, please, and we can finish up. Is there any special color cast you'd like, Maggie? We've got pink, white, red, lime green, blue, black—"

"Black," Maggie said. "I'm not feeling particularly festive at the moment. And if I can't walk on the cast, how will I get around?"

"Crutches," the doctor said, snapping on latex gloves. "Although, looking at you, I'd think a walker would be safer. You fall often, Maggie?"

She looked at him in confusion. "No. Why? Do I look clumsy?"

He shook his head. "Never mind. Just some private research for my own benefit. You're holding onto the litter with both hands, as if you might otherwise fall off. I've noticed that sort of reaction from people who fall often."

Maggie wet her lips as he bent her ankle so that her toes were pointing slightly upward, and went for humor. "I'm afraid of heights, of falling. I get dizzy on a deep rug. I fell down the stairs, when I was a kid. Top to bottom. I can still remember that feeling of pitching straight into the air . . . rolling head over heels . . . lying at the bottom of the stairs with my mother looking down at me, yelling that I'd broken my neck."

"And had you?"

"No," Maggie said, thinking back to that day, and the expression on her mother's face. As if breaking her ten-year-old neck would inconvenience the hell out of the woman. "Are my friends out there?"

The doctor asked the nurse to check the waiting room and bring Saint Just and Sterling back to see her. "So I can give them the same sermon I'm going to give you again about keeping that foot off the floor. No weight-bearing, absolutely none. I'll know if you cheat, too, because the bottom of the cast will be flattened. And, like I said—Tuesdays and Fridays."

"Bet you aced your Bedside Manner course, huh?" Maggie grumbled, watching as he did his magic with white padding and the black wrap he wound around her from the base of her toes to just below her knee, her foot bent up at about a forty-five degree angle, so that if she did try to put her foot down, all that would touch would be the heel. "Ten days?"

"Or eight weeks. It all depends on you and that little bone," he said, putting both hands around her calf and squeezing the still-soft cast, molding it to her leg. "Now, something else. You're going to itch under here, partly because that happens, partly because you know you can't scratch the itch. Do not stick anything down the cast. No chopsticks, no rulers, no knitting needles, no nothing. Believe me, I've seen them all. I've found pennies when I've cut off a cast. Gummi-bears. Toothpicks, crochet hooks. I could write a book about things people stick down their casts."

"Couldn't everyone? Write a book, I mean," Maggie said, pretty sure the arch of her foot had begun to itch. "So what do I do if I get an itch?"

"Think good thoughts, offer the itch up to the poor souls in purgatory? Seriously, just don't think about the itch, and it usually goes away. If it gets really bad, turn the hair dryer on the spot. Ah, and who's this?"

Maggie looked toward the door to see her friend and editor, Bernice Toland-James, sweeping into the room on a cloud of scent and Armani. "Bernie, what are you doing here?"

"Are you kidding?" Bernie gave a quick shake of her head, serving only to fluff out the cloud of bright red hair that was her trademark. "My bestselling author takes a header, where else would I be? Will she live, Doctor?"

"Probably another sixty or seventy years, if she doesn't smoke and she eats all her green veggies." He looked up at Maggie, still holding onto her leg, still pressing on the cast, which was beginning to feel warm and uncomfortably tight. "An author, huh? What do you write?"

"A mystery series," Maggie said, not eager to tell him her pen name, just to have him say he'd never heard of her. She was depressed enough, without that.

"She's Cleo Dooley," Bernie supplied unhelpfully. "You're working on a very famous person, Doctor."

"Lucky me," he said, grinning. "I'd ask for your autograph, but I'll need your real name on the check when I send you my bill. There, all done. My nurse will be in with the walker. She'll give you the prescription for pain that I won't forget to write, a few lessons on how to navigate, bathe, and you're good to go. Ladies, a pleasure," he said, and then he was gone.

"Never do that, Bernie," Maggie said, glaring down at the cast that felt as if it weighed fifty pounds. "Nobody ever knows me. I don't know who's buying my books, I swear I don't, because I never meet any of them out here in the real world. Oh, and how did you get here? Did Alex call you?"

"I'm to take you home," Bernie said, opening and closing drawers and doors in the large metal cabinet on the far wall of the cubicle. "You want a bedpan? There's a nifty one in here. How about some peroxide?"

"Would you stop!" Maggie said, laughing. "That's probably a five-hundred-dollar bedpan. I'm so upset. I can't put weight on this thing, Bernie. I'm going home for Christmas. How the hell am I going to be any use to—oh. Wait a minute, I'm having a flash here. Yes, a definite flash, followed by a warm, fuzzy feeling. I'm not going to be any use to anybody, am I?"

"And? You're smiling, Maggie, and it's an evil smile. Since it 'tis the Season, I'd have to say you're looking a little like the Grinch as he leered down at Whoville. What are you thinking?"

"I can't help trim the tree at my parents' house. I can't set the table. I can't wash the dishes. Nobody can tell me I'm doing everything wrong, because I won't be doing *anything*." She was chanting now, and fighting the urge to rub her palms together like the Wicked Witch of the West. "I can't run errands, I can't shop for groceries, I can't wrap presents—well, Mom never lets me wrap presents because I can't make hospital corners on the boxes. I can't do anything but sit on the couch, watch TV with my dad, and eat what everyone else cooks. I'm going to be totally useless, and Maureen and Erin will be doing all the work and taking all the flak for not doing any of it the way my mother wants it done. There *is* a God!"

"There's a bright side to everything, I suppose," Bernie said. "Not to your mother, granted, but good for you, making lemonade out of lemons. Me? I'm going to Vail tomorrow morning, where I'm going to do absolutely nothing, too, except without the cast. That would be a huge impediment to my favorite indoor sport."

Knowing what Bernie's favorite indoor sport was—and it didn't waiver, whether she was in Manhattan or Vail or anywhere else—Maggie had a sudden, fairly depressing thought. "Where's Alex?"

"I'm not sure. He said something about a house. About buying a house, or having dinner over a house—something like that. Alex is buying a house?"

"No, I'm—well, *we're* buying a house, right here in Manhattan."

"We? As in you and Alex?" Bernie put a hand to her ear. "Hark! Are those wedding bells I hear? Or are you going to live in sin? I highly recommend the latter, unless you two fall out and he dies, leaving you with a million-dollar life, taxes-paid-up-front, insurance policy. May both my deceased husbands continue to rest in peace between shifts in the Devil's coal mines."

"No, Bernie, we're not getting married. We're not even living together. The house is huge, and we'll share it, all of us, Sterling included. The condo is just too small for me, that's all."

"Sweetie, that condo is too small for your cats. And you can use the deduction."

"That's what my accountant said. Where's that nurse? I want to go home, find out how Alex did with Kiki the Wonderbra."

Bernie raised her carefully plucked eyebrows. "A female Realtor? Ah, no wonder you sicced Alex on her. Good thinking, Mags. Although you could probably threaten to sue, breaking your ankle and everything, and get her down on price that way."

"It's my foot, and why didn't I think of that?" Maggie groused as the nurse drew back the curtain and came in, carrying an ugly metal walker. "Omigod, I can't use that. That's for *old* people."

Bernie patted her shoulder. "Don't worry, sweetie. I'll take it to our art department and have someone paint it, or wrap ribbon around it, or something. Maybe something red and green? You know—for Christmas?"

"Bah, humbug," Maggie muttered as the nurse opened the sides of the walker and began demonstrating how Maggie was to hop, hop, hop for the next ten days. . . .

Meanwhile, back at the ranch ... er, sorry. Meanwhile, back at the brain trust plotting the perfect crime ...

Severed brake lines?

The city's flat as a ruler. Severed brake lines were for the high, twisty hills of San Francisco. Here? The car would roll half a block, maybe, and then stop.

Oou! Oou! Poison!

Drain cleaner? Mercury? Poison mushrooms? Nah, I read about poison mushrooms somewhere. Somebody's already done that.

A push off a bridge? A roof?

Okay, okay. That seems workable.

Except he's bigger than me.

Surprise. That's what's needed. The element of surprise.

Like, hey—surprise, you're dead!

Chapter 4

"Would you peel a grape for me, Alex?"

"Sadly, no."

"My hero. Jeez."

Saint Just looked up from the mortgage application he was currently perusing to smile at Maggie, who was ensconced on one of the overstuffed couches in her living room, clad in sky blue flannel pajamas with small white sheep on them, and looking delightfully slothful.

Although he might soon politely suggest she find a way to take a shower.

"I wasn't aware you ate grapes, my dear."

"I don't. But if I'm forced to just lie here like a lump, the least you could do is wait on me."

"Thank you. But, again, no. Sterling is doing an exemplary job of dancing to your beck-and-call these past days. I wouldn't wish to depress his enthusiasm by intruding on his joy. Now, I'm afraid I will need your attention for a few minutes. You haven't taken any more of those pills today, have you? Not that I'm even mildly averse to listening once more to all one hundred verses of that ditty you called *Ninety-nine Bottles of Beer on a Wall*."

She shook her head. "I'm still in pain. Agony, even. But I really liked those pain pills, which is why I'm not taking them anymore. I'm being a good little soldier. Stiff upper lip, and all of that. Don't you feel sorry for me?"

"I've been feeling sorry for you for a week, although around verse eighty-six last night, I began to see the benefits of us not sharing the same domicile. At any rate, I believe it's time you began putting on a brave face."

"I don't want to. I want to lie here and play Camille. I've no more new Lee Child books to read, *Oprah*'s a rerun, and the news only depresses me, except for Keith Olbermann, and he's a rerun tonight, too. Nobody works over the holidays. How the heck do you rerun the news? And how could my mother still insist that we show up tomorrow? And she's *mad* at me, Alex. Like I broke my foot on purpose, just to ruin her life."

Saint Just averted his head. "I do believe I read somewhere that there are those who believe there are no accidents. That, in point of fact, you may have broken your foot in the hope that you then wouldn't have to travel to Ocean City for the holidays."

Maggie struggled to sit up higher on the couch. "That's ridiculous. Nobody breaks a bone on purpose—especially not an *important* one. Do you have any idea how hard it is for me to get that damn walker through the bathroom doorway? I can't shower because I can't do that on one foot without slipping and killing myself, the cast inside a stupid trash bag. I can't bathe because I don't own a tub, and if you offer one more time to help me with my sponge bath, I may have to hurt you. And this cast? I go to bed with it, I wake up with it—I *hate* it. I'd have to be a masochist, to break my foot on purpose."

"Then again, there's the rather recent, um, development, between us. A deepening of our relationship, a new closeness . . ."

"Whoa. You just hang on a minute, Alex. Are you saying—suggesting—that I broke my foot because you and I have been . . . well, you know, and that maybe I'm having second thoughts?"

"It's only a theory," Saint Just told her, amazed to find himself feeling not quite as calm and collected as he would like her to believe he always was. The idea of a true romantic attachment was new to him, completely outside his experience. He was also evolving, as he reminded Maggie whenever possible, attempting to become more his own man rather than simply her creation, and this evolving business had turned out to be slightly uncomfortable. How on earth did people function, feeling insecure about themselves? He much preferred the confidence of a hero.

"Well, you can take that theory and—never mind. I did not break my foot on purpose. I broke it on a doorstop, which is bad enough to admit. Can we change the subject now, please?"

Saint Just, as eager to change the subject as she, held up the thick sheaf of papers he'd been reading. "Perhaps you can fill in these forms, just to take your mind off your misery? For some reason, your bank feels it necessary to know everything about you from the time you were in the cradle, and they want this information all verified by a second party."

"That's because I'm a self-employed woman, and one who actually makes money. Nobody really wants to admit that's possible. Bankers are all male chauvinists, Bernie says so. They'd believe you before they'd ever believe me, and you aren't even real. But you're a man."

Maggie held out her hand for the papers and Saint Just gratefully turned them over to her, and then continued on his way to the drinks table, to pour himself a restorative glass of wine. Maggie was the delight of his life, but all-in-all, it had been a long week.

"Maggie? We could pool our resources, you know, and simply pay over the purchase price. *Fragrances by Pierre* has been exceedingly kind to me."

Maggie was bending over the top page, frowning. "No, we can't. I need the deduction. And we have to do this in my name only because I was only joking before—your forged documents only take us so far."

"And so far so good, as I've heard the term. I am a most upstanding citizen of this metropolis. I look forward to filing my federal income tax forms in a few weeks."

"Yeah, yeah. Right now you're *upstanding* in my light while I'm trying to read this. Go sit down."

He did as she had commanded, only because it suited him to sit down—he hoped she was clear on that.

"You know," Maggie said, eying the application, "much as I hate to say it, Alex, you did a heck of a job with Miss Kudzu of 1998. What a great price. Do I want to know how you managed it?"

"Charm, wit, my usual undeniable attractions," Saint Just told her, smiling over the rim of his wineglass. "I stand in disbelief of the power a simple kiss on the hand is to you American women. I should really give lessons on the proper way to court the modern female."

Maggie rolled her eyes. "Yeah. You could have your own TV show: *Regency Eye for the Hapless Guy*. Gimme a break. Oh, hello, Sterling. Flowers? For me?"

Sterling Balder carefully nudged the door closed behind him as his hands were full, holding tight to a rather large crystal bowl filled with exotic cut flowers. "No, Maggie, I'm so sorry, but no. These just arrived for you, Saint Just, but I thought Maggie might like to look at them, shut in as she is."

"They're for Alex? Put them down over there on the table, Sterling, and give me the card."

Saint Just got to his feet. "I believe I'm capable of reading my own card, thank you, Maggie," he said.

But for a woman who spent most of her days with her casted left foot riding the top of the couch, Maggie had become very fleet of *arm*, and she had already snatched the card from the bouquet as Sterling walked past her.

She swiveled her body so that she was in a seated position and pulled the small card from the small envelope. She read the few lines, then glared at Alex.

"Tell me again. How did you get such a good price?"

"Ah. Then I can assume that those lovely blooms are courtesy of Miss Rodgers?"

Maggie flipped the card in his general direction, and he snagged it neatly out of the air.

Loved working with you, sugar, he read, and then smiled at the three lines of numbers—Kiki's home, office, and cell numbers.

"Oh, stop grinning like the village idiot," Maggie told him, jerking on the walker until she had it where she wanted it, and then got to her feet. "You're impossible."

"On the contrary, I'm irresistible. Just as you made me. Miss Rodgers vows I have a career in selling, and I'd have to agree with her, if it weren't for knowing my title would be reduced from Viscount to Salesman. Posing for photographs cannot really be considered work, not in the least smelling of the shop, an anathema for those of us whose bloodlines can be traced back to William the Conqueror. There are only so many sacrifices one man can be expected to make, you understand, no matter what his altered circumstances."

Maggie jutted out her jaw. "Listen to me, Alex. One more time. You're . . . not . . . a . . . real Viscount. You're a figment of my imagination, you and Sterling both. Got it?"

"Oh, I say, Maggie, that was rather cruel. Wasn't it, Saint Just?"

Saint Just looked to Maggie, who had been in the act of rising to one foot with the aid of the walker. "Maggie?"

She sat down once more. "I'm sorry, Sterling, sweetie. You're real. You really are. And I'm a pig."

Sterling, who had risen to his feet as Maggie tried to stand up, then subsided onto the facing couch when she plopped down, got to his feet once more. "No, you're not. Police are pigs. I remember distinctly."

"Alex?" Maggie pleaded, looking desperately at Saint Just.

"With pleasure, my dear," he said, bowing to her. "Sterling, *pigs* was a term often used in the Regency Era to describe the local constabulary. Bow Street Runners, Bow Street Pigs. The term was considered offensive then and it is deemed to be even more offensive now. Please do not employ it again."

Sterling's eyes squinted behind his spectacles. "But Maggie just used it."

Saint Just inclined his head slightly to the love of his life. "Punting to you, my dear, as they say."

As Maggie tripped over her own tongue, explaining to the very literal Sterling the ins and outs of modern day slang, Saint Just watched his friend in some amusement.

Dear, dear Sterling. His short, pudgy, balding counterpart, the perfect counterpart, in point of fact, to the sometimes sarcastic, arrogant Saint Just. The foil, the comic relief, the *human* part of the Saint Just Mysteries. Why, the man had a quite impressive online fan club.

Sterling. The innocent. The always kind, fiercely loyal, never judgmental, Sterling.

They weren't, Saint Just had decided, exactly Batman, Robin, and Batgirl, but, together, the three of them were actually a rather formidable force.

"So you can *say* you're a pig, or call someone else a pig, but only if that someone else isn't a member of the police force? Like Lieutenant Wendell?"

"Exactly," Maggie said, looking at Saint Just. "And, speaking of Steve, he phoned this morning to tell me that he and his girlfriend are driving up to Stowe for the holidays. They're going skiing, and asked if we wanted to go along. Fat chance of that, huh, with this thing stuck to my leg?"

"And with your parents expecting you at Christmas dinner, yes," Saint Just said, picking up the mortgage application one more time and handing the papers to her. "We really need you to fill these out before we leave for Ocean City."

"We? What *we* needs me to fill out these papers? You and me, we? You and Kiki, we? The *kingly* we? What's the hurry, Alex? I checked the listing online again, and the house has been on the market for over eighteen months. That's unheard of in Manhattan. Nobody's going to buy it out from under us a few days before Christmas. It's not like anyone could tuck it up in a stocking, as a last minute Christmas gift."

Women had never been a mystery to Saint Just, until he'd joined Maggie's world. "Pardon me, my dear, but wasn't purchasing this house *your* idea?"

"I know, I know. But now that I've had time to think, I'm wondering why Kiki jumped at the price you offered."

"Loathe as I am to bring this up again—I am fairly persuasive."

"Oh, shut up. Granted, you're cute and all, but business is business. And Kiki was in a mighty hurry. Did you try turning on the water, Alex? Or the lights? I was so busy being impressed with the size of the place, the woodwork, the stained glass, that I didn't jump up and down to see if the floorboards squeak, or check for faulty plumbing. There's something wrong with the place, right? It's a lemon."

"But that's a fruit."

Maggie wrinkled up her nose. "Sorry, Sterling. Yes, a lemon is a fruit. I think it's a fruit. Maybe a vegetable. No . . . no, a fruit. So, maybe the house is a dog—scratch that, too. Alex, do you think something's wrong with the house?"

Saint Just took back the papers. "Perhaps it's haunted?"

"Yes! It could be—no, Sterling, don't look like that. Alex is kidding. Alex, tell Sterling you're kidding, for crying out loud. You *are* kidding, right?"

"I was being flippant, Sterling. My most profound apologies. And, as I don't believe we're making very much progress here, I think I'll just toddle off to your bedroom, Maggie, and pack for you, as Sterling has performed that kind office for me. Not quite a gentleman's gentleman, definitely not on a par with Sterling, but I believe I'll manage."

Maggie hastily grabbed the walker, struggled to her feet. "The hell you will! Stay out of my drawers!"

Chuckling, and repressing an insane urge—a suicidal urge, actually—to retort that it was too late for that particular warning, Saint Just entered the bedroom a good minute ahead of Maggie and her now gaily decorated walker, and was removing delicate undergarments from her top dresser drawer when she bounded into the room, hopping so fast she ended by falling onto the bed on her back, to glare up at him.

"Comfortable, my dear?"

"I'd be a lot more comfortable if you were in China," she groused. And then, to his profound relief, she burst into tears. He'd been waiting, less and less patiently, for her finally to give in to her emotions.

He was sitting beside her in an instant, stroking her hair back from her face. "And more than time for a good cry, my dear," he told her. "He phoned me this morning, as well."

She stopped crying to look up at him, her Irish green eyes awash in tears. "Dad? My dad called you?"

"After he spoke with you, yes. He's quite maudlin."

Maggie reached for something to use to wipe her eyes, then saw that she was using a pair of lovely ivory-colored silk unmentionables and threw it toward a corner of the room.

"He's going to be all alone for Christmas. Mom disinvited him to Christmas dinner. Maureen barely talks to him, Erin refuses to return his calls. And Tate is just as bad—worse, because he's supposed to be the fair-haired boy. Yeah, right. This is going to be the worst Christmas ever, Alex—and that includes the three years I spent the day with stomach flu. Cripes, my mother took video of me throwing up into the box my Barbie Dream House came in, and she shows it every damn year. I can't go home. I don't want to go home. And now . . . now I have to *hop* there."

Saint Just retreated from the bed long enough to take a box of tissues from the dresser and hand it to Maggie, then sat down beside her once more, bending to place a kiss on her forehead. "He did have an affair, my dear. Not many women can forgive such a thing, not when you Americans all believe in marriage for love, not simply convenience."

Maggie pushed away his hand and sat up. "That was Regency England, Alex. That was rich dukes marrying penniless young beauties and then the two of them falling madly in love by Chapter Twelve. We're not talking fiction, we're talking about my parents. My parents! My own father! He goes bowling. He watches sports on TV. Last time I checked, Mom still trimmed the fat off his meat, for crying out loud. He doesn't have *affairs*."

"If I recall correctly, Evan only indulged in the affair because he'd learned that your mother had succumbed to the thrill of an . . . well, of an adventure outside the marriage vows some years ago."

"Please don't keep giving me creepy mental pictures that will keep me up nights. And that *adventure* of hers was about, what, ten years ago? Probably a menopausal aberration, and why she finally decided to tell him about it last month amazes me. Happy wedding anniversary, Evan—I had an affair a decade ago. Jeez. Still, wasn't it a little late of Dad to be playing the game of payback's a bitch? These are people in their middle sixties, for crying out loud. I didn't think people in their sixties even *had* sex anymore. Fat lot I know, huh?"

She grabbed the walker and pulled herself upright. "That's it, it's over. I'm not going. I can't stay in that house, chowing down a big turkey dinner while my father is eating cold baked beans out of the can in his bachelor pad. Don't answer that," she warned tightly when the phone began to ring.

"Hello, Kelly residence," Saint Just said, picking up the phone.

He smiled, held it out to Maggie. "Exquisite timing. Your mother. Now you can inform her as to your decision."

Maggie hopped backward a good three feet even as she shook her head furiously; she really was becoming more proficient with that walker of hers. "Tell her I broke my leg and you had to shoot me."

"You broke your foot, and she probably heard you anyway. I seem to have forgotten to depress the Mute button."

"Oh, hell," Maggie muttered as she hopped back to the bed and snatched the phone from him, pasting a large, patently artificial smile on her face as she said, "Hi, Mom!"

Saint Just returned to his task, that of packing up Maggie while she was powerless to stop him, pretending not to listen to Maggie's side of the conversation, even if she did little more than mumble the occasional, "Uh-huh."

Maggie's mother, if she had existed during the time of the English Regency, would have been a be-feathered matron, tall and rawboned, her proud pigeon chest puffed out, her manner abrupt, condescending, and, to be frank, fairly obnoxious. That she was Maggie's mother was a constant astonishment to Saint Just.

In point of fact, Alicia Kelly was one of the myriad reasons Saint Just had felt it necessary to poof—as Maggie insisted on so inelegantly terming his truly impressive feat—into her life.

He was, he had long ago decided, the part of Maggie that she had felt missing from her life. The confident part, the brave and daring part; a creation of her imagination, one composed of all the elements of herself that she believed she lacked.

And what Saint Just lacked, what Maggie believed she also lacked, had been completed with the creation of their own dear Sterling Balder, who was all heart, and caring, and almost child-like devotion.

What Maggie didn't realize was that she couldn't possibly have created Saint Just, created Sterling, and made them both believable to her readers, unless she herself was made up of all those virtues she felt she lacked.

By herself, Maggie was intelligent, yet unsure of herself. With him—with Saint Just, and with Sterling—she was at last complete. It was the stuff of fiction, but it worked. It worked enough for Saint Just to be able to join her, bringing Sterling along. It worked enough for the three of them to exist together on the same astral plane, or whatever such things were called.

Not that Maggie was a frail flower, but she had never quite mastered how to deal with Alicia Kelly's rather overbearing personality, feeling more attuned to her father, the hapless, straying Evan Kelly. With her father out of the house, cast out of the family, Maggie would be spending Christmas with the strangers who were her mother and siblings.

It was all rather sad.

"Yippee!"

"I beg your pardon?" Saint Just said, catching the tossed phone in self-defense. "Did I miss something, or is that the usual ending to the sort of monosyllabic dirge you've been chanting for the past ten minutes? *Yippee*?"

Maggie fell back onto the mattress once more, but this time she looked much more the inviting picture than she had earlier. The pout was gone. The tears were gone. "Tate's bringing another couple with him, so Mom says we can't stay at the condo. She can't toss Erin out without her throwing some huge hissy fit, and God forbid Tate and his pals could find a hotel, so I'm the natural choice. We're bunking in with Dad. Isn't that fabulous? Why didn't I think of that in the first place?"

"You're not upset that your mother would deny you a place at the family hearth, giving that place instead to some friends of your brother's?"

"Upset? I'd be doing handstands, if I could. For once being the black sheep of the family is showing some benefits." She turned her head to look at Saint Just, caught in the act of removing a few sweaters from one of the drawers. "And speaking of black, pack the black cashmere sweater, please. You like me in the black cashmere. Oh, I feel *so* much better."

"How gratifying, I'm sure. So there will be no more pouting?" Saint Just asked facetiously.

"I've still got this *thing* on my leg. Don't expect unmitigated bliss here. But, no, there will be no more pouting. Tomorrow it's under the river and through the Pine Barrens, to celebrate another Kelly Dysfunctional Christmas. But we'll be doing it mostly from Dad's apartment, *not* the condo. With any luck, we'll actually get through the next few days with nobody murdering anybody. And for our family? Hell, that'll be ... it'll be like a Christmas miracle."

*And now a few words from
our Shadowy Figure lurking
in the background ...*

Yes! Yes, I've got it.
   The perfect way.
The perfect crime.
The perfect answer.
The timing has to be right. Maybe the weather, too, but probably not.
All that I've ever wanted, soon to be mine, mine, mine!
It's coming. My moment.
I probably should get a haircut. . . .

Chapter 5

Maggie leaned her forearms on the steering wheel and looked to her right, past Alex, to see the full flight of wood-slat stairs leading up to her father's borrowed bachelor pad.

She should have realized. Lots of the houses nearest the ocean were built on pilings, to allow parking beneath them, off the street, and to avoid flood damage during nor'easters and the occasional hurricane.

"Great. How am I supposed to get up there? Fly?"

"It would be an interesting phenomenon if you could, and one I'd be delighted to witness. Or I could volunteer my services," Alex suggested, opening the car door. "But I believe I'll first reconnoiter, ascertain if your father is indeed at home and receiving visitors. Much as I adore you, sweetheart, the idea of carrying you up those stairs, and whatever stairs may lay beyond the door, just to carry you back down again, does not really appeal."

"I'd be insulted, if you weren't right. Going up I can handle. Coming down again is another story, not that I don't trust you not to drop me. Okay. He's in 2B. Sounds like the second floor, huh? Damn."

She waited, tapping her fingertips on the steering wheel, for Alex to return to the car. It would have been easier, logistically, to stay at her mother's house (no longer her parents' house), but she'd rather have to bump herself up two flights on her fanny than admit that to anyone.

Sterling leaned on the back of the front seat. "What will we do if your father isn't at home?"

Maggie opened her mouth to say they'd just have to suck it up and go to her mother's, and then changed her mind. It was stupid, putting off the inevitable, but she was a devout coward, and it was time she owned up to that sad fact. "I don't know, Sterling," she said brightly. "You said you wanted to go to Atlantic City again. We could do that."

"Oh, yes, that would be above all things wonderful. Do you think they still have the dancing woodpeckers?"

Maggie frowned, trying to decipher that statement, and then smiled. "Oh, right, the dancing woodpeckers. On one of the nickel slots you played last time. I remember now. I'm sure they do, Sterling. Ah, here comes Alex. So?" she asked as he climbed back into the front seat.

"There's a note on his door—his second-floor door, so I believe you'll, as you say, owe me big time, before this visit is concluded. I look forward to that. He's at the dentist for something called a crown, and doesn't expect to be home for a few hours. We just missed him, as a matter-of-fact. But he did leave a key under the mat, which is either a testament to the citizens of this small city or a remarkable lapse in judgment by your father."

"No comment. Did you take the key?"

"No, I did not, as your father might then wonder what had happened to it. Or are you ready to go upstairs?"

"With Dad not there? I don't think so," Maggie said. It would be odd enough, seeing her father in a bachelor apartment. Invading that apartment without him there was just plain creepy.

"Excuse me, please. A crown?" Sterling said, quite predictably, from the backseat. "That doesn't mean what it should mean, does it?"

Maggie put the car in gear as she explained that, no, her father wasn't about to become royalty, and then told Alex her brilliant plan. They'd drive up to the Borgata, only eight miles away. Sterling could play the nickel slots, Alex could try his hand at baccarat again, and Maggie, who didn't gamble, could wait patiently until they were ready to go to the buffet for prime rib and coconut macaroons.

"A capital idea, my dear. Directly after we stop in at your mother's house, to assure her you actually have made an appearance rather than running off to join the circus."

"I'm not even going to ask what that means," Sterling grumbled from the backseat, clicking on his seat belt.

"Yeah, right. A drop-in visit with Mommy Dearest, only three hours after she called to tell me that she's being run off her feet—her words—because I'm not there to help her and won't be able to help her when I am there. Go see her now? Uh-uh, that's not going to happen until it has to happen, thank you. And tomorrow's soon enough to see everybody else, too," Maggie told him, stopping at the red light. She watched idly as three cars went past her along Wesley Avenue, and then leaned forward as a long black limousine entered the intersection, the back window rolled down. "Oh, would you for crying out loud look at that!"

Alex, who had been unfolding a map of New Jersey he'd taken from the glove compartment, looked up and smiled as the limousine glided out of the intersection. "Why, hello, Tate."

"He hired a limo. He hired a freaking *limo*," Maggie said, shaking her head. "And Ninth Street is the way in from the Expressway—Wesley is the way to Atlantic City. He was in Atlantic City, dollars to donuts. Lording it in the casinos with his important friends, whoever they are, and now he's on his way to sponge off my mother. A limo, Alex. And I'm going to arrive in a rented Taurus. There is no justice in this world."

"Hesitant as I am to point this out, Maggie, *you* could have employed a limousine service. If you weren't," he smiled, "so economically prudent."

"I am *not* cheap," Maggie said, turning the corner once the light turned green, and probably stepping too hard on the gas with her good foot. "I'm buying a mansion, for crying out loud."

"True. And a bargain, at that."

"I would have paid full price," Maggie said, holding out her hand for change for the toll. "Maybe. And I'm still wondering why I got it so cheap."

"It could be haunted. I must say, I like that idea better than thinking about poor drains or small insects gnawing on the floorboards, and all of that," Sterling supplied from the backseat, earning himself speaking looks from both his friends.

Alex handed over a dollar bill even as he surveyed their surroundings, low marshland to their left, the fairly dark waters of the Atlantic to their right. "I seem to recall that we're to bear to the left once we're beyond this bridge, and then quickly to the right."

"I know where I'm going," Maggie told him, even as she squinted a bit in the deepening dusk. "You don't need that map. Why does Jersey insist on making all its route markers so small? It's almost like they don't want you to know where you're going."

"I'll read the signs for you, Maggie," Sterling said helpfully from the backseat.

True to his word, Sterling read every sign as they passed through several small towns, until they were at last in Atlantic City.

"We could use the tunnel, Maggie. I think we're fairly close now," Alex said, pointing to a small sign—a ridiculously small sign—vaguely labeled *Marina*, when anyone knew the smarter thing to do would be to have the sign printed with the word *Tunnel* on it.

Traffic was slow, impeded by the light blue jitneys that seemed to stop wherever and whenever the driver felt like it.

"Where do I turn? Sterling? You're reading the signs, remember?"

"Oh, my, yes. And they're all so big and pretty, aren't they? So many lights. Look! Do you see that sign? Sir Elton John is coming to town? How wonderful it would be for you to have a nice visit with a fellow peer, Saint Just. Wouldn't it be wonderful if we could—"

"You missed the turn, Maggie," Alex pointed out quietly as the Taurus was cut off by a tour bus with a Pennsylvania license plate. "Let's see. Next up would be Martin Luther King Junior Boulevard. I believe that if you were to turn left at that intersection we would have no problem in—ah. Sterling, wave a fond farewell to Martin Luther King Junior Boulevard, would you?"

"If you'd only *talk faster*," Maggie groused as she switched on the windshield wipers to swipe away the light snow that had begun to fall. She was pretty sure their next stop would be the ocean, if she didn't find somewhere to take a left turn. "And this is stupid, anyway. Just another one of my very bad ideas. I can't hop through a casino. I should just turn the car around and face the music—no, Sterling, don't say anything else!"

"I won't. Except that we just passed a small purple fingerpost with the name Borgata printed on it. If-you-were-to-quickly-turn-left-we-might—that's the ticket, Maggie! Just like Nascar. She feathered that corner just like an established whip, didn't she, Saint Just? That's probably why automobile aficionados speak of *horses* beneath the hood, yes?"

Alex retrieved the map from the floor and replaced it in the glove box. "I must remember to apply for a driver's license the moment we return to the metropolis. Either that, or take up daily prayers. Ah, and there it is, the Borgata, shining golden in the distance. Sterling, I believe we're in for some fairly spectacular good luck. The omens are all there."

"They are?" Sterling scrambled out of the backseat with the folded-up walker as Maggie pulled to a stop in the valet parking line, having decided that people who can qualify for a three-million-dollar mortgage probably have left the self-park garage behind, at least on Christmas Eve. "What omens, Saint Just?"

Alex handed a ten dollar bill to the attendant before Maggie could pull a one dollar bill from her purse, and escorted his friends inside, explaining, "We survived to arrive here, didn't we? I consider that a good omen."

"Bite me," Maggie said, hopping through the opened door and then sagging against the walker at the sheer vastness of the casino floor in the distance.

"Excuse me, miss? Might I suggest a motorized cart? We rent by the day, quite reasonably."

Maggie looked up at the casino employee, ready to refuse. After all, she wasn't even going to gamble. But she'd only hopped about thirty feet, and she was already exhausted. "It's a deal."

Ten minutes later, with only a short tutorial on the thing, Maggie was zipping ahead of Alex and Sterling, still giggling over the idea that, when she put the cart in reverse, it beeped like she was backing up a semi.

"I could get used to this," she told Alex, unfortunately taking her eyes away from where she was going as she neared the end of a double row of spectacularly tall slot machines.

The head-on collision with the cart turning into the aisle wasn't horrendous, but it was definitely humiliating, causing Maggie to paraphrase in her best Dustin Hoffman/Ratso Rizzo voice: "Hey, I'm driving here."

The man mountain on the other cart backed up a good three feet . . . and rammed her again, hard, as if they were on bumper cars at one of the small amusement parks on the Boardwalk. "Get out of my way, wise mouth. That's my machine, and if I don't get it because of you, I'm going to run you over like a bug."

Maggie looked to her left and right. To her left were six empty machines. A like number of the same machines were to her right. But the guy seemed to have his eyes on the second machine from the end on the right. "Which machine? I don't see a name on any of these machines. Or is your name Big-Wheels-o'-Bucks? No? I didn't think so. Back up, buster."

"Maggie, I think you might have been in the wrong," Alex told her in his best-accented English, placing his hand on the handlebars. "Excuse us, sir. My friend here is still learning how to navigate."

"Yeah? What was your first clue, Jeeves?"

"Now, now, no need to take umbrage. If you'd be so kind as to reverse your conveyance just a tad more, we'll move on now. Won't we, Maggie?"

"The hell we will, Jeeves," Maggie said, feeling suddenly stubborn. She hadn't had the best day. Face it, she hadn't had the best week, or even the best month, as someone had tried to kill her not so long ago. Tomorrow was Christmas, and it didn't look to be any better than any other day in her recent memory.

If this guy wanted to make himself a target for all her pent-up anger, she was more than willing to take out her miserableness on him. She'd already had a good cry, more than one good cry. That was enough with the pity parties! Maybe it was time figuratively to punch something . . . and the bozo on the go-cart was as good as anything else.

She grabbed onto the back of the nearest seat and held on as she planted her right foot and hopped around until she could sit in the chair. "This is *my* machine. I'm staying right here."

"You can't do that! That's *my* machine! I play that machine every time I come here."

"Yeah? And like I said, I didn't see your name on it. Still don't. So, the way I see it, I'm sitting here, and that makes it *my* machine," Maggie said, settling herself. She felt stupid, mulish, but the man was really getting on her nerves. What did it matter which machine he lost his ten bucks in, anyway? She shot her left arm into the air, palm up. "Alex, give me some money."

"I'll be back with an attendant to boot you out of here. And you'd damn well better not win while I'm gone," the fat man said, beep-beeping as he backed up and tore off in the opposite direction, all but leaving skid marks on the carpet.

"You just go do that, see if I care," she called after him, and then lost her smile, because she was pretty sure she'd already lost her mind. "God, what have I done?"

"You've a heart of gold, Maggie," Alex told her, bending to kiss the nape of her neck as he inserted a bill into the machine. "But I don't believe this particular side of you is very appealing."

She sagged in the chair, all the fight gone out of her. Her casted leg hurt, her right foot felt black-and-blue from hopping on it for days on end, her arms seemed as weak as the proverbial wet noodles, her palms were throbbing from holding onto the walker—and she was pretty sure she was developing calluses.

She'd kill to take a real shower rather than washing at the bathroom sink, body part by body part, then balancing on one foot at the kitchen sink to wash her hair, half the time missing with the sprayer and having to one-handedly wipe down the cabinets when she was done.

And she refused to take any more pain pills because they made her feel too good, and if she could get addicted to cigarettes, maybe she was an addictive personality, or whatever, so she'd flushed the pain pills.

Except for two of them. They were in her purse. Lurking there, the way her cigarettes used to lurk there, calling to her.

And her leg ached like a son of a—

Maybe if she only took one? She could still drive back to Ocean City in a couple of hours, if she only took one.

Leaving her one more for Christmas Day and the Kelly family dinner. Painkillers should be de rigueur for Kelly family dinners.

Oh yeah. All in all, she felt like crap. She'd been really rude to that idiot on the go-cart. Hell, in the mood she was in, she probably would have beat up Santa Claus if he'd looked at her crooked. "I know, I know. That was inexcusable, even if the guy is a card-carrying jerk. Call him back, Alex. You know I don't gamble. He can have his damn machine."

"Nonsense. Just because you were rude does not excuse his boorishness. The initial collision was an accident, most probably your fault, but an accident nonetheless. It was he who backed up to give it another go, hit you again. You stay here with Sterling, gamble away my money, and I'll seek out the baccarat tables, all right? I think it's safer for yourself and possibly the general population if you remain in one place."

Maggie nodded, feeling heat come into her cheeks. "It was seeing Tate in the limo, Alex. Showing up like the Grand Poobah with his friends who will be sleeping in my bed. I think that one put me over the top. That and Mom knowing I'm in a leg cast, and kicking me out, sending me to stay in Dad's second-floor apartment anyway. There's a certain lack of maternal caring there, Alex. Definitely."

"Take people as they are, my dear, rather than hope they'll live up to your expectations of what they should be, and your own life becomes less stressful."

She searched in her purse for the small bottle of water that she always carried, and then spoke to Alex around the pretty hot-pink pill she'd plopped onto her tongue. "Yeah? Where did you read that?"

"It may have been the Cryptoquote in this morning's newspaper, actually. Now, are you comfortable?"

She swallowed the pill, instantly regretting having done so. "I haven't been comfortable since this cast went on, but I'm all right. I'll just sit here, put my leg up on the end seat, and if the guy comes back, I'll move to another machine in the row. I only came here for the macaroons, anyway." She leaned forward to inspect the machine. "But maybe I'll lose your money for you, just because I'm taking you *as you are*. How much did you put in here, anyway?"

"The first bill I found," he told her. "A one hundred dollar bill."

Maggie's eyes threatened to pop out of her head as she saw a number one followed by two zeroes lit up in red on the *Credits* line of the machine. "A hundred bucks? Are you nuts? Get it out of there. How do you get it out of there?"

"It's all right, Maggie," Sterling said, sitting down beside her. "Look, they're only nickels. And the operation of the machine itself is quite simple. You just press the button labeled *Max Bet*, although I have no idea who Max is, do you? He may have invented the machines, don't you think? At any rate, just push the button, and the machine does everything else. Isn't that correct, Saint Just?"

"It is. However, this isn't a nickel machine, but a dollar machine. The maximum bet, as I have deduced, is three dollars."

Maggie held her hands out in front of her as if figuratively backing away from the machine. "There is *no* way I'm going to play three dollars at one time, Daddy Warbucks, even with your money. No freaking way."

"So speaks the woman who just bought a several million dollar house in order to prove that she's gained confidence in her own worth and that of her career."

"Don't use my own words on me, Alex. Gambling is stupid. How do you think they build casinos like these? I'll tell you how. Because the only people that really win in casinos are the people who own them. Now get that money out of there. Look for a Refund button, or something. There must be a way to get it out of there."

"Oh ye of faint heart. You could win, you know. Sterling, push the button if you please," Alex instructed, and Maggie watched as the three reels began to spin, then stopped, one by one.

The machine had proved her point for her. "And you're both happy now? You'll never see that three dollars again."

"I'm not ecstatic," Alex told her, "but I am delighted to know that you'll stay here, not causing any more uproar, while I try my own luck. And, if it makes you feel better, we can agree to divide whatever you win three ways. Sterling, don't let her move from here."

"I'm not a baby, you know," Maggie groused, scrambling in her purse for her nicotine inhaler. Her pacifier. Oh, hell. Why didn't she just give it up before somebody thought they had to burp her. "Just go, Alex, knowing that no matter what you win, I'll be here losing your hundred dollars. It won't be any different than if I set fire to the money. Pushing that button just takes longer."

"Always the optimist. And it's now officially *our* one hundred dollars you'll be *burning* through the machine. Good luck, my dear."

"Yeah, thanks," Maggie said, scowling at the machine, now

showing ninety-one credits, as Sterling had been busily pressing the Max button. "This is looking better and better, isn't it? Sure, I believe I could win. And my foot could magically heal itself overnight so I can dance the lead in the *Nutcracker*. Go away, Alex. I'm not fit company."

Meanwhile, back at the—oh, right. We already did that one . . .

*H*e picked up the photograph, recognizing the woman he'd seen parked at the curb, in the No Parking/Loading Zone out front.
Pretty girl.
Too bad for her, huh?
And not much more time to get what he came for.
Nice of Evan to tape that note to his door, though.
Nicer of him to keep a key stashed under the mat.
Schmuck.
Okay, okay, luck is good, but luck runs out. Nobody lives eight miles from Atlantic City without knowing that one, right?
So get what you need and go. Don't think, just act. The first act, that leads to the second act, that leads to—oh yeah. Time to boogie.
Get the show on the road.
Four more hours, that's all.
Four more hours, and it's party time.
Now, where the hell does he keep it . . . ?

Alas, dear reader, this is the last time we will delve into the twisted mind of our Shadowy Figure. Because said Shadowy Figure isn't kidding—no more thinking of any great consequence is going to happen inside that particular brain any time soon.

Figuratively, from this point on, it is as if Shadowy Figure's mind, like Elvis, has left the building.

Chapter 6

Saint Just strolled casually but purposefully toward the well-appointed baccarat tables, his first and only previous visit to a modern day casino still a fond memory, and with every confidence his luck would likewise be "in" today.

He'd only just bowed politely to the dealer, his hand reaching inside his cashmere sports coat for his billfold, when . . . well, when all hell seemed to break loose around him.

Bells rang. Lights flashed, strafing wildly across the unadorned ceiling. People began running from everywhere, and all seemed to be headed in the same direction.

"My immense powers of observation to one side," he joked to the dealer, "it would appear that something's happened?"

"Yeah, you could say that. Somebody hit a big one. From the way people are running, I'd say it's probably the Big-Wheel-o'-Bucks machine. Sir? Why, thank you sir."

Saint Just had already tossed a twenty-dollar tip on the table and joined the herd of people making their way back across the floor to where he'd left Maggie and Sterling.

He was stopped by a man wearing a jacket with the logo *Security* on the breast pocket and told that he could go no farther.

"Yes, of course," Saint Just said, craning his neck to see what he could see. "But I left my friends at those machines, and I wonder if you could answer a question for me, my good sir?"

"Sure. You think they won?"

"I have no idea. Is it possible that the winner is sporting a black orthopedic cast on her left leg, and accompanied by a con-genial, pudgy, balding man wearing an astonished expression?"

"Yeah, that's them. Well, that's her, because she was the one at the machine. Why don't you come with me, sir. I'll get you through to her."

Smiling quizzically, Saint Just followed the security man, who was now following a small gaggle of casino employees, two car-rying copious numbers of balloons, the rear brought up by a third man who was doing his best to make his way while holding onto a ridiculously large facsimile of a check.

A check with no name written on the Payee line.

A check with *Three million two hundred eighty-three thousand dollars* written on the Amount line in fairly impressive calligraphy.

Saint Just smiled.

And then he saw Maggie, and he began to laugh.

She was still sitting where he'd left her, and the stunned-ox ex-pression she wore was absolutely priceless.

She saw him, and began waving to him frantically, calling his name as if she might be drowning. Which, for Maggie, was prob-ably how she felt.

He'd almost gotten to her when his ankle was clipped by the wheel of a motorized cart and he turned to his left to see the man they'd encountered earlier, bullying his cart through the crowd.

His expression was neither astonished nor of the stunned-ox variety.

It was more like that of a rabid boar crashing through the under-growth, and all but foaming at the mouth.

"That's mine! That's mine! She took my machine! I told you guys, and you wouldn't do anything. Now look! That bitch took my jackpot!"

"Excuse me," the security guard said to Alex before taking off after the man who had now somehow gained possession of the oversize check and was swinging it above his head, clearly in an attempt to attack Maggie physically.

But Saint Just was faster, and had already grabbed hold of the check at the other end, deftly pulling it from the man's hands.

Which only momentarily diverted the fellow, who was now aiming his cart directly at Maggie.

Maggie sort of *eeked*, and quickly moved her casted foot out of the line of fire.

The motorized cart seemed to go into second gear.

Sterling, who'd only recently vowed to never be a hero again, manfully leaped in front of Maggie, taking the full force of the oncoming cart, and then folded like a broken flower when Saint Just reached into the cart and turned off the power.

At which point Maggie pushed herself up on one foot, held onto the back of the chair for balance, declared, "You ran into my friend!" a heartbeat prior to delivering (Saint Just knew from watching HBO *Fight Night*) what was a stunning right cross directly to the flabby jaw of her attacker.

Women screamed.

Men laughed.

Camera phones flashed.

Saint Just swooped Maggie up into his arms and she held on tight. "Look what I did. I hit that stupid man. This is all your fault," she told him, in typical Maggie-style. "Sterling? Are you all right?"

"As rain, Maggie, thank you," Sterling said, behind her.

Security personnel surrounded the main participants, hauling the man in the cart—now bleeding profusely from the nose—away from Saint Just, the recovering Sterling, and K.O. Kelly herself, while others formed a phalanx to lead the way out of the crowd.

Within moments they were all locked behind large doors in a well-appointed room just off the casino floor.

The sudden silence was rather overpowering as a half dozen rather senior-looking Borgata employees ushered them all to chairs.

"We're back in control," said one. "I thought I'd seen it all, but *that* was different."

Maggie shifted herself on the soft leather couch, moving away from Saint Just. "Not if you lived in my world lately," she muttered, glaring at her *hero*. "And all for what? I know I did something right, when all three lines had the same thing on them, but all that showed up in the little box listing credits won were a bunch of three's. Or maybe Es. They kept flashing on and off.

And so, what? I won a little over three thousand dollars? That's great, it really is, even if it punches holes in my theories that nobody really wins—but why the big fuss?"

Saint Just coughed slightly into his hands. "You didn't win three thousand dollars, Maggie."

She shifted on the couch, to look at him. "Oh, okay, *we* won three thousand dollars. You and Sterling will get your cut. Jeez. But I still don't see why we needed lights, camera, action—and balloons. I think we could have safely dispensed with the balloons."

Saint Just could see that she was clearly woozy, her eyes slightly unfocused. It might have been better if she hadn't taken that pill. "Are you in pain, Maggie?"

"God, yes, my leg still hurts. I probably let it hang too much today, in the car, and here, too. I wonder if these people would mind if I sat sideways and lifted the cast up onto the back of the couch."

There was, Saint Just was about to say, only one way to find out. But Maggie had already lifted her leg onto the back of the couch.

"Ma'am?"

Maggie looked up at the rather tall blond woman who had entered the room. "Sorry," she said, lowering her leg.

"That's quite all right, if you'd be more comfortable that way. But I overheard you a moment ago, and I think you should know that you didn't win three thousand dollars. Big-Wheels-o'-Bucks is a progressive slot, connected to many casinos. You played the maximum amount and won the progressive jackpot. So, not three thousand and change, but three *million* and change."

"Oh, I did not. That's ridiculous." Maggie retorted rather angrily, but then grabbed Saint Just's hand. "I did? We did? Holy— that is, *Alex*?"

"Beside you, as always, my dear," he told her. "Sterling? That was an exceedingly brave thing you did, shielding Maggie from that ridiculous man. I am once again forever in your debt."

"Oh, right," Maggie said, blinking rather furiously. "Sterling, you saved me, you really did." Then she looked back at Saint Just in a panic. "That man! I stole his machine. I stole the winning machine! Oh, Alex . . . and pooh on him, he tried to run me over. And me an invalid, for crying out loud. *Three million dollars*?"

"Excuse me?" the blond woman inquired. "Are you referring to the gentleman who attacked you? May I ask how you stole his machine?"

But Maggie wasn't really listening anymore, as anyone could plainly see. Her eyes had gone rather wide and unblinking, her expression amazingly blank; her hands were twisting together in her lap, and she had begun to mumble.

It was Saint Just's opinion, gained from watching medical documentaries on The Learning Channel, that she'd slipped into some sort of shock. She probably shouldn't be disturbed, as that could be injurious to the poor thing.

Then Maggie began to smile, rather inanely. Smiling, and chanting quietly, "Three million dollars. Three million bucks. Three million smack-a-roos. Three million. Three million? Three *million* . . ."

It was left to Saint Just to explain the contretemps, and the woman visibly relaxed. "Unless you physically removed him from the chair while he had credits on the machine, then used them to win the jackpot, he has no claim. And our eye in the sky caught everything, and I'm sure will prove what you're saying is true. We're holding the gentleman in another room. Do you wish to press charges?"

"*Three* mill—what? Oh, God, no," Maggie said, slumping back against the soft leather. Saint Just was pleased to see that she'd begun to blink once more. "It's probably more than enough that I ruined the poor guy's life."

"All right, then," the blond woman said, accepting a rather thick stack of forms from the man who stood behind her. "On behalf of the Borgata, let me congratulate you on your truly spectacular win. There are just a few formalities we'll need to go over . . ."

When Saint Just next pulled his gold pocket watch from his pants pocket, two hours had slipped by, and Maggie was signing yet another paper after posing for photographs with Borgata officials who stood on either side of her holding up the large check, now made out to Margaret Kelly.

He would not admit that he was bored with all the excitement, but there was really precious little to do once Sterling had an ice bag on his shin and Maggie had been taken off for photographs. The baccarat tables still called to him, but he was rather loathe to present his face in the casino. Most especially now that one of the casino employees had been kind enough to turn on the television set so that he could see the entire happy event replayed on the local six o'clock news.

Someone had been very adept with a camera phone, and there were lovely still pictures of Maggie swinging at her attacker, of Saint Just swooping her up into his arms and carrying her to safety.

As heroes will do.

There had also been a live interview with the gentleman in the mobile cart, one Henry Novack, of Weehawken, who seemed quite able to stand on his own two feet as he roundly accused Maggie of stealing his jackpot. He was going to contact a lawyer. He was going to sue.

Poor Maggie. Life never seemed to be an unmitigated joy for her. There was always something or someone lurking about to throw a spanner in the works, even in the best of times.

But now he was here with her, the perfect hero, the knight in shining armor she'd dreamed of since shortly after puberty. He would slay her dragons, stand in front of her or watch her back. Whatever she needed, and even if she didn't need him, or want his heroics.

Because that's what heroes do . . .

"And we had this one lady who used to toss pixie dust in the air before she hit the button when she thought she was due to be lucky."

Saint Just had snapped out of his reverie. "I beg your pardon, Miss Hatchard?"

The young woman who had obviously been assigned to babysit Saint Just and Sterling had been prattling on to his friend for some minutes, but this last statement caught Saint Just's attention.

"Oh, yes. Pixie dust. Pretty, sparkly stuff, except that she made a mess from one end of the casino to the other. We finally had to ban her. That was a shame, because she used to make dozens of brownies for us on holidays. Like I was telling Sterling here, we get them all in here at one time or another. People who rub the screen, like, you know, *caress* it? That's creepy. And then there's those who prop photos of their kids on the screen. But it's the ladies who put photos of their dead husbands up there that get me, though. It's like, you know, hey, George, look what I'm doing with your 401k. That'll teach you to play golf every weekend and leave me home alone with the kids. It's like, well, like payback, you know?"

"Forgive me, my dear, for not really attending. Everything you've said is fascinating. I once had the acquaintance of a gentleman who believed his fairly homely pug dog brought him luck at the tables. Took him everywhere. The dog eventually grew aged and died, and the gentleman had him stuffed, still brought him to the clubs, much to the consternation of the other members."

"The glass eyes, you understand," Sterling explained. "They were rather, um, *protuberant*. Always thought they were staring at me, didn't I, Saint Just?"

"Yes, Sterling, thank you. But that was another time, another place. Miss Hatchard, do you know if Maggie will be allowed to leave soon?"

"I'll just go check," the young woman said, quickly getting to her feet and heading for one of the other rooms in the large suite of offices.

"What's a troll, Saint Just?" Sterling asked, still holding the ice bag to his shin.

"A troll, Sterling? Why, I believe those are most unfortunate fellows who live beneath bridges. Something like that. Why?"

"Because back when you weren't really attending, Miss Hatchard said that some people stick little trolls on top of the slot machine they're playing. For good luck, you understand. But if trolls are forced to live beneath bridges, I can't see how they'd be much help in the good luck department, can you?"

"I don't know, Sterling." Saint Just stood, and began to pace. "I believe I'd be more interested in where anyone *locates* a troll in the first place. How do you feel? Better?"

Sterling put down the ice bag. "Oh, yes, much better, thank you. It was a trifling thing, really, and I'm sure if I'd thought about it sufficiently I wouldn't have tossed myself in that man's path. I'm not a hero, Saint Just, much as Maggie says I am. I just don't think quickly enough to save myself."

"Anyone else, Sterling, and I'd say you were angling for a compliment. But you are a hero, my friend, in every way. Ah, and here comes our lady of the moment. Maggie? You were featured on the local television news an hour ago."

Maggie's expression instantly went from happily dazed to completely panicked. "No! Oh, God, I didn't sign any release to have my name and face shown. I know I didn't. They wanted me to, but I'm not a complete idiot. Those photographs were just for the Big-Wheels-o'-Bucks people. They promised to block out my face if they show the pictures. Who needs the world knowing you just won three million dollars? Which I get in yearly increments for twenty years, and that's after the Feds take a big chunk straight off the top. Not that I'm complaining. Did you see the broadcast?"

"There's quite a lot to address in all of that, but let's begin with the most important question. You are yet to be called anything but *the lucky winner*. That, I would say, would be the good news."

Maggie hopped over to him. "And the bad news?"

"Sales of camera phones have climbed into the stratosphere, I would say. If we were to piece together all of the various photographs I've just recently seen displayed on the television screen, I believe the result would be a movie taking us from your initial confusion, to Mr. Henry Novack's shouted accusations and attempt to run you over with his electric cart, to the moment I, well, the moment I rescued you from the fray. Oh, yes, and one fairly magnificent photograph of you in the act of punching Mr. Novack."

"Oh, God. I'm a dead woman," Maggie said, bowing her head over the walker, and looking rather abject for the winner of a three-million-dollar jackpot. "You know it's only a matter of hours before someone sees my face and recognizes it. And my mother? What's she going to say? No, don't suggest anything. I can already imagine what she's going to say: 'Margaret? Can't you do *anything* without making public spectacles of us all?' I think I'm going to be sick."

"Ah, yes, but not now, my dear. Miss Hatchard has promised us all a most wonderful repast at the restaurant of your choosing. I've taken the liberty of narrowing those choices down to one owned by Bobby Flay, who I enjoy watching on the *Food Network*, and—"

"I want to go to the buffet. I want coconut macaroons. I'll go nowhere that doesn't included coconut macaroons. I have *earned* some coconut macaroons."

"I don't think it would be comfortable for you in such a public area, Ms. Kelly," Miss Hatchard supplied helpfully. "But I'm certain I can get you a nice bag of macaroons to take with you. If you're positive that you won't accept the Borgata's hospitality and a complimentary suite for the night?"

Maggie looked at Saint Just, who merely shrugged his shoulders. "No steps, Alex," she pointed out. "Everything free. I'm tempted. But no. We have to go back to Dad's, right? He's probably wondering where we are, and my cell phone doesn't work in here, which means nothing, because I forget his number at the apartment anyway. What time is it? I'm sure my pill's through my system now—I hurt bad enough again to know it's gone—so I'm safe to drive. We'd better go, right?"

Minutes later, they were back in the Taurus, Sterling reading all the signs, Saint Just studying Maggie's face in the darkness inside the car.

"You're feeling guilty, aren't you, my dear? Happy as you are, and I'm sure you're over the moon, as are we all, you're feeling guilty."

She shot him a quick look, eased across the wide intersection and onto Martin Luther King Junior Boulevard. "Don't be ridiculous. Guilty? Why should I—oh, all right, yes. I feel guilty. I'm Irish, I'm Catholic—I'm good at guilt. I have, over the years, elevated guilt to an art form, I know that. But, Alex, he called it *his* machine. He probably played it every time he came to the casino, just waiting for it to pay off—and I come hopping in and win the whole jackpot. On Christmas Eve, no less. That poor man."

"That poor man, Maggie, called you an unpleasant name and not once but twice attempted to run you down with his motorized cart. Not to mention his clear intent to behead you with that oversize check."

"Well, yeah, there is that," she said, turning onto Atlantic Avenue, so that Saint Just felt fairly certain they'd make it back to Ocean City without a detour into Pennsylvania, or some such thing. "You said his name, didn't you? What is it?"

"Henry Novack, a fairly innocuous name. Why?"

"I don't know. I thought maybe I could send him some money. What do you think?"

"I think the day has been too much for you, my dear. That would be tantamount to admitting that he deserves the money, and not you. You did nothing wrong. The machine was there for the taking, and you took it."

"And we're splitting the winnings three ways, I know. I can't believe this has happened to me, to us. I've never even won a door prize or a free ham, for crying out loud. If only I could have remained the anonymous winner. It's like I told them all, who cares if some famous author—yes, I said that, much as I hate saying stuff like that—wins a jackpot? I know I wasn't all that choked up when J-Lo's mom won a big jackpot here in Atlantic City. Them what has, gets, that's probably what I said—and she only won two-point-four million."

"*Only*, Maggie?"

"Yeah, well, you know what I mean. It's only a good story if some retired kindergarten teacher wins big and says she's going to pay off the mortgage on her house and set up trusts for her six grandchildren before joining the Peace Corps, you know? People will hate me for winning."

"Fame and fortune. Such terrible curses. Such a burden you carry, Maggie," Saint Just said, motioning for her to pay attention, as they were nearing the turnoff leading up to the bridge into Ocean City.

"Go ahead, mock me. And remember that this money isn't coming to us in one huge lump. And I already know what I'm doing with mine. I'm giving it to someone who deserves it. Someone who, through no fault of his own, has no income at the moment. I'm giving my yearly share to Sterling."

"I beg your pardon?" Sterling said, leaning front as far as his seat belt would allow. "*Me?*"

"A splendid idea for both of us, Maggie," Saint Just agreed, delighted for his friend. "Sterling deserves to live in the style to which he was accustomed in our books. A yearly allowance is just the thing."

"My books. Not our books, *my* books. You get all the fun, I get all the heavy lifting. Remember that. Now, tell me what I'm going to say to my mother when she asks me if I'm happy with the way I've once again disgraced the family. And come up with the right words before the eleven o'clock local news, just in case she missed the early broadcast."

But Saint Just wasn't really attending to Maggie's words, as she'd just turned the corner and he could see flashing red and blue lights up ahead. "There may have been an accident," he said as Maggie slowed down, obviously also seeing the lights, the shiny white police cars blocking most of the street.

"That's Dad's place," she said, easing the car to a stop a good thirty yards away from the apartment building. "And the front door is open, and there's cops all over the place. Oh, cripes. Do you think Mom showed up and someone called the cops for a domestic dispute? I may be saved yet, if Mom did something dumber than I did."

She pulled the car ahead, stopping inches from one of the patrol cars, and yelled for Sterling to get her walker out of the backseat.

"Stay with her, Sterling. I'll go inquire as to what is going on."

Saint Just had only walked halfway to the door when he stopped to see Evan Kelly being led out onto the porch, then down the stairs. There was a policeman on either side of him, and his hands were cuffed behind his back.

Obviously Maggie saw her father as well. "Daddy!"

Saint Just grabbed at Maggie, keeping her upright as she attempted to move the walker fast enough to keep up with her frantic hops. "Panic aids nothing, sweetheart. Stay here with Sterling, and I'll go see what's happening. Whatever it is, I'm sure it's a mistake."

Evan Kelly was already ensconced in the rear seat of one of the patrol cars, and a policeman was walking toward Saint Just, ordering him to move the Taurus.

"In a moment, officer," he told him. "Mr. Kelly's daughter wishes to know the nature of the charge against her father."

The officer looked past Saint Just, to see Maggie balancing behind the walker, her beautiful face stark white in terror. "We don't give out that sort of information. His kid, you said? And who are you?"

"A close friend of the family. It's Christmas Eve, officer. Surely there are exceptions to the rule, on Christmas Eve."

"Yeah. Yeah, okay, don't get me all misty. The way I hear it, Kelly's a slam dunk for murder one, okay? That's all I got for you. Now move that damn car or I'll have it impounded." The officer then tipped his hat slightly and smiled. "And, oh, yeah—Merry Christmas."

Chapter 7

"Margaret. You are here then? And you've heard about your father? Well, of course, I should have known. Like I've always said, your middle name should have been Trouble. . . ."

Maggie suppressed a flinch, and kept her back to the door of the police station. She'd been hoping there could be a way to make whatever was happening all go away before her mother found out about it. So much for luck—except bad luck. "Hi, Mom. Fancy meeting you here."

"Actually, I'm the one who figured you'd probably be here somewhere, Maggie."

Maggie's upper lip curled only slightly. She swiveled on the uncomfortable wooden bench that reminded her of a church pew, and looked toward her brother, who appeared to be his usual buttoned-down arrogant self. "Tate. *Figured* that out all by yourself, huh?"

"How did you break your foot?"

"I stepped on a doorstop," Maggie told him grudgingly.

"Get out. Nobody does that."

She felt her temperature rising. "Okay, okay, if you think it's important at a time like this. I was crossing Broadway and didn't look where I was going and my foot got run over by the lead car of the president's motorcade."

"No! My God, did they stop? Did you get his autograph?"

Maggie rolled her eyes. "And Mom says you're the smart one . . ."

There was a sort of *flutter* in the doorway, followed by an anguished female cry. "*Maggie*! Oh, God—*Daddy*! This is *terrible*!"

Maggie smiled slightly at her sister, the baby of the family, who had taken refuge behind a fist-size wad of already soggy tissues. Maureen was really good at playing the baby of the family, too. All the Kelly children, Maggie had decided long ago, had been typecast by their mother at birth. Erin, the oldest, therefore infallible. Tate, the only boy, the heir, the one carrying on the family name. And Maggie, the middle child—she'd been preprogrammed to be the odd one out.

"Hi, Maureen."

Her sister looked her up and down. "Mom said you broke your foot. 'To annoy her,' she said. How did you do it?"

Sometimes it took Maggie a minute or two to learn. But then she learned fast. "Rappelling down the Matterhorn."

"Wow."

"Yeah. Wow. Guess the gang's all here, huh, except for Erin. She parking the car?"

Alicia Kelly collapsed onto the bench beside Maggie. "Don't be facetious. And Tate drove us in my car, as he'd already sent away the limousine he'd hired. Erin had to cancel yesterday morning, poor thing, although we can only be glad she isn't here, as she's too sensitive for something like this. Gavin has the flu, or something. She's devastated not to be here, but her husband's health comes first."

"Sure, it does. Yesterday morning, Mom, you said? Leaving you time to call me, tell me that we could stay at the house, right? I mean, you did call me yesterday afternoon. Of course, that was only to remind me to keep Dad away from the house tomorrow, so he couldn't ruin Christmas dinner."

If Maggie had expected her mother to blush, or look sheepish, then she really was asking for a miracle for Christmas. "Always finding fault, aren't you, Margaret?"

"Yeah, that's me. I'm sorry, it wasn't important. Well, it was, I guess," she waffled. "But not really, huh? Not right now, anyway. Who's that over there with Tate?"

Mrs. Kelly was sitting ramrod straight, repeatedly snapping and unsnapping the clasp on her huge black purse. "His friends, of course. And how embarrassing for Tate, to have to come down here to bail out your father."

Maggie felt strange. Almost as if her backbone was getting stronger. Now why was that?

"Yeah, poor Tate. Hard to impress his important pals, what with his daddy in the slammer and all that. My friends, on the other hand, don't count," Maggie said, rolling her eyes at Alex, who had just stepped back into the nondescript lobby that, Maggie had noticed earlier, smelled like a branch office of Dunkin Donuts. "Alex? Did you get hold of her?"

"I did," he told her, inclining his head to Alicia. "Mrs. Kelly, how pleasant to see you again, no matter the circumstances."

"I'm always happy to see *you*, Alex," Mrs. Kelly answered. Very nearly purred. It wasn't easy, putting a purr for Alex and a shot at Maggie in the same sentence, but the woman was a master.

"Right," Maggie said tightly, still amazed that even her mother was not immune to Alex's perfect-hero charm—although having bought the woman a diamond bracelet after his initial win at the baccarat table over the Thanksgiving holiday couldn't have hurt. "Is she coming here? Does she have a license to practice in Jersey? What did she say?"

"She—meaning, Mrs. Kelly, our good friend and exemplary criminal attorney, J.P. Boxer—informs me that the weather in Aruba is wonderfully balmy, although a tad windy at times, which made her full-body massage on the beach a fairly risqué affair at one point. There are times, I'll admit, when I wish I didn't inspire such confidences from the fairer sex."

Maggie's stomach did a small, sick flip. "Oh, God. She's in Aruba? She can't be in Aruba. What the hell is J.P. doing in Aruba?"

Alex smiled. "She told me you'd say that, almost word-for-word, actually. She also told me to tell you that she's in Aruba because that's—pardon me, Mrs. Kelly—that's damn well where she wants to be right now, considering the fact that snow and slush are unheard of in that particular climate."

"But she promised me free legal advice for life. Did you remind her of that, Alex?"

"Unnecessary, my dear. J.P. is well aware of her promise. She also instructed me to tell you that she lied."

Maggie sagged in her seat. "Of course, she did. Never put your trust in lawyers, unless they're already on a hefty retainer. Didn't Shakespeare say something like that?"

"Shakespeare said many things, Maggie," Alex told her. "I fear I have not committed them all to memory."

"No, just most of them." Maggie was very aware of her mother, sitting beside her. For some reason, one she'd have to figure out later, she had this insane impulse to shield the woman, take the burden all on her own shoulders. Okay, and on Alex's shoulders. "So now what? We're in this alone, right? Give me some ideas. How do we get Dad out of here?"

"A stout rope tied to the prison bars, a stouter bumper on your car, and I suppose we could manage it. Unless you're aware of a source for a few sticks of dynamite, hmm?"

"If that was meant to amuse me, you missed the mark, bucko. I'm serious. Daddy can't stay here all night. It's Christmas Eve."

"J.P. did give me a few names, other attorneys we might be able to contact. Although it is as you said, Christmas Eve, Maggie, so I don't know that we'll be able to spring your father from the hoosegow much before Boxing Day."

"Hoosegow?"

"Something Sterling said to me. It would appear he's quite taken with the term. I rather favor it myself, it's amusing. And rather rolls off the tongue, don't you think? *Hoosegow.*"

"Not now, Alex, please. I don't need *amusing* right now." Maggie looked over to the desk where the booking officer or whoever he was sat, talking to Sterling. "What's he doing over there anyway?"

"Sterling? Why, being his usual amiable self, I imagine. Leave him be, Maggie. If anyone can arrange for a way for us to speak with your father yet this evening, it will be Sterling."

"Not really, Alex," Mrs. Kelly said, getting to her feet. "Tate's friend's wife is arranging bail now. Or releasing Evan on his own recognizance, as I believe she called it. After all, it's not as if he could have done anything too terrible. Not Evan. He isn't capable."

Maggie goggled up at her mother. "Cripes, Mom. Nobody told you why Daddy's here?"

Alex put his hand warningly on her shoulder, speaking quietly.

"Tread carefully, Maggie. We're muddling along with precious few histrionics, save your dear sister, that is. We're not flying up into the treetops. Yet. Let's attempt to remain this way as long as possible."

Maggie considered Alex's warning, and then nodded her head in agreement. They'd start slow, that's what they'd do. Daddy had been arrested. Her mother was coping with that fairly well. Why rush into telling her *why* he'd been arrested? What was that old joke? Something about *the cat was on the roof* . . . ?

She looked toward Tate, now standing with the man who'd come in with him. But the woman was gone. "She's a lawyer, Mom? The guy's wife?"

"Much more than just a lawyer, Margaret. She's the senior partner in a very prestigious firm in Basking Ridge."

"And she does criminal law?"

Mrs. Kelly didn't answer, but just waved Tate and his companion over to them. "Sean? This is my daughter, Margaret. Margaret—Sean Whitaker." She shot a look at Maggie. "Sean's a Realtor."

Maggie waited a beat, for her mother to say, "And Maggie's a famous writer."

When the silence stretched out for a good five seconds, with no word coming from Alicia Kelly, Maggie put out her hand and had it thoroughly wrung by the handsome blond-headed man who looked like he'd just stepped out of a Calvin Klein ad.

"A pleasure, Sean. And your wife is an attorney?"

"She is, Margaret, yes. Cynthia Spade-Whitaker. You may have heard of her? She just successfully defended several charges against—well, names don't really matter, do they?"

"In Jersey? Not unless the name is Soprano, right? Bada-bing," Maggie said, knowing she was being snarky.

Then again, it had been a long day, and it wasn't over yet.

And she may have inadvertently hit the target, as handsome Sean seemed to turn a little green around the gills. "Everyone deserves a good defense. I'm really very proud of her. So," he added, much too brightly, "how did you break your leg?"

"My foot, actually. I broke it chasing down a purse snatcher who'd grabbed some old lady's bag as she came out of Barney's. Got him, too. The mayor's giving me a commendation next week. I do try, but it's hard to be humble."

Alex coughed into his fist.

"Really? That's . . . that's very heroic of you. Ah, and here comes my wife now."

Everyone turned to watch as the blond-haired sylph with eyes as green as grass glided into the room, a self-satisfied smirk on her artfully made-up face. "All done, kiddies," she said—crowed. "I found us a judge who . . . well, let's say he owes our firm a favor. Mr. Kelly will be released in a few hours. Just as soon as our judge comes here and arraigns him in a special private session and someone posts bond, of course. Tate, I'm sure you can manage that. The bail bondsman will want ten percent—fifty-thousand dollars."

Sometimes being the outsider had its benefits. Maggie could stand back, unnoticed and forgotten, and observe her fellow humans, as writers tend to do. Like now, when Maggie could watch Tate's nostrils flare, watch his Adam's apple climb his neck as he swallowed rather convulsively.

She couldn't resist: "Oh, that's great, Tate. To the rescue, as usual. Mom, isn't Tate great? What a guy."

Alex pulled her back down onto the bench and then sat down beside her. "Neither you nor your brother should ever consider playing at cards for money, my dear. I can read both your faces quite easily. Tate doesn't have fifty-thousand dollars he can readily convert to cash—and you know it. But remember, Maggie, this is not about sibling rivalry. It's about Evan."

"I do know that. I'm trying not to think about Daddy back there somewhere behind that door, half swallowed up by some horrible orange jumpsuit and sharing a cell with a bunch of Christmas Eve drunks. I'll let Tate off the hook in a moment, post the bail. But would you look at Mom? She's beginning to get a sort of deer-in-the-headlights look. Not that it isn't about time she went a little crazy. She can't believe Daddy's been tossed in jail for parking tickets or littering. Not with a five-hundred-thousand-dollar bail."

Her mother was looking around the room, as if applying for some sort of assistance but not knowing whom to ask. And then, much to Maggie's surprise, Mrs. Kelly walked back across the room to sit down beside Maggie.

She covered her mother's hand with her own. "Mom? You okay?"

Mrs. Kelly shook her head slowly. "Fifty-thousand dollars? What did the man *do*? The officer who called me didn't say. But I assumed . . . that is . . . I thought it was something minor . . . something typically stupid . . ."

Maggie looked up at Alex, who nodded to her, and then squeezed her mother's hand. "It isn't something minor, Mom. They say . . . um . . . they say Daddy killed somebody."

Mrs. Kelly pushed Maggie's hand away and shot to her feet. "That's ridiculous! Evan may be an idiot, but he wouldn't step on a bug. Tate! Someone's made a mistake. Get your father out here this minute."

But Tate was standing with his friends, gesturing nervously, probably explaining that his funds weren't "liquid," or some such drivel.

"Mom, they aren't kidding. They say he killed someone." Maggie got to her feet, put her arm around her mother, then stood with her arm still outstretched as Mrs. Kelly shrugged off the offer of comfort. "Alex? What's the man's name?"

Alex took a pristine white linen handkerchief from his pocket and handed it to Maureen, who was now comforting her mother.

Maggie noticed that Maureen was allowed to do that. How silly she'd been, to try to step out from her typecasting. But, with a new clarity that had come from somewhere, Maggie wondered if that was her problem—or her mother's. And, if it was her mother's, then the woman had to be going nuts knowing that her husband, safely in his assigned "role" all these years, had suddenly stepped out of character.

"The victim's name?" Alex said, frowning. "I don't know that I have that, actually. Give me a moment to confer with Sterling."

He was back in a less than a minute, smiling slightly. "Sterling is now a junior detective, Maggie. He showed me his badge."

Even with her mother beginning to fall apart—a phenomenon Maggie could not remember ever witnessing—she had to smile as she glanced toward Sterling, who was proudly holding up a plastic badge. "Isn't that cute? I'm guessing they give them to all the kids," she said, waving and nodding at the lovable Sterling Balder. "So? The name?"

"Yes, of course. The deceased is one Walter Bodkin."

"Bodkin? There's a name for you," Maggie said, and turned back to her mother. "Mom? Do you recognize the—hey now, how about we sit you back down, okay? You're looking a little pale. Alex?"

Alex immediately guided Mrs. Kelly back down onto the bench, even as Maureen subsided beside her, also looking faintly sick.

"Mom?" Maggie asked again. "You knew this Bodkin person?"

Maureen giggled inanely, then burst into sobs.

Mrs. Kelly blinked, then blinked again. "My God, he did it. He killed him. And it's all my fault." She reached up blindly, grabbing for Alex's hand, clutching it tightly. "You're always involved in something scandalous, aren't you? You and Maggie? You and Maggie have to do something. You have to fix this. You have to help Evan. *He killed him, and it's all my fault.*"

"Jeez Louise, Mom, why don't you say that a little louder—I'm not sure the cop at the desk heard you."

"But he did it, Margaret. Evan killed Walter. He did it for *me*."

It was like bad soap-opera dialogue. Maggie half expected the scene to freeze in front of her and then fade to black as the network went to commercial.

"Maureen," Maggie commanded, grabbing her wrist and giving it a shake. "Fall apart later, okay? Help me get Mom out of here before some cop hears her and wants to take a statement. Alex? Talk to the blonde and find out how I bail Dad out of this place. Mom? Come on, Mom, up an' at 'em. That's the girl. Let's walk you outside and let Maureen get you home . . ."

Chapter 8

Saint Just perched at his leisure beside Maggie on the arm of the chair in Alicia Kelly's large and rather floral living room, observing.

It had been more than two hours since he'd last seen Mrs. Kelly, and the woman seemed to be back under control. Which probably had gone far in reassuring Maggie that the entirety of her world hadn't turned upside down at the moment of her father's arrest for murder.

Just ninety-nine percent of it.

They'd seen Mrs. Kelly off with Maureen, and then rejoined the others in the police station, Saint Just more than willing to take charge of the situation. After all, that was why he was here in the first place, on this plane of existence. To be a supporting prop to his beloved Maggie.

Who, as it turned out, hadn't seemed to need him at all.

He smiled now as he remembered how she'd employed her walker to cut Cynthia Spade-Whitaker effectively from the herd, asking pertinent questions and then efficiently handling the phone call to the bail bondsman. She'd not so much as blinked when the attorney then named her exorbitant fee for services, promising to have funds transferred to the woman's firm the day after Christmas.

No, she hadn't even blinked. Maggie, parting with huge sums of money without an obvious show of pain. Truly an amazing sight to behold. One he should probably treasure, as he doubted it was something he'd see again any time soon.

But she'd gone beyond that, daring to push at the sergeant behind the main desk, badgering him until she was allowed to write a note to her father, inform him that he would soon be released.

She'd told Tate to go back to the house because their mother would probably want to see him, and then ordered him to stop somewhere and find some donuts and coffee for everyone, as they'd probably be awake the rest of the night.

She'd called their mutual friend, Manhattan police lieutenant Steve Wendell, and told him to take off his skis and get himself to Ocean City, because she needed him to get some of the Ocean City cops to talk off the record about the details of the alleged crime.

Her cell phone stuck to her ear seemingly forever, Maggie had also called Bernie, to warn her that Evan's arrest was bound to hit the newspapers within a few days' time, and that they could unfortunately count on Channel 5's Holly Spivak to make the connection between Evan Kelly and Maggie Kelly. And oh, yes, by the way, she'd also seemed to have won three million dollars, and that would probably make the newspapers, too.

A second warning call went to Tabitha Leighton, Maggie's literary agent. That one took longer, as Tabby and Maureen seemed to share a similar affection for tearful hysterics. Tabby had cried for "poor Evan." Then cried again at Maggie's jackpot win. The woman was an equal opportunity crier. Although, as she was first and foremost an agent, she had rallied enough to begin tossing out plans to somehow capitalize on the jackpot win—perhaps with an appearance on *Letterman*?

Maggie had called Socks, their friend and doorman, telling him they'd be extending their stay in Ocean City indefinitely, so could he please make sure to feed the cats as well as Sterling's mouse, Henry, and watch out for the package from Tabitha. Tabby always sent fresh fruit, always mailed it too late to arrive for Christmas, and she didn't want the box put in a warm room so that the condo smelled of overripe grapefruit when she got home.

Her attention to detail fairly boggled the mind. But she was, as the saying went, running hard on all cylinders, and he had never been quite so proud of her.

General Kelly, commanding her troops. She didn't *ask* anyone. She *told* them. She had been short, none too sweet, and to the point.

In precisely sixty-eight minutes, Evan Kelly was walking toward them via a doorway at the back of the small police station, blinking at the bright overhead lights and looking small, older than the last time Saint Just had seen him, and infinitely bemused.

He wore baggy mud-brown slacks that looked as if he regularly slept in them, and a gray sweater with patches on the elbows, buttoned up over the collar of a garish yellow shirt. His left shoe was untied. His left sock was blue. His right sock was black. His mostly gray brown hair stood up straight on the back of his head, as though he'd been sleeping. He carried an unfortunate-looking wool tweed coat over his arm.

If this was what two hours of incarceration had done to the man, clearly he could not be allowed to be returned to prison. Although that was still no excuse for the man's inexorable taste in clothing. "Batching it," as the man had been doing for the past nearly two months, since his separation from his wife, clearly had taken its toll. Perhaps Alicia Kelly had formerly laid out his clothing for him each morning.

Maggie had seen him, closed her cell phone on the conversation she'd been having with Lieutenant Wendell, to whom she'd been giving directions to Ocean City, and crossed the room to embrace her father.

She'd cried as she'd hugged him, audibly sobbed, but then quickly stepped back, wiped at her eyes, took a steadying breath, and got back down to business.

They were shed of the discomforts of the hoosegow in less time than it took for Maggie to swipe a chocolate-covered glazed donut from the sergeant's desk.

Sterling was now ensconced in her father's bachelor apartment, watching over the man as they both dug into large bowls of puffed rice cereal, and Maggie and Saint Just had just begun reporting what they knew to the rest of the family at the Kelly residence.

Unfortunately, what they knew wasn't much, as Evan Kelly had been less than cooperative.

Yes, he'd gone to the dentist's office to have his new crown put on his front right bicuspid. He'd pulled back his lip to show them all, and it was indeed an impressive tooth, although unfortunately whiter than the abutting teeth. However, as evidence, it was at least noticeable.

Yes, he'd then come home, ascertained that Maggie had not yet arrived to share the evening with him. Which was fine, because there had been a message on his telephone answering machine: Any members of the Majestics—Evan's bowling team—who had time to kill on Christmas Eve were welcome to free lanes from six to eight, when the alley would close for the holiday.

Evan had donned his Majestics shirt and headed for the lanes—thus explaining the bright yellow shirt collar Saint Just had winced at, but did not, to Saint Just's mind, explain the two thick black stripes running down the front of said shirt, the black short sleeves, or the black velvet letters spelling out *Majestics* on the back of said shirt. There was nothing within the wide scope of Saint Just's sartorical knowledge that could possibly justify such an abomination.

In fact, if Saint Just had been forced to name one good thing about said shirt, it would have to be that the material seemed impervious to wrinkles. Of course, he would then be forced to add that the polyester fabric might also be impervious to soap, water, and, possibly, atomic fallout.

At any rate—hideous shirt to one side (please, God)—Evan had gone off to the bowling alley, to see two other members of the Majestics there, the only other single members of the team, also obviously with little to do on Christmas Eve. They'd bowled three games before he and the other members—yes, one had been Walter Bodkin—had exchanged wishes for a happy holiday and parted ways in the parking lot outside the bowling alley. No, Evan couldn't remember if anyone had seen either of them get into separate cars and drive out of the parking lot.

After that? Well, after that, no matter how Maggie badgered the man—and she did badger him—Evan Kelly refused to comment as to how he'd spent his time before returning to his apartment only minutes before the Ocean City police were banging on his door.

Now, having given their report, Saint Just believed it might be time he and Maggie asked some questions.

Beginning with why Alicia Kelly had blurted out that Evan had murdered Walter Bodkin for her.

Saint Just was collecting his thoughts, planning precisely how he might broach the subject, when Sean Whitaker, who had taken himself upstairs to watch CNN, bounded down the stairs and raced across the living room to switch on the television set.

"You've got to see this," he said, looking to the set, turning to grin at Maggie and Saint Just. "Oh, damn, they've already gone to commercial. Tate—what channel shows MSNBC around here? They'll probably have it, too. Come on, come on—talk to me, Tate."

Maggie reached up and pinched Saint Just's arm. "You know what he just saw, don't you? With all that's happened, I actually forgot about, you know, the money? But it looks like we made freaking CNN, if that idiot's stupid grin means anything. This is *not* going to be pretty."

"It certainly wasn't, the first time I saw it," Saint Just supplied, turning toward the television screen even as Maureen returned to the living room, carrying a small tray of cookies.

"Oh, no," she said, subsiding into a chair. "Daddy's on TV?"

"No, not Dad," Maggie began, inching closer to Saint Just. "Sean? Can you please not bother channel-surfing and turn that thing off? Mom? Everyone? Something happened today . . ."

"*Omigod, it's Maggie!* Look, everybody—it's *Maggie!*"

"Never mind," Maggie said weakly as Maureen's high-pitched outburst had every head in the room whipping eyes-front to the television set.

"Courage, my dear," Saint Just whispered as he lifted her hand to place a kiss in her palm. "And please try to remember—winning over three million dollars, for most people, is considered to be a good thing."

"Yeah? Watch. I have a feeling that your *most people* doesn't include many of the people in this room."

Having already seen the footage that had appeared on the local station, Saint Just listened to the commentator and kept his gaze roaming the Kelly living room, doing his best to interpret the varying expressions of the faces of the other occupants.

". . . definitely will be a Merry Christmas this year for the lucky winner of the Big-Wheels-o'-Bucks jackpot in Atlantic City earlier today . . ."

Maureen had put down the tray of cookies on the couch beside her and now had both hands clamped to her mouth, her eyes going the size of saucers.

". . . until Scrooge arrived in the form of a fat but not quite jolly gentlemen. Watch closely, folks. Ouch! That had to hurt . . ."

Tate, sat down. On the tray of cookies. "Damn it!"

". . . The lady with the great right cross declined to give her name, but sources in Manhattan have verified that she is none other than Cleo Dooley, bestselling author of something called the Viscount Saint Just Mysteries. A nearly constant name on the *New York Times* bestseller list, Ms. Dooley is in fact one Margaret Kelly. The man you see carrying her off-screen remains unidentified, but we do know the name of our Scrooge with the bloody nose."

Alicia Kelly's expression was unreadable. Saint Just considered this to be a blessing that wouldn't last.

". . . *pushed* herself in front of me and grabbed my machine. That was *my* machine! Margaret Kelly, huh? Kelly, you hear me! This isn't over! That's *my* jackpot!"

Now Saint Just did turn his attention to the screen, as the man he knew as Henry Novack seemed to have a new song to sing. A threat, actually. And there he was, live, on a split-screen with the reporter, shaking his fist in the air, his face nearly purple, spittle gathered at the corners of his mouth.

The reporter seemed to agree with Saint Just's assessment: "Is that a threat, Mr. Novack?"

Henry Novack pushed his face closer to the camera. "It's whatever you want it to be! I know who you are now, Margaret Kelly. You've got my three million bucks, cupcake! I'm gonna sue. You hear me? I'm gonna sue your miserable ass—"

Henry Novack's face disappeared, and the reporter was full-screen once more.

"Yes, Merry Christmas, Margaret Kelly, Cleo Dooley—*cupcake*. And now onto the real news. I've just gotten word that Santa Claus has been sighted over Newfoundland. His ETA in your town tonight, with skies remaining fair over the Northeast, is—"

"Turn that off."

"Yes, ma'am, Mrs. Kelly," Sean Whitaker said, aiming the remote at the screen.

"Margaret?"

"Yes, ma'am," Maggie said, sounding like Sean's echo. "It wasn't my fault, Mom. My leg hurt, and that guy was being a real pain, and I just sat down, and Alex put this damn hundred dollar bill in the—"

"Why do you do that?" Alicia Kelly asked her, interrupting Maggie not a moment too soon, to Saint Just's mind. "Why do you always assume I have nothing good to say about anything you do?"

Maggie shot Saint Just a quick, astonished look. "Uh . . . because you *don't*?"

"That's cruel, Margaret, and untrue," Mrs. Kelly said.

Now Saint Just shot an astonished (for him) look at Maggie's mother.

"I'm sor—no. No, I'm not sorry, Mom. You hate my books. You complain that I don't come home enough. Okay, okay, you have a point there. You tell me I'm fat, you tell me I cause you embarrassment. You . . . you never hung up my Perfect Attendance plaque I got in the fourth grade."

"That last might have been dispensed with, my dear," Saint Just whispered to her.

"Right," Maggie agreed, shifting on the seat of the chair, her posture belligerent. "You never read one of my books. Never. None of you. You just condemned them because they were *romances*. Filth, you called them—and you never read them."

Maureen raised her hand. "I did. I mean, I do. I read all of them. I get them from the library."

"Well, there's a mixed blessing, sweetings," Saint Just whispered, close by Maggie's ear. "She reads them, but she doesn't buy them."

"Margaret, are you quite finished?"

Maggie looked up at Saint Just, who nodded.

"Yeah, Mom, I'm done. And now I do apologize. I fell into a trap, one people under stress fall into all the time. We don't want to think about Daddy, about the trouble he's in, so we fight about anything we can fight about. I'm sorry."

"As well you should be," Mrs. Kelly said, falling back into her more recognizable form. "Now, tell us how much of this jackpot you get to keep, dear. I seem to have missed that. Enough to pay Cynthia to find a way for your father to beat this rap?"

"Beat this—uh." Maggie gave her head a quick shake. "Well,

yeah, sure, Mom. I have enough money to help Dad prove his innocence. But not from the jackpot. I'm giving my winnings to Sterling. He . . . um . . . well, he was the one pushing the Max button. I'd found the Cash-out button, and would have pushed it, but he was having so much fun that I let him keep pushing the button, and it wasn't as though it was my money we were wasting, you know, so in some ways it is Sterling's win, not mine. And that guy, that Novack guy? I did take his machine."

"My congratulations, my dear," Saint Just told her as everyone else in the room opened their mouths, but it was as if Maggie had hit some sort of invisible Mute button, because no words passed anyone's lips. "They've been struck dumb."

It was Cynthia Spade-Whitaker who rallied first. "Margaret, here's some free legal advice. Never say that again. Any of it. To anyone. *Ever.*"

"She'll be very careful, I assure you," Saint Just said, at last pushing himself up from the arm of the chair, as sitting close beside Maggie hadn't seemed to do much to protect her from her family.

"Good, because some ambulance-chasing lawyer would jump all over that statement. By the way, how did you break your leg?"

"Maggie . . ." Saint Just muttered beneath his breath warningly.

"My foot, you mean? Well, it's the silliest thing. I was jogging in Central Park when this man came running by yelling '*The sky is falling, the sky is falling.*' And he was naked. Did I mention that he was naked? And this cop comes out of nowhere, to throw a tackle on the guy, and the guy rolled into me, we both went down—bam, broken foot."

"Really? You could probably sue, you know. I represented a similar case not six months ago. Smithers *v.* the City of New York City, and—"

"She made that up, Cynthia," her husband told her, glaring at Maggie. "She writes fiction, Tate said, remember?"

Cynthia coughed slightly. Shook back her shoulders. "Very amusing."

"Yes," Saint Just said. "Our Maggie is easily amused. Now, if we might return to the subject of the murder?"

"The alleged murder," Cynthia corrected. "The detective refused to give me any pertinent information as to TOD, MOD, COD. The whole thing could have been an accident, and this arrest-happy cowboy just took it from there."

"Time of death, manner of death, cause of death, right?" Maggie asked Saint Just, who merely nodded. He watched The Learning Channel faithfully, as well as all the *CSI* programs, and was familiar with all of the terms.

"Ah, but we do have at least a preliminary cause of death," he told everyone. "Evan and I had a small coze before Maggie and I adjourned here, and we deduced, from the questions posed to him from the detective, that Mr. Bodkin succumbed to a blow to the head with a heavy object. Several blows, to be precise, as I understand that Evan saw the murder weapon that had been sealed in a heavy plastic evidence bag, and was told that what he saw on the weapon was blood, bits of bone, and gray matter."

"Oh, yuk," Maggie said, wrapping her arms around her midsection. "So, what was the weapon?"

"A bowling ball," Saint Just told them, watching them in turn as he paused, let the tension build. "A bowling ball inscribed EEK: Evan Edward Kelly." He looked over his shoulder at Maggie. "Nearly as unfortunate as your We Are Romance writers organization, yes? Do you Americans never think of these things?"

"Did they read him his rights before they showed him the bowling ball? Did he identify the bowling ball as his? That's why they showed it to him. Has to be. If they asked him, they're out of line."

"That, Attorney Spade-Whitaker, I could not say."

"I can get any confession thrown out," Cynthia told them confidently, sitting back and crossing her long legs. "If they'd taken him straight to Cape May, let the county prosecutor's office handle everything from the get-go, or even called in the state police, we might have more trouble. But they didn't, not on Christmas Eve. With any luck at all, we can have this whole thing tossed, at least for a few weeks, until they have more than a bloody bowling ball. The weapon might be Kelly's, but that doesn't mean they can prove he had possession of the ball at the time of the murder. OJ got off with a lot more against him."

"So if the bowling ball doesn't fit, they have to acquit?" Maggie asked, then rolled her eyes at Saint Just.

"You're being very encouraging, counselor," Saint Just complimented, ignoring Maggie. "But I think we have a sticking point
here. Mrs. Kelly seemed to believe, at first blush, that Evan murdered the late Walter Bodkin *for her*. Mrs. Kelly? Would you care
to explain that statement?"

Maureen muttered something under her breath, picked up the
tray of crushed cookies, and escaped toward the kitchen. Saint
Just watched her go, something about the woman's reaction
whenever Walter Bodkin's name was mentioned in relationship to
her mother niggling at him. Combined with her blurted giggle at
the police station, it was enough to make him believe that he'd
have to speak with the woman sometime soon.

"No. I don't care to explain anything to you," Mrs. Kelly said,
also getting to her feet. "It's late, I'm tired, and don't want to think
about any of this any more tonight. Tate, see to your guests.
Margaret, go take care of your father. We're done here."

And that was that. Maggie might be his general at the moment,
but Alicia Kelly clearly remained commander-in-chief.

Chapter 9

Maggie and Alex had walked the long block from her father's borrowed bachelor apartment to her mother's condo. Well, Alex had walked it. Maggie had hopped it. They now retraced their steps slowly, by necessity, Maggie with her chin tucked into the collar of her new winter coat against the late December wind off the ocean as she hopped, stopped, rested, hopped again.

"Smell that, Alex? I really like this city, much as I was glad to get away from home. I miss the smell of the ocean," she said during one of her rest stops. "But I think I enjoy it more in July, when my teeth aren't chattering. At least it isn't snowing tonight. No white Christmas this year."

"It will be midnight in another minute," Alex told her, slipping his arm around her waist during one of her long pauses to catch her breath, drawing her against the side of his body. "Happy Christmas, sweetings."

She peered up at him in the light from a streetlamp. "Our first Christmas together, a house of our own, my stupid foot, a jackpot, a murder. I guess we'll never forget this first one, huh? Alex?"

He pressed a kiss against her forehead. "Yes, my dear?"

"There's something you should know."

"There are many things I should know, beginning with why your mother seems to, as you say, *freak out* every time Walter Bodkin's name is brought into a conversation."

"Well, yeah, we need to know that. Definitely. And did you notice Maureen? She went sort of ape herself, don't you think? Even her little pink pills couldn't disguise that she was—well, that she's hiding something. If we can't get Mom to talk with us tomorrow, she'll be my next move."

"Ah, Maggie, we're splendid together, do you know that?"

"Meaning? Oh. So you saw it, too. Maureen's reaction. Even for her, it wasn't quite right."

"Was there really any question that I would notice?"

"No, I suppose not. The great Viscount Saint Just is on the case. And, for once, I'm not arguing with you or telling you to butt out. But that's not what I wanted to say to you right now. I just think you should know something. Not all families are like ours. You know—wacko? They really aren't."

"Then those families must be exceedingly dull and uninteresting," Alex told her as they turned the corner on Thirty-seventh Street, heading up the sidewalk for one short block, to Evan's apartment.

"We're dysfunctional, textbook dysfunctional," Maggie pushed on, needing Alex to understand. "Doctor Bob said that to me, first thing. Although he'd be proud of the way I stopped myself when I started off on that tangent about being the unappreciated middle child—although finally putting at least some of how I feel into words, and saying those words to Mom, really was liberating there for a moment. But it was also petty. I'm learning, Alex, I really am. I'm a big girl now, and I have to accept my past, understand it, forgive it, and then move on. I can't just keep blaming my unhappy childhood for everything and never become my own person."

"And you made a great leap in that direction this evening, my dear, no pun intended. My felicitations."

"Yes, I think I did. And they love me. I know that, somewhere down deep inside. And I have to acknowledge that every hang-up I have can be pretty much laid at their doorstep, but if I believe that, then I also have to believe that anything *good* about me also came from them."

"A reasonable conclusion, yes."

"If I hadn't wanted so badly to get away from them, prove myself, I might never have gone to New York, might never have written one book, let alone all the books I've written. I might still be living here, maybe working in a bank, or something, and popping little pink pills, like Maureen."

"You're thinking that you might never have imagined me, aren't you, Maggie?"

She felt her cheeks grow hot, even in the fairly frigid breeze. "According to you, I've been *imagining* you since I hit puberty, in one way or another. Which is fairly disturbing. Like I've been looking for, and imagining, a white knight for most of my life. I'm an independent woman. A modern woman."

"A hopping woman."

"Now you're laughing at me," she said, pushing herself out of his light embrace and hopping ahead of him before turning about to face him once more—man, she was getting good on this walker. If they made walker-hopping an Olympic sport, she might just capture the bronze.

"Indeed, no. Don't you realize what you did this evening, sweetings? You took charge. In the usually daunting face of authority, in the face of the policeman's uniform, in the face of your mother's anger, your brother's usual ridiculousness, Cynthia Spade-Whitaker's cool condescension—I could go on—you stood tall, you stood your ground. You were, in a word, magnificent. A modern Boadicea. And all by yourself. Or may I take any of the credit? I'd like to think I could."

Maggie let him put his arm around her again. "It is nice, knowing you have my back," she admitted. "Does that give me a new problem—I'm nothing without a man?"

"I have no idea what that means," Alex told her. "Are you tired? I can carry you, you know."

Maggie looked at him, so handsome in the light from the streetlamp. He wore his long black cashmere topcoat with flair, as he wore every stitch of his clothing with flair; the creamy ivory silk scarf hanging loose around his neck setting off the perpetual light tan of his face beneath the wide, flat brim of his black hat that always reminded her of one worn by a young Clint Eastwood in those spaghetti westerns. Black leather gloves, his gold-topped sword cane—the man was, as they had said in the Regency, well set up, and definitely well put together.

On most other men, the clothes might look like a costume. But Alex was so self-assured, so comfortable in his own skin (and designer clothes), that all a person could do was be impressed. Damned impressed.

She certainly was impressed.

And he was going to be bunking in with Sterling, just as he had when he and Sterling had first poofed into her life. After a few lovely weeks of sharing her bed. Was she an unnatural child to think about that right now, rather than concentrate on her father's terrible problem?

Well, yeah.

But that's life.

Maggie looked up the block, to see that they were only two doors away from the stairs leading up into her father's building. "No, I can make it, thanks. I don't know about those steps, though. I might let you play Sir Galahad this time, and carry me up them, instead of me bumping up them on my fanny. Alex?"

He fell into step with her once more. "Hmm, yes?"

"I miss you."

She didn't turn her head to see his smile, but she could feel it.

"I miss you, too, sweetings. As incentives go, I believe being denied the pleasure of watching you fall asleep in my arms will go a long way toward the speedy resolution of your father's dilemma."

"You watch me sleep? Oh, God, Alex, don't do that. I probably drool."

"No comment, as I pride myself on being a gentleman. Which means, naturally, that I also refuse to mention the occasional soft snore."

"Bite me," Maggie said, and then hopped around in a half circle so that she had her back to the wide wooden steps. She lowered herself down, slowly, carefully. "Wanna neck a while before we go in? That is, my hero, do you wish to partake of a small, necessarily limited romantic encounter?"

"I thought you'd never suggest it," Alex said, sitting down beside her and pulling her into his arms. "You're more than usually beautiful in the moonlight, sweetings. Your eyes seem to shine with a special light."

She blinked once, and then smiled up at him. "It's not the moon, it's the streetlamp. But don't let me stop you. Tell me more about my eyes. And don't use any lines I've put in your mouth over the years."

"Never. Let's see," he said, trailing the tips of his fingers down her cheek. "Where do I begin? With the soft velvet of your skin . . . the pertness of your perfect little nose . . . the lush, sweet fullness of the most delectable lips I've—stay here."

"Huh?" Maggie opened her eyes as Alex rapidly stood up, unsheathing his swordstick and pointing it into the darkness beyond the circle of light cast by the street lamp. "Alex, what in hell are you—oh, shit . . ."

"Google," Henry Novack said proudly, sitting in the street, perched on his stupid motorized go-cart. He wore a bright green nylon ski jacket over his considerable bulk, one with orange Day-Glo reflector stripes on the sleeves, and a huge orange woolen cap—with earflaps. He looked, to Maggie, like a cross between a duck hunter and the logo for the Orange Bowl parade.

"Google what?"

"*The* Google, the one on the Internet. All you need is a name. Okay, and a city helps. Evan Kelly. Ocean City. And up pops the address. I followed you here from there. Man, you move slow. You and me, Kelly, we're gonna deal."

"Oh, yeah? Really?" Maggie said, pushing herself to her feet— foot, anyway. "I'm on one foot, sure, not able to run away. But tell me something, Novack. Did you happen to notice this guy with me, huh? The tall, athletic one with a freaking *sword* in his hand, pointed at you? We're not going to do anything I don't want to do. Not now, not ever. Not unless you want me to sic him on you."

"I begin to believe, sweetings, that this hero-to-the-rescue business has begun to go to at least one of our heads," Alex told her dryly, not taking his eyes, or his sword, off Novack. "I remember a time when you weren't quite so comfortable depending on me."

"Yeah, well, I wasn't hopping around in this stupid cast then, either," Maggie pointed out, still rather heady with her earlier bravado at the police station and at her mother's house. "Novack? You still here? Why are you still here? Oh, I know. You want to ask me how I broke my foot, right?"

"What the hell do I care how you broke your damn foot?"

Maggie grinned. "Don't do that. I could begin to like you,

Novack. Tell me something—how many miles a charge do you get on that thing?"

"You stole my machine. You stole my jackpot."

"Mr. Novack," Alex said, lowering the sword to his side, "you become wearisome, not to mention redundant."

"You've got money," Novack went on, as if Alex hadn't spoken. "I Googled you, too. The great Cleo Dooley. You didn't need that jackpot. I *need* that jackpot. Sam says you'll pay me, just so I don't sue. Just so you can keep your face out of the papers and off the news, because the great Cleo Dooley can't be seen as cheap, and a cheater. Especially not with her daddy in the slammer for murder. And me handicapped, too. That's the topper."

"Who's Sam?" Maggie asked, subsiding onto the wooden stair once more. She'd had worse days, but she couldn't think of any of them at the moment.

"My *lawyer*, that's who Sam is," Henry Novack crowed in some satisfaction. "My brother's second daughter's husband's cousin—and he's smart, too."

"It's possible, seeing as how he's not your blood relative," Maggie said, reaching into her pocket for her empty nicotine inhaler.

"Sam says Fox News eats up stuff like this. And that blonde with the bulgy eyes on CNN? Her, too. What's her name? I can't remember. Haircut like she belongs on one of them Dutch Boy paint can labels. Now there's a real barracuda for you. They'd all want me on the air."

"I'll just bet they would," sparing a moment to think of Alex's "pal" at New York's Fox News, Holly Spivak. She wasn't Nancy Grace, thank God—the barracuda—but she sure did love a juicy bit of scandal. Maggie searched through her purse for her very last, hoarded, nicotine cylinder. And people who couldn't get through stressful days without their caffeine or their daily booze wondered why other people smoked . . .

"Every week, I play that machine. Every week since the day the machines went in. Do you know how much money I've put through that machine?"

"Maybe you should have used that money to join a health club instead," Maggie muttered under her breath, figuring the man weighed four hundred pounds if he weighed an ounce. No wonder he used a cart—he could have used a U-Haul.

"Mr. Novack," Alex said, stepping in front of Maggie. "Impressed as we both are by your tenacity, if not your arguments, we would appreciate it greatly if you were to, um, retire from the field for the night. Now, what would it take, Mr. Novack, for you to do just that, hmm?"

"Here it comes," Maggie muttered, then sucked on her inhaler.

"I want to talk, that's what I want. I want to *deal*. You deal, you do right by me, and I won't talk to reporters anymore."

"Oh, God, Alex," Maggie moaned. "Can't I just pay him?"

"Hush, sweetings." He stepped closer to the street even as he sheathed his sword, sliding it back inside the cane. "As you have told us you know about Miss Kelly's other problems, and as tomorrow—today—is Christmas, I believe we would like very much to postpone our conversation until Boxing Day, if that's agreeable to you."

"Boxing Day? When the hell is that? There's no fights scheduled at Caesar's until January, I know that much. Is there one at the old Convention Hall? Who's on the fight card? Any heavyweights?"

Maggie eased back against the steps, giggling. Sometimes, she thought almost hysterically, you just had to *roll with the punches*.

"December the twenty-sixth, Mr. Novack," Alex explained. "Somewhere discreet."

"Oh, okay. Why didn't you just say so? Boxing Day? That's some English thing, right? And I'm not a monster, ya know," Henry Novack said, his go-cart beeping as he backed away from the curb. "I got feelings, too, ya know. I just want what's mine. Okay, okay. Day after Christmas, right here in Ocean City, up on the Boardwalk. We'll meet in front of the Music Pier, off Eighth Street. Nobody's going to be there at night. Too cold, right? Midnight good for you? It's good for me."

"Oh, for crying out loud, Alex. The guy thinks he's freaking Deep Throat on a go-cart, or something. And not on the twenty-sixth. That's the day of my appointment to get this foot X-rayed, get into a walking cast, remember? I have to drive back to the city. Make it the twenty-seventh. At eight o'clock. Otherwise Dad would want to know why we're going out so late."

Novack put the go-cart in drive, bumped at the curb. "Now you're putting me off, aren't you? Hoping I'll go away. Not happening, cupcake. You go to the city, sure, but you'd better come back, because I know where you live. Wherever you go, whatever you do, I'm going to be watching you. I'm your worst nightmare."

Okay, fun was fun, and all that, but fun time was now over. Maggie grabbed the walker and stood up. "Buddy, you don't even come close to being my worst nightmare, so just take a number and get in line, okay. I said we'd be there, and we'll be there. The twenty-seventh, eight o'clock, at the Music Pier. Pin a red midsize Buick to your lapel, so I recognize you. Now *go away*."

Alex watched until the go-cart had turned the corner before walking back over to Maggie and allowing her to steady herself against his shoulder while he folded the walker, slid it up and over his shoulder, then lifted her into his arms.

"A midsize Buick?" he asked her, the corners of his mouth twitching slightly.

"I know. That was pretty good, wasn't it? But he made me so mad."

"You're not meeting with that lunatic, you know," he told her as he carried her up the stairs. "I'm meeting with him."

Maggie snuggled her face into his neck. "Are we going to fight about this? Because I'm going. I know I don't owe the man. Not really, not legally. But I do feel sorry for him. I never would have sat down at that machine if he hadn't been such a jerk."

"You can't give him money, Maggie. He'll keep coming back for more, over and over again. He's gone beyond a rather pathetic man with bad luck, and graduated into stalking and a strange form of blackmail. That cannot be countenanced. Reach down and open the door, if you will, please."

Maggie did as he asked, then held on tight as Alex climbed the first half flight, turned on the landing, and mounted the second half flight leading to her father's door. Bless the man, he wasn't even breathing hard when they reached the second floor. That did a lot for her female ego. "So why did you suggest we meet with him? Are you planning to scare him off somehow? Threaten him?"

He put her down, opened the walker for her. "I've not as yet formed a strategy. Are you planning to adopt him?"

"No, of course not," Maggie said angrily, grabbing the walker. "I'm . . . I don't know what I'm planning. Cynthia says I can't pay him. You say I can't pay him. I don't know what to do with him. I just know I don't want him following me around everywhere in that stupid go-cart like some motorized Lassie until we figure out some sort of solution that makes him go away. Did you take the key with you when we went to Mom's?"

Alex shook his head. "It's probably open," he said, reaching past her to turn the handle, which turned easily. "Ah, what a trusting man your father is, Maggie."

"And not a killer," she said, hopping into the dark living room. "Anybody with half a brain could figure that out in a millisecond. Hit the lights, will you? No, wait. Look, over there—the message light is still glowing on Dad's answering machine. Not blinking, like with a new message, but just glowing, because Dad didn't erase the messages he has stored on it. The cops should have taken that, shouldn't they? You know, for the message Dad said was on the machine? The one telling him about the free bowling?"

"Very true," Alex agreed, snapping on the large overhead lights that were a part of an equally large ceiling fan shaped like palm fronds. "The message is the reason Evan gave for going to the bowling alley last evening."

"Yes, and he said he and Bodkin and someone else were the only three to show up. How many people are on a bowling team, anyway? So maybe the real killer set up the meet, then took it from there. We may have the real killer's voice, right here, on the answering machine. God, this is going to be easier than I thought. I adore stupid criminals." Maggie hopped as fast as she could, eager to get to the machine, and pressed the Message button:

"You have one old message. Message One: *Hi, Evan. Free bowling for all Majestics 'til eight tonight. Tournament's next week, so we need the practice. Be there!* Message received December twenty-four, at four-fifty-three P.M. End of messages."

The call was short, the voice was male, with considerable background noise placing the origin of the call as most probably being the bowling alley. But someone might recognize it. Maybe.

Maggie collapsed into the chair beside the table holding the answering machine. "Well, there it is. Time stamped and dated. The police were sloppy, not taking the machine. Dad was *lured*. Right, Alex? He was lured, and if we can voice-print whoever called him with that message, we have our killer. He followed Dad, copped his bowling ball somehow, and used it to bash in the other guy's head. Walter Bodkin's head. Right? Right?"

"It seems plausible. Especially if we're fortunate enough to find a similar message on Bodkin's machine—if the man didn't answer his own phone. But, not to rain on your parade, my dear, it would seem, as another member of the team also was there for this free bowling exercise, that the entire call would be dismissed by the police as irrelevant. And one more thing—wouldn't your father have noticed if his bowling ball went missing?"

"Yeah, you're right. He'd notice. He loves that bowling ball. I gave it to him, you know, on his last birthday. He had to have taken it with him to the bowling alley. And a person notices if he's carrying a bowling ball bag with a bowling ball in it or a bowling ball bag with no bowling ball in it. Dad uses a twelve-pound ball, as I remember it. Twelve less pounds in your bag as you're heading for the parking lot? You'd notice."

Maggie felt tears stinging at her eyes again, when she'd thought she'd gotten them out of her system. She needed to be all business, concentrate on the facts. Even as she had to believe in her father's innocence.

"He didn't do it, Alex. I know he didn't. We have to make him tell us where he went after he left the bowling alley. We have to make Mom tell us why she thinks Dad killed Bodkin for *her*. We have to . . ."

"We have to go to bed," Alex said, shifting the walker to one side and holding out his hands to her.

She took them, and pulled up to balance on her right foot, then gasped as Alex lifted her high against his chest. "I can walk to the bedroom," she told him even as she curled her arms around his neck.

"Just as I can find my way to the chamber I'm sharing with Sterling before the sun rises in a few hours. In the meantime," he said, stepping inside the door to Maggie's assigned bedroom and toeing shut the door, "where was I when we were so rudely interrupted? Ah, yes, I believe I was about to describe the remarkable beauty of your mouth . . ."

Chapter 10

Ocean City, New Jersey, is accessible by main bridges at Ninth and Thirty-fourth Street and smaller bridges that dot the scenic highway that runs along the coast both north and south.

The island is long rather than wide, and the north-south blocks are about as long as city blocks in Manhattan, with the east-west blocks running short.

The numbered streets run east-west, from the bay to the ocean.

With land at a premium, the building lots are for the most part narrow and long, the houses built on them fitting from the street to the alleys that run parallel to the north-south streets.

Is this important? Well, yeah. Maybe.

If your house is on First Street, you are one heck of a long haul from, say, Fifty-fifth Street. But if someone lives on Wesley near Thirty-eighth (as did Maggie's mother), and you reside on Thirty-seventh (as did Maggie's father), chances are you could gaze out your back window, look down the alley, and wave to your neighbor a full city block away on Wesley.

As Saint Just was finding out to his surprise and amazement at eight o'clock on Christmas morning.

"Interesting," Saint Just remarked as he stood in the kitchen alcove, nursing his morning cup of coffee, squinting at the sunlight glinting off what he was fairly certain was the lens of a pair of binoculars.

He heard the clump-clump of Maggie's walker on the tile floor behind him. "Maggie, good morning, my dear. Would you care to hobble over here, perhaps see something interesting?"

"Only if it's yellow, and scrambled, comes with toast and bacon, and I didn't have to cook any of it," Maggie grumbled as she stumbled into the kitchen, stopped, scratched at her—well, Saint Just would delicately call the general area of her scratching her derriere.

His Maggie was a true lady, she really was. But probably not before her morning coffee and toilette.

"I think it's possible that someone is observing us," he told her as she made her way over to him, taking her by the shoulders and placing her in front of him, turning her body so that she had a clear sight down the length of the alleyway. "There you go. Your mother's condo is light green in color, correct? With the kitchen to the rear of what you Americans call the second floor? Look for the flash of sun off glass, if you please."

Maggie leaned her head forward and squinted, as if pushing that particular appendage two inches forward would give her a better view. "Okay. I see it. What am I seeing?"

"That flash of light, I believe, is caused by the sun hitting the lens of a pair of binoculars trained in our direction. Held, one could suppose, by your mother. Would you care to wave?"

"Holy cripes!" Maggie ducked out from beneath Saint Just's hands and, scuttling like a five-legged crab on her walker, all but plastered her back against the refrigerator door on the far side of the room. "She's watching? She's been watching him—*spying* on Daddy? She could see us just now, too, if she's been watching? She saw us seeing her? Are you sure? You can't be sure, you're only guessing. How do you know the sun's hitting binoculars?"

"So many questions, all of them meaning much the same thing. As for my conclusion, it is an educated guess, actually," Saint Just told her, putting down his coffee cup. "Earlier, on a hunt for spoons, I opened a few drawers, and found this." He opened the bread drawer and pulled out . . . a pair of binoculars.

"And now that's just sick. He's watching her, too? While she's watching him? No wonder I'm a borderline nutcase. It's in my genes. What is the *matter* with these people?"

"I've been considering that very question. I would imagine your mother has been monitoring your father in hopes—or dread—of seeing him with a guest present. Carol is her name, yes? The paramour who is employed, as I believe your mother said, at the best jewelry store in Ocean City."

"I stand by my first impression. That is *sick*. So what's my dad been looking for?"

Saint Just picked up his cup of coffee once more. "Similar evidence of marital infidelity?"

"No, that can't be it. That makes them both voyeurs. I can't live with that, so I'm not going to believe it. They're just nosy. And don't correct me. I write fiction. I like fantasy, happy endings. Anything else is too real, especially this early in the morning. Lower the blinds, will you? I don't like being on display. Or would that be too obvious?"

"Too obvious by half, yes."

"Damn, I think so, too. Well, then let's just behave normally, like we don't know she's out there. And, boy, is she *out* there. Oh, good," she added, raising her voice, "there's more coffee. You made the coffee, Alex? Thank you so much. I believe I'll have some coffee now."

"Yes, I did indeed prepare the coffee. There's really no end to my talents, once I apply myself. But, as you playact, sweetings, remember that we are only, in a way of speaking, on video, and not audio."

"You'd hope so, wouldn't you. I don't know how good Mom is. They sell a lot of weird things at Radio Shack these days. Do you think Mom can read lips from that distance?"

Saint Just smiled at her pained grimace. "Sterling, by the way, has gone in search of donuts, as your brother failed so miserably to do so last night. Your father went with him. I've asked that they procure copies of all the morning newspapers, as I'm convinced you'll wish to read them."

"I guess I have to. As long as a picture of my dad doing the perp walk in leg shackles isn't above the fold. Anyway," she said, balancing on one foot as she spooned three sugars into her coffee as Saint Just manfully suppressed a wince, "Dad can't be watching to see if Mom is up to any hanky-panky. Walt Hagenbush died three years ago."

He took her coffee cup and placed it on the table for her. "I beg your pardon? Who?"

"Thank you." Maggie slid onto the slick, curved plastic cushion of the built-in bench and table that fit below a rather lovely bow window. The garishly flowered plastic, however, seemed an unfortunate choice. "Mom's *lover*, Alex, remember? That's what started all of this in the first place."

"Ah, yes, I believe I can recall that now," Saint Just said, sitting down across from her as she scooted farther onto the bench and rested her casted leg on a display of unnaturally large begonias. "Vaguely."

Maggie slid her forearms forward on the tabletop, the mug with the words "Lefties Do It Better" grasped between her palms. "On the occasion of their fortieth wedding anniversary this past summer, Mom decided to make a clean breast of things and tell Dad about an affair she had with Walt Hagenbush ten years earlier. That's when everything started to go off the rails. Coming clearer now?"

"Yes, it is. I had attempted to banish such intimate knowledge of your family's domestic travails from my memory, I'm afraid. Your father, worried over the admission of your mother's foray into infidelity, decided that the only way he could ever find it in his heart to forgive her would be if he had an affair of his own. Enter Carol, the jewelry shop clerk."

"The little chippie, as Mom calls her, yes. And exit Dad, to this place, when Mom found out about it," Maggie said, lifting the coffee cup to her lips. She took a sip, frowned, and asked Saint Just to please bring the sugar bowl and the spoon over to the table for her.

This time, as Maggie added another heaping teaspoonful of sugar to the cup, Saint Just did wince. But he did politely refrain from pointing out that it might be easier if the dear woman simply poured coffee into the sugar bowl, rather than the other way round.

"So your father couldn't have been watching your family home to ascertain whether or not your mother had taken up a romantic association with the late Walt Hagenbush once more. Leaving us to assume that he may have been watching the condo and saw her—"

"Playing house with Walter Bodkin," Maggie finished for him, subsiding against the back cushion of the banquette. "What is it with men named Walter, anyway? Does my mother have some kind of a name fetish? No, don't answer that. And I mean that sincerely. A daughter should never say the words mother and fetish in the same sentence, not if the daughter hopes ever to be able to look that mother in the face again."

"We have to look at this thing logically, Maggie."

"I know that. But it's not easy for a daughter to think sordid and Mommy and Daddy at the same time. Hell, I think I was twenty-one before I'd finally given up the fantasy that my parents had four kids, which meant they'd had sex four times. God, Alex, I'm going to be seeing Doctor Bob every week for the rest of my unnatural life, I swear it."

"But you are thinking about the situation now, correct? I'd forgotten the late and unlamented Mr. Hagenbush, but this might come down to your mother having an affair, your father having a revenge affair, and your mother then launching a double-revenge affair. You know, Maggie, this scenario has all the earmarks of a two-part Doctor Phil special."

"Bite your tongue! So what you're saying—what you think the cops could say—is that Dad saw Mom and Bodkin—we'll just call him Bodkin, because Walter is too confusing—and *offed* him?"

"They might think that, yes. Shall we dispose of the binoculars? Or, at the very least, relocate them?"

"Tampering with evidence. We can't do that," Maggie muttered, her brow creased, as she appeared to be deep in thought. "Besides, this is a pretty small town, especially in the winter, with the tourists gone and half the condos empty. If Mom was . . . with Bodkin, someone would have seen them, and someone would most probably have told Dad. Mom said Dad did it for her— killed Bodkin for her, that is. Not because of her, because she was having an affair, but *for* her. That doesn't quite fit, does it?"

She looked toward the doorway. "He's got to talk to us this morning. Be honest with us. He looks guilty, refusing to tell anyone where he was last night. And Cynthia is just going to tell him not to say anything to anybody, so we have to get to him first. How long ago did he and Sterling leave?"

Saint Just glanced up at the wall clock. "No more than forty-five minutes ago, I'd say. I wasn't particularly paying attention.

That was lax of me. Perhaps I was still quietly rhapsodizing about the woman I'd just left and the pleasant memory of a most remarkable interlude."

"We had sex, Alex. And this damn cast didn't make it easy, either," Maggie said, rolling her eyes as she struggled to stand up. "So enough with the romantic interlude business, and definitely enough with sitting here, pretending we don't know Mom is playing secret agent with us in her sights. Take my coffee cup into the living room for me, will you, please? My leg will be more comfortable on the couch. I can hop, but I still can't juggle worth a darn."

His Maggie was so easily flustered in the daylight. Thankfully, not once they were alone together, in the dark. But it was early days yet, he'd give her all the time she needed. Saint Just brushed his fingertips across the back of her neck as he led the way past the doorway, and into the living room of the condo. "Call it what you will, sweetings. I know what it was."

"Yeah, well . . . okay," Maggie said, tagging after him, her casted left leg bent at the knee, her right foot bare, and probably cold on the tile floor. "Hey, where are you going? Aren't you going to stay here with me? Aren't we going to talk about this some more?"

"Then you do wish to discuss our romantic interlude?" Saint Just inquired, pausing at the short half flight of steps that led up to the three bedrooms in the condo apartment. "Anything you wish, Maggie."

She fell backward onto the couch, then struggled to sit upright, grabbed her coffee mug once more. "Ha. Ha. I meant Dad. And Mom. And the two of them spying on each other. That's creepy. Don't you think that's creepy? If they don't care about each other, why watch each other?"

"Because they *do* care about each other?"

Maggie pointed a finger at him. "Aha! That's what I think. Mom fell apart last night, at least as far apart as I've ever seen her since the day I swung my softball bat in the dining room and took out her grandmother's pedestal vase that the woman brought here from County Clare."

Saint Just looked at her levelly. "You weren't an easy child, were you, Maggie?"

"Another subject, for another time. I don't go to my high

school reunions, though, if that gives you any indication of how well I dealt with being a teenager. *Anyway*—it stands to reason that Mom and Dad do still love each other, or whatever has ever passed for love between them. And, no, I don't really want to go there, either. But, if Dad still loves her, and if Bodkin did something to her, or even tried to do something to her . . ."

"Such as?" Saint Just asked her, taking a seat in a nearby chair. He thoroughly enjoyed watching Maggie's mind work. He believed he could almost hear the gears turning inside her head.

"I don't know. They've been separated since around Thanksgiving. She might have started dating? After all, Dad was—maybe still is—dating that Carol woman. Bodkin might have brought Mom home, gone into the house with her, made a pass at her in the kitchen, where Dad could see—"

"We can see clearly into the side windows of the kitchen, Maggie. I had the chance to tour the entirety of your mother's condo when we first visited last month. If you'd raised your gaze slightly, to the next floor, you'd realize that we could also see into what I believe is the master bedroom."

"Worse!" she said, plunking down the now empty mug. "Bodkin wormed his way upstairs, attacked Mom, she had to fight him off. Now she's afraid of him. Dad figures that the way back into Mom's good graces is to play the hero for her, confront the guy, warn him off. They have words, it gets physical, yadda-yadda. Oh, damn, Alex. I'm building the prosecutor's case for him, aren't I? Oh, hi, Dad, Sterling. Merry Christmas!"

Saint Just got up as the two men closed the door behind them. As they shrugged out of their coats, they stamped their feet as though to rid themselves of the cold air they'd walked through. "Yes, Happy Christmas, everyone."

"Thank you, Saint Just," Sterling said, pulling a face as he repeatedly shot his gaze toward Evan Kelly.

But Saint Just hadn't needed Sterling's worried expression or eyeball gymnastics to ascertain that Evan Kelly was not quite as jolly as the red and white Santa cap on his head.

"Daddy? What's wrong?"

"Nothing, sweetheart," Evan said, handing the bag of donuts to Sterling before heading for the steps to the bedrooms. "Merry Christmas. Everyone. Please excuse me."

"Sterling?" Maggie asked as he handed several newspapers to Saint Just, who saw nothing alarming on any of the front pages. That was, until he'd rifled through the first one to find the first page of the Local section, to see Evan Kelly smiling at him as he held up a bowling trophy. Saint Just knew it was a bowling trophy because the copy beneath the photograph supplied that information. The garish thing had, to him, looked like something one might employ to prop open the door of a brothel. The headline read: Police Arrest Local Man in Murder of Bowling Buddy.

"No perp walk, as you termed it, my dear, but I doubt there is anyone in Ocean City who is unaware of your father's dilemma."

"Oh, yes, Saint Just. Everyone knows. It was terrible, Maggie," Sterling said sadly as he subsided into a chair, still holding his red knitted hat with the pom-pom on top—the pom-pom he was doing an admirable job of shredding in his agitation. "It took us some time to find a shop that was open on the holiday, and it was quite crowded. People *looked* at Evan. Nobody spoke. They just *looked*. And then they turned and walked away."

"The cut direct," Saint Just said, sighing. "I should have realized. It's as Balzac said, 'Society, like the Roman youth at the circus, never shows mercy to the fallen gladiator.' "

"Oh, God. Poor Daddy. What did he do?"

"Lifted his chin and ordered a dozen glazed, seemingly having forgotten that I'd told him I prefer powdered, with that lovely jelly filling," Sterling said, and then shook his head. "That is, he stood up manfully, Maggie. Until this person approached him. I'm afraid I didn't get his name, but he spoke to Evan, just for a moment, and then he, too, turned on his heel and walked away. Evan, well, Evan just stood there, looking as if he'd been poleaxed. I brought him straight home."

"Do you know what the man said, Sterling?"

"Yes, Saint Just, I do. The man told Evan that he is no longer to consider himself a member of the Majestics. I can't be sure, unaware of the level of prestige the Majestics may hold in this community, but I gather this must be the way Byron felt when the *ton* delivered him the cut direct at Almack's that night—you know, before he was forced to leave England entirely. He's a broken man, Saint Just, his spirit crushed by this terrible turn of events."

"They threw him off his bowling team? Daddy *lives* for his bowling team."

"Yes, Maggie," Sterling agreed. "I thought I saw a tear in Evan's eye, although that may have been from the cold and wind. In any event, we must do something. We must do something very soon."

Chapter 11

"Margaret? *Margaret!*"

Maggie pushed herself to her feet and hopped into the kitchen. "You bellowed—that is, I'm here, Mom."

Yes, she was *here*. And she'd been *here* for five hours now. Five hours that seemed like five days.

The Christmas tree was lit, decorated as it had always been decorated, in early after-Christmas-clearance items. One thing she had to say for her mother, though, she did faithfully hang up every ornament her children had made for her over the years.

Unfortunately, that included the one Maggie had made in sixth grade, with her school picture glued to the center of a gilt elbow macaroni frame. The photograph of her grinning manically in pigtails and teeth braces. Saint Just had gone up to it as if guided there by some sort of radar, and she'd glared at him, just daring him to say something, anything, that would force her to beat him heavily around the head and shoulders with her walker.

The nativity scene was spread out on top of the spinet, as always. The shepherd boy's flute was still missing its front end, the guardian angel's wing still oddly glued back in place where it had been broken the year their cat, Tuffy, had been frightened up onto the piano when Tate tried out his brand new drum set.

The lighted village—the one with the animated skaters whirling around a pond made out of a mirror—had been set up on the sideboard.

There were candles everywhere, none of them ever burned, of

course, some of them slightly misshapen as a consequence of being stored in the hot garage.

The Santa candle's face had, for instance, melted slightly, so that it looked now as if he was leering at Mrs. Claus with an eye toward slipping away with her to someplace private for a little one-on-one celebration.

Maggie's whole day thus far, her surroundings, had been one big trip down Memory Lane, and if her father had been there, wearing his silly Santa hat, ho-ho-ho-ing from time to time from his favorite chair in the living room for no apparent reason, Maggie would have been a reasonably happy camper.

But he wasn't there. He was back at his apartment, behind the locked door of his bedroom, refusing to come out, refusing to talk to anyone.

Her mother could have taken a hint from that, and done the same . . .

"Margaret, I asked one thing of you. One."

"Three, actually," Maggie said, still fairly delighted in her new-found knowledge that her mother no longer held the power to intimidate her. All of her life, Maggie had held her mother in awe. She was big. She had a big voice. She had a big bosom—but Maggie didn't think she really needed to number that among her problems with her mother.

Her mother spoke in absolutes. She had a way of cutting a person to ribbons if she scented blood in the water.

Her mother, as Doctor Bob had pointed out, was pretty much at the bottom of Maggie's problems with authority, with those who wielded their authority or their supposed knowledge like hammers, with those who yelled louder, were physically bigger . . . etc., etc., etc.

Stupid, really. A childhood trauma she'd carried with her into adulthood.

But, hey, not anymore. She was free. Free at last, free at last, thank God Almighty—etc.

And all it had taken was to have her father arrested for murder. *Jeez.*

"You asked me to slice the carrots and celery, which I did. You asked me to take a bowl of potato chips into the living room, which any id—which I couldn't do. And you asked me to lift the turkey into the roasting pan for Maureen as long as I was just sitting at the kitchen table, taking up valuable space, so that she could then slip it into the oven, which I did do, although it wasn't easy. Smells, good in here, doesn't it? Is it ready?"

Mrs. Kelly had been standing in front of the stove, her hands on her hips, her expression unreadable. Now she stepped to one side, half facing the stove. She gestured at the roasting pan and the lovely, golden brown turkey inside it. "Where are the breasts, Margaret?"

"Hmm?" Maggie asked, moving the walker forward as she hopped closer to the stove. "There's the legs. And the wings," she said helpfully. "Aren't the breasts nearby?"

"No, Margaret, they're not. Maureen, I can understand. One more of her little pills and she'll be sliding onto the floor, dribbling saliva out of the corners of her mouth. But you should have noticed."

"That we had a flat-breasted turkey? Oh, I don't think so, Mom. I don't really cook, remember? And if I had noticed, it probably would have been impolite to point it out, don't you think? Isn't it enough we killed it and we're going to eat it? Do we have to insult it, too?"

Mrs. Kelly eyed her suspiciously. "How much of that boxed wine have you drunk, Margaret?"

"Clearly not enough," Maggie muttered, although she had noticed a sort of *glow* about the world around her after her last glass, and looked at the turkey again. "So. Where are the breasts?"

"They're *under* the bird, that's where they are. You put the turkey in the pan upside down!"

"Get out!" Maggie thought back to the moment. She'd been sitting in a kitchen chair. The big, empty black roasting pan had been in front of her, the unwrapped turkey to her right. Her mother had told her to lift it into the pan for Maureen, and Maggie had braced her good foot on the floor, hefted the raw, slippery twenty-pound bird the best she could with the rotten leverage sitting down allowed her . . . and sort of dumped it, shoveled it, into the pan.

Yeah, that kind of meant turning the dumb bird over, didn't it?

Oops.

Well, you'd think Maureen might have noticed.

Maggie leaned closer to the stove, smiled. Laughed out loud. "Upside down? Really? I thought the drumsticks should, you know, sort of stand up in the air? Upside down. Oh, God, that's hysterical! It's definitely a Kelly bird, huh, Mom?"

Alicia Kelly sort of tottered to the nearest chair and sat down, buried her head in her apron. Her shoulders shook, and she was making rather weird sounds behind the apron.

Maggie hopped over to her, held out her hand, thinking to put it on her mother's shoulder, to comfort her. She got close but, for all her recent strides, she just couldn't do it. She was too worried her gesture wouldn't be appreciated. "Mom? Ah, Mom, I'm sorry. Don't cry."

Her mother lifted her head and looked up at Maggie. True, there were tears in her eyes. But the smile that all but cut her face in two told Maggie that they were tears of mirth. "A Kelly bird! It is, it *is*! We're all upside down anymore, aren't we?"

And then, which was much more reasonable, Alicia Kelly's face rather crumpled, and she began to cry.

"Damn this stupid cast," Maggie growled, wishing she could hug her mother. Do *something*. But all she could do was to bellow, "Alex! I need you in the kitchen *now*!"

Within minutes, Saint Just had taken in the situation and had led Mrs. Kelly to the sunroom behind the kitchen, poured her a nearly full glass of wine, and he and Maggie (who had managed to carry an open box of tissues with her, in her teeth) sat facing her, waiting for her to dry her eyes one more time.

"You okay now, Mom? Tate and his friends are still gone wherever they went, and Maureen won't be back for a while from John's parents' house. Can we talk now, hmm?"

"The breasts will be fine," Mrs. Kelly said, wiping at her eyes. "In fact, they should be quite moist, don't you think, cooking in their own juice?"

"I'm sure the meal is going to be delicious. All of it. But that's not what we want to talk about, Mom. We need to talk about what you said last night, at the police station. About how Daddy . . . well, how you thought maybe Daddy had killed Bodkin for you. Remember?"

Mrs. Kelly sniffed, sat up very straight, once more the *mother*, the *authoritative figure*. "I spoke out of turn. I was upset. I didn't mean any of it. No, not at all. Certainly not. Don't be so cruel, Margaret, throwing a weak moment in my face like that."

"Mom . . ."

"Mrs. Kelly, if I might be so bold," Alex said quickly, before Maggie could say anything else—not that she had been able to think of anything else to say. "Who, exactly, is Walter Bodkin?"

Maggie's mother had begun shredding the tissue in her hands, much the way Sterling had been pulling his pom-pom apart. But Sterling had been upset. Alicia Kelly was stalling.

"One of Evan's bowling friends. They're on the same team. The Majestics. They have been, for years and years."

"Yes, thank you," Alex said kindly. "I deduced as much from the stories in the morning newspapers. And were they friends, as well? Away from the bowling establishment?"

Mrs. Kelly shook her head. "Walter doesn't—Walter didn't have many friends. He had . . . a very busy life."

"Really. I read that he was the proprietor of quite a substantial number of properties here in Ocean City. Rental units, I believe they're called?"

"Yes, that's right. He was a landlord. He . . . he owned a lot of buildings. Not the big, fancy ones close to the ocean or the bay. The smaller ones, more inland, more downtown. A few of them were sort of run-down, but they all made him money. And he had a lot of them. Maybe a dozen or so."

"And he'd rent them to summer vacationers, is that correct?"

"High school and college kids, mostly. He said he could cram them into the buildings a dozen or more at a time. They didn't care, he said, because not many people would rent to them in the first place, so they took whatever they could get. Walter wasn't always . . . scrupulous."

"I don't see where this is going, Alex," Maggie said.

"Everything leads somewhere, my dear. Eventually," he told her, and Maggie subsided. She was too close to this whole thing, she had to let Alex take the lead. He could be more objective.

"Walter was a good landlord. I shouldn't speak evil of the dead. He kept the places in fairly good repair," Alicia Kelly said when the room fell silent. "He was very good . . . quite, um, talented with his hands."

Maggie winced, tried to banish her mother's last few words from her brain's memory banks.

"And therefore also a strong man, Mrs. Kelly? To carry out his own repairs on the buildings. Was he also a large man?"

She nodded. "He used a sixteen-pound ball."

"Dad uses a twelve," Maggie explained to Alex, happy for the change of subject, away from Bodkin's talented hands. "When I ordered it, the guy told me a lot of women use twelve-pounders, but men go a little heavier. But Dad liked the loft he could get, I think he said, with a lighter ball. But sixteen pounds? Wow, Bodkin must really have been a strong man."

"And tall, Mrs. Kelly? Was Mr. Bodkin tall?"

She nodded her head. "He was a . . . a very active man."

Maggie sat back in her chair. "So he was tall, strong, active. We know, from the newspaper story, that he was sixty-three, same age as Daddy. My dad isn't exactly short, Alex, but no one could call him a giant. He's in his early sixties, and I saw one of those rubber disks in one of his kitchen drawers. You know, Mom, the kind you use to help get the top off jars?"

"I always have to open his pickle jar for him," Alicia Kelly said, sighing. "He probably hasn't had a good gherkin in months."

"Right," Maggie said quickly, as her mother looked ready to cry again. "One's tall, strong, one's medium height, no Schwarzenegger back when he was on steroids. So how, Alex, did my dad conk Bodkin over the head with his bowling ball? He would have had to carry a footstool with him."

"Not if he first disabled the man, swinging the ball at Bodkin's knees, for instance, so that the man was down when Evan delivered the fatal blows."

Maggie shot him a fierce look. "Don't help anymore, Alex. I'm trying to prove that Dad couldn't have done it."

Alex got to his feet. "In which case, my dear, we'll have to wait for more information, won't we? Where it happened, when it happened, the logistics of the scene. The results of the autopsy. Perhaps there were bruises, contusions, elsewhere on Bodkin's body. We know the cause of death from the blood and bone evidence on the bowling ball itself. We know his skull was badly smashed. But we don't know all of it, do we?"

Mrs. Kelly put a hand to her mouth and ran out of the room.

"Well, that helped, big mouth. You had to talk about the autopsy? We haven't learned a damn thing."

"On the contrary," Alex said, getting to his feet. "We know your mother had feelings for Walter Bodkin. And, if we know, it's more than possible that your father knew as well."

Maggie's mouth dropped open. She looked to the doorway, where her mother had disappeared, and then back to Alex. "Cripes, Alex, my mother is a little chippie!"

"Shhh," Alex warned, walking over to the now opened doorway. "Ah, your sister has returned. Good cop or bad cop, Maggie?"

"Hmm?" she asked, still struggling with the idea that her mother might have had not one, but two affairs. It was difficult to believe there were that many men in this one small town who'd had the courage to take her on.

"I said, your sister has returned. We've agreed that we need to speak to her, yes?"

"We do," Maggie agreed, turning her walker in the direction of the kitchen. "But not now, Alex. I know you want to troll for clues, but Tate and his friends will be back soon, and people still have to eat. Let's get all of that out of the way, and then grab Maureen later and grill her. Tate already announced that he's taking his pals up to Atlantic City for some show at seven. John will be snoring on the couch by then, and we'll have a free shot at Maureen."

"Agreed. Now, where do I hide this box of wine, so that we can hope she'll still be reasonably coherent by that time? And then please explain to me again why anyone would purchase wine that comes in a *box*."

Chapter 12

As much as Saint Just was anxious to speak with Maureen Kelly Burda, he was infinitely more eager to speak with Attorney Spade-Whitaker, who seemed to be evincing a remarkable lassitude when it came to consulting with her client.

Yes, it was Christmas, a holiday even for lawyers, he imagined, but it seemed imperative to speak to Evan as quickly as possible, if nothing else to warn him not to speak to anyone.

Save Maggie and himself, that is.

As he stood outside the condo with Sterling, enjoying one of his favored cheroots after partaking of Christmas dinner, and being quietly amazed at the amount of food the tall, painfully thin John Burda could consume without bursting open like an overripe melon, Saint Just began to review what he knew of the murder of Evan's bowling partner.

"Sterling, walk through this with me, please?"

"Where? You want to go down to the shore? Isn't it a bit nippy for that this late at night?" Sterling asked, already rising from the wrought-iron chair situated on the ground-level porch at the front of the condo.

"Perhaps we could stroll there tomorrow, Sterling," Saint Just said kindly. "I was, however, referring to the events of last night, as they pertain to the murder of Walter Bodkin and the erroneous subsequent arrest of Maggie's father. I believe I should like to put as much of the chronology in line as possible before we confront Evan once more, and attempt to beat down his refusal to speak openly with us."

"Oh, of course. My apologies. I'm afraid my mind was elsewhere. I've been sitting here, in point of fact, wondering how rude it would be of me to loosen my belt a notch."

Saint Just had already been mentally retracing the steps they'd all taken since driving up to the scene of Evan's arrest, but Sterling's words pulled him back to the moment. He looked at his friend with new interest. "I beg your pardon? Would you repeat that, please."

"Certainly. I know it isn't polite, especially in company, but as I said, I was thinking about how I would like to loosen my—Saint Just? Why are you looking at me that way?"

"Stand up, Sterling, if you'd please," Saint Just said, and then slowly walked around his friend, motioning for him to remain still as he circled him. And then circled him again. "Sterling, you're gaining weight."

Sterling pushed his hands against his chest and attempted to look down at himself. "I am? By George, Saint Just, you're right!"

He looked at Saint Just in the yellow light of the porch lamp, the expression on his mobile features one of mixed elation and confusion. "But . . . but we don't change, Saint Just. Not unless Maggie changes us in our books. You said so. No matter how I first hoped to diet away this belly of mine, no matter how much I indulged in my favorite Ding Dongs, I am destined never to gain weight, never to lose it. We are and will remain as Maggie imagined us. I remember it all quite distinctly."

"Yes, yes, I also remember, Sterling. The scar on my shoulder was given to me by Maggie. Just as she gifted you with your delightful way of looking at life. Everything we are, we are because of Maggie. But we are as we are in our books. We don't age, we don't change."

Sterling sat down again, patting his stomach. "But I am changing, Saint Just. Perhaps that's because of how you have been striving to evolve, urging me to evolve, attempt to become more of my own man? By God, Saint Just, it's working! Does that mean we're staying, remaining on this plane, and all of that? It does, doesn't it? We aren't going to *poof*, as Maggie worries so about us doing. And . . . and we're becoming free to be who we wish to be. Not that I wish to be anyone other than I am. I rather like myself, you know. And my Ding Dongs."

Saint Just smiled indulgently. "You're a good man, Sterling. No matter what happens, now matter how you evolve, you will always be a good man. Goodness is at the very center, the heart of you. I, however . . ."

"You're also a good man, Saint Just," Sterling protested as Saint Just's voice trailed off. "You're a hero, remember? An upstanding member of the *ton*. The compleat gentleman, and all of that."

"I've killed a man since we've been here, Sterling," Saint Just reminded his friend. "I thought, at the time, that I was being myself, protecting those in my charge, persons for which I feel a responsibility. And if I had to revisit that same situation, knowing now of Maggie's horror at the time, I'd do it again, without compunction. Does that mean I haven't evolved . . . or that I am becoming more the twenty-first century man than even I would feel comfortable being?"

"I don't know, Saint Just. Such a discussion requires much more concentration than I feel capable of at the moment. Pardon me for being so shallow, but do you think, if I am truly evolving, that this time, if I try one of those hair-growing miracles as advertised on the television machine, I would have a better chance at success?"

Saint Just shook himself back to the moment. "I can't imagine it would hurt to try, Sterling."

"Oh, capital, Saint Just! And I can exercise on Maggie's treadmill to lose weight, and cultivate a beard if I so chose, and learn how to play the guitar—I've harbored that wish for some time now, you understand. Oh! And I can cease and desist being *not in the petticoat way*, as Maggie created me. I think I should like to chase a few petticoats, not that the ladies wear them anymore, I suppose."

Saint Just tossed his cheroot toward the street, watching it soar into the darkness and disappear. "You—we—are also going to begin to age, Sterling. We will, if I've been correct all along in my assumptions, begin to grow older. Suffer aches and pains. We will have become . . . vulnerable."

Sterling was silent for a few moments, and when he spoke, it was quietly, and in some awe. "What will it be like for you, Saint

Just, to . . . to go into battle if it becomes necessary, knowing that you could . . . well, you know? Die?"

"A very good question, Sterling," Saint Just said, leaning against one of the porch posts. "I am not by nature a cowardly man, I don't believe. But I will say that, over the course of our varied experiences since arriving here, I've taken more than a modicum of solace from the idea that, no matter what I did, no matter what perils I might face, I would prevail. And survive."

"Gives a person pause, don't it?" Sterling asked, biting his bottom lip. "I imagine you feel rather as that super fellow did, when he discovered the existence of kryptonite, hmm? You'd think it would be lowering enough to be forced to fly about in those horrid blue tights."

"I beg your pardon? No, never mind, I imagine we can dispense with an explanation of that last statement for the nonce. Yes, indeed, Sterling, this revelation does give me pause. Which is why, Sterling, Maggie is not to know this. Any of this. Do you understand?"

"I believe so, yes. She won't let you be a hero if she knows you could be hurt, will she?"

"She'd attempt to wrap me in cotton wool and put me figuratively on a shelf, at the very least," Saint Just agreed, frowning. He needed some time now. Time to think about this evolving business. Time to remember why he had thought it so important that he do so, for one.

He would age. Along with Maggie, he would age.

He rather liked that. Maggie would be ecstatic, having more than once complained that she'd be collecting social security and playing shuffleboard in Boca, and he'd still be thirty-five, and vital, virile, chased by all the women who weren't slowed down by arthritic hips and bifocals, like her.

Maggie had such an interesting imagination. . . .

He would die. Along with Maggie, he would one day die.

He didn't really mind that. Life without Maggie would be a hell on earth, or whatever plane of existence would be left to him once she was gone, once her imagination no longer kept him and Sterling alive.

He could live with all of that. Die with all of that.

But how was he to live with the idea that he was no longer the perfect hero? Indomitable. *Indestructible*.

Capable of—egad!—failure!

How quick would he be to unsheath his swordstick, knowing that he could suffer a fatal injury as well as inflict one?

And why now? Now, when Maggie needed him more than ever, to save her father? Why did he have to discover all of this now? How could he possibly fail her now?

"Saint Just! We can get the sniffles now! Toothaches! Why, the list is endless, isn't it?"

Saint Just shook himself back to the moment. "And this pleases you, Sterling?"

"Yes, I suppose it does. We're *here*, my dear Saint Just. We're here, and we're not going back. Not poofing back into Maggie's mind, into the pages of our books." He giggled, actually giggled. "I am Sterling Balder. I am a *real* person—hear me roar!"

"I'm sure you know just what that means, my friend," Saint Just said, deciding to give up his own less amusing thoughts, as none of them quite pleased him. "Only you must remember, Sterling. Maggie isn't to know."

"I'm not such a booby, Saint Just. My tongue doesn't run on wheels. I've not got loose lips, and all of that. Not a word, I promise. But she will notice, you know. Eventually."

"And eventually is more than soon enough. Now, to get back to the problem at hand. Is that possible for you, Sterling?"

"I suppose so," he said, loosening his belt slightly. "Ah, that's better. Um . . . what was the problem at hand, Saint Just?"

Saint Just mentally retraced the conversation, and realized that he hadn't said anything of any importance prior to realizing that Sterling's waistline had expanded, not beyond, at least, a suggestion that they review events since last evening.

"It wasn't really important, Sterling," Saint Just said, pushing himself away from the post. "I believe I'd like to go back inside now, speak with Attorney Spade-Whitaker before their party leaves for Atlantic City."

"I suppose that's a good idea. Although, wouldn't it be better if Attorney Spade-Whitaker was speaking to Evan?"

Saint Just turned just as he was about to open the door, and smiled at his friend. "Yes, Sterling, you are evolving, aren't you? Not that you haven't always had a fine mind, one I admire vastly. But that hint of sarcasm in your voice as you made that last suggestion? That is new, my friend. My felicitations."

"Do I thank you now? Or was that also sarcasm?"

"Don't hurt your head, Sterling. You've nothing to prove," Saint Just told him, and then stood back in the shadows, as Tate and his small party were approaching down the spiral staircase leading to the front door, Tate speaking quietly, almost, one could say, conspiratorially.

Not that Saint Just was an advocate of eavesdropping.

Unless the opportunity fell into his lap.

"So now you've seen all of it, Sean, top to bottom. Five bedrooms, four and one-half baths, the large living and dining area above us, a fully equipped kitchen—with island. And then this smaller, completely equipped apartment down here, on the lowest level, with its own small kitchen. It could be walled off somehow, don't you think, given its own entrance? Make this a two-income property? Oh, and the dumbwaiter. I showed you the dumbwaiter?"

"Yes, Tate, I've seen the dumbwaiter," Sean said, slipping a fur coat Bernice Toland-James would have committed deviant sex acts to acquire, over his wife's shoulders. "A good idea, that, with the building having so many levels. Especially with the kitchen on the second floor. You've got two parking spaces out back, off the alley, but no outside under-cover parking."

"True, true," Tate said, his tone bordering on the defensive. "But it's a two-car garage."

"With no separate storage for body boards, bicycles, strollers. By the time all that paraphernalia is stored away, there's only really a one-car garage. The house sleeps ten—fourteen with the two sofa beds. But, in reality, you only have off-street parking for three cars. At the height of the season, parking is at a premium here. A discerning buyer will notice that."

"Wesley's quiet up here, near the end of it. There's never any trouble, parking out front, not even in the summer," Tate argued. This time he wasn't being defensive. He was whining. "You're looking for reasons to go low on the price, Sean, but you can't do it. Parking's not an issue."

"All right, then. The Boardwalk. You're a long way from the Boardwalk, Tate. I'm rather surprised you didn't think of that when you bought this place."

"This very *green* place," Cynthia Spade-Whitaker interjected. "It reminds me of lime Jell-O. I detest lime Jell-O. But it is a nice kitchen, Sean, and well equipped, unless all those pots hanging over the island are your mother's and will leave with her. Still, it isn't all terrible."

Saint Just listened to Tate's nervous laugh, and was glad they couldn't see him, standing just outside the door, keeping it open just a sliver with the toe of his shoe, so that he could hear clearly.

"And it's off-season, so prices are a little lower. You forgot to add that," Tate grumbled. "Anything else? Or are you going to hit me with a price?"

"Don't get all bent out of shape, Tate," Sean said. "Cyndy and I were playing with you. It's a great condo. I know what you paid, I know how long ago you bought the place. We both know the market has cooled off a bit, that interest rates have climbed more than a point. All that said, I think I can promise you a half million-dollar profit, including my commission. Not bad for a four-year investment, right?"

"That much? Okay, that's good, that's good. Hell, Sean, that's great! Let's do it!"

"I'd like to stage it, though, Tate. You know, get all your mother's things out of here, furnish it more like a seashore condo—at your expense, but we'll take that out of the proceeds. Get all the personal things gone. How soon did you say she could be out?"

"I don't know. How soon can you talk her into filing those divorce papers, Cynthia?"

"Soon, Tate. But all work and no play doesn't make Cyndy a happy camper. You did promise us some fun when you invited us, remember? I don't call it fun, being yanked down to the local police station on Christmas Eve."

"You'll get him off, right?"

"I'll get him off before there can be a trial, don't worry about that. But I'm also going to enjoy dipping deeply into your jackpot-winning sister's purse while I'm at it. Do you mind?"

"Me? Hell, no. And the more you drag it out, the more Mom is going to want to sell, maybe even leave town to get away from the scandal. I can get her something fairly cheap in Florida, take another profit—you know . . . later on."

Saint Just felt he had heard enough. More than enough. He opened the door and stepped inside, his face (he hoped) a reflection of his pleased surprise at seeing the three people standing there in the foyer. "You're off, then?" he asked, smiling. He held the door open. "Sterling? Are you coming in?"

Sterling strode into the foyer, his own face beet red, and not from the December chill. "I'll be upstairs, perhaps making dear Mrs. Kelly a pot of tea," he said tightly as he brushed past Tate and his friends, an act of rudeness the Maggie-created Sterling would have been incapable of pulling off without faltering, apologizing, and blushing even more deeply. Especially if he realized that the belt as well as the top button of his corduroy slacks were hanging open.

"We're driving up to Atlantic City, yes," Tate said, looking at Saint Just in a way that showed he was afraid he'd been overheard discussing the sale of his mother's house out from under her. "Um . . . do you and Maggie want to go with us? I can't promise Maggie another jackpot, but it could be fun."

"Thank you, no. Maggie will wish to get back to her father, I believe. Your father, that is. Your collective father," Saint Just said, apologetically, feigning embarrassment at his verbal faux pas. "Have you . . . have any of you spoken with him today?"

"You mean me, don't you, Alex?" Cynthia said in her usually clipped, crisp professional tone. "It's Christmas Day, remember? Nobody's going to be asking me to bring him back in for voluntary questioning until tomorrow, at the earliest. I'll speak with him tomorrow. He's to do what I said—talk to no one. Has he talked to you, Alex?"

Saint Just had never struck a lady and never would. But he realized that, evolving as he was, outraged as he was at all he'd heard in the last few minutes, the idea did hold some appeal. "No, Mrs. Spade-Whitaker, he has not."

"Good. I like an easy client. Alex?"

"Yes, *Cyndy*," he returned cordially.

"Tate was telling me about your . . . your exploits. Yours and Maggie's. In fact, Maureen pulled out a scrapbook Maggie's mother keeps on your press coverage. It made for interesting reading. The two of you seem to have a penchant for getting mixed up in murder investigations."

"We've had our moments, yes."

"Yeah, right," Cynthia said, pointing a finger at Saint Just, coming within inches of his nose with her index finger. "Here's the deal as I see it. Maggie's the daughter. You're the concerned friend. And that's *it*. Don't go poking around like amateur detectives. Not in this case, not with me on board as attorney of record. Because I don't work with amateurs. Have I made myself clear? Are we clear on this, Alex?"

"As crystal, madam," Saint Just said, bowing to her. "Everyone, enjoy your evening."

Cynthia and Sean swept through the doorway, leaving Tate behind, looking at Saint Just.

"Um . . . about what you heard . . ."

"Heard? Did I hear anything?"

"I don't know. Did you?"

"I heard Attorney Spade-Whitaker—as I've heard it said on numerous crime programs on the television—warn Maggie and me off the case. Was there anything else?"

"Uh, no, no, not if you—you heard, didn't you? I can see it in your eyes. About selling the condo?"

"Of course I did. You have lovely friends, Tate," Saint Just told him, turning the screw, just a tad. "A lawyer and a Realtor. A redoubtable pair, although you might have added one other profession to the mix."

Tate swallowed down hard, glared at Saint Just. "Oh yeah? Which profession?"

"Why, a physician, of course," Saint Just purred, taking his quizzing glass from his pocket and holding it up to his left eye, the black grosgrain ribbon dangling.

He then took a single step forward, looked Tate up and down, as if inspecting the man for flaws—and finding them. "Because, if you somehow manage to force Maggie's mother out of this house before she is ready to go, I will personally find you, corner you, and cane you to within an inch of your selfish, pathetic little life— a caning, Tate, as you are too low and loathsome, for a gentleman such as myself to even think of directly soiling my hands on you. And as I inflict this beating, I will enjoy your every squeal and whimper to the top of my bent. So," he ended, smiling, "as your attorney friend asked me just a moment ago—are we clear on that, Tate?"

Tate opened his mouth to say something—Saint Just was fairly sure it would have been something astoundingly stupid, such as "Oh, yeah?"—but then shut it again and bolted out of the house.

That had gone well. And employing snippets of dialogue Maggie had fed his imaginary self for one of their books into his little monologue had bordered on the delicious, actually.

"Remarkable," Saint Just said to himself as he lightly rubbed the quizzing glass against his sweater, polishing it. "Although an idiot, Tate Evans is tall, young, and exceedingly fit. He could probably give, or at least think he could, as good as he got. Yet, knowing that, I was, and am, more than willing to take him on. Even eager. Once an unremarkable reaction, but not now, having so recently discovered my own vulnerabilities. By God, I'm still a hero."

Satisfied, and not a little elated, Saint Just walked through the living room, eager to find Maggie, steal her away somewhere for a moment, and kiss her quite soundly. She was such an intelligent puss. Not only had she gifted him with looks and brains. She'd gifted him with a strong backbone, one that did not bend, even as he grew more mortal.

Chapter 13

Maggie looked across the kitchen table at her baby sister, who was sitting with her head lowered, her eyes cast down, playing the victim better than any French aristocrat riding the tumbrel on the way through the streets of Paris to the guillotine.

Maureen used to be fun. She really did. Well, fun in the I-lead-she-always-follows way of older sisters who talk younger sisters into stealing the cigarettes out of their mother's purse, and who will also then sneak a slice of cake upstairs when her older sister is grounded and sent to her room for talking the younger sister into copping Mom's Parliaments.

Maureen had let Maggie dye her hair orange for Halloween—with permanent dye. Maureen had helped her sneak into Tate's room one night and try out the experiment of submerging his hand in a glass of water so that he'd—and he did, too! Maureen dug in her heels and had eloped with John even when her mother told her she was making a big mistake in wanting to marry a garbage man.

Maggie's dad had helped then, stepped in, actually shut up Alicia Kelly by saying that when the rest of the world thought it was too good to collect somebody else's trash, the last garbage man in America would be a very wealthy man. Then he'd aimed the clicker at the TV and gone back to watching a documentary on prairie dogs, not to be heard from again for the next decade, Maggie was pretty sure.

Maureen used to have a spine, damn it!

What had happened to that Maureen? The silly, always ready for adventure Maureen? Where had she gone? Why did she go?

Now she was a mouse, a frightened, gray mouse. Walking quietly, on her toes, so that no one would be disturbed by her footsteps.

Now she wore an apron all the time, maybe to cover her swollen shape—when she'd always been slim, athletic.

Now she carried those damn little pink pills with her everywhere she went.

"Maureen? Reenie? It's me, only me, remember? And it wasn't a hard question," Maggie said now. "Who was Walter Bodkin?"

Maureen lifted a hand to twist at her hair, her hand shielding her face as she held it in profile. "But I don't know. He was a man, that's all. He . . . he owned a lot of houses."

"And that's it? That's all you've got?"

Her sister finally looked at her. "He was a Majestic?"

Maggie looked to Alex, who had been standing quietly, his back to the kitchen counter, sipping a glass of wine. He'd found a bottle in the crisper drawer of the refrigerator and deemed it passable, and a clear cut above the boxed wine Maureen had made such inroads on during dinner.

"Help?" Maggie mouthed silently.

Alex approached the table and bowed his head slightly, wordlessly asking for permission to join them. Maggie rolled her eyes at him, still amazed at the man's dogged adherence to Regency Era manners. When they suited him, that is.

"Maureen, my good lady," he said once he'd sat down. "I am not, by and large, a particularly observant person—"

Maggie choked on her sip of diet soda.

He looked at her owlishly. "But I do believe I noticed your rather unusual reaction last night at the police station. Let me see if I can recollect the exact moment, shall we? Oh, yes. Maggie inquired of her mother if she was acquainted with Walter Bodkin, and you . . . well, you giggled. You giggled, and then you burst into sobs. Do you recall that, my dear?"

Maureen looked at her sister, then down at her hands, which were twisting in her lap. "No, Alex. I don't remember that. I giggled? I didn't giggle, did I, Maggie? You're wrong. Really, you're wrong. I'm sure of it."

"Indeed. My apologies. So you never really knew Walter Bodkin, or of any association he might have had with, say, your mother?"

Maureen giggled . . . and then quickly clapped both hands over her mouth, her eyes wide as she looked to Maggie. For help?

"You really have to stop taking those pills, Maureen," Maggie told her, reaching across the table to touch her sister's arm. "And something else. You have to stop lying to us. Dad's in big trouble, sis. If you know anything, you have to tell us. Good or bad."

"I can't, Maggie. I can't tell you. I'd rather *die* than tell you."

"Oh, for God's sake, Maureen, stop whining."

Maggie and Alex looked up to see that her mother had come into the room. She'd changed out of her clothing and into a deep sapphire blue caftan that didn't do a heck of a lot for her. But she looked comfortable. At sixty-three, maybe comfortable was enough? Maggie hoped not.

"Mom?" Maggie asked as Alicia Kelly held out her hand for the glass Alex was holding, and then downed the remaining contents in one long gulp.

"Ah, that's better. Wine in a box. Sometimes Tate can be so cheap. A limo for his friends, wine in a box for his family. Don't think I don't notice. Maureen, scoot over to the next chair and let me sit down. It's time we talked."

"But, Mom, you can't," Maureen all but whimpered. "John's in the living room."

"And snoring fair to beat the band," Mrs. Kelly said, shaking her head in disgust. "It's the tryptophan. In the turkey, you know? I read about that somewhere—it makes you sleepy. Considering he ate half the damn bird, he should be unconscious until New Year's."

Maggie shot a look toward Alex, who only shrugged. Big whacking help he was being. Didn't he know how she hated family conversations? Still, at least tonight her mom was being sort of an equal opportunity sniper, already taking shots a Maureen, Tate, and John. Could a swipe at Maggie be far behind?

Yeah, well. If she was going to be the new Maggie, the one who didn't buckle under every time things got a little sticky with her mother, now was the time to prove it, right?

"Why can't John hear what we're saying, Mom? What's somebody going to say? I don't get it."

"Nobody expects you to, Margaret, not without an explanation. Alex," she said, turning to spear him with her eyes. "I wouldn't do this, would never do anything so embarrassing, except that you and Margaret have had some success in solving crimes. Four of them, as I recall."

"Five," Maggie interjected. "Bernie's ex—well, both her exes— the murders at the WAR conference, and over in England, and the rat killer. More than five, if we just count bodies. Let's see, there was—"

Alicia Kelly sighed. An exasperated sigh, Maggie was pretty sure.

"But who's counting, right, Mom? Sorry for the interruption. You were saying?"

"I had an affair with Walter Bodkin," Alicia said, just throwing it all out there, with no preamble, so that Maggie sucked in her breath until she realized she was feeling a little light-headed.

"Oh, Mom . . ." Maureen said, lowering her head onto her crossed arms.

Maggie recovered her breath enough to say, "You had *two* affairs? Walt Hagenbush *and* Walter Bodkin?" She shot a look at Alex. "Maybe I was right. You know, about the Walter fetish?"

"Shh, Maggie. I don't think your mother's quite finished. Please, Alicia, go on."

"I never had an affair with Walt Hagenbush, Margaret," her mother told her, her chin still high, her eyes defiant. "My God, the man had halitosis that could stop a Mack truck."

Had to say this for her, Maggie thought—the woman had brass ones. And was that something to be proud of, in a mother? Hmm . . . ?

"When . . . when I felt it necessary to confess my indiscretion of a decade ago to your father—"

"Yeah, while we're on the subject, Mom," Maggie interrupted. "Why in God's name would you do something like that?"

Maureen let out a choked cry—rather like a chicken in the midst of a neck-wringing—and ran out of the room.

Alica Kelly shook her head. "Never had half your spunk, did she, Margaret? I told your father because I was leading up to telling him something else."

"Something else?" Maggie looked to the doorway. "Let me guess. Something about Maureen?"

"I wanted, still want, to pay for Maureen to go to some sort of therapy. John's insurance doesn't cover more than three visits, and, well, we all know three visits isn't even going to scratch the surface, don't we?"

Thinking of her own visits to Doctor Bob that were well into their fifth or sixth year now, Maggie only nodded her head.

"Your father didn't think therapy was necessary."

"You needed his permission? Wow."

"I need your father's permission for nothing, Margaret. I wanted his agreement. And, perhaps, I needed him to under-stand. Because . . . because I wanted to go into therapy myself. I wanted us to go into therapy as a family. And maybe even the garbage truck jockey, too," she added, shrugging.

"*You* wanted to go into therapy?" Maggie was fairly certain her eyes were popping halfway out of her head, and was sure they were when Alex cleared his throat delicately as he kicked her, ever so slightly, beneath the table. "Okay, okay, I'm sorry. I just had this flash. You know, this throwback, to a late-night rerun of that old show, *The Odd Couple*? Remember that one, Mom? With Felix Unger and Oscar Madison? Well, those were the names of the characters."

She turned to explain to Alex. "Felix was a fussbudget, a neat freak. He and Oscar were roommates. Oscar was a slob, and Felix was always picking up after him, always nagging him, driving him crazy. So Oscar got a stomach ulcer, and Felix—he was a hypochondriac, too—worried that he was going to get a stomach ulcer as well. But the doctor told him, that in the world of stom-ach ulcers, Felix was what one called a *carrier*. Get it, Alex? Felix wouldn't get an ulcer—he *gave* ulcers."

"Very amusing, Maggie," Alex told her. "And you'll now ex-plain the relevance?"

Maggie opened her mouth to do just that, but then realized that she was going to say that her mother didn't go to therapy—she sent others running there. "Nevermind. I guess it was funnier in the episode where Felix Unger kept writing Oscar notes and signing them with his initials, and Oscar couldn't figure out if it was Felix's initials, or an insult. You know—Felix Unger? F for Felix, U for—go on, Mom. Sorry for the interruption."

"I've been watching *Dr. Phil*," Alicia Kelly said as Maggie did what she was pretty sure was a good Maureen impersonation—lowering her head, looking at her entwined fingers. "Some of it is pure drivel. But not all of it. I'm not blind, Margaret. I know there are problems here, in our family."

"Let me count the ways ..." Maggie muttered under her breath.

"Tate is—well, Tate is becoming a disappointment, after all my high hopes for him. I don't know if Erin is a disappointment, as I haven't seen her in nearly a year. I expect her husband will come down with bubonic plague just in time for her to back out of Easter dinner. Maureen? God, we all see Maureen. In fact, Margaret, you're the only one who seems to be ... normal."

"Me? Surely you jest—and don't call me Shirley," Maggie blurted, and then wished she could kick herself.

"Your mother keeps a scrapbook, Maggie, concerning our exploits," Alex told her, an overload of information, considering all her mother had just said.

Maggie's head was reeling. "A scrapbook. Of me? Wow. That's ... that's so *normal*."

"You're not perfect, Margaret, so you can stop grinning like an idiot over there. You embarrass us on a depressingly regular basis with your shenanigans. And, of course, those dirty books of yours."

"You've never read any of my books."

"And I never will. A mother must retain some illusions. Maureen, however, destroyed many of them."

"And we're back to Maureen," Maggie said, grateful for the shift. "What happened to her anyway, Mom? The past three or four years she's been—weird. Spacey. Jumpy, too."

Alicia Kelly looked to Alex. "Where was I? Margaret will insist on going off on tangents. She was always like that, if only hoping to prolong the inevitable. But not this time. The inevitable must be said, if you two are to make sure Evan doesn't end up doing hard time as somebody's bitch."

"As somebody's—o-o-o-*kay*," Maggie said, reaching for her nicotine inhaler. "So tell us, Mom. What do we need to know?"

"I had an affair with Walter Bodkin."

"You really don't have to keep saying that, Mom, we got it," Maggie said, then inhaled deeply on her plastic pacifier, hoping like hell there was still some nicotine joy juice in the cylinder.

"But I told your father I'd had an affair with Walt Hagenbush."

She turned to Alex, a plea in her expression. "I started to say Bodkin, but Evan looked so crushed, and yet so angry, that I couldn't do it, I couldn't say it. So I said Walt Hagenbush instead. Walt was dead. Evan couldn't go beat him up if he was dead, right? And the problem was still the problem. What difference was there in a name?"

"Oh, brother," Maggie said. "Mom, it makes all the difference in the world. Doesn't it, Alex?"

"I don't know, Maggie, as we've yet to be told the details of this problem, remember?"

"It was a quick thing, a stupid thing. Ten years ago. We'd been looking to buy a new condo, and your father was never home to go look at them with me, so I went by myself—with Walter as our Realtor. We were together a lot, had lunch a few times. He was . . . he was very smooth. And all those condos. All those bedrooms. It . . . it just happened."

Maggie looked quickly from left to right, her knuckles white on the edge of the table as she tried to hold onto her sanity. "Anybody got a barf bag around here anywhere?"

"Maggie, hush."

"But it was over and done, and I tried to forget about it." Alicia Kelly looked to Alex again, and he took her outstretched hand in his, gave it a reassuring squeeze. "And then . . . and then, about three years ago, Maureen and John decided they wanted to buy a condo."

"Sweet Jesus in a cherry tree—*Maureen*? Maureen hopped between the sheets with Walter Bodkin?"

Alicia bit her lips together between her teeth, nodded. "I think she was regretting the garbage man, not that I hadn't warned her. I noticed the change in her during those weeks—the giddiness, the sudden, unexplained smiles—and I was fairly certain I knew why she was giving me excuses not to ask me to come along when she went looking at condos. So I finally confronted her, told her of my affair with Walter, hoping to warn her off before she did something stupid . . ."

"But she'd already done something stupid," Maggie said, sighing. "It's like you said, Mom. All those condos. All those bedrooms. Reenie had an affair with her mother's former lover. Two generations of Kellys, in the same sack with the same man. Oh, yuck. Oh, double yuck. No wonder she's popping all those pills. That's sick."

"Perhaps, Maggie, you should leave the room, just until you can compose yourself," Alex suggested quietly.

Maggie squeezed her eyes shut, tried to block the images that seemed determined to lodge forever in her brain. "I'm sorry. You're telling us important stuff, Mom, and I'm being a jerk. So, um, so you fudged this summer, when you went to Dad with your big confession. You told Dad, but you told him Hagenbush, not Bodkin. That wasn't so bad, really, and the problem was still the problem—that you and Maureen had both been—at separate times, separated by whole years, right?—both been seduced by Walt Bodkin."

"I'd hardly say seduced, Margaret," Alicia Kelly said in an aggrieved tone. "That would make us both silly, vulnerable women. I'd like to believe we knew what we were doing. Or at least I did. Although I will admit I stopped taking those hormone pills Donald Helsing insisted I try to be rid of hot flashes. I had some very strange thoughts when I was taking those pills, I tell you."

"Doctor Helsing? He's still practicing?"

"Donald? Of course he is. My goodness, he's only a few years older than your father and me."

"Wow," Maggie said, once again steering toward a side road, because it was easier to take the information her mother was handing her in small doses. "I used to think he was ancient. So much for a child's perspective on the world—something I should have remembered five Doctor Bob years ago."

"Excuse her, Alicia," Alex said. "As you've already pointed out, she will do this sort of thing from time to time. So, if I might put a voice to some things I've been thinking as we've spoken?"

"Of course, Alex," Alicia said, her voice almost girlish.

Maggie curled her upper lip. No woman was immune to Alex. Although she was giving hopping down to see Doctor Helsing tomorrow for an immunization shot some serious thought at the moment.

"You told Evan about your long-ago affair, begged his forgiveness even as you gave him the name of a dead man instead of the person actually responsible . . ."

"So he wouldn't go after him, try to fight him," Alicia said. "Evan gets some strange ideas sometimes."

"Yes, I understand. You were protecting him. Totally understandable. You then told him that Maureen also had an affair with the man, and had been—what is the word?—*traumatized* to learn that she had made the same mistake her mother had made."

"She freaked," Alicia said, looking at Maggie, and impressing her daughter again with her terminology. "She went to bed for two weeks. Wouldn't talk to anyone, wouldn't eat, kept showering all the time. Then she stopped that, and began eating. All the time. She's gained forty pounds, Margaret."

"I noticed, yes."

"Every pound she put on, I felt worse. My baby, my youngest, and I'd done that to her. I began to think of what else I . . . I might have done. To anyone else. Confession was the only thing I could think of that might help me. But still I couldn't bring myself to tell your father all of the truth. I'd said Walter, but then I said Hagenbush, not Bodkin. I was, am, a coward."

"Don't beat up on yourself, Mom. Alex? This is why Daddy won't talk to us. He doesn't want us to know about Maureen. I'll bet that's it. But did he know about Bodkin anyway, did he find out on his own somehow? Mom? Is that why you said what you said last night? You think Daddy found out it was really Bodkin, not Hagenbush, and he went nuts? Bopped him over the head with his bowling ball?"

"It would be as silly as going off to have that affair with his little chippie, just to punish me. Yes, he knew it was Walter Bodkin, not Walt Hagenbush. He's known for a few weeks now—and I've been worried sick. You don't know your father, Margaret. You think I'm the horrible woman who browbeats him, keeps him under her thumb. But your father needs to be under someone's thumb. Trust me. He's no Wally Cox."

"Pardon me?"

"He's no wimp, Alex," Maggie explained, and then looked to

her mother once more. "Mom? You're telling me that underneath that gray button cardigan and orthopedic shoes, my father is a wild man?"

Alicia Kelly sat back, folded her hands beneath her ample breasts. "Ask Walter Bodkin. Oh, wait, you can't, can you? Because he's dead."

Maggie's head felt ready to explode. Information overload. Definitely. But something was knocking at the back of her skull, and it wasn't just her headache. "But Daddy couldn't have known. You have to be wrong on that. He wouldn't have bowled with the guy last night, if he'd known. Would he?"

Alicia shrugged. "He said they'd settled things between them. They're—they were—teammates on the Majestics, remember? Nothing and nobody can come between the members of the Majestics. I could hate him for that, except that the Majestics are all Evan has, especially now that he's taken early retirement."

"Damn. So how did he know? How did he find out?"

"Maureen told him. She didn't mean to, but when your father finally went to her, to tell her he wouldn't go to therapy with her, but he would pay for it, she opened her big mouth and said Walter's name."

"And when was that, Alicia?" Alex asked her.

"Two weeks ago? Three? I think Evan thought that if he made some sort of gesture, like paying for Maureen's therapy, I'd forgive him, let him come home."

"And you said they'd settled things between them? That he confronted Bodkin? Two, three weeks ago?"

"It was about then, yes. They rolled around in the parking lot of the bowling alley like two idiot teenagers, hitting at each other, making fools of themselves. But then it was over, or at least I thought so."

"Yet you said Evan killed Bodkin for you."

"Yes, Alex, I did, and I don't know why I said that. They made up, didn't they? Evan prizes the Majestics over me, over his own daughter. Men are asses. They think they can hit each other and then go off to bowl together. Or so I thought."

"That'd put me in therapy," Maggie said, feeling sympathy for her mother. "How could Daddy bear to be in the same room with the guy?"

"Because he's a man, Margaret. Men fight, and then they go on with what they want to go on with—like your father's stupid Majestics. I can't honestly believe Evan killed Walter, but if he did, he did it because he thought it would make me happy. I wasn't happy, you understand, when he told me he'd fought Walter, and then they'd made up as if nothing had ever happened. The man actually said to me—*water under the bridge can't be called back, Alicia*. He forgave me, he said. He forgave Walter. Can you imagine? But I was wrong, I'm sure of that. Evan couldn't have killed Walter. He can be difficult, but he's no killer. And he'd never lie to me. He wouldn't dare."

"Mom?" Maggie would return to the idea of her father being a wild man, difficult, some other time. For now, she had a much more important question. "Did anyone see them fighting? Were there witnesses?"

"It was a Friday night, Margaret. League night. Of course there were witnesses. Dozens of them. I stayed away from the supermarket for a week, too embarrassed to show my face. And nobody knew why your father and Walter had been fighting. Now they'll know it all, the whole world will know. If I didn't have a fully stocked freezer, we'd all starve to death."

"This isn't good," Maggie said, sighing. "Well, none of it is good. But, damn, Alex, people saw Daddy fighting with Bodkin."

"Yes, I understand. And at least one of them will have contacted the police no later than tomorrow, eager to share that very information," Alex said as Maggie sat back in her chair, dragging hard at her nicotine inhaler . . .

Chapter 14

"No, let's not go up yet, Alex," Maggie said as he put his foot on the first step, having won the battle and carrying her from the car rather than to stand back, helpless, watching her hop on one foot. He believed himself to be the perfect hero, but Maggie seemed to continue having some difficulty fitting herself into the role of the swooning, helpless heroine.

"You're tired, Maggie," Saint Just told her, hesitating. "One way or another, it's been another long day. You've been on that foot too much. It won't help your father if you have to take to your bed for a few days."

"I know, but Dad's up there. And my mind is still racing. I really need to talk to you, and I don't want to have to whisper. Please, put me down so we can sit a while on the steps."

He did as she asked, taking off his coat and spreading it on the step before she sat down. He then retrieved the walker from the car and sat down beside her. "We have to speak with him at some point, you know. We really can't go much further in any direction without his cooperation. And, as characters on the current police dramas on television say, the clock is ticking. Most homicides, unless solved within the first forty-eight hours, remain unsolved. A good thing no one said that during the Regency, or our books would all be short stories."

"Very funny. And I watch the programs with you, so I know about the forty-eight hour thing. I'm delaying right now, stalling. We'll work on him tomorrow, when I'm not feeling like such a wimp. For now, with any luck, he'll have gone to bed before we get up there. Alex?"

He was lightly rubbing at her shoulders, as she'd told him more than once that they ached after a day navigating on the walker, and had even teased him that she'd soon have shoulders like a fullback. "Hmm?"

"We're doing a really good job, you know, unearthing evidence. Clues, to you. We learned a lot today. The problem with those clues is that we should be working for the prosecution. Everything we've learned just points to Dad crushing Bodkin's skull for him."

"I was wondering when you might stumble over that conclusion, my dear, no pun intended."

"Ah, that feels good," Maggie said, hunching her shoulders as he worked on her neck, as he pressed his lips against her neck. But if his touch only felt *good*, obviously a romantic interlude this evening was out of the question. Pity.

"It could feel better, but I suppose not."

She ignored that statement, or just hadn't heard it. Yes, definitely Maggie had to work on the swooning, grateful, can't-help-herself-but-falls-into-his-arms aspects of being a heroine. "We have another suspect, though. Three, if you want to push it to Mom."

"John, if he is aware of his wife's indiscretion, and Maureen. Yes, I have deduced that much. But attempting to include your brother-in-law may be pushing the envelope. The man sleeps the sleep of the innocent—"

"Or the tryptophan stuffed."

"True. And Maureen doesn't strike me—again, no pun intended—as the sort who could cold-bloodedly kill anyone. Your rather redoubtable mother, on the other hand . . ."

"I know. She's freaking amazing, isn't she? Even in that horrible blue caftan, she commanded the room, didn't she? Or, as I used to say before I knew she actually keeps a scrapbook of our press clippings, like a normal mother—that is one scary broad. But she wasn't faking going all white and nearly fainting when she heard Bodkin was dead. Nobody's that good."

"Bringing us back to your father."

"Unfortunately, yes." Maggie leaned her head on Saint Just's shoulder. "You know what we need, Alex? We need to broaden our investigation. We need more suspects."

" 'The more the alternatives, the more difficult the choice.' "

Maggie nodded against his shoulder. "Yeah, like that. We dig up enough suspects, maybe even feed some of them to the press, and the police can't just pin it on Dad and not investigate other possibilities. We make this as hard as we can for them, right? Very good, Alex."

"I blush to say that I'm not the first to utter the words. You had me quote the Abbé D'Allainval in *The Case of the Pilfered Pearls*, remember?"

"Are you kidding? You're the one I gave the steel-trap brain, not me. I have at least a half dozen thick quote books in my office. I get an idea, look through them for a key word, and then steal like crazy. You don't really think I commit all that stuff to memory, do you?"

"Another illusion cruelly shattered by my pragmatic heroine," Saint Just said, pressing a kiss against her hair. "And here I thought you were a walking encyclopedia of knowledge."

"Only if I pushed a set of encyclopedias in front of me in a shopping cart. But people seem to think I have it all in my head, and ask me questions about obscure stuff I may have found, and written about, but then forgot. And they get all torqued when I don't remember. It's like walking up to comedians and demanding they say something funny. It just doesn't work that way."

"Is this going anywhere?"

"No, Alex, I don't suppose it is. I'm just saying, I'm not a genius. You, by association, are not a genius. Good, even great, but not a genius. We just do the best we can with what we've got. And what we've got right now is bupkus. That's nothing, Alex. Bupkus."

Saint Just knew he had to agree. Other than to supply even more motive that could send Evan Kelly, as Alicia had said, 'up the river to become somebody's bitch,' they really hadn't accomplished anything at all concrete a full four-and-twenty hours after the murder.

But he had learned something.

"Maggie," he began slowly, "there's more going on here than Bodkin's murder and your father's arrest. Loathe as I am to add to your burden, I believe I must tell you that I overheard your brother discussing his plan to sell your parents' home out from beneath them."

Maggie sat up straight, looking at him in the yellow light of the street lamp. "What? He's doing *what*?"

"Sean Whitaker is a Realtor, Maggie. Tate invited him for the holiday so that he could come into the house without being too obvious, inspect it, and then set a sale price."

"Why, that sneaky, no-good, son of a—"

"You'll want to hold onto that righteous anger a moment more, sweetings, as there's more to tell. Cynthia Spade-Whitaker, as you already know, is an attorney. *She* has been invited along as Sean's wife, but also to assist in preparing divorce papers Tate hopes your mother will then sign. Now, feel free to rant."

But Maggie didn't say anything. Not a single word.

"Maggie? Are you all right?"

"No," she said, her voice small. "God, what a twisted, sick family we are, Alex. Maybe Mom's right, and I've turned out to be the only normal one. And if I'm normal, sitting here, talking to my imaginary perfect hero somehow come to life, then the rest of them are freaking certifiable!"

Saint Just chuckled quietly at that bit of self-deprecating wit. "Are they, Maggie? Ready to be carted off to Bedlam in their own straight waistcoats? Your sister Erin, whom I haven't yet had the pleasure of meeting, seems to have found her own path. Granted, one that leads away from her parents."

"But she lies about why she doesn't come home. You're not normal if you can't just stand up and say, no, folks, you make me nuts, and I'm not coming home anymore."

"Really? You come back here, while longing to stay away, because you can't say the words you expect Erin to say."

"I hate when you're logical. Erin lies and hides, I try to lie, and eventually buckle. Okay, so Erin and I are maybe working out the same problem, each in our own way. But Tate? Mom and Dad have always treated him like the golden child. Tate this, Tate that, Margaret, why can't you be more like Tate—all of that. And yet he's the one trying to pull the rug out from under them."

"You once told me that Tate bought the condo for your parents as a business investment."

"And to score points with Mom and Dad by telling them they could live in it as long as they wanted. Don't forget that one, Alex. Tate's all about scoring points, keeping score."

"Like a dog with a bone, aren't you, sweetings? But to return to my hastily assembled theory, if you don't mind? He may have suffered some business reversals, Maggie. If you'll recall, he rather blanched at the idea of producing the fifty-thousand dollars necessary for your father's release from the police station last evening. Selling your parents' house may give him the money he needs. Sean mentioned a half million-dollar profit."

"So Tate's cold-bloodedly planning to kick Mom and Dad to the curb—for money? Why didn't he just come to me? He knows I have money."

Saint Just smiled in the darkness. "Would you apply to your brother for funds, if you found yourself in need?"

"Are you kidding? I'd rather eat dirt."

"Yes. And it is to be assumed that your brother feels likewise. I could pity him, except for the fact that I believe he sees your father's current difficulties as a prod to induce your mother to file the divorce papers and leave Ocean City, and her embarrassment, behind."

"He's a snake," Maggie sneered. "My mother has nurtured a snake at her bosom."

"A very poetical if rather dated turn of phrase, one common to the Regency. And here you protest that your knowledge of the era runs into and out of your mind as if it is a sieve. We will not, of course, allow Tate to succeed in his plan—both his plans—so let us put the subject of your scaly brother to one side for the nonce."

"A worm. A wiggly, squiggly, slimy, filthy little—oh, okay, I'm done now. For the moment. Because I'm not finished, not by a long shot. Tate's going to pay for thinking he can dump Mom and Dad after promising them they had that condo for life. That limo? He hired that for show. Maybe it took his last money, but he did it to impress his *pals*, make them think he's loaded and doesn't need the profit from the condo. God, I hope so. I hope he's down to his last penny. The bastard. I don't know how, but he's going to pay."

"He will cower in a corner beneath the force of your righteous wrath, tremble in his boots, yes. I look forward to the sight."

"You bet! And when I say *pay*, I mean with money. Real money."

"But if he's already embarrassed for funds . . . ?"

"Then I'll pick his last pocket, for his last dime. Money, Alex. It's the one thing Tate loves. He used to keep his money shoved up in the bottom of the lamp in his bedroom. Pulled off the felt thingie on the bottom, and shoved his weekly allowance up into the base, put the felt back on, all nice and neat."

"Clever."

"As you'd say, too clever by half! Then he'd fib and say he didn't have any money, or he'd pull out a ten for a gumball and whine that he couldn't bear to break it, and Maureen or Erin or I would end up buying him his damn gumball. He did it all the time. But Mom? Mostly it was Mom who paid, let him off the hook, just warning him that he'd have to learn to be better with his money. But I knew better, because I'd see his smile when Mom turned her back, handed over the money for whatever it was Tate wanted. It took me a while, but I finally found his stash, and took it, hid it under his mattress, where I was sure Mom would find it when she changed his sheets."

"Pardon my interruption, but just how old were you when you formed this Machiavellian plan?"

"I don't know. Six? Seven? I was precocious, okay? He never even suspected it was me who'd done it. Although I'd love to tell him someday. Maybe soon, huh?"

"Amazing. And what happened?" Saint Just asked, intrigued.

"And she took the money. Put it in the bank for him—over one hundred bucks! Wouldn't let him touch it. God, was he mad!" She smiled at Tate. "It's one of my happiest childhood memories. Yeah, that's it—money. I have to call Bernie in the morning, pick her brain. She's sneaky enough, and knows enough about finances. She'll come up with something."

"Maggie and Bernie on a Tate hunt. I almost find it in my heart to pity the fellow. But not quite."

"Good, because I'd have to hurt you. Okay, now, who's left on the Kelly hit parade? Oh, right, Maureen. Boy, there's a mess, huh?"

"We have to speak to her again, I'm afraid."

"But not me, Sherlock. It wouldn't get us anywhere. I don't want to look at her, and I doubt she wants to look at me. Not until we both get used to the idea that I know she was bopping Mom's ex-lover. Oh, God, there goes my stomach, turning over again."

"Very well, I'll speak to her tomorrow, while you and Sterling are in the city to see your surgeon."

"Doctor, Alex. Don't say surgeon. If this stupid bone moved, I'll be in surgery on Tuesday. Think miraculous healing, think nifty walking cast. God knows I am. Are you sure you don't want to go back with me?"

"Someone has to remain close to your father, my dear. And, if I'm delicate enough—which I have no doubt I will be—and with his daughter gone for the day, he may just confide in me. We must know where he was from the time he says he left Bodkin in the parking lot of the bowling establishment and the time the police arrived to arrest him. Clearly Cynthia Spade-Whitaker isn't rushing to establish an ironclad alibi for the poor man, put an end to this nonsense. J.P. can't return from her vacation soon enough to please me."

"Agreed. You'll have to tell him that you know about Mom and Maureen and Bodkin. That won't be fun."

"I will have spent more pleasurable hours, I'm sure, yes, but I will persevere." He put his arm around her shoulders. "You're beginning to shiver. Let me carry you upstairs."

"Not yet. I want a cigarette," Maggie said, regarding nothing. "I'd kill for a cigarette, Alex. I've been good, I've been brave, but I don't think I can hold it together much longer, not without outside help. Give me the walker, will you? I'll bet that convenience store down on Ninth is open. I'll get dizzy, the first couple of drags, because I did before, that time I quit for a whole week last year, but I can fight through it."

"Maggie . . ."

"*Mag-gie*," she repeated, dripping sarcasm. "I need the real thing, Alex. It helps me think. It has been medically proven that, only seven seconds after taking a hit, the brain sort of, sort of *perks up*. If we're going to get Dad out of this mess, I need to be able to think, and on all cylinders. *Please*?"

"You've been so strong, for so long," he pointed out to her, part of him feeling sympathy for her, the other part knowing that she'd broken her addiction and she would hate herself if she slipped back into it now.

"Yeah, big deal. I made the world happy, I quit smoking. And now New York is after my trans fats. What's next for them, Alex, hmm? What are they going to stand up on their sanctimonious pedestals and condemn next? Because they're not done, not now that they've tasted success. Give the do-gooders a hand, and they take the whole freaking arm."

"Maggie, you're digressing."

"No, I'm not. I'm speaking the truth, Alex. They won't be happy until the rest of the world is miserable, and all marching in lockstep for what they want, what they see as best for everyone else. I see regimented, mandatory exercise in our futures, Alex, no lie. And book burning. And an official national religion. They'll just take, and take, and take. We never should have let them get away with the No Smoking crap. That was the first mistake. They're heady with power now. You'll see, everyone will be sorry when their own personal ox gets gored. They came for my neighbor's Marlboros, and I said nothing. They came for my other neighbor's french fries in saturated fat, and I said nothing. *And then they came for me . . .*"

"Maggie, now you're obsessing."

"Damn straight, I'm obsessing. I have a right to obsess, to go a little nuts. My mother and sister were banging the same guy, and my dad's going to be on trial for killing the bastard. My brother's a worm. Erin bailed out years ago and won't be any help. Maureen? Get real. She's less than worthless right now. It's on me, Alex. It's all on *me*. And I can't even have a crummy cigarette."

"You've got me. And Sterling. You know you've got us standing at your back. You're not alone in this, Maggie."

"I can help, too, you know."

Saint Just grabbed onto Maggie's shoulders as she visibly jumped, and they both looked up to see Henry Novack standing on the sidewalk, holding onto the street lamp.

"Well, I can. Nobody knows me here. I can scoot around, asking questions, keeping one ear to the ground. Maybe find out things you two can't. For a price, of course."

"I don't believe this," Maggie said, pulling the walker open and bracing herself against it as she stood. "What are you doing here, Novack? And where are your wheels?"

"Back at the van, around the corner. Gets heavy, lifting it in and out, you know."

Saint Just looked down the street, then at Novack. "You don't need the cart, Mr. Novack? You're not infirm?"

"Hey, watch it. Obesity is an infirmity. You're not blind, sport, you can see what I look like. I'm morbidly obese. Four hundred twenty-seven and a half pounds at my last weigh-in. They weigh me on a fucking meat scale, pardon my French. I got good reason to have that cart. Is it my fault my mother overfed me, pushed food on me twenty-four/seven, huh? Set me up for a miserable life like this?"

"Mothers really can screw you up, can't they, Novack?" Maggie said, hopping toward him. "But you have to acknowledge that, forgive your past, and move on. Take responsibility for your own actions."

Henry Novack looked past Maggie to Saint Just. "Women. Always got an answer, don't they?" He turned back to Maggie. "You want my help or not?"

"Not," Maggie said, turning the walker and heading back to the steps. "Now go away."

"Come on, come on. I'm on Disability. I could use the extra bucks. Under the table, like, you know? Okay, here's the thing. I'll go out hunting tomorrow, give you something for free. I give you something, prove myself, and I'm on the payroll. Is it a deal?"

"Will you go away if I say yes?" Maggie asked as Saint Just coughed into his hand to hide his amusement. They were like children, squabbling. He should probably give one a carton of cigarettes, and the other a joint of beef to gnaw on, before things turned nasty.

"With some money, you know, I could go into one of those treatment centers? One of those fat farms? I'm forty-two. I have a life to live, somewhere inside me. Where the thin person lives.

You took my machine, cost me my jackpot, cost me my chance. You *killed* me, Maggie Kelly. Now you have to save me."

"Oh, for crying out loud. Just what I need, another guilt trip. Alex?" Maggie bleated. "Help me."

Saint Just got to his feet. "You make a convincing argument, Mr. Novack," he told him. "Now, how can we use you, hmm? I know. Tomorrow, why don't you take yourself over to the bowling alley, listen to people talking, and then come back, tell us what they said? I agree, Maggie and I both would be too obvious. And, although it would be impossible to say that you, Mr. Novack, would blend into any crowd, I do think you wouldn't arouse any suspicions, now would you?"

"Not if he hangs out at the snack bar," Maggie grumbled, balancing rather precariously on her good foot. "Can we go upstairs now? I think I've just about had enough for one day."

"When do I meet you?" Novack asked, pushing away from the streetlamp, his enormous face shiny with sweat in the December chill. "Not the Music Pier, but maybe here? Same time, same place, tomorrow night?"

"Yes, that would be fine. But please bring your cart. You don't look well, Mr. Novack."

"I'll look a lot better when the thin guy gets out," he said sincerely.

And then Henry Novack shuffled off down the street, his massive corduroy slacks *swush-swush-ing* together audibly between his thighs, his shape in the fading light reminiscent of one of the balloon characters Sterling had so admired in the recent Macy's Thanksgiving Day Parade in Manhattan.

"The entire world has problems, Maggie," Saint Just told her as she leaned against him while he folded the walker. "And we all deal with them in our own way. Mr. Novack eats."

"And I smoke. Someone else crawls into a bottle, or hits things, or shops for fancy cars they can't afford. I get it, Alex, you don't have to hammer the nail all the way in. I'll make it through this without the damn nicotine, I promise. He's really something, isn't he?"

Saint Just lifted her up into his arms. "You're going to give him money, aren't you, sweetings? You've always been planning to give him money."

"I took his machine, Alex. You can say I didn't. The people at the casino can say I didn't. But I did. I saw him look at it, and I took it. With malice of forethought, you could say."

"Well, at least now we can pretend that he's earned whatever largesse with which you propose to shower him, hmm?"

"Works for me," Maggie told him, snuggling close. "At least something's working out . . ."

Chapter 15

Socks ran out into the street to assist Maggie from the rental car, helping her hop to the curb and then stepping away from her, bowing to her three times, his arms stretched out in front of him. "All hail, all hail!"

"What the hell do you think you're doing, Socks?" Maggie asked as Sterling brought her the walker from the backseat.

"I'm bowing to brilliance, of course. Maggie Kelly won the big jackpot. Three-point-something *mill*-ion dollars. Quick, rub my arm. Give me some of your luck."

"You're an idiot," Maggie said, pushing past him. "You have no idea how much trouble that jackpot has caused me." But he took hold of her arm, holding her back.

"I think I do, Maggie. You don't want to go in there. Not until I clean out the place."

"Clean it out of what?" Maggie asked him, eying the doorway to the condo building with some trepidation. "And don't tell me someone else mailed me a rat. That joke isn't funny anymore."

Socks looked to his left and right, as if expecting attack from some unknown quarter. "No. Not rats. Leeches."

Maggie grimaced, feeling sick. "That's not funny, Socks. Rats aren't funny. Roaches aren't funny, either, but at least most of them are native New Yorkers and will outlive us all. But leeches aren't funny. Not even a little bit."

"I know. And these are human leeches. They started showing up here the minute the newspapers identified you as the big winner in A.C. I've been keeping them out, keeping them away. But it's cold, you know, and I felt sorry for a couple of them. Such sad stories, Maggie. Every one of them had a sad story, and every one of them thought I needed to hear it. I think they were practicing on me."

Maggie hopped backward, planning a hasty retreat. "You've got people in the lobby now, Socks? That isn't allowed. Damn it, Socks, it's not allowed." That last was, unfortunately, even to her own ears, a bit of a whine.

"Okay, okay, so give me a minute to get rid of them, all right? It's just the guy with the warts all over his chin and Mrs. O'Reilly. She wants a bus ticket to Las Vegas, to visit her grandson—plane fare, if you can see it in your heart to keep an old woman off the bus. Except I don't really think her name is O'Reilly, and I don't think she has a grandson. And I guess I don't have to tell you what the wart guy wants, huh? Money for wart removal. Hey, I told you anyway! Sorry."

"Warts all over his—? Never mind, just get rid of him. And the grandma, too. Wait. I'm going to regret asking this—but why don't you think her name is O'Reilly?"

"Because she keeps saying *begorra*, and *blessin's o' the Irish on ye, mate.* With a Brooklyn accent you could slice salami with. You stay here, you and Sterling—hi ya, Sterlman—and I'll boost them out of there."

"Your first thought, and still a good one," Maggie said, balancing on the walker and longing to be upstairs, in her own condo, maybe with a hot cup of tea, *begorra*.

"I'll stand in front of you, Maggie," Sterling offered valiantly. "Block you from sight, and all of that."

"Thank you, Sterling. People are crazy. You know that, Sterling? People are just plain *nuts*. Do they really believe they can make up some sad story out here, on the street, and I'll reach in my pocket and throw money at them?"

"Saint Just said you're going to pay the man in the go-cart."

"Maybe. *Maybe* I'm going to pay the guy in the go-cart. But that's different, Sterling. At least he offered to work for the money. It's what people do, you know. They *work*. Most of them."

"I don't," Sterling said quietly, "and you and Saint Just are going to give me all of the money. That doesn't seem fair. I don't think I'll take it."

"Oh, jeez." Stupid, stupid! She should have seen that one coming. Maggie lowered her head, wishing she felt less harassed, wishing she felt more human, wishing herself out of the cast and her father out of trouble. Maybe then she could speak without putting her remaining good foot in her mouth. "No, Sterling, sweetheart, it isn't the same."

"How isn't it the same, Maggie?" Sterling asked, shielding her as a red-haired woman (clearly a recent, and unfortunate, dye job) and a tall, thin man with what looked to be bits of macaroni glued to his cheeks and chin exited the lobby, Socks prodding from the back.

"I could have made better warts with Silly Putty," Maggie grumbled as Socks herded the people all the way to the corner, and then looked at Sterling once more. "It isn't the same, Sterling, because . . . because . . . I'm freezing, Sterling, let's go inside while the coast is clear."

They made it to the elevator before Socks trotted back into the lobby. "Maggie? I read in the paper that you don't get the whole three million right away, that they divvy it up over a bunch of years. Maybe twenty? Is that true?"

"I think that's right, Socks," Maggie told him, the look on the doorman's face warning her that another shoe was ready to drop. As it stood now, she had enough footwear falling on her head to open her own shoe store. "Why?"

"Oh, nothing. So, after the Feds take their share, and the rest is split up over that many years—you didn't really win much, did you?"

Maggie grinned at him. "Why, Socks, I didn't know you were from the glass-half-empty school of thought. I think I still get pretty much. I mean, it's better than a poke in the eye with a sharp stick, right?"

"She's giving it to me," Sterling told him, his expression pained. "For doing nothing."

"Not for doing *nothing*, Sterling. I already have money. Alex has his own money now that he's modeling for *Fragrances by Pierre*, not to mention the money he gets from his Streetcorner Orators and Players—not that I ever like mentioning that because I still can't believe the profit he's pulling in with that deal.

Anyway, it's only fair, since you're here, that you have some money of your own, too."

"Since I'm here?"

Maggie looked at Socks, and then rolled her eyes at Sterling warningly. "Later, okay?"

"Since I just happened to come along, Maggie? I didn't ask to come along, you know. I only thought Saint Just might need me. I didn't know I was such a *burden* to you both."

Socks looked from Maggie to Sterling. "Guess I'll . . . I'll go see if anyone wants a taxi, huh?"

"Yeah. Why don't you do that, Socks. We'll talk later." Maggie hopped onto the elevator when the doors mercifully opened. "Sterling? Come on, honey. Come upstairs with me."

"If I'm wanted," he said, showing Maggie a heretofore unknown dramatic bent.

The doors closed on them and she turned on him. "What's going on, Sterling? You don't pout. You don't sulk. You're the happiest man I know. And you were happy when Alex and I said we wanted to give our share of the jackpot to you. You already had one third of it, remember?"

"I don't know what's wrong with me, Maggie," Sterling said as he held open the elevator doors when the car reached their floor. "I'm being ungrateful, aren't I? Yes, that's what I'm feeling. Put out. Ungrateful. *Snarky?* What an uncomfortable feeling. My goodness, how do you people stand it?"

Maggie extracted her keys from her pocket and opened the door to her condo. "Let's go inside, Sterling. Talk about this some more," she said, looking over her shoulder at him, as he was about to open the door to the condo he shared with Alex, and leave her. "Please?"

"I should check on Henry."

"Henry will be fine for another five minutes. Oh, cripes, and here comes the thundering herd," she said as Wellington and Napoleon charged out of the kitchen, to tangle themselves around the legs of the walker. "I'd think you loved me, you fuzzy little rug rats, but I'm guessing this just means you're sick of the self-feeder dry stuff and want a can of the smelly stuff, right?"

The Persians, tails lifted straight in the air, turned as one and padded back toward the kitchen, just as though Maggie would naturally follow, eager to please them. Which she would do. But not until she and Sterling had a small talk.

"Your mail, Maggie," Sterling said, picking up a fairly thick stack of mail that included the familiar red stripe-edged white envelope from Toland Books.

"Probably Christmas cards from people I forgot to send to," she said, sighing. "And that big one? That's fan mail forwarded from Toland Books. It can all wait, Sterling. Come on, sit down. Let's talk about this."

"Must we? I'm feeling quite the ape now, thank you. I'd much rather take myself off to be by myself for a while, attempt to understand what's happening to me that I'm so upset with you and Saint Just for—well, for being you and Saint Just. I only want to apologize for looking a gift horse in the face."

"Mouth. But I know what you mean, Sterling. We love you, you know that. You're most certainly not anything like those two people downstairs, or even Henry Novack. You never ask for anything. That's why it's so terrific to be able to give you everything. Okay? We're okay now?"

"We're fine now, thank you," Sterling told her, but his smile was strained, and Maggie watched him leave, his steps slow and dragging, and fought the urge to call him back.

Because something was really strange here.

Sterling wasn't being Sterling. Well, who else could he be, for crying out loud? She made him as Sterling, hadn't she? He'd popped into her mind all those years ago, and then popped out of it, and into her living room a few months ago, as Sterling Balder. Sweet, lovable, naïve, trusting, never angry, never petty, always kind Sterling Balder.

Maggie plopped herself down on the couch beside her stack of mail and sat back, chewed on the side of her thumb as she looked at the closed door.

"So if I know who and what and how Sterling Balder is—who the hell just walked out of my condo?"

She was still sitting there five minutes later, still gnawing on the side of her thumb, when there was a knock on the door. Oh, thank God! He'd come back, and they could talk some more. "Come in, Sterling."

"It's Socks, Maggie."

"Oh," she said, and did her best to push her unproductive thoughts about Sterling out of her mind for a moment. "It's open, Socks."

He entered slowly, bent forward a little, and if he'd been holding a hat, the brim would probably have been clutched in both hands in front of him. He looked like a supplicant timidly approaching the throne.

"Oh, cripes, Socks, not you. Please, not you."

He stopped a good ten feet away, lowered his head. "You're right, I'm sorry. What was I thinking? I wasn't thinking, was I? I'll go now."

"No, no, don't go. Come on, come sit down," Maggie said, waving to the facing couch. "Now tell me what's on your mind. And how much."

Socks rubbed at his wonderfully sculpted chin, which hadn't lent him much help landing a part on Broadway. Nor had his singing skills, or his dancing skills. But what Socks lacked in talent, he made up for in desire. At least to Maggie. "You're giving the money to Sterling."

"*We're* giving the money to Sterling," Maggie corrected. "It was Alex's hundred bucks, Sterling's finger on the button, and my butt in the seat. That jackpot was a community effort, but Sterling gets the money, because Sterling is a wonderful guy who couldn't get a job in New York if everyone else left town, and the one time he did try to do something good he got mixed up in a terrible scam and could have been hurt. And why am I explaining any of this to you?"

"So that I won't leave here and go straight across the hall to put my proposition to Sterling?"

"Good point," Maggie said, shifting on the cushions. "Would you please do me a favor and feed the cats for me before they mutiny? The cans are in the long cabinet beside the stove. Oh, and I'd love a drink of water. From the refrigerator door—but no ice. Thanks."

Socks hopped to do her bidding with a bit more alacrity than she found comfortable, and Maggie passed the time by picking up the large envelope from Toland Books and ripping it open.

Fan mail was fun. It didn't used to be. It used to be like a grab bag that could have goodies inside, or a chainsaw waiting to shred her always threadbare confidence in herself as a writer.

But then someone at the publishing house started vetting the mail first, and sending along only the good stuff. The bad stuff got tossed in the circular file, Maggie knew now, and the really bad stuff got filed away in Toland Books' Losers and Loonies file. In fact, if it hadn't been for that file, the rat thing a couple of weeks ago could have been a lot worse. . . .

She frowned when she realized that none of the six envelopes had been slit open, which meant that nobody had screened the letters. The way employees came and went at publishing houses, it was no big surprise that a probable new hire hadn't gotten the word yet, and just sent out whatever had been addressed to Maggie in care of Toland Books.

Well, how bad could they be? She had real fans, not just nuts. Maggie opened the first envelope.

I never wrote to an author before, but I just had to tell you how much I love Saint Just . . .

Okay, that one was good. She'd put it aside to read the rest of it later, when she could enjoy it.

I guess you hear this all the time, Ms. Dooley, but I have written a book and I think you'd like to publish it if you'd only read it. I've had the most interesting life, and I think the world would be better for hearing my story. And if you like it and think it needs work, I'd gladly share the profits if you rewrote it for me. If you would send me your address, I'd send you—

"God, some people's kids," Maggie yelled to Socks, tossing the second letter back into the large envelope. "They think I actually publish the books. They think I do the artwork. They think I write the back cover copy. And they think I should write their books for them while I'm at it. When the hell do they think I find time to write my own books?"

She looked toward the kitchen, but Socks was still out there, talking to the cats—who were talking back to him, one of the reasons she so loved Persians—so she picked up another letter, hoping for two good ones out of three.

She read. She read again. And then she threw her head back and laughed out loud, causing Socks to run back into the room to ask what was so funny.

"Read . . . read this," she said, waving the letter above her head. "Out loud. I want to hear it out loud."

Socks took the letter and frowned at it, and then grinned. "It's short and to the point, isn't it, Maggie? You really want me to read it out loud?"

"Yes, please," she told him, wiping at her eyes with the sleeve of her sweater. "God, how I needed that laugh. I should have the thing framed. Talk about keeping me humble."

" 'Dear Ms. Dooley,' " Socks began, and then looked at her. "Do you ever get used to it, Maggie? Being called Ms. Dooley? Cleo Dooley?"

"No, not really. I was being a little crazy when I made up the name, but now that I've got it, I'm sort of stuck with it. And I still do like the Os."

Socks nodded. "Sort of the way my pal Jay got stuck with Jayne when he started doing the drag queen thing. He said he did it off the top of his head, but now he's stuck with it, now that he's so popular in the clubs. He really wanted to be Raquel. I don't know, I think Jayne's okay, don't you?"

"Raquel might be a little over the top," Maggie agreed, doing her best to keep a straight face. She'd never been lumped in with a drag queen before. It was kind of neat, seeing how Socks's thought processes worked.

"Yeah, it probably is. Anyway, I'll read the letter now: 'I am a new reader and just love your Saint Just Mysteries series books. I do not like regular historical romances and understand you started out writing them, and so I'm wondering if there is a way I can get a list of the regular historical ones you wrote to make sure I don't buy them when I shop at the used bookstore?' "

It was just as good the third time, and Maggie clutched her stomach as she rolled with laughter. "I'm supposed to send her a list of my historicals. To be sure she *doesn't* buy them! A kiss and a slap, Socks. Two slaps—considering she buys used, and I don't get a bent penny out of the deal. I love it!"

"Maggie? Are you all right? It's funny, sure. But it isn't *that* funny," Socks said carefully.

"I know, I know. Okay," she said, wiping her eyes once more. "I'm under control again, I promise. You know I have a car picking me up out front in an hour, to take me to the doctor's office? Good. Now, tell me about your idea. Because you have one, right?"

Socks sat down once more, perching on the edge of the couch cushion, his back ramrod straight, his hands folded in his lap. "It's Jay and me, both. Who got the idea, I mean. We've been thinking about it for a long time. I mean, Jay's pushing forty, and belting out *Over the Rainbow* every night is getting a little old, you know? And I'll never make it on Broadway, I know that. I've known that for a while."

"I'm sorry it hasn't worked out for you, Socks. So you two are looking to switch careers."

"Yeah, that's what we're looking for. Do you remember my mama's pies, Maggie?"

Maggie had to shift mental gears, but she managed it. "Sure, I do. She makes great pies. Why?"

"Well, I've got all her recipes. Her grandmama's recipes, that is. And her fried chicken recipe. And her—well, lots of recipes. You know when I go to auditions? I usually take some of Mama's pecan brownies or her fig bars with me. Everybody loves them. I almost got a part in the chorus of *Wicked*, the producer liked her pralines so much. She makes the best pralines."

"Is this going anywhere, Socks?" Maggie asked, as she had pulled a few more pieces of mail out of the pile, and saw that they were all personal letters from people she didn't know, four of them addressed to the "The Jackpot Winner." And there'd been only one mailing day since she won, what with the Christmas holiday. If this was today's mail, what would tomorrow bring?

"Jay? Well, Jay cooks. I don't cook, but Jay does," Socks went on hurriedly, obviously aware he was in danger of losing his audience. "We'd need a place, of course, and some start-up money for inventory, things like that. We already went to the Small

Business administration for a loan, but they give most of them to single moms and like that. Not a lot of loans out there for a gay tap-dancing doorman and a cross-dressing Judy Garland impersonator. Jay says it's discrimination, but I don't know. Anyway, we were thinking—"

"You were thinking about asking me for a loan," Maggie finished for him, hating to see him so nervous.

"We'd pay you back, you know that, right?"

Maggie smiled. "I know that. Do you and Jay know that about seventy percent of all small businesses fail in their first year? And restaurants most especially? It's like Yogi Berra said about a restaurant one time, 'Nobody goes there anymore, it's too crowded.' One minute a Manhattan restaurant is hot, and the next minute it's the new parking garage."

Socks nodded as if he understood, and then blew it. "Who's Yogi Berra?"

"Okay, so we've ruled out the Bronx near the stadium as a spot for your restaurant," Maggie said, grinning. "Where do you want to put it?"

Socks coughed into his hand. Choked, actually. "Well . . . you know that house you bought?" Then he looked at her, blinking like the innocent she knew he wasn't. "I should have waited, shouldn't I? But, no, I had to go and open my big mouth. He said he'd talk to you while you were in Jersey. Didn't Alex talk to you about that yet?"

"We've been a little busy. Didn't Alex talk to me about *what* yet?"

"About the bottom floor," Socks said, getting to his feet. "Well, I've already been gone too long. Can't leave the lobby unguarded, right? I'll go watch for that car for you, buzz you when it shows up, okay?"

"Sit . . . down."

Socks danced in place as he short of shuffled his arms toward the door. "I'd really rather . . ."

"*Sit!*"

"But I really need to . . ." Socks looked at Maggie, whose eyes were most probably popping out of her head. "Oh . . . okay . . . sure thing," he said, plopping back down on the edge of the couch.

"Now talk."

Socks cleared his throat. "Okay. But Alex is going to be pis—er, he probably wanted to talk to you himself. The house? That big building? It's mixed zoning, or something like that. He asked that Realtor lady, and she said it would be okay. Even the way the place is built is really terrific—with the squared off first floor, and the rounded ones sort of climbing on top? And four whole floors? Alex says nobody needs to live on all four floors, not even the three of you. You, Sterling—"

Maggie rubbed at her aching forehead. "I know who I'm going to be living with, Socks. Unless I kill Alex, that is. But then there will be even more room, won't there? For *what*?"

"Well . . . on the one side, our S&J Pies and Soul Food shop. It was a dream, you know? Having the place maybe, but not the money. Not until you won the—well, we won't talk about that anymore. Except for one thing. Not a restaurant, a shop. Takeout, you know?"

"Charming. So, as your landlord and your banker, I guess I wouldn't starve, huh?"

Socks spread his arms wide, his smile even wider and said fervently: "All the free food you'd ever want, definitely!"

"Uh-huh," Maggie said, mentally collecting rent, which she knew was prudent of her, but which she knew Alex would call just being herself—cheap. "I hadn't thought of the house as income property. It makes it all seem less an indulgence, doesn't it? But you said *one side*. What would go on the other side?"

"I can't, Maggie. I really can't. Alex will tell you."

"Oh, Alex is going to be telling me a lot of things when I get back to Jersey, trust me."

"Right, you have to go back there," Socks said, looking at her sympathetically. "How's your dad doing, Maggie? A killer? Somebody's got to be totally off their wheels, thinking that. But Alex is there, hunting for clues, right? He'll take care of this. Doesn't he always?"

Maggie attempted a confident smile. "Yes, that's our Alex. Always riding to the rescue . . ."

Chapter 16

Ocean City was a pleasant metropolis, if rather thin of company in the winter months, but it didn't hold a patch on Brighton, where Saint Just had often been a guest of the Prince Regent during the Season.

The prince's pavilion, of course, had been an architectural marvel. Why, his royal majesty's horseflesh had been housed better than most of his majesty's subjects, their stalls lit by the huge crystal chandeliers that hung suspended from the vaulted ceiling.

And the food? Ah, say what you will about the spendthrift heir to the throne, the man most certainly knew how to entertain. Course after course, delicacy after delicacy. Poor Sterling, he ate with his eyes, often allowing much more to be piled on his plate than he could possibly consume comfortably. But, if it was on the fine china plate, it must be eaten, unless he wished to insult his host. Sterling had always persevered, even if he had to take to their rented townhouse for the entirety of the next day, existing on nothing more than watered wine and bits of toast.

Of course, none of it was real, not to Saint Just, because the Viscount Saint Just was not real. The pavilion? Yes, that had been real, was still real. The Prince Regent had been real, or as real as historical research could make him. It had been Maggie, however, who had given poor Sterling his uncomfortable post-banquet bouts of dyspepsia.

Maggie had taken her creations, Sterling and himself, and paged through her research books as she recreated the pavilion and the prince and all the others.

It was still difficult, from time to time, to wrap his brains around all of it—what had been real, what he had only lived, experienced, courtesy of Maggie's imagination. They'd have to travel to Brighton one day, tour the pavilion, and he could then see for himself how correct Maggie's descriptions had been.

Or perhaps not. He had memories of the prince's Carleton House, too, but that had been ripped down not too many years after the Regency had ended. So depressing.

Still, he was here, and not in Regency England, and he should enjoy this seaside resort for what it was.

He'd come up onto the Boardwalk to reconnoiter, as it were, the Eighth Street Music Pier, where Mr. Novack had suggested they meet tomorrow night. The assignation might have ended in being canceled, but it was always best to be prepared for any eventuality.

The pier jutted out toward the shoreline, but didn't quite reach it, unless a higher tide might push water against the large pilings upon which it had been built. A cursory inspection, however, was all Saint Just needed to ascertain that there would be precious little space for Novack or anyone else to hide, as three sides of the Pier were fenced off, unavailable to the public.

There was only an area to the right of the structure, lined with wooden benches, where a person might hide himself in the shadows. It had a clear view of anyone approaching from either side or from the front, via a long ramp leading off the far side of the Boardwalk and down to Eighth Street itself. A convenient access for Mr. Novack's go-cart?

Saint Just raised his cane, let it rest on his shoulder as he looked up the Boardwalk that ran to Twenty-sixth or Twenty-eighth Street—not that it mattered—and then to the north until it reached past First Street. There were a few other people braving the wind off the water and the winter chill, riding on bicycles or in wheeled surreys they propelled with pedals.

A young boy on Rollerblades skated by, calling for Saint Just to get out of his way—how Sterling had failed at that particular mode of transportation brought a smile to Saint Just's face. Perhaps, next time they visited the resort town, Sterling would wish to bring his motorized scooter with him?

Most of the shops had closed for the season, but there seemed to be life going on inside a shop bearing the sign Mack and Manco's, and Saint Just made his way there, now lured by the aroma of freshly made pizza.

The place had the look of a local eating spot, a year-round place for tourists and the citizens of the town. Saint Just was not surprised to see the tables nearly all occupied, and more than a few gentlemen sitting on stools, their elbows on the counter, chatting among themselves.

He joined them, tipping his hat to the red-haired man who turned to look at him curiously before returning to his conversation.

Saint Just ordered a slice, amended that order to two slices, added a request for a glass of ice water, and then pretended an interest in the plastic-coated menu.

He listened to the conversation going on beside him. After all, two things were certain to him: men gossip as much or more than women; and two, the murder was probably the main topic of that gossip in a town as small and quiet as this one.

And his deductions were quickly rewarded.

"I told you—I *told* him. Saw him yesterday, showing up to buy donuts, just like regular people. I went up to him and I said—I said, 'Evan, you're gone. Out. Tossed. His-*tor*-ee.' "

"Damn! Just like that?" the man beside him asked, hunching his shoulders as he cradled a mug of coffee between his hands. "After all these years? Man, that's tough. I'd go nuts, Joe, you know?"

"Yeah? Well, *we're* going nuts, so just screw Evan. We've got the New Year's tournament coming up with Sea Isle, and we've got to go with two alternates. Raw, untested."

"I know who one of them is. Frank Kelso, right? He's first alternate?"

"Eight years now, right. He should be okay, I guess. He took over those two weeks last year when Pete had that gall bladder thing, remember?"

"So who's the other guy? Tiny?"

"No, not Tiny. He's third alternate. Barry Butts." Joe made a face.

"Oh, man, that's rough. Butts isn't as good as Tiny."

"Tell me about it," Joe said, and then drained his coffee cup, held it out to the kid behind the counter for a refill. "But seniority is seniority, Sam, and rules are rules. Butts has been on the list for eight years, too, but six months less than Frank. It's his turn."

"I can't believe you guys. You're all so good, you know? What other team could have a waiting list eight years' long? And keeping the trophy from the New Year's tournament all those years, too. Man, it'd be a pisser, having to give it up."

"Tell me about it," Joe said, obviously a man with a limited repertoire of verbal comebacks. "I'm the captain, and it's me who'd have to turn over the trophy to those bastards if we lose. Fourteen years we've held that trophy. Fourteen frigging years. Makes me sick. So you want to talk tough? *That's* tough." He repeatedly poked at his chest with one pudgy index finger. "*I'm* the one who's got *tough*."

"You still got Pete, though, right? Between the two of you, you should be all right. You know, carry the new guys?"

"I don't know," the one named Joe said sourly. "Pete's such a woman. Saying we should cancel. You know, out of respect for Walter's passing."

"Pete *is* a woman, Joe," the other guy said, laughing. "At least she was, last time I checked."

"You checked? Jeez Louise. Then you're a braver man than I am, Sam. Especially with her sprouting that mustache a couple of years ago. Walter used to say she was a—well, you know. But he probably said that because he couldn't get her into the sack. Not that anyone I know would ever want to get Pete in the sack. But you know Walter."

The other man chuckled again. "Yeah, we all knew Walter."

The aproned youth behind the counter slid a paper plate containing two hot slices of pizza in front of Saint Just.

"May I have a knife and fork, please?"

Joe and Sam leaned forward on their elbows, eyes shifting left, their amazed gazes on Saint Just.

"Excuse me," Joe said, grinning. "You English?"

"Why, yes, how astute of you. I am."

"So you English eat pizza with a knife and fork?"

Saint Just reached for the utensils. "I cannot speak for the general population, but I do, yes."

"Tastes better when you eat it with your hands," Sam told him.

"Then I'll have to try that, won't I?" Saint Just said, laying down the knife and fork and lifting the first piece of pizza. He took a healthy bite and spoke around it. "Hmm—good."

Inwardly, Saint Just was cringing. He imagined the one hundred or more guests at one of Prinney's Brighton Pavilion banquets all eating with their fingers, and then smiled. He wasn't in Regency England anymore, was he? And he wasn't going back. He took another bite.

"So, what're you doing here, in Ocean City?"

Now this could be tricky. If he said he was here with Maggie, visiting with the Kelly family, Joe and his friend Sam could back away from him. As it was, they were being quite friendly.

"Indulging in my love for baccarat, actually. My travel agent told me it would be less costly to book a room in a hotel in Ocean City during the off-season, rather than to stay at one of the casinos."

Joe nodded. "Yeah, that's true enough, I guess. Where ya staying?"

Saint Just hooked his thumb toward the south. Lord knew there were hotels enough to make it a reasonable gesture. "Oh, about a block that way," he said, and took a drink of water.

"Ninth Street? Oh, okay. My cousin's wife's aunt—something like that—she owns that place."

"What a splendid coincidence, then." Saint Just beat down the urge to wipe his fingers on the—unfortunately—thin paper napkin. "Lots of excitement here, isn't there?" he asked. "I mean, the murder?"

"Yeah, me and Sam were just talking about it. Can't remember the last time we had a murder around here."

"And they were bowling companions, I believe?" Saint Just prodded, hopefully not too hard, but just enough to keep the men talking. "Would that be lawn bowling?"

"On the *grass*? Hell, no. It's regular bowling. You know, *American* bowling? With lanes? We're in the middle of the season."

"Ah, I see," Saint Just said, shaking his head. "And you lost two of your company, then, didn't you? That must be a great loss."

"Yeah, tell me about it," Joe said, shaking his head. "They were both on the Majestics. That's my team. One dead, one arrested. Whole damn team's been des-des—you know."

"Decimated," Saint Just provided helpfully.

"Yeah, that. I had no choice, you know, being the captain. I had to throw the guy off. I mean, he killed Walter, right?"

"Did he? I thought the American way of justice was innocence until proved guilty?"

Joe leaned closer, rolled his tongue around the inside of his lower lip. Obviously some sort of information was about to be forthcoming. "They found Walter on the beach. Right down there, between Seventh and Eighth. Head bashed in, Evan Kelly's bowling ball just sitting there in the sand, right beside the body. Doesn't take a genius to know who done it, right?"

"On the beach?" Saint Just knew as much from the articles in the morning papers, but feigned surprise. "What on earth would lure a man onto the beach in this weather?"

Sam leaned back, put his hand on Joe's back to hold him in place, and whispered, "We heard it was drugs. You know, making a deal down on the sand? Walter liked his weed." The man then brought his point home by holding his forefinger and thumb to his lips and audibly sucking in air. "Our guess is Evan was his contact, and the . . . the *meet*, you know? It went bad."

Saint Just attempted to picture Evan Kelly selling marijuana. No, the image wouldn't come. "So this Walter person—the victim?—was a drug user? He doesn't sound like a very exemplary citizen."

Joe hit at his friend, pushing him forward on his stool once more. "Jeez, Sam. You don't know Walter was using drugs."

"I do, too," Sam protested. "He offered me some, just a couple of weeks ago. Said it, you know, *enhanced* the experience."

"I thought he took those little blue pills," Joe whispered, but the man's whisper wasn't all he'd probably hoped it could be, because Saint Just had no trouble hearing him. "You know, that Vigor thing?"

"Had to stop. Woke up half blind one morning. Bummed him out, because he liked the pills, but he told me he likes to see who he's doing. Get it, Joe? See *who* he's doing? A real card, that was Walter, all right."

"Wow," Joe said, shaking his head. "Okay, so maybe it was a

meet for drugs. But I don't know, Sam, I don't see Evan pushing weed. Had to be something else. Something bigger."

"Yeah, like that fight they had, remember?"

Joe turned to glance at Saint Just, who still maintained his look of polite interest, and then leaned in close to his friend.

"We told the cops, Sam. We don't have to tell the world."

"A fight? A disagreement of some sort?" Saint Just asked, starting on his second piece of pizza. "I don't think I read that in this morning's newspaper. You all must be very close to the investigation. I'm impressed, truly."

It would seem that Joe was not immune to flattery. "Yeah, well Walter and Evan, we all go back a long way. On the Majestics, you know? Coulda knocked me down with a feather when I came out of the lanes, saw the two of them rolling around in the parking lot like a couple of kids. But they made up. Hell, they went bowling together Christmas Eve—just before Evan killed old Walter."

"You coulda gone, right, Joe?" Sam asked. "Free bowling and all. You coulda seen them go off together, maybe? A witness, right?"

Joe shook his head. "The wife would have had my head in a sling if I said I was going to the lanes on Christmas Eve, free or not. I had to put together that wagon for little Joey, remember?" He swiveled back to Saint Just. "My grandson. He's three. Wanna see a picture?"

"I would greatly enjoy viewing a photograph, thank you," Saint Just said, and spent the next five minutes looking at an entire foldout string of pictures of a rather pudgy little creature sitting naked in a metal washtub.

But he and Joe were friends now—pals, he imagined Joe might say—and that made it easier to ask the man more questions.

One of the answers Saint Just received two cups of coffee and an hour later, however, shocked even the usually unflappable perfect hero. . . .

Chapter 17

"Maggie? What happened?" Socks raced to the curb to help her out of the car when he saw the walker come out first, pushed out of the car by Maggie, and helped along with a short, pithy swear word. "I thought you said when you left here that you were going to get one of those walking cast things?"

"So did I," she told him, pulling herself to her feet. "Surprise, surprise. My idea of a walking cast isn't the stupid doctor's idea of a walking cast. I'm allowed to put the foot down, sort of, but still supporting about ninety percent of myself on this damn contraption while I do it. Six more weeks, Socks. I have to have this stupid thing for six more weeks."

"Gee, that's a bummer. Where'd you get the neat bicycle horn? I had one of those things, when I was a kid. Let's hear it, okay?"

Maggie gave the silver horn attached to the walker two quick squeezes on its large red ball end.

Oooga-oooga.

Socks laughed, gave the ball two more squeezes. *Oooga-oooga. Oooga-oooga.*

"Bernie's idea of a joke. It was in the overnight package you brought up earlier. You'd think she had better things to do, wouldn't you?"

"But you put it on the walker."

"Yeah, I know. I'm as pitiful as she is. A person has to get her jollies somewhere, right? I'm going to go upstairs, now, to shoot myself. Socks, you know anybody who has a gun?"

"Well, didn't J.P. have one?" he suggested, following after her, holding onto her purse.

"Are you kidding? Ask J.P.? She'd probably offer to pull the trigger for me." Maggie almost made it to the door when, in the damp dusk that had fallen over the city, suddenly the sun shone bright.

Except it wasn't the sun. It was television lights, and Holly Spivak was pushing a microphone in her face. Maggie quickly averted her head, shielding her eyes as best she could while trying to maintain her balance.

"And here she is, *Fox Live at Four* family, our very own Big-Wheels-o'-Bucks jackpot winner, Manhattan's own Maggie Kelly! Maggie, tell my audience, how does it feel to break the bank in Atlantic City?"

"Go . . . away," Maggie said, keeping her head turned away from the lights, hoping the cameraman wasn't zeroing in on her backside. Didn't everything look bigger on television?

"Ha-ha," the blond newscaster-cum-predator trilled into the microphone, and then quickly lowered the thing, covered it with her hand. "Work with me, Kelly. We're live here."

"Yeah? How you'd like to be dead here?"

The newscaster laughed nervously. "Always such a card, folks. She's only kidding. Maggie and I go way back, don't we, Maggie. Why, just last month—"

Oooga-oooga-oooga!

Holly put the microphone to her mouth once more even as she raised her right hand to her ear as though listening to someone speak into the earpiece she wore. "What? Oh, right, Miranda. It *is* time we go to a break. Gotta pay the bills, folks! But we'll be right back with our exclusive interview with the woman who won over three million bucks and had her daddy tossed in the pokey for murder, all in the same day! And you think you have a crazy life? Not compared to Maggie Kelly. Stay tuned, it's a great story. Back to you, Miranda!"

"We're out. Nice juggle. Two minutes, Holly," a disembodied voice called, and Holly grabbed Maggie's upper arm, gave it a squeeze.

"Look," she said, her pleasant on-air voice dropped into its usual flat, Midwestern tones. "You're news, Maggie. You're always news. You and Alex."

Oooga-oooga. Oooga-oooga.

"Sorry, Spivak. Can't hear you."

"Will you knock that off? Where is he, anyway? Alex? My ratings go up when I can put that gorgeous face of his on-air. Now come on, we've got two minutes—less than that."

"My heart breaks for you. Go away."

"I'm not going anywhere, and neither are you. All I want are a couple of comments. You know, on winning? And maybe on your dad? Tough break there, huh? But I'm betting you and Alex are going to get him off. Look how you got your editor friend off— the crazy redhead? Great ratings on that one, let me tell you. Work with me, Maggie, you know Alex would. You want some sympathy for your old man? I can do it. Just let me ask a couple of questions, and I'll have everyone feeling sorry for you. Who knows, you could hit Larry King with this one."

"Gee," Maggie said, resting against the side of the building. "Not Bill O'Reilly? I've always wanted to talk to him. Ask *him* a few questions. You know, like—who the hell ever let you out from under your rock, Bill-o?"

Holly looked toward her cameraman. "Time? Okay, we've still got some time. It's longer, on the half-hour break. Maggie, not now, don't fight me now. Be a bleeding-heart liberal on your time, not mine, please. I'm trying to help you here. Look over there— see that woman over there?"

She pointed toward the curb and, against her better judgment, Maggie looked. The trim, fairly pretty blond woman of about fifty, balancing precariously on the curb at the moment, smiled at her, waved. "Who's that?"

"Her name's Carol something-or-other. *Name!*"

"Carol Heinie. Honest to God!" some guy yelled back at her.

"Heinie? Man, I'da changed that in a heartbeat, wouldn't you?" Holly said, turning back to Maggie. "Carol Heinie, Maggie. She works in a jewelry store in Ocean City."

Oooga-ooo—"What? *Who?*"

Maggie did what she knew had to be a classic double take, goggling at the woman now walking toward them, being gently pushed from behind by a short, fat guy wearing a headset.

"Sixty seconds, Holly."

"How on earth did you—" Maggie asked, getting her first real look at her dad's . . . her dad's what? Paramour? Lover? *Little chippie?* Oh. God.

"She came to me," Holly said, preening. "Totally unsolicited, although I'm going to say I found her, of course. They all come to me, sooner or later. Don't you know that, Maggie? Now come on. A piece of fluff on the jackpot, and then we'll let Carol tell her story. Sound good?"

"How the hell should I know? What's she going to say? What did she tell you?"

"That your dad—Everett, right?"

"Evan," Maggie said, her heart pounding.

"That's good, too. Evan. That he couldn't have murdered this guy in Ocean City, because he was with her, in her apartment with her, at the time of the killing. Good, huh?"

"I think that depends on whether you're Dad's defense lawyer, or his wife," Maggie said, caught between elation and forming a mental picture of her mother's meltdown when she heard the news. No wonder her dad hadn't wanted to tell anyone where he was Christmas Eve. He was protecting Carol. Or himself. Again, depending on who found out—the cops, or Alicia Evans.

"Five minutes, Maggie, *Fox Live at Four*, on-air in the tristate area, and your dad's off the hook. Ironclad alibi, and she's here to tell everyone her story. It's a gift, Maggie, a gift I'm giving you here."

"Thirty seconds! Talk faster, Holly!"

"Well, okay, I guess it's—wait a minute! You said she came to you. Why to you? Are you *paying* this woman?"

"Fox doesn't have to pay for news," Holly said, her tone one of righteous indignation. "Perhaps a small appearance fee, her transportation, a night in a hotel here in Manhattan, a little wardrobe help. That's all."

"Crap! Crap and double crap! Spivak, you know what you just did? You just tainted that woman's testimony. Now get out of here before I thrill your viewers by giving you a hefty belt in the chops. I did it before, you know. You've probably already run the tape a million times. Out of my way. *Move!*"

"And five . . . four . . . three . . . two—throw it back to the studio! Throw it back!"

"You got that? Tell me you got that," Holly Spivak said, picking herself up from the pavement, as Maggie had been a little violent when she'd shoved her walker forward, and the tangle of cords caught on one leg of the thing, she pulled, and the reporter (holding tight to the microphone) had gone down.

"Close the door," Maggie told Socks, hopping into the foyer because that was still faster than trying to roll lightly on her left foot. "And lock it!"

"You want to let your dad's alibi in?"

"What's the point?" Maggie asked, carefully walking toward the elevator. "They'd put her on the stand, let her tell her story, and then ask her if she'd been paid for her story. End of credibility. Is Sterling upstairs?"

"Yeah," Socks said, looking out at the commotion on the sidewalk. "Wow, Spivak's really mad, Maggie. And she's got the other blonde standing with her now, and she's asking her questions. I think maybe you should have—"

"I know, I know," Maggie said, holding open the door to the elevator. "First I did, then I thought. But it's too late now. I could kill Alex for being friends with that bloodsucking blonde. Is he okay?"

Socks was mugging for the camera, which was now focused on the locked door. "Hmm? Oh. Sterling? I don't know. I asked him why he didn't go with you to the doctor and he said he didn't think you really needed him. And then he bailed on going to lunch with me. When does the Sterlman not eat lunch?"

"I think he's catching a cold," Maggie lied quickly, and let go of the door, not frowning until it was closed and she was on her way up to her floor.

It was only when she was standing in front of her door that she realized that Socks still had her purse. With her keys in it.

"Damn! Can my life get any more screwed up?"

The ding of the elevator at the end of the hall pulled her attention, and she looked hopefully down the hall for Socks.

But it was Lieutenant Steve Wendell who emerged, carrying her purse by the strap, as if it was a poisonous snake. "Hi, Maggie. Saw Holly Spivak doing one of her on-the-spot deals downstairs and figured you had to be home. The amount of stories she's been doing on you, she must think you're her ticket to the big time. Socks handed me this. How's it hoppin'?"

"Funny," she said, grabbing the purse from him. "Aren't you going to ask me?"

"Ask you what?" Steve leaned against the wall, watching as she struggled to extract her keys from the purse.

Saint Just had carried her. Steve watched while she struggled.

And was there anyone in the civilized world who might wonder why, when caught up in associations with both men, she'd opted for her imaginary hero with the lovely Regency Era manners and the belief that women were to be treated with every courtesy?

"Thanks for the help," Maggie said, sort of glaring at him when Steve finally leaned over and pushed open the now un-locked door. "Oh, cripes!"

Steve caught her before she could tumble over the huge box just inside the door.

"Steady," Steve warned, and then slid through the doorway to lift the box out of the way. "Wow, this is heavy." He leaned his face down toward the top of the box. "But it smells good."

"Sterling!" Maggie called out loudly, and a moment later Sterling poked his head out of the doorway across the hall. "The box?"

"Oh, oh yes," he said, hurrying across the hall. "Mr. Campiano sent it for you. It arrived a little while ago, a belated Christmas present. We've got one as well. I've opened ours. Meatballs—Saint Just's favorites. Isn't that a lovely, thoughtful present?"

"Hey, at least it's not a horse's head in your bed," Steve said, depositing the box on the dining table. "And it's not everyone who gets a box of meatballs from New York's premier mobster. Caroline's right, Maggie—you live a strange life."

"And you're happier being out of it, right?" Maggie said, finally managing to make it to the couch, where she sat down heavily. "How is your girlfriend, anyway? You two had fun on the slopes?"

Steve blushed to the roots of his shaggy light brown hair. "We . . . uh . . . we never really made . . . made it to the slopes."

"You couldn't locate them?" Sterling asked as Maggie gave it up and began to laugh. What was the matter with her, poking at Steve that way?

Although she'd liked the guy, sure, she'd chosen Alex. But Steve, unbeknownst to her, had been choosing Caroline-the-orthodontic-assistant or whatever she was at the same time Maggie had been realizing that, although Steve was nice, and normal, what she really wanted was Alex. Maybe that's what bugged her. Which was stupid, and entirely too female a reaction to make her feel good about herself.

"You said I was going to ask you something, Maggie?" Steve reminded her as she sat there, thinking her stupid thoughts.

"Hmm? Oh, right. Aren't you going to ask me how I broke my foot? Because I've got some real zingers lined up."

Steve grinned, making his handsome, boyish face adorably appealing. She really did like him. He just had come into her life at the wrong time—which was at the same time Alex had poofed into it. "I already know how you broke it. Sterling told me when I called one day last week or so. But hit me with a couple anyway. I know you're dying to."

"No, that's all right," she said, waving her hand dismissively. "Well, okay. Just one. I tripped trying to get out of Donald Trump's way when he spied a dime lying on the sidewalk."

Steve nodded. "Okay. Not great, but okay. You have more?"

"You didn't like that one? I thought that one was pretty good. Okay, one more. I tripped trying to get out of the way when Donald Trump ran away when he saw Rosie O'Donnell coming down the sidewalk?"

"Don't give up your day job, Maggie. Stand-up comedy doesn't need you."

"Yeah, well, I'm working under a handicap," she said, shrugging.

"Your foot?"

"My dad's arrest," Maggie said, forgetting her foot, and the stupid nonwalking walking cast that was going to be her constant unwelcome companion for the next six weeks.

"Right, your dad." Steve was looking nervous again.

"You're here because you're going to go back to Ocean City with me, right? Talk to the cops there? Cop to cop?"

He shook his head. "I can't, Mags. That's what I came to tell you. I didn't want to do it in a phone call, and I've only got a minute, but I wanted you to know. I was up for the next case, and got hit with a triple homicide this morning. I'm primary, can't get out of it. I'm sorry."

Maggie bit her lips between her teeth, nodded. "It's okay, Steve. We'll . . . we'll manage."

"You and Alex? You'll have half the Ocean City police force putting in for early retirement before you're through," he said, and then laughed without much humor. "But I did call down there for you."

"And?"

"And . . . not much. They pretty much told me they don't have more than circumstantial evidence against your dad. That's probably why he got bail so easily. They knew they probably didn't have enough to hold him too long, but since he was all they had, they put the collar on him anyway, trying to look good for the morning papers. Amateur hour, you know?"

"Did they tell you what they have?"

"Yeah, they did. Professional to professional. Bloody bowling ball at the scene, his prints on the ball. Hearsay about him getting in some knockdown with the vic a couple of weeks previous to the murder. But then some woman came forward with an alibi for him. So they're probably going to have to drop the charge, refile if they get something else. They're still digging. But he's still their Number One guy—since they don't have anyone else."

"Holly Spivak threw money at the alibi," Maggie told him, and watched as he winced as if in real pain. "Yeah, I know. Not good, right?"

"Not great, no. Is Bernie here? I thought you said something to me on the phone about calling Bernie to come home. She might be able to help."

"She's not coming. Or Tabby, either, who's visiting her in-laws in Nebraska or some other godforsaken place. Not that I could figure out why I'd need my literary agent at a time like this—but you know Tabby. She worries," Maggie told him as Sterling—hopefully back to his helpful, uncomplicated self—handed her a glass of cold water. "Thanks, Sterling. And Bernie's not coming because she met somebody, some international banker who will probably turn out to be an international jewel thief, or an international gold digger."

"A miner?" Sterling sat down on the facing couch. "I would imagine that would be a very interesting occupation."

Maggie smiled at her friend. "I love you, Sterling."

"I love you, too, Maggie," Sterling said. "I said something silly and entirely inappropriate again, didn't I?"

"Uh . . ."

"Gotta go, Mags," Steve broke in, slapping his hands against his thighs as if he was about to turn to his trusty horse, mount up, and gallop into the sunset. "You need anything, you let me know."

Maggie waited until Steve had closed the door behind him before speaking to Sterling once more. "You don't say silly or inappropriate things, Sterling. You say very entertaining and sweet things. You're extremely . . . literal. That's how I created you to be. You can't help it. You're only being you."

"Yes, I suppose so," he said, getting to his feet. "But I shouldn't be. Not now that I'm . . . er, um . . . will we be driving back to Ocean City yet tonight, Maggie? I should imagine we should start soon, then, as I was listening to the weather birdie box chirping and there may be snow soon."

"The weather birdie—oh, right. That weather box thingie you bought. Yes, sure, we'll go back tonight. Nothing keeping us here, and maybe Alex found something out today, snooping around."

"Saint Just doesn't *snoop*, Maggie. He *detects*."

"By snooping," Maggie said, pushing herself to her feet. "You were going to say something, Sterling, a moment ago? It seemed important."

"Me? No, not me. I rarely ever say anything important," he said, walking over to the large box. "I know what's inside this box, Maggie. A lovely Crock-Pot—that's what Mr. Campiano's man called it—filled to the brim with meatballs from Mr. Campiano's favorite restaurant. Saint Just complimented them when they dined together, remember? They're still hot, and soaking in a lovely fragrant red gravy. Shall we take them with us?"

"Two Crock-Pots full of meatballs? Hey, why not," she said, smiling slowly. "We'll take one to Dad's place . . . and I think I have an idea of where to deliver the other one. Give me ten minutes, Sterling, and we'll leave."

"You look like the cat with canary feathers protruding from the corner of her mouth, Maggie. What are you planning?"

"Oh, nothing much. And it will all be entirely innocent. Only I doubt the person on the other end is going to think so. Sterling, you are a sweet, kind, loving person. Believe it. But me? I'm mean. I'm mean to the bone . . ."

Chapter 18

Maggie hesitated, the fork speared through half a meatball almost to her mouth as she sat in her dad's small kitchen a few hours later. "Come again? There's a *what*?"

Saint Just smiled, motioned for her to eat the meatball, which was dripping sauce on the tabletop. "Yes, that was rather my reaction, as well, although I, unlike you, managed to hide my dismay. Not without effort, I admit. I said, they have formed a club. Or at least my new friends Joe and Sam believe that. I've yet to approach your sister about the thing, feeling the subject to be rather delicate. I waited for you, and will allow you to broach the question."

Maggie spoke around the meatball, her third. "Gee, thanks—you coward. And how the hell do I do that? I mean, it's a real wowzer of a subject, Alex. Alex? What was that? Don't tell me you—"

"Oh, but I did." Saint Just had also heard the knock on the door, and stood up. "I'm confident you'll figure out exactly what to say. And that you'll be sympathetic, even kind. Sterling has your father nicely occupied at the movie theater, if you'll recall, so I'll go personally welcome her in, shall I?"

"Now? You invited her here now? Why did you do that? *Now*? I'm not ready for this. I'll never be ready for this."

He hid his smile, being a prudent man. "I had assumed you'd be returning earlier than you did, affording us more time to discuss the matter and formulate some sort of delicate approach. My apologies. But rough ground is to be got over as quickly as possible, yes?"

"I'm not riding a freaking horse, Alex. Damn, she's knocking again. Go let her in."

Saint Just inclined his head slightly to Maggie and walked to the door, opening it to see Maureen standing in the hallway, her seemingly ever-present apron visible beneath her opened coat, all of her looking sad, regrettably dumpy, and exceedingly nervous.

"Ah, good evening, my dear. Thank you so much for coming," he said, surprising himself by leaning forward to kiss Maureen's ice-cold cheek. "Maggie's in the kitchen. Do you like meatballs?"

"I . . . uh . . . I guess so," Maureen said as Saint Just took her coat. "I still don't understand why you wanted me to come over here, Alex. Is Maggie all right? I know she went to the doctor today. Does she need my help getting into the shower, or something? I know when John broke his leg I had to help him tape a garbage bag around his cast so it wouldn't get wet in the shower."

She turned to Saint Just, wrinkled up her nose. "They smell something awful when they get wet, you know. You don't want to be anywhere near when they finally cut off Maggie's cast, believe me."

"I'll be certain to keep that in mind, thank you," Saint Just said as, with a graceful sweep of his arm, he indicated that Maureen should precede him into the kitchen. At least the woman appeared talkative, not her usual quiet self. Could that be a good sign? Or a sign that she was highly nervous? Perhaps he hadn't been as cryptic as he'd hoped when he'd phoned to ask her to stop by the apartment.

Ah, well, Maggie would cope. She wouldn't like it, but she would cope. Pluck to the backbone, that was his Maggie. Unfortunately, she was also now armed with that ridiculous horn, and had been squeezing it whenever she didn't appreciate something he said.

Maureen didn't seem to be finished with the subject of the trials and tribulations relating to casts. "And with Maggie? No, she won't want you there when the cast is cut off. Especially not when she hasn't been able to shave her leg in—oh, hi, Mags."

"Hi, Reenie." Maggie waved weakly to her sister, and then

glared at Saint Just. Obviously she hadn't as yet quite formed a definite plan of attack. "Want a meatball?"

Maureen slid onto the plastic seat opposite her sister, eying Maggie's plate with barely hidden trepidation. "You made those?"

"Me? Right. Would I be eating them, if I made them? No, they were a gift. Alex, get Maureen a plate and a fork, please."

"And . . . and a glass of water?" Maureen added pitifully as she reached into the pocket of her apron. "I, um, I think I need to take a pill."

"Maureen, you do *not* need to take a pill," Maggie told her firmly. "I don't need a cigarette, you don't need a pill. Oh, okay, I want a cigarette. You want a pill. But we're not going to give in, either of us."

"I really need a pill," Maureen said, looking up at Saint Just, her eyes filled with pleading.

"Allow the woman her medication, Maggie," Saint Just said, placing a plate, fork and small glass of water in front of Maureen. When had he become a member of some personal Maggie wait staff? How lowering. If only Maggie could make the character of Clarence, his butler, as *real* as she'd made him and Sterling, so that good man could join them on this plane of existence. And the man definitely had a way with boot black and the pressing iron . . .

"Thank you, Alex," Maureen said, pulling a ridiculously small chip of pink pill from her apron, removing the lint on it, and popping it into her mouth. She drank the water. "I'm very careful to ration them. Ah, that's better."

"What's better, Reenie? What was that, a quarter of a pill? And it hasn't even hit your stomach yet. You know what those pills are? They're a crutch, that's what they are. You don't really need them. You just think you need them."

Saint Just sat down beside Maggie, said softly, "Someone's digressing. And preaching. You've stopped smoking, and that's wonderful, commendable. But perhaps it's true, as I once heard someone say, that converts are usually the most righteous. And the most annoying. Ah, wait a moment. That was you who said those particular words, wasn't it?"

"Okay, okay, point taken, so knock it off. You don't have to hit me over the head with everything I ever said," Maggie said, pushing away the plate in front of her. "Maureen, we have to talk."

"About Daddy?"

"Well . . . sort of about Daddy. More so about Walter Bodkin."

"No! I don't want to do that. I came here to help you take your shower." Maureen shot to her feet, clearly ready to bolt for the door.

"Reenie, don't do that, don't run away," Maggie said, holding out her arm, unable to reach her sister. "Alex, make her sit down."

"From doorman to wait staff to warden. How much further can a London gentleman possibly fall in one short evening, do you suppose? Maureen? Please retake your seat—this is for your father. You wish to help him, don't you? Maggie and I believe you possess the power to help him."

"I do? How?" Maureen sniffled, but sat down once more, folded her hands together tightly on the tabletop. "I don't think I know anything, but I want to help Daddy. I really do."

"That's the girl," Maggie said encouragingly. "We found something out today, Reenie. Well, Alex did. Something that might help Daddy. You see, so far he's the police's only suspect. We'd like to give them more suspects to choose from. That make sense to you?"

"No," Maureen said quietly. "You think I'm a suspect?"

"Hell, no."

"But I had . . . had an affair with Walter. I know Mom told you. I could . . . I could be the woman scorned."

Maggie and Saint Just exchanged looks, and Maggie pushed on. "But you weren't the *only* woman scorned, right?"

Maureen's eyes went wide. "Mom's a suspect?"

"You might want to speed this up a bit, my dear, thus limiting erroneous conclusions on your sister's part," Saint Just suggested, wishing himself sitting beside Sterling at the movie theater, possibly even partaking of some popcorn. Or, better, a large box of those lovely chocolate-covered raisins.

"Alex found out today that Bodkin was a . . . that he was . . . that he got around. *A lot.*"

Maureen lowered her gaze. Shrugged. "He got around to Mom and me. So I guess you could say that."

"Alex also found out that there are people in this town who believe that some of the women who Bodkin, well, you know, that some of the women actually formed a club. Is that right? Do you know anything about that?"

Maureen nodded. But said nothing.

"I feel like I'm pulling teeth here," Maggie muttered to Saint Just.

"Patience is usually rewarded. You're doing fine."

"Thanks. I guess that means you're just going to sit there, and not help. Okay, if we're playing Twenty Questions, it's time for another one. Reenie? Do you belong to that club?"

Maureen nodded once more and began digging in her apron pocket again.

"Is Mom a member of that club?"

Finally, Maureen looked at her sister. "Mom? Are you kidding? Nobody knows about Mom and Walter. Well, except for me. And Dad, since I slipped and said something. And you guys . . ." She began to blink furiously. "People really know about the club?"

"They're just guessing, I'm sure. But now *we* know for sure. So tell us about the club. What do you do in this club?"

"It's the W.B.B."

"Pardon me?" Maggie asked, looking increasingly frazzled.

Saint Just felt it was time he stepped in. "The *Weeb*, Maureen? I don't understand."

At last Maureen smiled. "That's what we call it. It's really the W.B.B. Weeb?"

"Ah, like your WAR, Maggie," Saint Just said, sitting back against the cushions. "So the letters mean something?"

Maggie held up a hand. "Wait. Don't tell me. I want to guess. W.B.B? We . . . um . . . Women Who Boinked Bodkin? No, too many W's. Hey, and try saying *boinked Bodkin* five times, fast. Talk about your tongue twisters."

"Maggie!"

"Sorry, Reenie. Do I get another chance? Best two out of three?"

"Maggie, sweetings, you are perhaps being a little bit—"

"Snarky," she interrupted. "Yeah, I know. But consider the subject matter, for crying out loud."

Maureen got to her feet, taking her empty glass over to the dispenser on the refrigerator door. "It's actually We Banged Bodkin, but nobody really says that. It's too embarrassing. We tell people we're the Women's Bible Babes, and that we get together once a month to read scripture." She sighed deeply. "We're all probably going to Hell, aren't we?"

"Not my call," Maggie said, spreading her hands, and then bit her bottom lip. But not before a small giggle escaped.

"Pete named us and she's . . . well, she's sometimes crude, although she's a lovely person, really."

With an unfortunate growth of hair on her upper lip, Saint Just remembered, and then quickly discarded the thought.

"Allow me, please, Maggie. After spending much of the early afternoon with Joe and Sam—I'd rather not identify them beyond that—I fear I am now a veritable font of information. Pete," Saint Just interjected, "is one Mae Petersen. She bowls as a member of the Majestics."

"I need another meatball," Maggie said, pushing her plate at Saint Just. "And maybe the better part of a fifth of Scotch. A woman named Pete bowls with my dad and boinked Bodkin. My sister and my mother boinked Bodkin. Enough women in this burg boinked Bodkin to form a club. At least it isn't the Triple B, or some such idiocy. You know—Bopped *By* Bodkin? Do you gals feel less like victims saying it your way? Is that it? And what in hell does a W.B.B. club *do*? And skip the reading scripture business, okay?"

Maureen sat down again, sipping at the glass of ice water. "Well, like I said, we meet once a month, except in the summer. Too many of us going on vacations, you know? We play Hearts, we have a covered-dish supper twice a year. We . . . we counsel new members. We're, basically, I guess you could say, a mutual support group. A recovery group?"

"Hold the meatballs," Maggie ordered, shaking her head. "I think I'm feeling a little sick. How many members are in W.B.B., Maureen?"

Maureen looked up to the ceiling, as though mentally taking roll at the last meeting of the W.B.B. "At last count? Fifteen? Susan Powers moved to Cincinnati this past October, and Hilda Klein died, poor thing. So fourteen. Maybe fifteen. Is that important?"

Maggie leaned forward on her elbows. "Hilda died? She's dead? When? How old was she?"

"Maggie, I don't think we're looking at a serial killer here," Saint Just told her.

"Hilda was seventy-eight. Her son said her heart just gave out," Maureen said. "We W.B.B.s collected for a lovely flower arrangement."

"Seventy-eight? Bodkin was what—Alex?"

"Sixty-something. Sixty-three? Clearly a man of eclectic tastes."

"Clearly an immoral son of a—Maureen, how could you have done this? I saw the photograph of Bodkin in the newspaper. He wasn't exactly George Clooney. More like George Burns. I don't get it. What was the big attraction?"

Maureen was now wringing her hands together, clearly agitated. Saint Just knew he wouldn't have asked that particular question of the poor woman, had he been in charge of the . . . the inquisition? But, clearly, this last inquiry of Maggie's had been purely a female reaction.

"He . . . he was kind," Maureen said at last. "He understood women. He opened car doors. He knew no woman should live without a dishwasher or an adequately-sized hot water heater. He . . . um . . . he complimented us. And he . . . and he . . . in bed, you understand? He knew just how to . . . well, John? John seems to think *I* should, but that *he* should never have to—you know, like on his birthday? Must I do this, Maggie?"

Maggie looked at the meatball she'd speared, and then put it down on her plate again. "No, you don't have to say anything else, Reenie. Really, I think I've—we've—heard enough." She looked at Saint Just, her expression pained. "More than enough. Alex?"

"Are you handing the questions over to me, Maggie?" Saint Just asked her, watching as she pulled out her nicotine inhaler, had the cylinder nearly to her lips, and then quickly stuck it back in her pocket, blushing.

Ah, the modern American woman. What a delight they all were.

"No, never mind, I can do this. Reenie—we need a list of names. All the members of your little club."

"Why? I can't do that. Nobody knows about the club."

Maggie pulled a face. "We've already been through this part. They *know*, Reenie. They talk about it at Mack and Manco's over a pepperoni slice. We need suspects. Women scorned are great suspects. So give us the names."

"But *my* name would be on that list! You'd turn me in to the cops, Maggie? Your own sister?"

Maggie looked at Saint Just, who decided—cravenly, he knew—that he really wasn't a part of this decision.

"And nobody from W.B.B. would have killed Walter. We *loved* him."

"O-*kay*," Maggie said, motioning for Saint Just to move so that she could slide out of her seat. She grabbed at her walker and pulled herself to her feet. "They *loved* him? I'm outta here, Alex. She's all yours. There are just some things sisters don't need to know, you know? I think that last asinine statement just about tops the list."

Saint Just waited until Maggie's clomp-clomps with the walker could no longer be heard, and then crossed to the refrigerator to take out the bottle of wine he'd opened earlier for dinner.

He retrieved two glasses from the dishwasher (his increasing domesticity amazed even him), and poured himself and Maureen each a generous measure of the zinfandel. He placed one in front of her before sitting down with his own glass.

"Thank you," she said, grabbing the glass and downing half its contents. "I've shocked her, haven't I? I'm her baby sister. I'm supposed to still be playing with dolls, or something."

"Maggie will be fine, don't worry about her," Saint Just said reassuringly. "But I will admit to being confused. I thought you said, earlier, that your small organization is in the way of support for each other. Mr. Bodkin hurt all of you, correct? And you joined together, companions in your misery?"

"I did sort of say that, didn't I?" Maureen's smile was unexpectedly wicked, her eyes shone, and Saint Just at last saw the physical resemblance between Maggie and her sister. "That was a big fib. Maggie wouldn't understand. We liked Walter. All of us. He made us feel special, and important. And pretty. Oh, we all knew that Walter was using us—he thought he was using us—but we really didn't mind, not all that much. Because we were using him, too."

"Amazing. Utterly amazing," Saint Just said quietly, thinking about his varied and quite substantial romantic exploits in his

Saint Just Mysteries. All the women he had bedded. And left. Perhaps Maggie would understand. But he doubted that. Maggie wrote fiction . . . she didn't want to *live* a fiction.

If he, today, tomorrow, in twenty years, had so much as the glimmer of a notion of behaving with other women as he did in their books, he felt one hundred percent certain his now evolving, mortal remains would be found somewhere, with Maggie's hands still clutched convulsively about his neck.

"Alex? What's wrong? You're looking at me funny. You think I'm crazy, don't you? You think we're all crazy. Not hating Walter for what he did to us? And maybe we are, but we're all better for it, you know? Well, except for me, once I found out that Mom—you know."

Saint Just took another sip of wine, for his throat had gone slightly dry. "Your mother, Maureen. How did she feel about Mr. Bodkin? Was she as forgiving, as . . . grateful to him?"

"Mom? She never said. I mean, not about what it was like when Walter was paying attention to her. I don't think she was *proud* of what happened. When . . . the day she came to me, warned me away from Walter, and then found out that I'd already—you know? She was pretty upset that day. Said how dared he go from mother to daughter. What a bastard he was. Like that, you know? Said she'd kill—oh! She didn't mean that," Maureen went on quickly. "She said it. But she didn't really *mean* it."

"No, no, of course not," Saint Just assured her. "Maggie and I have already eliminated your mother from our list of suspects."

"But not me? Not the other girls? I didn't kill Walter. I couldn't!"

Saint Just heard the clump-clump of the walker as Maggie returned, and suppressed a relieved sigh. He'd faced down angry men intent on killing him. Stood toe-to-toe with deadly weapons unsheathed, without a blink. But this conversation? Clearly there were some things gentlemen, at least those of his particular, Regency Era sensibilities were better off not knowing.

"I heard that," Maggie said, clomping to the table to stand looking down at her sister. "You're something else, you know that, Reenie? You go out and have yourself an affair, and then go all wacky-wacko when you find out your own mother got there first. You start popping pills, you let yourself go, you turn into this timid little mouse who belongs to a club filled with other idiots like yourself—you have covered-dish suppers, for the love of heaven. But, no, we know you didn't kill Bodkin."

Maureen sagged against the cushions in relief. "Thank you, sis. So you don't still want the list?"

Maggie rolled her eyes as she sat down beside Saint Just. "Yes, I do still want the list. You may say everyone else felt like you do, not really angry with Bodkin. But what if you're wrong, Reenie? What if one of them was just faking it? We won't give the list to the police, I promise. But Alex and I have to talk to these women. You see that, don't you? The police may not have all that much on Dad, but they might have enough. Juries are weird. The only way we can be sure to clear him, keep this business about you and Mom and Bodkin out of it, is to find the real killer. Fast."

"Well, put, Maggie," Saint Just said approvingly. "Although I believe we'd probably be better served to look to the husbands, if there are any. Swinging a bowling ball with enough force to crush a man's skull like that is probably beyond the strength of many women."

"Not Pete. She's a plumber, she's strong as an ox," Maureen said idly, and then blanched. "Do you guys think—"

Saint Just shook his head. "It's early days yet, Maureen. We're merely gathering clues at this time. But we most certainly will be speaking to Miss Petersen, won't we, Maggie?"

"Yeah. You can be charming, and I'll grill her. That should work. And not a word, Reenie, not to anybody. Reenie? Are you listening to me?"

Maureen looked at her sister, her complexion deathly pale. "You're going to look at the husbands? That's what you said, Alex, didn't you? You're going to look at the husbands? Oh, God, what have I done!"

Maggie opened her mouth to say something, but Saint Just touched her arm, shook his head. "Maureen, my dear," he asked gently, "does John know about your indiscretion with Mr. Bodkin? We'd wondered, but we couldn't be sure."

Maureen nodded her head furiously, and then buried her face in her apron. "I . . . I wanted him to go to therapy with me. We were all going to go, Mom said, before Mom threw Dad out. If Dad knew, then John should . . . you know. *Know?* I told him a couple of months ago."

"Oh, cripes," Maggie said, grabbing Saint Just's wineglass. "What is it with this family? First Mom, and now you? Confession is good for the soul? Is that what you thought? What a bunch of bunk! Alex, if I tried passing off this plot in a novel, nobody would believe it."

" ' 'Tis strange—but true; for truth is always strange; stranger than fiction.' "

"Don't quote Byron at me, Alex. Not now."

"Ah, you recognize the quote, and know the source. And here you insist on saying you write, but you do not retain. You're so self-deprecating at times, my dear. You might want to work on that with Doctor Bob in *your* therapy sessions."

"Bite me," Maggie growled at him, and then reached over to her walker as she punctuated her suggestion. *Oooga-oooga.*

Chapter 19

"Alex?"

He made a low, purring sound and continued to stroke her hair as she rested her head against his bare shoulder. Wasn't he sweet? She felt a little like purring, herself.

But they really had to talk.

"You really should get married."

Alex sat up, dislodging Maggie from her comfortable spot. "I beg your pardon? Is this a proposal?"

"No, not exactly, sport. Let me try that one again, okay?" Maggie scooted backward against the headboard, pulling the sheet with her, pushing her hair out of her eyes. "Not to me. Not here. Not yet. In our books, Alex. That's what I'm talking about. You should be married. Think of all the hearts you'd break. One a book. I'm writing book eight now. That's eight broken hearts. That's terrible. And I'm—cripes, I'm your *enabler*."

"I don't know that this is a problem. The dear ladies all seemed happy enough as I gave them their congé—gifting them with diamonds and the like. Bracketed to one woman, I might be boring. Think of our readership, sweetings. There's nothing more lethal than a boring hero."

"Right. That's why I decided you needed to be sarcastic sometimes. And with a little touch of larceny in your soul. Man, both of those have come back to bite me a time or two, haven't they?"

"So we're finished with this subject?" he asked, settling back against the pillows.

"I don't know. I don't think so. I've thought about this before, you know. A couple of weeks or so ago? That maybe it's time you evolved in our books. You're always talking about evolving here, with me. Growing, changing, all of that stuff? Not that it's worked so far. Maybe, after eight books, it's time Saint Just also grew, evolved. Got married, set up his nursery. If you evolve in the books, it stands to reason you might begin to evolve here, too, yes? Be less inclined maybe to *poof* one day?"

"One advancement at a time, please. I see no crushing need for a nursery in the near future."

"True. One thing at a time. And it's not like you'd have to get married all at once. I could . . . I could introduce a new character. A woman. You could, I don't know, you could strike sparks off each other. Liking each other sometimes, not so crazy about each other at other times. Build the relationship over the course of a few books, and then, bam, you get married."

"And live happily ever after? How boring. Are you planning on abandoning the *Saint Just Mysteries?*"

Maggie wished this conversation didn't sound so much like she was talking about Alex and herself. Except that she was. Sort of. He had to know it. "Being married doesn't mean their adventures would be over. I can think of a bunch of series where being married worked. The Nick and Nora Charles movies and books, for one. *Hart to Hart*, on television—that's an oldie, not as much of an oldie as the Nick and Nora Charles things—but they both worked. Oh, and Nora Roberts has a great series going now with a man and his cop wife. You and . . . you and your bride could solve the mysteries together. There'd still be plenty of sex," she added, feeling her cheeks going hot, darn it. "The mysteries, the sensual interludes, the perfect hero being a perfect hero to his own woman now as well as in general? I think I like it."

"Maggie. Dearest. Are you by any chance feeling even a tad jealous of my heroines?"

"Don't be ridiculous! They're fiction. Why would I be jealous of your fictional bed partners?"

"I don't know. Perhaps because that particular fictional character is sitting beside you in *this* bed, talking to you? If moving onto this plane of existence was possible for me, for Sterling, could it one day be possible for one or two of your other characters?"

"Yeah, right. And with my luck, it would be one of the villains."

"An unhappy thought," Alex agreed, slipping his arm around her shoulders. "But never fear, I would dispatch him immediately—and then kiss my lady wife and take her to bed."

"Very funny."

"I doubt that any of this is amusing to you, sweetings," he said quietly. "I do *not* doubt that much of what we're discussing has to do with your sister and Mr. Bodkin. Am I correct?"

"Well, yeah. Maybe. Sort of . . ."

"You're comparing me, the Viscount Saint Just, to Walter Bodkin? I may go into a sad decline."

"There aren't that many differences. Not when it comes to how you treat women. How your character treats women, that is. You know—love 'em and leave 'em?"

"More than merely taking to my bed in despair, I fear. If you'll excuse me now," Alex said, a chuckle in his voice, "I do believe I will locate my sword cane, find a deep woods somewhere, and walk inside, fall on my sword. It's all you've left me, Maggie."

"Oh, shut up! You're not anything like Bodkin, and you know it. But, man, Alex, that ditzy sister of mine? The guy seduces her—and half the county—and they're not mad at him. If Bodkin isn't going to come off as the bad guy, then what does that make my sister, and all those other women? *Dopes*, that's what it makes them. Willing to be used, discarded. I never looked at the heroines in the *Saint Just Mysteries* that way before, but that's what they are, too. Everyone knows Saint Just is a—well, not exactly a womanizer . . ."

"Thank the good Lord for small favors," Alex grumbled, adjusting the sheets over them. "Next you'll be calling me a cad."

"No, you were—are—a man of your time. Rich, titled, wickedly handsome, faintly bored, on the lookout for adventure. Very appealing to the ladies. Irresistible."

"I can think of one who resists me with unsettling regularity."

"We're *not* talking about us, Alex."

"Yes, sweetings, I'm very much afraid that we are."

"All right, okay. Yes. We are talking about us. At least a little bit. Do you know how hard it is to write your love scenes, now that you're here? That last manuscript? It was bad, Alex. Toss in the circular file bad, which is where it went. Now I've started again, and this one is going to be terrible, too, I can just feel it. I need to give you a heroine. One heroine. Listening to Maureen tonight proved it to me. What you do now is a fantasy, okay for fiction, but at some point you become a farce, a man out only for his own pleasure. And that's *not* a perfect hero, Alex, not to today's woman, today's intelligent reader. Saint Just has at least to begin to evolve."

Alex put a hand to his ear. "Hark! I believe I begin to hear an echo."

Maggie pushed at his hand. "You said *here*, Alex. You said you had to evolve *here*, with me, in this world. You never said you had to evolve in your—our—books. I should have seen that for myself, you know, just as a writer, I should have seen that. There may be people out there who don't mind reading the same book over and over again, but I give my readers more credit than that. Saint Just has to evolve."

"I'm so grateful we've had this discussion of what you've already decided," Alex said, his grin wicked. "So Lady Prestwick is to be introduced as my love interest in our next book? Blond, buxomy? Seems workable."

Maggie looked at him levelly. "Kiki the Kudzu Queen is *not* going to be your love interest, so just forget it. Not happening, trust me."

"And we wave a fond farewell to our Realtor. May I suggest an alternative?"

"You can't have Angelina Jolie, either," Maggie said mulishly.

"So classically beautiful. A pity," Alex said, sighing. "I do, however, have someone else in mind, as you have this habit of borrowing attributes from famous persons, movie actors."

"You mean a conglomeration, the way I did with you?"

"Or just one actor, molded slightly to fit your requirements. I would suggest a woman not precisely classically beautiful, but rather unique. One with the ability to appear regal, haughty, and yet also more than willing to, shall we say, roll with the punches if it became necessary. Flutter a fan, wave a pistol, glide through the waltz, tackle an escaping miscreant and wrestle him to the concrete floor of a parking garage without any thought to her own safety, leap without hesitation into dark, cold flood waters—"

"There aren't any parking garages in Regency England, Alex. And leaping into a flood—*me*? You're talking about me? Putting *me* into our books? Who are you comparing to me, for crying out loud? I don't look anything like a movie star. I mean, that's the sort of thing you notice, right?"

"In your case? Apparently not, no. So, my vote, and I do believe I should have at least equal say in the matter, would be for our new heroine physically to resemble . . . of course you may not agree . . . and, as both Saint Just *and* Alex, perhaps I should have two-thirds of the—"

Maggie pushed at his chest with both hands. "Out with it!"

Alex grinned, even as he rubbed at his abused chest. "Ashley Judd."

"Who?" Maggie closed her eyes, tried to picture the actor. "She was in *Double Jeopardy*, right? That one with Tommy Lee Jones? She's—" Maggie slammed her lips shut over the words *skinnier than me*. What woman in her right mind—and Maggie liked to think she was still at least semi-sane—would admit to anything like that? "You think we look alike? You think I look like Ashley Judd? Really?"

"You object?"

"Object? Hell, no!" Then Maggie mentally slapped herself back to reality. "So you want Saint Just's love interest to look like me—like Ashley Judd? I don't know, Alex. That's bringing this whole thing really close to home. I write fiction, not memoirs. It's kind of spooky. I'll have to think about this. Maybe next month. For now, turn your back, Alex. And I mean it!"

Maggie jabbed him in the side, hard, with her elbow as she pushed herself forward, left the bed. Balanced on her walker, her pajamas slung over the top rail of the thing, she clomp-clomped her way to the bathroom.

Once she'd maneuvered the walker and herself inside the small space and the door was closed behind her, Maggie let her shoulders slump. As exits go, that one couldn't have been very graceful. Ashley Judd couldn't have looked graceful hopping naked to a bathroom.

And Angelina Jolie couldn't have fared much better, so there.

But Alex was a gentleman. He wouldn't have looked. She could count on him for that.

She could count on him for a lot of things. And she did.

That she now seemed to be counting on him to make her life complete was more than a little frightening.

She thought she might know where the problem lay. She hadn't been mad at him, exasperated with him, for a while now. Probably too long. It was easier, keeping her emotional distance, when she was mad at him.

But now that they were lovers? Kind of hard to get mad at a guy who wasn't just the perfect hero, but also the perfect lover.

And he actually thought she maybe looked a little like Ashley Judd? Ahhh, that was so sweet of him.

Maggie shook her head, shook off the flattery. Refused to look at herself in the mirror, hunt for traces of the movie star. Promised herself she was going to stop acting like . . . like such a *girl*.

Maybe what she needed right now was a good fight, to help keep her perspective.

"Okay," she said as she reentered the bedroom a few minutes later, having finally inched her pajama bottoms up and over her cast, "let's talk about something else."

"An excellent suggestion," Alex said, motioning her to one of the chairs near the sliding glass doors to a small, iced-over balcony. "Feel free to select a subject."

He'd dressed, not in pajamas—because perfect heroes know pajamas are unnecessary for them—and looked his usual fabulous self in black slacks and a black cashmere pullover sweater.

Comparing her blue pajamas with the white sheep on them—the baggy legs were the only ones that fit over the cast—to his sartorial perfection was enough to get her just a little bit mad at him. But he didn't seem to mind at all when she looked like she'd been dragged through a hedge, backward, so how could she get mad at him about that?

She needed something else. And then she remembered . . .

"Let's talk about Socks, why don't we? Socks, and pies, and soul food."

Saint Just slipped the black grosgrain ribbon of his quizzing glass over his head and lifted a length of it, allowing the quizzing glass to swing lazily back and forth at midchest level.

A sure sign that he wasn't feeling quite as composed as he'd like her to believe. She knew the signs. She'd given him the habit, hadn't she?

"Socks was on duty when you visited the metropolis? And how is our mutual friend?"

"He's okay. I won't tell you about my visit to my condo, because I'm trying to forget it, but Socks is fine. And he'll get his foot out of his mouth soon, I'm sure of it."

"I was going to tell you myself in time, Maggie. Discuss the idea with you, that is."

"You were? *After* you decided, you were going to tell me. How very Regency-chauvinistic of you, Alex."

"It was only an idle conversation, Maggie, an exchange of ideas one late evening over coffee and cakes at Mario's. Socks and Jay don't have the wherewithal actually to set up such an establishment. Indeed, the entire thing was much more in the realm of fiction. You know, sweetings, as you deal in fiction. It was a conversation of *what if*."

"Uh-huh," Maggie said, tempted to squeeze the bicycle horn, give him a nonverbal opinion on the happy horse poop he was shoveling at her. "So let's play *what if*, shall we? What if Socks really wants to do this? What if he needs money to do this. Get ready, because here comes the biggie. And what if Maggie wins three-point-something-million dollars in A.C.?"

"Oh, dear, this is unfortunate," Alex said, dropping the length of ribbon. "He applied to you for a loan?"

"Him and the rest of the free world," Maggie groused, rubbing at her aching thigh, as carrying the cast around with her had begun causing aches and pains in other areas. "Why should Socks be any different?"

"True. But you told him that Sterling is going to be the beneficiary of your good luck, I imagine."

"I did, and then I warned him not to go asking Sterling for a loan. But that's not the point here, Alex. The point here is your plans for the first floor of my new house."

"Yes, I would imagine so. Again, Socks and I were in the realm of *what if*. I knew you had begun to fret about the cost of our new lodgings, and hence the idea of the bottom floor—clearly once employed commercially—producing some sort of income for you. To offset the cost of the mortgage. I shall disabuse him of the possibility the moment we return to the city."

And that was the problem. Alex knew her so well. How could she turn down the possibility of offsetting some of the cost of the house by renting out the bottom floor? She couldn't, wouldn't turn it down. She just wasn't built that way. Not after years of struggling financially. Her parents would probably call it having a Depression mentality, like so many people who had lived through the crash of 1929 and the lean years that followed. Whatever it was, she had it, and she couldn't seem to shake it.

"No, don't do that. It's having the idea tossed at me like that. That's what bothered me. It's probably a good idea. And I can even see Sterling working with Socks and Jay. The poor guy needs something to do other than stand around and be comic relief for you, the way he is in my books—our books. And he could eat all the pie and soul food he wants and not gain weight, right? The lucky dog."

Again with the quizzing glass? Lifting it, swinging it. Hmm, what *was* the man's problem?

"Alex? Right?"

"As rain, my dear. Then we're settled? I, of course, will front— the word is front, correct?—half of the funds Socks and Jay feel necessary to their project. Again, forgive me for not speaking with you before Socks could broach the subject."

"No problem. But I do have a problem, Alex."

"Other than your father, your mother, your sister—not to mention your conniving brother?"

"Yeah, well, they're all going to have to take a number and get in line for a minute. Because I want to know, Alex, what you're planning for, as Socks called it, the *other side* of the ground floor."

Come on, Alex, it's time for you to say something outlandish. Make me mad. I function better when I'm not feeling so damn lovey-dovey. Get me back on point, able to think about more than how we can get alone together, out of here, and the heck with anything else.

"Ah, sweetings, I don't think you really want to know. We've enough on our plates at the moment, don't we?"

She sagged against the back of the uncomfortable rattan chair. Why did beach furniture have to be so damn uncomfortable? And with pictures of shells and lighthouses on every damn wall? "That's okay, Alex," she said sweetly. "There's room on my plate, any time, to hear what you're thinking. You have such interesting ideas. I'm just hoping this one's legal."

"One of the very things I wished to discuss with you, yes."

"Oh, jeez . . ."

"Now, now, don't be so quick to fly up into the boughs, my dear. Allow me to expound a moment. You like to watch the older television shows on cable late at night, don't you?"

"You know I do. I'm still thinking about writing a book called *I Learned Everything I Ever Needed to Know on 'Seinfeld.'* You know—close-talkers, low-talkers, being sponge-worthy, never to do anything George Costanza might think is a good idea. What of it?"

Alex stood, walked over to the sliding glass doors, looked out toward the ocean view that would be there if two blocks of condos weren't in the way. "I happened to find, and become rather enamored with, the premise of one particular show: *The Equalizer.*"

He turned about to look at her. "You've seen the program?"

Maggie felt her stomach drop to her toes, and stay there. "I've seen it. The guy's ex-CIA or one of those agencies, and he puts an ad in the Classifieds. Something about people losing hope, feeling out of options, and suggesting they call the Equalizer. Then he goes out and solves all their problems and saves the day. Usually by killing somebody."

"There is a level of violence at times, yes. But all in honorable causes. The man has abilities, certain talents, and a profound belief that he employ them to help his fellow man. I admire that."

"Yeah, I'll just bet you do, Sparky," Maggie said, feeling more than a little fatalistic. "So you want to set up shop, be the Equalizer now?"

"I'm very blessed, Maggie. A man so blessed may feel the need to give something back. Help mankind."

"Uh-huh. Pull up the pants legs, Maggie, it's too late to save the shoes."

"Excuse me?"

"Old saying. You'd say, 'Pull the other one, it's got bells on.'

But the meaning's sort of the same. You want to help people—I believe that. But you also want to get your jollies. You *like* trouble. You *thrive* on it."

"And you don't?"

"No! No, I don't. Do you think I'm having fun here—watching my dad get arrested for murder? Watching Bernie get hauled off for murder a while ago? Finding that stupid writer hanging outside my bedroom window? Having some guy send me a dead rat? No, I don't like trouble. I *hate* trouble. But ever since you . . . since you *got here*, there's been nothing but trouble."

"Very well. I'll abandon the idea."

That was quick. Probably too quick. Maggie opened her mouth to say *good, terrific*. But then she closed it again.

"Maggie?"

"Don't push. I'm thinking here. You do the *Fragrances by Pierre* thing. Good money—great money—but you only need to work a couple of times a year for it. You've got the Streetcorner Orators and Players, but you've got Mary Louise and George and Vernon and probably two dozen more like them by now, who do the real work. Are you bored, Alex? Is it boring, being here? Being with me?"

"Do I miss the excitement of my former plane of existence, you mean? The balls, the routs, the gaming, the bruising rides, the mills, the court intrigues, the constant murders and mysteries to be solved? No, not really. We've been fairly well occupied here, Sterling and myself."

"So you weren't pulling my leg? You really feel like you want to give something back? Just plain old help people?"

His handsome face bore an adorably honest expression of resolve and bafflement. "It's what heroes do, Maggie. I am as you made me."

"And I wanted to be mad at you," she said quietly. "You're not helping here, Alex. I need to be mad at you, not like you more and more every damn day."

"*Like* me, Maggie?"

"Yeah . . . well . . . you know . . ."

"I do, yes. My dearest Maggie. So articulate in our books, so very tongue-tied at any other time, when it comes to subjects remotely emotional. We'll leave the subject for now, shall we? What do you think of my idea, hmm? Not calling myself an Equalizer, but something else. Something that defines the service I wish to offer my fellow citizens of Manhattan—and the boroughs, of course. Shall we think about that, instead?"

"Regency Man," Maggie said, happy to move on to another subject. Any other subject than the sort of words she might use to categorize her feelings for Alex. "No, that's not good. What are some synonyms for help? *The Assister*? *Bleech*, that's dumb. *The Neutralizer*? No, that sounds like an air freshener. We could maybe do a play on Saint Just. You know, like *The Saint*? Damn, that was a television series title, too. It's like book titles—all the good ones are already taken. You know, Alex, this could be fun. We are pretty good at this solving problems stuff. Will we charge for our services?"

Did she just include herself in his crazy plan? Yup, she had. And he hadn't blinked, either, so he'd been thinking the same thing. Well, hell, if she was going to be his fictional heroine anyway, why not? It could be fun. Not quite Nick and Nora Charles . . . but, as long as they seemed to go from trouble to trouble now anyway, why not make it a formal agreement?

"Collect fees, you mean? Not necessarily, no. Does that upset you?"

"Not necessarily, no," she repeated, still hung up on a name. Titles always drove her nuts. She'd find one she liked and Bernie would nix it. She'd give Bernie a dozen alternatives, and she'd nix them. That's why she'd called her books about Alex *The Saint Just Mysteries*. The title was all hers, and nobody else would have it, Bernie couldn't really fight it. Anything she could do to not end up with another sappy title like *Love's Lustful Embers* or *Miranda's Sweet Seduction*. *Gawd*! How many people never read a good romance novel because they didn't want to carry around a book with such a sappy title, and with a nursing mother cover to boot? "Wait, I've got it! *The Samaritan*. You like?"

"Very biblical," Alex agreed. "We'll consider it. For now, perhaps you should consider coming back to bed. We've another long day in front of us tomorrow, one way or the other. Speaking with your father, for one, as I was never able to get around to that today. Avoiding our friend on the go-cart, for two."

"Visiting all those women from the W.B.B., for three. I'm not looking forward to that one, although I guess you are. Laying on the charm, and all of that."

"One does what one does best," he told her, helping her to her feet and then sweeping her up high into his arms, returning to the bed. "And practice, I firmly believe, keeps one perfect . . ."

Chapter 20

Saint Just tucked Sterling's collar over his wooly scarf and gave the lapels a small tug. "Outfitted quite to a turn, my friend, and ready for all that winter can toss at you. Do you mind entertaining Evan for an hour or so, while Maggie and I try once again to find a way to work ourselves through this muddle?"

Sterling pulled his earflaps down and snapped the strap beneath his chin. "Not a bit of it, Saint Just. Evan and I are rubbing along famously. And there's nothing like a brisk walk on the boards, the sea air in our faces, to clear a man's head, and all of that."

"On the boards?" Saint Just smiled. "There was a time, you know, when we would think that meant to trod on the stage, emoting, rather than strolling along the seaside in search of any small shop that might have stayed open beyond the season. Our slang has changed, Sterling. So much of *us* has changed."

"But Maggie isn't to know that," Sterling said, nodding his head. "I remember. I'm to dub my mummer, correct?"

"Keep your mouth firmly closed on the subject, yes. Ah, Evan, you're looking much more the thing this morning."

"What thing?" Evan Kelly asked as he walked toward the small foyer, looking confused—a circumstance not entirely caused by Saint Just's words, or even the man's current legal and familial problems. Alas, for the man, since first Saint Just met him, had always borne that same nervous, faintly baffled expression. Without Alicia Kelly, the man seemed rudderless, adrift. Perhaps, as he might propose to Maggie at some point, her father needed his wife's firm hand.

"You look remarkably fine this morning," Saint Just expanded, helping Evan into his heavy tweed wool coat. "You don't mind accompanying Sterling on his daily exercise?"

"If he doesn't mind being seen with me, no," Evan said, and then sighed. "Do you English know that saying—he looks like he's just lost his last friend? Well, that's me. Lost my last friend. Every friend I ever had. They either think I killed Walter, or they don't want to be seen with the guy everyone else thinks killed Walter. You know what that means, Alex?"

"No, Evan," Saint Just said kindly. "What does that mean?"

"It means I never really had any friends. I thought I did. I thought I had lots of them. But I don't. Not if none of them will stick by me. My wife, my kids—except for Maggie, and maybe Maureen a little—my bowling buddies, the guys I have coffee with every morning up at The Last Sail? You name 'em, and they're gone. Fair-weather friends, fair-weather family."

Then he turned to smile much too brightly at Sterling. "Ready to go?"

"Evan, a moment if you will?" Saint Just said as Sterling, looking perilously close to tears, opened the door. "I'd like to show you something."

Evan stuffed his hands in his pockets, came out with a pair of obviously hand-knitted mittens. Love was in every stitch, Saint Just concluded, and talent in every fourth or fifth row of those stitches.

"When, Evan, you come upon one of these people—these fair-weather friends—I want you to do this. I will be you, and you will be the boorish idiot who dares to judge you. Watch carefully please."

Saint Just turned his back, and then turned around again, walked forward two paces and then stopped, as though suddenly aware of Evan's presence.

He opened his mouth, just slightly, breathed a silent *ahhh*, and then looked straight into Evan's eyes for precisely two seconds. He then pointedly raked his gaze downward, to Evan's toes, and slowly upward once more, again looking into Evan's eyes. Closed his eyes for a moment, opened them again, continued what was a look completely devoid of recognition. "So sorry, I momentarily mistook you for someone I once admired."

Then he lifted his chin slightly, turned his head to the left, and walked on, all the way past Evan, to the door.

He wheeled about on his heels, smiling. "Can you do that, Evan?"

Sterling clapped his hands in approval. "Not the cut direct. A cut above the cut direct. A combination of the cut direct and a verbal insult meant to depress any man's pretensions. Bravo, Saint Just, bravo! The quizzing glass to your eye would make it even better, as I've seen you do it, but good enough for Ocean City, and all of that."

"Thank you, Sterling," Saint Just said, and took a small bow. "You must strike first, however, Evan. Take the initiative, remove any chance of being snubbed before you deliver your insult."

"I don't know, Alex. I think I could . . . maybe? I'm mad enough, I really am. I may not look it, but I'm really, really mad. If I looked more like you, there's maybe a chance I could pull it off . . ."

"Done and done," Saint Just said, reaching for his sword cane and tossing it to the man. "Strike a pose for me, Evan. Legs slightly apart, the cane between them—no, not that close to your body. Ah, better. Lean one hand on top of the other—first ridding yourself of those mittens, please. Lovely as they are, I believe they do lack a certain *elegance*. Yes, much better. Now gaze out at the winter-dark sea, your thoughts lofty, even heroic in nature."

He held out his hand, motioning for Evan to raise his chin. "Higher . . . higher . . . and *perfect*. You see it don't you, Sterling? Appearance may not be everything, but it is far superior to walking about with one's head hanging down, one's feet shuffling. Never look the victim, Evan. Always, always, the warrior."

Evan kept his chin high as he turned for the door, forgetting to move the cane and nearly tripping over it. But as he passed through the doorway he took a moment to turn, look at Saint Just. "I'll do the best I can. I have to live here, don't I? I have to stop hiding."

"You are innocent of any crime, Evan," Saint Just reminded him. "Not a victim of a mistaken police, but an innocent man, unafraid of any charges because you know that, in the end, you will prevail. Head high, chest out—the world is not on your shoulders, Evan. You walk on top of the world!"

The door closed behind Sterling and Evan, and Saint Just let out a long breath. "I've just sent two innocents out onto the ice floes. Heaven help the both of them," he said, walking toward the kitchen, where Maggie was working on the list of names Maureen had brought over earlier.

"Dad's gone?" Maggie asked, putting a finger on a spot halfway down the list and looking up at him.

"He and Sterling both, yes. Off to suffer the slings and arrows of outrageous fortune and deflect them and all assault with the indomitable weapons of truth and innocence."

"He's going to do all of that? Dad? *My* dad?"

"I tutored him in the way of the cut direct and pointed insult, and then armed him with my sword cane."

Maggie's eyes went wide. "You didn't tell him you've got that sticker inside the cane, right? Alex?"

"Please, credit me with some small intelligence. Sending your father out with what he knew to be a sword cane would be rather like handing you Sterling's crepes pan. You might look fairly competent, holding it, but the results, were you to attempt to employ it, would be disastrous."

"Funny man," Maggie grumbled, motioning for him to sit down across the table from her. "I've been working on this list. Maureen finally figured it was fourteen women, remember?"

"I recall the number, yes. But you've drawn lines through some of the names, I see."

"Reenie crossed out two of them. Widows, and past the age of swinging bowling balls. Along with Pete, they were the charter members of W.B.B. Then we went through the list together and crossed out five more. Two never married, three are divorced, and none of them, according to Reenie, ever had anything but the nicest things to say about Bodkin."

"And about his particular talents."

"Let's not go there, Alex. Not now, not ever again, okay? So now we've got seven—six, after we deduct Reenie."

"And John?"

Maggie looked at him, shrugged. "What do you think?"

"I think I'd compare your brother-in-law to your father, as far as homicidal tendencies go."

"Yeah, me, too. With a list this long, we've got to trust our instincts, eliminate wherever we can. Then, if none of the names we kept pan out, we can go back, punt to the others on the list."

"Your mind, sweetings, is a constant delight. If you weren't writing fiction, you might wish to become a detective."

"I'll leave that to you, *Samaritan*, thanks. So, we've got six names. All married. None of them older than forty, so their husbands are still able to heft a bowling ball over the head and swing it with force. Man, I can't believe the names on here. I went to school with three of them. Brenda, Joyce, Lisa. Cheerleaders, all three of them—real popular, had their own little clique. One I could get nowhere near, trust me. Lisa was the head cheerleader, and a real pain in the butt. But I outted her in our senior year. Another of my few fond memories of high school."

"Outted? I'm sorry. You did what to her?"

Maggie waved a hand in dismissal. "You don't want to hear it. I mean, I'm not quite as proud of what I did now as I was back then."

Saint Just leaned back at his ease against the plastic cushion, folded his arms across his chest. "I'll wait."

Maggie lowered her eyes to the page. "Wait for what?"

"For your professed maturity to melt away so that you can tell me what it is you did to this Lisa person."

"Oh, okay," she said, and Saint Just grinned—he knew his Maggie so well. "Here's the thing: Lisa stuffed."

"Am I supposed to understand what that means? Stuffed?"

Maggie leaned forward, her elbows on the table. "Stuffed, Alex. She walked around in her cheerleader sweaters, all hot, and pushing her chest out, you know? But one day I had to leave gym class early because I ripped my shorts sliding into second base—it was spring, and we were playing softball—and I was alone in the locker room. I'd had a private bet with myself since the ninth grade about Lisa, figuring she wore a padded bra, you know?"

"You do have this fascination with women's bosoms, don't you, Maggie? Have you ever discussed this with Doctor Bob?"

"You don't understand, Alex. Men in general don't understand. Women . . . women *use* those things. For power. It's ridiculous, but that's just the way it is and always has been. And don't tell me guys are any different. They couldn't be, or I wouldn't get a dozen spam e-mails a day asking men if they want to enlarge their—well, never mind."

"Yes, indeed. Never mind."

"Right. We're talking about Lisa here, remember? She'd gotten a note from her mom about how she was shy, and the school had to let her use a private shower and dressing area—there was a law, or something, that allowed her mom to insist. The rest of us walked around together like idiots, trying to cover ourselves with those small towels the school gave us. But not Lisa. She had her own damn shower. So I got dressed quick, and then I hid right next to her private shower area, waited for her to come in, strip for her shower, and then I checked. And she stuffed!"

"No, I'm sorry. I still don't understand."

"Tissues, Alex. Lisa stuffed her thirty-eight-D with *tissues*. Cripes, must have been half a box of tissues."

"How gratifying for you, to have been right."

"Damn straight. It was even more gratifying when I copped the tissues. And all the toilet paper in her hotsy-totsy private dressing area. *And* her socks. I was thorough, left her with nothing to use for stuffing. Lisa went to gym class that day a thirty-eight-D, and left it an hour later as a thirty-two-double-A." Maggie leaned back, sighed. "It was a shining moment in my life."

"I repeat an earlier observation, Maggie. I do not believe you were an easy child."

"I got a three-day suspension when Lisa went berserk and the gym teacher figured out what happened, and Mom had a cow when she found out. But it was worth it."

Saint Just was left with nothing much else to say to his beloved, so he slid the paper across the table and began to read down the list of names that had yet to be crossed out. "I may be leaping to conclusions here, but I would imagine that I will be the one to interview one Lisa Butts?"

"Ya think? She must have married Barry Butts. He was the captain of our football team—maybe captain of every team he was ever on. Big, blond, huge teeth, all athlete—certainly not a brain trust. A real legend in his own mind. If ever two people deserved each other, it's the two of them."

Maggie sat forward once more, grabbed the list. "Anyway, you can have Lisa, and Brenda and Joyce. I'll take Jeannette, Kay, and Jackie—they're older than me and hopefully won't remember me well enough to slam the door in my face. Now—what do we say to them? What do we ask them?"

"And therein lies our dilemma," Saint Just said, cocking his head toward the window beside him. "Did you hear something?"

Maggie shook her head. "I know. It's not like we can go knock on doors saying, hi, we heard you were bopping Walter Bodkin—so, did you kill him? And if not you, how about your husband? He handy with bowling balls? Okay, *that* I heard. What was that?"

"Pebbles striking the window beside us would be my guess." Saint Just slid himself across the plastic banquette and pulled back the vertical blinds. Looked down toward the alleyway. "Why, I believe we have a visitor, Maggie. One Mr. Henry Novack."

"You're kidding." Maggie scooted over to the window. "Nope, not kidding. Look at him, wearing that big white fuzzy coat with the *New Jersey Devils* emblem on it, straddling that go-cart. He looks like a Zamboni. You know—one of those machines that scrapes the ice between hockey periods? Oh, never mind. Get my coat for me, will you, please, Alex? Clearly we have to go down to him. If he tried to climb two floors he might explode like the Stay-Puff Marshmallow Man, and I'd have to clean up the mess."

"Feeling particularly mean today, Maggie?" Saint Just asked as he helped her put on her coat as she balanced on one leg.

"Well, he makes me so mad," she told him, jamming an arm into her sleeve. "Novack says he's fat because his mother overfed him. Is she tying him in a chair today, stuffing brownies down his throat? No, she is not. He's feeding himself. He's feeding himself right into that go-cart, and probably straight into a coronary. He can't keep blaming his mother for—oh, damn it!"

"Is that a bell I hear pealing, and so very close to home?"

Maggie rolled her eyes. "I know, I know. Looking at Novack is like looking in a mirror. Granted, a much larger mirror, but you know what I mean. It's probably why I get so mad at him—and feel so sorry for him."

"Far be it from me to attempt to stand in lieu of the esteemed

Doctor Bob, but I do think you're making something of a break-through here, sweetings."

"Yes, I know. I am, I know I am, and I'm here to tell you it isn't painless. And why now, Alex? I've got too much going on to go sit in a corner somewhere and contemplate my navel, or whatever. It's been three days since Dad was arrested, and we're nowhere. Less than nowhere. I can't stand to look at him, he looks so sad. I'm mad, I'm upset, I'm frustrated, and I'm looking for a target to take out all my aggressions on. Nobody is safe around me. Nobody. So consider yourself warned."

Saint Just took hold of her coat lapels, much as he had with Sterling earlier, but this time it wasn't to smooth an unruly collar. This time it was to pull Maggie closer so that he could capture her mouth with his own and kiss her with all the expertise eight novels extolling his romantic prowess had instilled in him.

She fought him, but it was a predictably short fight, and with an extremely satisfying capitulation at the end of it, as she lifted her arms up and around his neck, pulling him even closer.

"Am I safe around you, sweetings?" he whispered against her ear a few moments later.

"You don't play fair," she whispered back, her body melted against his. "I so admire that in a man."

There was another shower of pebbles against the window, this assault containing at least one fairly good-size stone that cracked hard against the glass.

"Unaware that I am perhaps saving his life, our co-conspirator becomes anxious," Saint Just said, helping Maggie as she steadied herself on the walker. "Ready now?"

"Ready to bump down two flights of steps on my backside to find out what Secret Squirrel has been up to at the bowling alley? Oh, sure. I've been itching to do this all day. Grab the list, will you? Maureen put the addresses on it. Might as well do as much as we can before I have to face the stairs again."

Chapter 21

Maggie made it to the bottom step on her own, wishing she'd let Alex carry her, and wondering if it was possible to develop calluses on one's backside.

Not that she'd ever ask anyone that question, as it was one of those questions that elicits too many questions in return.

She knew that because she'd been asking that sort of question for most of her life. Some kids in school, for instance, asked why the sky is blue. Normal stuff like that. But Maggie asked questions like, "If the sky is blue up there, and the grass is green down here—what color is the middle?"

Alex was right. She'd not been an easy child.

And life wasn't getting any easier now that she supposedly was an adult.

Case in point: one Henry Novack.

"Hi, Henry," she said as Alex steadied the walker and she got to her feet, because even wooden steps got cold in December. "Love the coat."

"Yeah?" Novack said, patting at it, as though checking it for flaws. "I got it on sale. I think it makes me look fat. You know, being white and all. Do you think it makes me look fat?"

"Don't," Alex whispered as Maggie opened her mouth. "Some things are just too easy to be fun."

"I heard that," Novack said, and then shrugged. "Hell, I am fat. Morbidly obese, right?"

"Stop saying morbidly, Henry," Maggie told him. "It's defeatist. It's also cold out here and I forgot to put a sock on over my cast and my toes are freezing. Where can we go to talk?"

"I got my van parked right over there," Novack suggested. "I can turn the heater on?"

"Terrific," Maggie said unenthusiastically. "Let's go. Does your heater work?"

"I don't know. I'm always pretty hot, so I don't really use it. Natural insulation, you know?" Novack said as he led the way across the street, his corduroy pants swish-swishing together between his thighs, the shiny white material of his jacket keeping up an accompaniment every time he swung his arms. He looked and sounded, to Maggie, rather like a windup toy—with only the key missing from his back. "You're going to like what I have to tell you, though. Well, probably not. But I did learn something."

"You reconnoitered at the bowling establishment last evening, Henry?" Alex asked as he helped Maggie pull herself up into the front passenger seat of the van.

"I hung out at the lanes, if that's what you mean. Don't you English ever say anything the easy way?"

Maggie grinned as she looked into the backseat of the van, watching Alex settle himself. "Alex got one of those learn-a-word-every-day calendars for Christmas, Henry. Today's word is *reconnoiter*. Right, Alex?"

Alex used his gloved hand to push several paper bags with the names of fast food restaurants on them to one side of the backseat. "Very true. And yesterday's word was *exterminate*. It has several meanings," he said, looking hard at Maggie. "Would you care for me to use it in a sentence?"

"I'll pass, thanks," Maggie said, turning around quickly, then holding onto the sides of the seat because Novack had gone around to the driver's side and climbed into the van, and Maggie feared for a moment that the thing would turn on its side. "You might want to consider new shocks, or springs, or something, Henry."

"I would, if I'd won three million dollars," Novack said as he pulled off his knit cap. "I'd buy a new go-cart, too, considering how the one back there," he said, indicating the rear of the van with a hitch of his thumb, "is all dinged up now."

"Oh, come on, I didn't hit you *that* hard," Maggie complained. "And you're the one who rammed *me* a second time."

"No, not you," Novack told her as he unwrapped a chocolate bar, getting it halfway to his mouth before Maggie grabbed it from him and tossed it out the window. "Hey!"

"It's for your own good, Henry. Isn't it, Alex?"

"I wouldn't know, my dear. I'm fully occupied attempting to decide if one of the many bags back here is moving."

"You guys aren't funny, you know that?"

"Sorry, Henry," Maggie said, wishing she'd taken a bite of the chocolate bar before littering the street with it. "Tell us what happened to your go-cart."

"And my jacket," Henry told them. "You know? The one I had on the other night? Sleeve's ripped all to hell now, which is why I look like the *Michelin tires* cartoon guy today."

"I thought a Zamboni . . . but, then, you were on the go-cart when I first saw you, so I—"

"Maggie, focus if you will," Alex said warningly from the backseat. "I do believe Henry is telling us he had some sort of misadventure last evening. Am I correct in that assumption, Henry?"

"There he goes again, but I think I got the gist of that one," Novack said, once more hitching a thumb toward the backseat. "The lot was full, even the handicapped spaces, so I had to park my van down the block, you know, and take my go-cart. Some jackass didn't see me when I was leaving and ran me off the road into a ditch. I don't call that no misadventure, though. I call that a dumbass who had too much to drink at the lanes, that's what I call it."

Okay, so it had taken her a while. But Maggie was paying attention now.

"Someone ran you off the road? Alex? You know what I'm thinking? Oh, why am I even asking? Of course you do."

"Yes, sweetings, I have already deduced as much myself. But let us begin at the beginning, shall we? Henry, if you would please tell us about your evening at the bowling lanes?"

"That's what I was *trying* to do, until you guys started asking questions, stealing my chocolate. But I promised you a freebie, remember? A slice, not the whole cake. Not for free."

"You have a freebie for us, Henry?" Maggie asked him.

"Yeah, I do," he said, his eyelids narrowing as he looked at her.

"Heard some guys talking in the bar. But, remember, you're not going to like it. The dead guy? He was maybe banging your mom. Or maybe your sister? One of 'em. All I caught was the name."

"Maureen," Maggie said hopefully. It would be bad enough, people knowing about Maureen. But her mother? That would be really, really bad.

"No, that's not it."

"Reenie?" Maggie suggested, this time desperately.

"Nope. Why don't I just tell—"

"Alicia?" Maggie asked. Squeaked.

"Jeez, if you'd just hold onto your undies, I'd tell you. Erin. The name was Erin."

"Steady, sweetings," Alex said, reaching over the seat to put his hands on her shoulders.

"If that bastard wasn't dead, I'd kill him myself," Maggie declared through clenched teeth and suddenly numb lips. No wonder her sister hadn't been home in years. "Man, when I moved to New York I must have screwed up Bodkin's personal scorecard, huh? And forget I said *screwed*."

Novack seemed oblivious to Maggie's pain, her Trauma of the Day. "So that's the freebie. I say anything else and it's going to cost you."

"And do you have anything else to say?" Alex asked, still rubbing Maggie's stiff shoulders.

"That's not the point. I'm talking generally here," Novack said, burrowing all of his chins beneath the collar of his jacket. But then he sat up straight, grinning. "You said you wanted to know everything, right? Everything that happened last night? You still want that?"

"I want to pretend I'm an orphaned only child," Maggie said, blinking back tears. But she had to stop this; there was no time for a personal pity party, although a long letter to Erin, once this was all over, was probably in order, damn it. "Okay, okay, how much will this cost me?"

"I don't know," Novack said, sounding unsure of himself for the first time since he and Maggie had "bumped into" each other. "What's the going rate for private detectives, anyway?"

"I don't know, Henry," Maggie told him, rallying. "But the going rate for guys in go-carts is twenty bucks an hour."

"Twenty bucks an—plus expenses?"

Alex chuckled in the backseat.

"Expenses? What expenses?"

"Well, I was at the lanes for about five hours or so, and the pizzas were twelve bucks a pop . . ."

"Pizzas? As in plural pizzas? Oh, hell, all right. Let's make it an even two hundred for the night, okay?"

"Cash?"

"I'll tap my card later at an ATM."

"What kind of later? Later today, or later this week?"

"Later today, unless you make me really mad. Which you're doing. Now start talking."

Novack was nothing if not obedient, at least where the prospect of getting paid to talk was concerned.

He'd gone to the bowling lanes at around seven o'clock, when the leagues first began, and did what Maggie and Alex had told him to do. Be inconspicuous, while keeping his ears open. He walked from alley to alley, sitting down sometimes, pretending to look for a ball at others.

And listening. He did a lot of listening.

The topic of conversation, wherever he stopped to listen, was always the murder. The murder, and Evan Kelly's arrest for that murder.

"Oh, and somebody's got a pool going," he told them. "It's pretty much five-to-three odds that your dad gets life without parole. Sorry."

He went on to tell them that he'd found the alley where the Majestics were practicing, and stood behind a pillar so nobody could see him—

Okay, so Maggie wasn't really good at turning a laugh into a cough, but she gave it her best shot. . . .

—And heard the team talking about the murder, and the New Year's tournament that was coming up in a few days.

The redheaded guy, Novack told them, was having a small cow as he tried to get the new members of the team to understand that the bowling order would remain the same as it had been when Bodkin and Kelly had been on the team: the redhead first, some guy named Kelso next, then the lesbian—

"Henry, I don't think that's necessary," Maggie interrupted him. "And you're wrong. Trust me on this one."

Novack just shrugged and continued to list the bowling order. After the *woman*, the last one would be Barry Butts. And Barry Butts—"wild name, huh?"—hadn't liked that. He wanted to bowl second, not last. There'd been a near fight, but then the *woman* settled it, sort of smoothed things over. Novack figured the fun was also over, and since he'd just seen a guy walking by with a plate of nachos that looked pretty good, he took himself off to the bar for his own plate of nachos and a brewski. Light beer, of course, as he was trying to watch his calories.

"And that's it?" Maggie slumped in her seat. "Not much for two hundred bucks, Henry."

"There's more," he told her quickly. "In the bar? That's where I heard about your sister, I guess it was, and about some others. The guy with the red hair? Him? He came in with the other two guys, not the les—not the *woman*, and they were making jokes about the dead guy unzipping his pants all over town. The hothead? That Butts guy? He said he'd have *paid* the dead guy to take care of his wife for him. I laughed at that, and he looked over at me, all wild-eyed and mean all of a sudden, and asked me if I wanted to sit closer, so I could hear better. Then all three of them looked at me, all madlike."

"Ouch. Busted, huh? Next time you might want to try a cloak of invisibility . . . pup tent of invisibility," Maggie said as Alex remained quiet in the backseat. He was probably thinking, and since Maggie couldn't think of a thing to think herself, that made her a little angry. Because he was probably thinking of some clue she'd missed. This was a thought that pretty much took the fun out of hearing that Lisa "She Stuffs" Butts's husband seemed to think the honeymoon was long over.

"Pup tent, huh? That's good, really funny, if I was a masochist. See, I know some big words, too. But, yeah, I guess they figured out I was listening to them," Novack agreed. "So I finished my chicken wings and left right after they did, picked up my go-cart—I chain it to stuff when I don't want to use it—and took off for the van. And got pushed off the road. Tapped right on the left rear fender and went, bam, into the ditch."

At last Alex said something. "Did you happen to see the driver of the car, Henry? The color of the car? The numbers on the license plate?"

"From where was I supposed to see any of that, huh? From the bottom of the ditch? He was a drunk. Blind drunk, because anyone else would have seen me. I've got reflectors, I've got lights. I got *me*. I'm not small, you know."

"Henry," Alex said sternly, "I thank you so much for all you've done, but you're now, as you Americans say, *out of it*. No more investigating, no more eavesdropping, nothing."

Novack shifted on the seat, once more sending the van's springs to protesting loudly. "What? You think somebody did that *on purpose*? You think somebody tried to—well, holy crap."

Maggie laid a hand on Novack's sleeve. "It could be a coincidence, Henry. But do we want to take that chance?"

Novack seemed to consider the question for a moment. "Well . . . yeah, I think so. I mean, how much fun do you think a fat man has, anyway?" He turned as best as he could in his seat, to look back at Alex. "What do you want me to do next? Price has gone up, though, what with the hazardous-duty pay rules and all. Three hundred an hour?"

"Absolutely not!"

"Maggie," Alex said quietly, "Henry is going to need repairs on his go-cart. I've been looking at it back here, and the paint is rather scraped. Henry, we are agreed. And here's what I would like you to do . . ."

Chapter 22

Because Maggie's rental was low on gas, Saint Just found himself sitting in the front seat of her father's car, holding onto the Crockpot filled with meatballs as Maggie drove the one short and one long block to her mother's condo.

"I really must procure an operating license of my own," he said as the seat belt warning system annoyingly chirped faster and faster while he tried, in vain, to hook the seat belt and not lose his grip on the Crock-Pot. "I do not believe I have the constitution of a passenger."

"Wrong," Maggie told him. "You don't like having a woman drive you around—that's your problem. That male chauvinism thing. You can't believe a woman could drive as well as you. You really need to work on that, Alex. Oh, and while you're working on that, work on this—we're in this thing together, you and me. So stop making decisions without me, okay?"

"Meaning?" he asked, knowing full well why she was upset. The poor dear, she was such a sentimental little darling. Now, piled atop all her other worries, she was worrying about Henry Novack.

"*Meaning*, Alex, that you had no right to send Henry off to try to talk to Mae Petersen."

"You believe she's our killer, Maggie?"

"No," she said, pulling in to the curb, and rolling the front passenger side wheel up and over it, which caused her to direct a daggerlike stare at Alex that told him he would be well advised to ignore her small logistical misjudgment. "My money's on it being a man, definitely. Women, as a general rule, don't go around bashing a guy's brains in. We're neater than that. Unless it was a crime of passion, which I don't think it was, not when Bodkin was found on the beach, when only an idiot would go walking on the beach at night, in late December."

Saint Just opened the car door, now suffering a logistical dilemma of his own, as he needed to put the Crock-Pot somewhere and go around the car, take the walker from the backseat, and unfold it for Maggie. "I concur, totally. Our killer is male. Anything else?"

"Yes, there's something else. On top of the beach, I mean. Because our killer set up my dad to take the fall, which also screams premeditation, right? Somebody had a big hate for Bodkin."

Saint Just decided to place the Crock-Pot on the Kellys' porch, and withheld his comment until he'd done so. Then taking the walker from the backseat, he unfolded it, and opened Maggie's door. Modern life was so much more complicated than merely waiting for the coachie to put down the steps and then magnanimously handing his lady of the moment down from the carriage. "Unfortunately, there are so many male somebodies who could hold this *big hate* for Mr. Bodkin."

Maggie turned neatly on the seat and rather gracefully pulled herself erect outside the car even as Saint Just prudently held his hand just above her head, as she'd more than once hit that head against the side of the roof as she attempted her egress. "Which is why we're going to do this quick, and then start knocking on some female doors."

"Yes, do this quickly," Saint Just said, following Maggie to the curb. "And may I inquire as to just what, precisely, we are about to do quickly?"

"You'll see. I had an inspiration while I was in the city," Maggie said, grinning at him over her shoulder. "Just grab that Crockpot and follow my lead, okay? You'll like it, trust me."

"I adore you, Maggie. I worship at your dainty feet, even while you lumber about in that cast. But trust you, sweetings? Not when you grin the way you're grinning now. I cut my wisdoms too long ago to be so gullible."

Saint Just did not feel comfortable in the role, well, the role played by the trusting Sterling in their books, but Maggie seemed happy, something she had not seemed in several days. So, after voicing his concerns, he did as she suggested, and promised to follow her lead.

Follow her orders, that was, which had to do with him leaving the Crockpot on a table on the ground floor and heading upstairs to collect Tate and his friends, the Realtor and the lawyer, bringing them back downstairs to a waiting—and still happily smiling—Maggie.

"Hi, guys," she said, fairly dancing on one foot as she gripped the walker. "Thanks for coming down. I didn't think I could take another flight of stairs on my fanny right now."

"Yes, well, we don't have much time, Maggie," Tate said, carefully placing himself on the far side of his friends, as distant from Saint Just as he could get—a move that gratified Saint Just no small bit. "We have an appointment, some business to attend to this morning."

"Really? You mean like Cynthia here going to talk to Daddy about the night Bodkin was murdered? Listen to his side of things? Tell him what to say and what not to say? You know, *confer* with him? That kind of business?"

Cynthia Spade-Whitaker rolled her heavily mascared eyes. "Are you once again hinting that I'm not performing my duties to your satisfaction, Maggie? Because if you are—"

"Oh, heavens, no, Cynthia," Maggie interrupted, and Saint Just raised one expressive eyebrow, having decided that Maggie had her target in her sights and it was not, as he'd supposed, her brother, Tate. "I'm here to give you this. Alex? Show Cynthia what we brought for her."

"With every outward appearance of pleasure, my dear," he said quietly, walking over to unzip the insulated cover and lift out the Crockpot that had spent the night in the refrigerator. He lifted the glass lid. "Cynthia? Even cold, do you smell that delicious aroma?"

Sean Whitaker leaned forward and looked at the contents of the Crock-Pot. And then, because, as Saint Just had already concluded, the man was not the sharpest arrow in the quiver, he announced unnecessarily, "Meatballs? You brought Cyndy meatballs?"

"Oh, no, I don't cook," Maggie said, laughing. "The last man I cooked dinner for ended up dead. It kind of put me off the idea.

The meatballs are a gift. I had to go to the city yesterday, you understand, to see my orthopod, and while I was there a friend stopped by with the meatballs."

"No," Cynthia said. "I still don't understand. If someone gave you a gift, Maggie, why are you now giving it to me? Certainly," she added, sniffing, "not in lieu of my fee."

Saint Just lowered the lid on the Crock-Pot, at the same time surreptitiously looking at Maggie, seeing the way her knuckles had gone white as she grasped the walker, putting the lie to her seemingly genuine smile. What on earth was she about to do?

"Oh, heavens no, I'm not regifting in lieu of your fee," Maggie said, laughing. "Jerry Seinfeld would be appalled, wouldn't he? Regifting? Get it? Or maybe you don't watch *Seinfeld* reruns, huh?"

Ouch. That laugh sounded forced. Saint Just stepped closer to her.

"No, when I told my friend what was happening, about Daddy being arrested," Maggie went on, "he asked me to allow him to send my gift to me at another time, and deliver this gift to you." She looked up at Saint Just, blinking innocently. "That Salvatore. He's such a dear man."

And that's when, as Saint Just considered such things, the penny dropped, and he realized what Maggie was up to. No good, that's what she was up to.

How he adored her.

"Ah, yes, our own dear Mister C.," he said helpfully, pivoting slightly to look at Cynthia Spade-Whitaker, whose complexion had gone quite pale beneath her makeup, so that the blush on her cheeks stood out in stark relief. "So devoted to his friends. Very nearly parental, wouldn't you say, Maggie? Protective."

"Uh-huh." Maggie moved the walker forward a few paces. "When he asked who was helping Daddy I told him about you, Cynthia, and how lucky we were to have you. And he knew your name. He said you had defended a dear friend of his some little while ago, here in New Jersey. A Mr. Nicky Palmetto from Newark, was it? Such a small world."

"Cyndy? Palmetto. Isn't that the name of the concrete company guy you—well, you know," Sean Whitaker asked, taking hold of his wife's elbow as she staggered slightly in place. "But you got him off, so that's all right. Isn't it?"

"Shut up, Sean. For just this once, shut up. Salvatore Campiano," she said quietly. "That's who you mean, Maggie, right? Salvatore Campiano? *Boffo Transmissions*? And *other* stuff?"

"Well, he's more Alex's friend than mine," Maggie said, "but, yes, that's who I mean. Alex did his family a favor a little while ago, and you know how some people feel about returning favors. I told him—Mr. Campiano—that you're doing the very best that you can do for my father. Because you are, aren't you?"

"Uh . . . well, yes . . . yes, of course," Cynthia stammered. "The absolute best that I can. So you told Mr. Campiano that? That I'm devoting every moment to your father's defense?"

"Let's just say I told him what you've done so far," Maggie responded, not sounding quite so cheerful now. "He," and here she paused, a very pregnant, portentous pause, Saint Just thought, "sends his regards."

"Oh, shit . . ."

"I beg your pardon? Shall I tell Daddy that you'll be by later, to talk about his case?"

"Huh?" Cynthia blinked several times, and then nodded. Furiously. "Oh, absolutely! Sean and Tate can go on without me. I mean, they're just going to go look at boats. Or yachts. Or something. Down in Cape May? It's much more important that I stay here, conference with my most important client."

"Yes, I rather think it is," Maggie agreed. Purred her agreement. "Alex? I believe I'm done here."

"Oh, wait a moment, Maggie," Cynthia said as Maggie turned for the door. "About that figure I quoted you as my fee?"

Saint Just discreetly coughed into his fist. If the woman wanted to, as the current saying went, *score points* with his beloved, she had most certainly chosen the perfect avenue.

"I've instructed my accountant to pay you the full retainer, yes," Maggie said, keeping her back turned to the lawyer. "You should have a check later this week or early next week."

"Yes, well, thank you, that's very . . . very kind," Cynthia said. "But you know, you're Tate's sister, and I feel just terrible, taking advantage of Tate's little sister, and of this sad, sad situation. And it's Christmastime, and . . . and, well, you know how that is. I was going to tell you later, but I may as well say it now. I've waived my fee. All of it. I'm going to defend your father pro bono. I couldn't feel comfortable any other way."

Saint Just hoped that Maggie wouldn't give in to impulse, and throw a fist high in the air or anything else so amateurish for a woman playing for all the chips. He wasn't disappointed.

No, outward glee wasn't going to give Maggie away.

But *got ya* did. The need to let Cynthia know she'd been bested did.

Females. So lacking in subtlety. They simply didn't understand the nuances of a gentlemanly game of one-upmanship or the joys of a quiet self-satisfaction.

Maggie turned her walker and looked straight into Cynthia's wide eyes. "Yes, I thought you might," she said, sarcasm fairly dripping from every syllable. "Don't choke on your meatballs. Alex, could you get the door for me?"

He waited until they were back outside to take hold of her arm and tell her, "You were brilliant, sweetings, right up until that last moment. Was it truly necessary to gloat?"

"You bet your sweet bippy it was," she told him happily as she pushed off toward the car. "You're the cool, controlled Englishman, and that works for you. But I'm more the rub your nose in it ugly American type. Personally, I like my way better. And now maybe she'll actually do her damn job and get my dad off the hook. Because she is supposedly very good at what she does. I looked her up online when I was in the city, which is how I knew about her last case. The ethics of a two-dollar hooker, but good at what she does. And now she's damn well going to *do* what she does."

"J.P. will be back in the city within the week. You could have simply terminated Mrs. Spade-Whitaker, informed her that her services were no longer required." Saint Just pointed out as he stepped forward to open the driver's door for the bloodthirsty love of his life.

"And what fun would that have been, Alex?" Maggie asked, grinning at him. "Plus, we aren't going to need J.P., unless it's to sue the police department here for wrongful arrest or general stupidity, or something. You and I are going to solve the case, right?

Get Daddy off the hook ourselves? But in a weak moment I'd agreed to that stupid retainer Cyndy demanded. I wasn't going to pay that if I didn't have to. Not with us doing all the work. I just didn't know how to do it, until I saw the meatballs from your mobster buddy. That guy does come in handy, doesn't he? And it worked. Don't you just love it when a plan comes together?"

"You're that persuaded of our chances for success?"

"I am, yes. I don't know why I am, but I am. Bodkin bedded one too many wives—what else could be the motive, right? One of the husbands did it, Alex. I just wish there weren't so many suspects to choose from, that's all. Once we're back in the car you can get out the list again, okay? I'll drop you off at Lisa Butts's place on Second, and then hit my first target—just find me a name somewhere in that same area—and we can meet up at Second and Wesley and . . ."

"Yes, you were saying?" Saint Just asked as he folded the walker yet again, resisting the impulse to inquire as to how she thought she'd fare, hopping, in an attempt to get the thing out of the backseat by herself. But Maggie was feeling powerful at the moment, in charge, and he was reluctant to burst her bubble of independence.

"Alex, keep the door shut," Maggie said, balancing herself with one hand on the rearview mirror as she pointed to the door. "Do you see that? Granted the car is silver, and the sun's beating on it, but do you see that? Right there, around the lock? Those are scratches, right?"

Saint Just propped the walker against the backdoor and bent closer to the lock. "Why, yes, I do believe those are scratches. Faint, but there." He stood up straight once more and said, "My felicitations, sweetings. It would appear you've discovered a clue."

"Somebody picked Dad's lock," Maggie said, nearly losing her grip on the rearview mirror in her excitement. "Somebody broke into his car, Alex. And you know what I think? I think Dad kept his bowling ball in the car. In the backseat, probably. I mean, if you live on the second floor, and you go bowling three, four times a week, would you lug the ball upstairs every time you got home, lug it down when you needed it again? I'm just surprised he locks his car. Cripes, Alex, Dad doesn't even lock the door to his bachelor pad. Come on, we have to go talk to him. Do you think he and Sterling are back yet?"

Maggie had her answer two minutes later as they pulled up in front of her father's building to see Evan and Sterling just mounting the stairs. Maggie honked the car horn and they both walked over to the curb as Saint Just lowered the passenger side window.

"And how was your morning constitutional, gentlemen?"

"Oh, Saint Just," Sterling told him, beaming, "Evan was brilliant, simply brilliant. He performed admirably at the restaurant, walking in with his chin high, his look every inch the warrior. I think it's your cane, frankly. Lends one such an *air*, and all of that."

"But then I blew it," Evan said, handing the cane in through the open window. "I gave the direct cut, whatever you called it, to a guy on the street, before I realized who he was. I see Father Forest from the back of the church, usually, and didn't recognize him right away. And he was all bundled up in his coat, you know, so I didn't see his collar or anything."

Maggie leaned across the seat to grin at her father. "You snubbed a priest, Dad? What did he do?"

Saint Just watched as Evan's cheeks colored. "He was very nice, actually. And then he reminded me that he listens to Confessions every Saturday from three to four and again from six to seven. There isn't anyone in this town who believes I'm innocent, Maggie. Nobody."

"We do, Daddy," Maggie said fervently. "Alex, tell Dad about the scratches."

"First things first, Maggie," Saint Just told her. "Evan? Could you tell us, please, where you secure your bowling equipment when it's not employed in your recreational activity?"

"Huh?"

"Sometimes I feel like I'm freaking translating from one language to another." Maggie nearly fell into Saint Just's lap as she leaned across the seat again. "The bag, Daddy, where do you keep your bowling bag?"

Evan lifted his hat to scratch just behind his ear. "Well, it's two floors, you know? So I keep my bag in the backseat of my car. Makes the finger holes cold, but the ball warms up fast. Why?"

"In a moment, Evan. And where was your bowling ball Christ-mas Eve, when you left the bowling establishment? In the back-seat of this vehicle?"

Evan nodded. "Since I didn't even go home, yeah, that's where it was. That's where I told the cops to look for it. The bag was there, but it was empty. That's when they arrested me."

"Yes, and as I recall the thing, that's when you refused to say where you had been that evening between the time you departed the bowling establishment and returned here," Saint Just said. "You're an honorable man, Evan."

"I'm afraid of my wife, Alex," Evan Kelly said with as much of a smile as a man laboring under the knowledge that his wife could probably pin him in the best two-of-three falls could muster. "But now that Carol has gone on television and told the world, I guess it doesn't matter anymore. The cops might not be so sure I killed Walter, but Alicia will never take me back."

Once again, Maggie leaned across the front seat. "But, Dad, now we know what happened. You went bowling, you put your bag in the backseat, you went to see your—you went to see Carol—and while you were there, somebody picked the lock on the car and copped your bowling ball to use it to bash in Bodkin's skull. This all could have been over Christmas Eve, if you'd just told the truth. You were set up, and the scratches on the car door prove it."

"The police just said I was a slam dunk, a truly stupid mur-derer, and once the prints from the bowling ball came back from the lab, I could just make everybody's job easier and plead guilty," Evan said, not looking convinced. "There really are scratches on my car door? How bad? Will I need to have the door repainted? I'm not sure if I should report that. It could raise my rates, you know, and repainting a door probably wouldn't exceed my de-ductible anyway. Let me come around and see how bad it is, okay?"

Maggie laid her head back against the seat. "He's worried about his insurance rates? We just get him off the hook, and the man is worried about his deductible? *Now* do you see why I left home, Alex, hmm? They're nuts. All of them. Even more nuts than I am."

She lifted her head when her father knocked on the window and pushed the button, lowering the glass. "Happy now, Dad? In the words of patsies everywhere, *youse wuz framed*."

Evan was still inspecting the scratches. "I don't know, Maggie. Can we prove when these scratches got here? Do they look fresh?"

"Your father has a point, depressing as the thought is, my dear. How do we prove that the scratches were made by someone attempting to break into the car? How do we, in point of fact, prove that *we* didn't make those marks, hoping to create evidence after the fact that will remove your father from any list of suspects?"

"I'm surrounded by killjoys, all of them poking holes in my balloon," Maggie grumbled, closing her eyes. "Damn the stupid cops! If they'd impounded Dad's car like it was evidence, or something, then everyone would know how those scratches got there. But, no, they take the bowling bag and leave the car."

"It was Christmas Eve, sweetings. Perhaps their minds were not entirely on their jobs. In any event, I concur. Your father has been deprived of exculpatory evidence," Saint Just said as, on his side of the car, Sterling sighed audibly.

"I was so hopeful there, for a moment. What shall we do now, Saint Just?" his friend asked as Evan rejoined him on the curb.

"Sterling, as our dear Maggie often says, I assume we now go back ten and punt. Maggie? I believe you said Mrs. Butts resides on Second Street?"

"Right, we go back to the original plan. Go upstairs, fellas. Eat some meatballs." Maggie hit the buttons that raised both front windows, put the car in gear, and pulled away from the curb, not saying another word until she stopped the car once more, on Second Street.

"We had it, Alex. We had the evidence. We had Dad off the hook." She sighed. "And now we don't."

"But we will persevere, Maggie, and we will prevail. We always do, don't we?"

"Yeah, right. Go see Lisa, see if you can charm her, and I'll meet you up at the corner on Wesley in, what, an hour?"

"As we've already planned, yes. And you will be visiting one of the other W.B.B. members in the interim?"

She shook her head. "No, much as I don't want to, I think it's time I talked to the little chippie . . ."

Chapter 23

Maggie sat outside the jewelry store, drumming her fingers on the steering wheel as she looked through the large picture window while Carol waited on a customer who seemed to need nothing more than a new battery in her watch.

Maggie was wondering just what in hell was she doing here? She didn't want to talk to the woman. She didn't even want to *see* the woman, not ever again.

What did she say to her? *Hi, I'm your lover's daughter—wanna do lunch?*

The customer was digging in her purse now to pay for the new battery, so Maggie knew she could no longer put off the inevitable. Not if she wanted to talk to Carol before another customer showed up.

She got out of the car, hopped on one foot until she'd managed to open the backdoor and pull out the walker, and then carefully made her way to the sidewalk. She could put her broken foot down as she walked now, no more than five percent of her weight, pushing hard on the walker to support the rest of her. It was stupid, but it was still better than hopping, the cast dragging heavily on her bent leg—unless she had to go up or down. The curb was up, and she couldn't rest her weight on her left foot while she got her right up onto the curb.

So she hopped.

So the wheels on the front of the walker slid on some ice she hadn't seen.

So her first meeting with Carol the chippie took place out on the sidewalk—Carol looking down at her in real concern, Maggie looking up at her and feeling like a first-class klutz.

"Hi, I'm Maggie," she said as Carol helped her to her feet.

"Yes, I know, dear. I saw you in New York, remember? Are you all right? Nothing's hurting you? Would you like to come inside? I was just about to put up the Closed sign, for lunch. Are you hungry? I brought cold turkey sandwiches again today, leftovers from Christmas. Why I roasted a turkey and all the fixings for one person I can't tell you. Well, I could, but I bought the turkey before Evan was arrested, and ended up eating alone, in front of the TV. I'd be more than happy to give you a sandwich. I'm already so sick of turkey."

Maggie kept smiling and nodding as Carol kept talking about the difficulties inherent in cooking holiday meals for one, and before she knew it, they were past a thick beaded curtain and in a small back room, and Carol was helping her into a chair.

"You know you shouldn't have done that, right?" Maggie asked her as Carol opened a large insulated bag and pulled out two foil-wrapped sandwiches. "Talked to Holly Spivak, I mean."

"I know that *now*, yes," Carol told her, grabbing two paper cups from a small cabinet and two cans of soda from the same refrigerator she'd taken the insulated bag from a moment earlier. She worked with a quiet efficiency that was only betrayed once as she attempted to open one of the cans and her fingers shook so badly she couldn't get a firm grip on the pop-top.

"Here, I'll do that," Maggie said helpfully, motioning for Carol to push the cans over to her.

"Thank you, dear. I'm *so* nervous. I just thought that if I made the whole thing public, then the police would have to drop their charges against poor Evan. Would you like more mayonnaise on that sandwich? I keep some in the fridge."

"Er . . . um . . . sure, fine, that's good."

Maggie wanted to slide under the table. She wanted to take off her coat and look at her elbow because it was probably broken.

But those were small things.

What she really wanted to do was figure out how to shut Carol up and make her talk, both at the same time.

Of course, then there were the questions:

So you're really my dad's lover? Girlfriend? Chippie?

Do you know he doesn't really love you and was just using you for revenge on Mom?

Do you know he loves my mom? I don't know exactly why he loves my mom, but he does, and she loves him back. But, then, who understands what goes on inside a marriage, right?

Did my dad tell you what went on inside his marriage?

What were you two doing at your house on Christmas Eve? Exchanging gifts? Exchanging something else?

Do I really want to know?

"I suppose you're here to talk about Evan," Carol said, unwrapping her sandwich.

"Yeah, okay," Maggie said, wishing herself at the North Pole or somewhere, but not until she'd eaten her own sandwich, because she'd unwrapped it, and Carol used really good marbled rye, and wasn't stingy with the turkey, and even had put lettuce and tomato on the thing, for crying out loud.

Maggie's idea of a sandwich when she was working consisted of two slices of dry, hopefully semi-fresh bread and whatever lunchmeat hadn't yet turned green in her refrigerator.

When this woman had lunch, she had *lunch*.

"He's really the sweetest man," Carol said, resting her elbows on the table, her fisted hands tucked beneath her chin. With her blond curls, her small, upturned nose, her neatly pressed Peter Pan collar peeking out from above a pink angora sweater, her single strand of pearls, she looked like Richie Cunningham's mom, Marion, the menopausal version. Pretty, fairly clueless, and totally harmless. Except, with Maggie's dad arrested for murder, these certainly weren't *Happy Days*, were they?

"Yeah, Dad's one of the good guys."

Carol smiled. "He didn't betray his vows, you know. Not with me. We were just friends. Very good friends, but no more than that. I think he thought he wanted more, *should* want more, when we first began seeing each other, but he didn't. I invited him up for coffee after we'd been out for dinner for the third time, and he didn't even know what that *meant*. Such a sweet man. He loves your mother very much, and she hurt him very badly."

"With Bodkin. Yeah, I know."

"Oh, good," Carol said, at last picking up her sandwich. "I'm so glad he's told you about that. Walter Bodkin was a bad man, a very bad man. I did my best to explain that to Evan, explain that your mother was a victim. The way . . . the way I was a victim." Maggie put down her soda can with an audible *thump*.

"Holy cripes, was there a woman in this town the guy didn't boink—I mean . . . well, you know what I mean. Sorry."

"Don't be. I was a grown woman, recently divorced, and horribly lonely. I thought I knew what I was doing. I doubt he lingered with any woman beyond a week or two, and then went on his merry way again. But few held that against him. As I told your father, Walter Bodkin had this, well, this *way* about him. By the time Walter was gone, I was also ready to move on with my life."

"Yeah, a way about him. I heard he was very . . . talented."

Carol looked down at her sandwich, her cheeks coloring becomingly. "*That* I didn't tell Evan. Walter was charming, convincing, even caring. Always a sympathetic ear, you understand? And before you knew it, he was—well, he was very good at what he did. A lonely woman appreciates feeling so . . . so, um, *catered to*. It wasn't until at least a year or so after Walter had moved on to greener pastures, and greener pastures after that, that I realized *I* had been used, and not the other way around. I had been looking for comfort, some sort of reassurance that I was still an attractive woman, and he gave me that gift. But Walter was also a predator. That was the whole truth. He was keeping score in his own sick, private game. Possibly the lonely women he romanced were as guilty as he was, and might not have blamed him too much. Because I can't honestly say he didn't provide . . . provide a service."

Maggie looked at her half-eaten sandwich and decided she'd lost her appetite. If she stayed in this town another week or so, she'd have lost all of the weight she gained when she quit smoking. "Mom blames the hormone pills her doctor gave her," she said, then wondered why the hell she'd said it, why she was defending her mother for doing something so completely stupid.

"We all had our reasons, I'm sure. I understand there are some women who were actually *grateful* to Walter, even after he moved on."

"The W.B.B.s," Maggie said, reaching for her walker. "It's a club. But you didn't join, did you?"

Carol smiled sweetly. "No, I didn't. I'd like to think I still had some pride, when it was over. But maybe a club isn't so far-fetched. Isn't that why wives are so unhappy? Men have their clubs, their activities. They golf, they fish, they bowl. My ex-husband made a second career out of sports, card games and beer, all with his friends. What have we women got? Our homes, juggled careers, children if we're lucky? *Oprah?* And nobody plays bridge anymore. We live in a small town, Maggie, and it's even smaller in the winter months, with the tourists gone. Walter was excitement. And I believe I got your father to understand that, understand what happened to Alicia. So when he came here Christmas Eve, it was to exchange presents, and to say good-bye. I'm moving to Colorado next week to be with my grown daughter and her children. I'll come back, if there's a trial, of course, to testify in Evan's behalf."

Maggie pushed herself to her feet, feeling better, much better. "You're a good friend to my dad, Carol. Thank you."

Carol also got to her feet. "I gave him a tie," she said as she walked with Maggie to the door of the store. "You know, Christmas Eve, when we exchanged presents. He gave me a food chopper. I don't know how I'm going to pack that and get it through airport security." She leaned over to kiss Maggie's cheek. "You're a good daughter. He's very proud of you. He talked about you all the time. You, and all the children."

Maggie blinked furiously as tears stung at her eyes. "Do you have any idea who might have killed Walter? My . . . my friend and I are trying to figure out who did it, to get Dad off the hook."

Carol sighed. "No, I'm afraid I don't. I wouldn't think your father had any enemies."

"Enemies? My father?" Maggie forgot her tears. "But it was Bodkin who was killed."

"Yes, dear, I know," Carol said, unlocking the door and holding it open for Maggie. "But out of the many men in this town, why was your father the one who was chosen, made to look guilty? Such a kind, gentle . . . well, such an almost timid man. Not a murderer at all. It seemed an odd choice for a—is the term *fall guy*? Evan called me yesterday, to tell me that you and your English friend are hoping to uncover the real murderer, and that you've done this sort of thing before, and are quite good at it. Maybe, when you find the person who really killed Walter, he'll answer that question for you: Why Evan?"

"I gotta go," Maggie said, her heart pounding. "I've got to meet, um, meet my English friend. Carol, thank you so much. Thanks for being there for my dad when my mom tossed . . . well, when he was vulnerable. Thanks for coming forward as his alibi, because I know that couldn't have been easy. I hope you're very happy in Colorado. But I've really gotta go . . ."

She hopped off the curb with more success than she'd managed in her attempt to climb it, shoved the walker into the backseat and just about fell into the front seat, trying to aim the key at the ignition at the same time.

Why Dad?

Dad had an enemy?

Oh God, oh, God, oh, God . . . why hadn't she and Alex thought of that possibility?

Glancing at the clock on the dashboard, Maggie realized she'd only been with Carol for about fifteen minutes. Alex would have just been getting into Second Stage Charming with Lisa Butts in that amount of time, but she'd drive past Second and Wesley anyway, just to be sure.

He wasn't there. She knew he wouldn't be there. Damn it, she needed to talk to him!

So where to now? She had at least a half hour to kill. It would be stupid to go back to her father's place, because it would take ten minutes to bump up the stairs, and she'd get to the apartment just in time to bump herself back down again.

Sherlock Holmes never had this kind of problem. . . .

She was just about to turn around, go back to Second and Wesley, wait it out there, when she saw Henry Novack's van parked in front of the donut shop.

Seeing Henry hadn't been on the top of her To Do list, but the donut shop wasn't a bad idea.

Maggie parked out front, in the loading zone, and waited only a minute or so before Henry came waddling out with a huge box of donuts. She beeped her horn and motioned for him to come over, join her in the car.

"You got any crème-filled?" she asked him as he wedged himself into the front seat, sucking in his breath until he could reach the lever that allowed him to push the seat back as far as it would go. "Not the custard cream, the white stuff. The sugary stuff?"

"I don't know, *boss lady*. How bad do you want one?" Henry asked, lifting the lid only slightly, then using it as a fan, to spread the smell of fresh donuts throughout the car.

"Don't toy with me, Novack. Do you or don't you?"

"If I did, and if my *boss* wanted one, that would mean I was on the job while I was in the donut shop, right? And then there's all my time getting to the donut shop, and my time now, of course. Hundred bucks? On top of what you already owe me for tracking down Mae Petersen and pumping her. Because I just came from seeing her."

The smell of powdered sugar was really getting to Maggie. And she had just saved that huge retainer she was going to pay Cyndy the Shyster. Besides, she really had to stop counting pennies—pinching pennies, as Alex called it. She'd been making strides in believing herself successful. She'd bought the house, she'd . . . okay, she'd bought the house. That was it, so far. Now maybe it was time really to let loose in all areas of her life. If nothing else, spending all this money was one sure way to get her back to her computer, and writing another book.

"All right, all right, it's a deal. Henry, have you ever considered a future in used car sales? Or maybe as a cemetery plot salesman? Politics?"

Henry laughed. "I like you, Maggie, I really do. You're so weird. Here you go—one crème-filled. I've got glazed, too."

"Keep it on the back burner for me," Maggie said around her first bite of donut. "Oh, God, this is good. Donuts, fudge, saltwater taffy, caramel corn—I can't get within a mile of the ocean without craving all of them. So, what did Mae have to say to you?"

"I get paid no matter if the information is good or not?"

"You want a written contract, Henry? I've got a hot-shot mob lawyer here in town on retainer. And she works cheaper than you."

"Naw," he said, Maggie's sarcasm sailing right over his head, "I trust you to pay me. I'm just rattling your cage, making a joke.

All fat people are jolly. Everyone knows that. Mob lawyer, you say? Hey, aren't they all? Here, take the glazed. It's still sorta warm."

Maggie looked at the donut, debated for a full two seconds, and then grabbed it. "Got any napkins? How did you approach Mae, anyway?"

"Ah," Novack said, wiping a bit of éclair custard from his chin, "that's the beauty of it. I skunked her. Well, first I stalked her, *then* I skunked her. Followed her to the supermarket and cornered her in the produce department. Told her I worked as a stringer— that's a publishing term, Maggie, *stringer*—for the *New York Post*, and was sent here to do a story on Cleo Dooley's murdering papa. Even took my digital camera along, to take pictures of her, you know? I had her pose with the persimmons. Let me tell you something, Maggie, the woman is no brain trust. She bought everything I said, hook, line, and sinker. I thought I'd never be able to shut her up."

Maggie sighed audibly. "I couldn't have run into a nun on sabbatical in the casino? Oh no, I've got to run into Henry Novack, man of many talents, blackmail not being the least of them. And she knew who Cleo Dooley was—is? That she's me, I mean? Isn't that terrific—not. But go on, what did she tell you?"

"Not much," Novack said, losing his grin. "All she really wanted to talk about were the Majestics. How they're the best bowling team in South Jersey, how the four of them have been together for, like, since forever, how somebody has to die before anyone on the waiting list gets to be on the team. I have to tell you, Cleo—I mean, Maggie—these people are seriously bent. Bowling? Get real. You throw a ball and knock over some pins. You have beer frames, and those might be fun. But—*bowling*? It's not even a real sport."

"Don't say that around my father, Henry," Maggie warned him before stuffing the last of the glazed donut in her mouth. "So that was it? You couldn't get her to talk about the murder? She didn't tell you if she thinks my dad did it?"

"Oh, she says he's guilty, all right. She saw the two of them fighting one night in the parking lot, a couple of weeks before the murder, you know? Said they were really going at it, except that your dad was kind of hitting the air a lot, and the dead guy was sort of dancing around, and laughing when your dad missed him."

"Did you ask her the question Alex wanted you to ask her? If she got a call on Christmas Eve, inviting her for free bowling? Did she tell you who called her?"

"Oh, right, that. Yeah, she got the call. From Bodkin."

"Damn. That's who Dad says called him. We even have the message on his answering machine. Fat lot of good that does us—the dead guy made the calls. And there's no way of knowing who called him, if anyone did. Which the murderer probably did, to get Dad and him to the lanes. To try get the whole team there, actually, then wait until Dad and Bodkin left, and he followed Dad, got the bowling ball, then somehow got Bodkin to meet him on the beach, in the dark."

Novack was working on his second éclair. "You talking to me, or to yourself?"

"I'm sorry, Henry. You did a fine job, really. But I have to go now, pick up Alex. What are you planning for the rest of the day?"

"I dunno. I thought maybe I'd go see if I can talk to the red-headed guy—Panelli, right? You know, the captain of the big bad bowling team? If Mae Petersen could believe I'm a reporter, I'll bet I can make him believe it, too."

"All right, I guess. Just be careful. We already know somebody thinks you're being too nosy. At least now, pretending you're a reporter, it makes your nosiness explainable."

"No problem-o, Maggie. I just hope we don't crack the case too soon. I want to get my go-cart repainted, and that doesn't come cheap."

"Glad I can help," Maggie said as Novack pushed his way out of her father's sedan. "As long as you're not stalking me anymore, I'm happy."

Chapter 24

Saint Just opened the car door and slid onto the front seat, feeling very much the conspirator. "She wants to talk to you," he said without preamble as he reached over to turn up the heat, as he'd been standing at the windy corner for more than ten minutes, and had begun to feel the chill. "Now."

"Who wants to talk to me now? Lisa? *Lisa* wants to talk to me?" Maggie's eyes were wide. "She hates me. She never talked to me in school. She didn't even know who I was until the day I unstuffed her, for crying out loud. Why on earth would she want to talk to *me*?"

"She didn't confide that information to me, but I think you should see her, Maggie. She's one of the ghosts from your past, isn't she?"

"Ghosts? Like I'm *haunted* or something? Don't go all Doctor Bob on me now, Alex."

"Lisa Butts is a very unhappy woman, Maggie. And, I believe, a considerably frightened woman."

"Lisa? She ruled the world, Alex. Well, our world."

"Time moves on, and the world changes. When I first arrived, introduced myself, she seemed wary, unwilling to talk. But I'd had the happy coincidence of arriving in the midst of a small meeting for refreshments—Lisa called it a coffee *klatch*? At any event, two of the women there were on our list of WBB members, although the third was not. Still, the topic of conversation was, as one would expect, the murder of Walter Bodkin."

"Hold it. Back up a minute, okay? How did you introduce

yourself? You never told me how you were going to get through the door."

Saint Just smiled. "Why, sweetings, I took a page from our books, you might say. I told them I was an author friend of yours in town with you for the holidays, and planning on writing a recap of the murder for my next true crime anthology."

"You're kidding. You have *got* to be kidding. You and Henry, both using variations on a theme? And they swallowed that?"

"I have no idea if any of them even know the definition of anthology. I have found, much as you dislike hearing such things, that once I've bowed over a woman's hand and complimented her eyes, there is nothing all that difficult about having myself invited in from the cold for tea and biscuits."

"It's a damn good thing you're no Ted Bundy."

"And now *I* have no idea what you mean. However, if I might return to what I've learned?"

"My irresistible perfect hero. I should give you a wart on the end of your nose in your next book, and maybe it will show up on your face here and—no, forget that. That would mean I'd have to look at the wart, wouldn't I? I'm not a masochist. Who were the other two women?"

"Jeanette Bradley and Brenda Kelso. As I said, both on the list of WBB members. Not that anyone volunteered that particular snippet of information. They both seem fairly innocuous women with uninspiring husbands, and I believe we can cross them off our list. In any event, we chatted about the murder for some minutes, Mrs. Butts lending very little to the conversation, as she seemed fully occupied in shredding her paper napkin and keeping her eyes downcast. It was only when the others left that she asked about you, asked me to bring you to her."

"And you said yes," Maggie said on a sigh. "Why? Do you think she knows something? Because of the way she was acting?"

"I do, yes. I know the good *Left*-tenant Wendell would remind me that feelings are not evidence, but as Steve is not here with us, I think we can go with my powers of observation and the conclusions I draw from those observations. At least for the nonce. Now, are you willing to face your ghost?"

"I really wish you'd stop saying that," Maggie told him as she put the car in gear and executed a very neat U-turn, heading back down Second Street to the gray two-story house sadly in need of fresh paint. "And, before we go in, I've got some information for you. Well, not exactly information, but something Carol said started me thinking that maybe we've missed something."

"Indeed," Saint Just said, looking at her in some interest. "How depressing to believe we are not infallible."

"I'm not writing this story, Alex, so get used to it—it's not like we're following some outline I've already gotten the bugs out of, plugged up all the plot flaws so you can look good."

"Ah, then it's not me that's no longer infallible, but you. Just so that we're clear on that."

"Bite me," Maggie said, turning off the car's motor. "Carol said, wondered, who Dad's enemy is. Not Bodkin's enemy—Dad's."

Saint Just reached inside his topcoat and extracted the grosgrain ribbon that held his quizzing glass, began swinging it idly back-and-forth at chest level as he considered Carol's question from every angle he could muster. "Hmm, an interesting twist on the thing, isn't it?"

"Right," Maggie said, unbuckling her seat belt and turning toward him on the seat. "The murderer could have set up anybody, well, nearly anybody, if we stick to our theory that the killer is married or was married to a WBB member. Or he—the murderer—could have just bopped Bodkin with a hammer or a tree branch, or any number of weapons, and not tried to frame Daddy or anyone else at all. Right? But he didn't. He went out of his way to break into Dad's car, steal his bowling ball, use it as the murder weapon. So why, Alex? Why did the murderer do that? And why Dad, just about the last person in the world anyone would think capable of murder?"

Saint Just lifted the quizzing glass and began tapping its edge against his chin, cudgeling his brains for an answer to that question as he looked toward the vast ocean, the water gray and cold with winter. "We had thought it could be because of that contretemps your father and Bodkin partook of in the parking lot outside of the bowling establishment a few weeks ago. There were witnesses, correct?"

"Yeah, I thought about that one. And I ran into Henry—not literally, not this time—and he talked to Mae Petersen this morning, and he said that what she told him about was seeing the fight. There probably isn't anyone in town who doesn't know about the fight."

"If I were to murder someone," Saint Just said, still tapping the quizzing glass against his chin, stopping only when he realized what he was doing, and how Maggie had written that affectation into their books, "I might consider it prudent to find a way to cast suspicion on someone else and away from me. Prudent, and plausible. Indeed, I might even first discover that idea after observing the man I wanted dead and another man rolling about a parking lot, beating on each other for all to see. But that would only be a theory, one not easy to prove."

"So you think Dad didn't have any enemy, that Bodkin's murder wasn't a two-for-one shot—kill one, convict the other and send him up the river and, bam, two enemies gone with one blow? I'm finding that scenario pretty hard to believe, myself. So, bottom line here, you think that the fight with Bodkin just gave the murderer the idea to try to pin the blame on Daddy?"

Saint Just considered this for a full minute. "Yes, the latter theory seems more logical," he said at last.

"But you aren't buying it, are you? Not one hundred percent."

"No, I don't think I am. At least not completely. The more I learn, the more I realize—we realize—that the late Walter Bodkin's amorous adventures may have been the worst-kept secret in this relatively speaking small town. There was no real reason to go to the trouble to select your father from so many possible suspects, so many cuckolded husbands. Indeed, if the police would only let go their grip on their conviction that your father is their *slam dunk*, they would probably have at least two-score names to put on their suspects list."

Maggie sank back against the seat. "So Daddy does have an enemy. That's what you're saying, isn't it?"

"I'm saying, Maggie, that we cannot discount the notion that your father could have been the real target, and Bodkin tossed in as the victim as a sort of two-for-the-price-of-one, thus getting rid of the local lothario at the same time. Even if I can think of only one other person of my acquaintances I would consider less likely to ever cultivate an enemy than your father."

"Sterling," Maggie said, smiling slightly. "You know, I think I must have unconsciously patterned Sterling a little on my dad. Minus the being browbeaten, I mean."

"I would say that we should curtail their excursions about town, except that as long as your father remains the primary suspect, he's probably safe. If the charges against him were to be dropped, however, and he truly does have an enemy who is also already a murderer, we'll have to rethink the situation. In the meantime, I believe we've kept Mrs. Butts waiting long enough."

"Oh, right," Maggie said, reaching over to pull down the sun visor in front of Saint Just and checking her makeup, pushing at her hair. "How do I look?"

"No longer seventeen and vulnerable," Saint Just told her, taking her chin in his hand. "But let's do something about that mouth, shall we?"

Maggie tried to look in the mirror again, even as he held her chin steady. "My mouth? What's wrong with my mouth?"

"I don't think it has been kissed in at least two hours," Saint Just said as he leaned closer, took her mouth with his own. He sucked lightly on her bottom lip, then slanted his mouth as he ran his tongue around the sensitive skin behind her upper lip, smiling against her as she moaned low in her throat and pulled him even closer.

When he moved away from her, it was to see her with her eyes still closed, her mouth soft, moist, and faintly bee-stung. "There. Perfect."

Maggie opened her eyes. "Well, that was interesting," she said, and then sighed.

"Hmm, yes, although you might wish to explain why you taste, delightfully, of sugar," Saint Just told her, taking his handkerchief from his pocket and brushing at the bits of white powder and small particles of sugar littering the front of her coat. "And then tell me why you seem to be *decorated* with it as well."

"Henry. He gave me donuts when I saw him. I didn't want them, but he forced them on me."

"Held you down and shoved them into your mouth, did he? The unmitigated cad! Do you think I should call him out? Gocarts at ten paces?"

"Aren't you a riot? I'm hunting a killer with a guy auditioning to be a stand-up comic." Maggie pushed his hand away and opened the car door. "We're keeping Lisa waiting, remember?"

Saint Just smiled as he walked around the car to extract the walker from the backseat, and then bowed slightly as he unfolded it and presented it to Maggie, who seemed to feel it was time she checked to be sure that the bicycle horn Bernie had given her still worked.

Oooga-oooga.

"Move it, Romeo. I want to get this over with and get home to Dad, ask him a few more questions."

"Such as?" Saint Just asked her as he followed her up the short brick walkway to the Buttses' domicile.

"I don't know yet. But I'll think of something. In fact, maybe we should take Dad over to Mom's, and sit them both down, ask them both some questions."

"Put them together in the same room? My, aren't you the brave one today. Or is what I'm seeing an example of what I've heard termed a *sugar high*?"

"You're like a dog with a bone, aren't you, Alex? Yes, I ate two donuts. No, I'm not sorry. Yes, I know I told you I'm still trying to lose those last three pounds I gained when I quit smoking. Okay, four pounds." She stood back as he reached past her to bang the knocker three times, smiling down at her as he did so. "All right, all right, five pounds. I still have to lose five pounds. Happy now?"

"I don't recall ever putting forth the notion that I am unhappy, sweetings. You're soft to the touch, and I like that." He leaned closer, his mouth a mere inch from hers. "I like that very much."

The door opened just as Maggie's lips parted slightly.

"Alex, you're—oh. Maggie? Maggie Kelly? Wow, you've really changed, haven't you?"

Maggie had pulled herself erect on the walker and was now smiling at Lisa Butts. "Well, I got my hair cut, put in a few high-lights, you know, and—um . . . you haven't changed a bit, Lisa," she said, her smile so bright Saint Just knew that the poor girl was positively cringing inside at what had to be a blatant lie.

After all, Saint Just considered himself to be a connoisseur of the feminine sex, and if Maggie and Lisa Butts were of nearly the same age, had graduated high school in the same year, then something had gone wonderfully right in Maggie's life in the intervening years, while something had gone depressingly wrong in the life of the former chief cheerleader.

Lisa Butts had lines around her eyes, lines that only seemed to accentuate the dark circles beneath those eyes. Her lips, although wide and full, pulled down at the corners, as if they had forgotten how to smile. Her brown hair hung rather limply to just above her shoulders, her body was clothed in a too-large gray sweatshirt and black knit pants that bagged badly at the knees. Her bare feet were pushed into frayed satin slippers that may once, long ago, have been white.

It did not, as Maggie would have said, take a rocket scientist to determine that the years had not been kind to Lisa Meadwick Butts.

The photograph he had seen on the fireplace mantel during his first visit to the house, that of a much younger, immeasurably happier Lisa Butts executing a truly impressive leap into the air while thrusting her arms and some large pom-pom type things high in the air, could also be considered a clue to Lisa's unhappy state.

But Saint Just preferred to think he would have known all of this without also seeing the photograph.

"You want to come in?" Lisa asked, turning away from the door she left open behind her. "I've got fresh coffee on. Just go in there, to the living room, and I'll bring it right in, okay? How'd you break your ankle, Maggie?"

"Foot," Maggie called after her as she maneuvered the walker toward the living room. "I fell out of a tree in Yosemite National Park while photographing a white-breasted nuthatch and . . ." she turned on Saint Just as Lisa disappeared down the hallway, whispering, "Holy cripes, Alex. What happened to her?"

"Life happens to people, sweetings. And life, I would deduce, has not been kind to Lisa Butts."

Maggie turned the walker and backed up until her calves were against an overstuffed chair covered in an unfortunate choice of imitation orange leather, and then sat down with a thump, sinking even lower as the sound of air being *hissed* out of the cushion was the only sound in the small room. "But she was head cheer-leader. She married the captain of the football team. She had a charmed life . . ."

"Here we go," Lisa said, reentering the room, this time carrying a tarnished silver tray holding the glass pot from a coffee-maker and three thick earthenware mugs. "I hope you take it black, Maggie. I'm out of milk and I can't go to the store until Barry—well, I can't go until later."

Saint Just neatly divested her of the tray and placed it on the table in front of the couch as Lisa smiled up at him, blushing, and sat down.

"Thank you, Alex," she said, resting her elbows on her knees as she leaned forward, spoke to Maggie. "I can't tell you how sorry I was to hear about your father. But I'm sure he's innocent. I heard you hired some hotshot woman lawyer. She'll get him off, won't she? Because I'm sure he didn't—well, I suppose you're sure, too, huh?"

"Thanks, Lisa," Maggie said, pouring herself a cup of coffee, and then lifting the pot and looking at Saint Just, who shook his head, declining her offer to pour a cup for him as well. "I think you're the first person we've talked to who believes Daddy didn't do it."

"I am?" She sat back quickly, almost as if she'd been slapped. Or said too much? If so, she wasn't done speaking. "Maybe that's because I remember your father from the Laundromat where I work on weekends. It's right next to Barry's shop, so it works out fine for us. He's so sweet, your dad, coming in with his laundry the last two months or so. He had absolutely no idea how to work the washers. In fact, he tried to put his clothes in one of the extrac-tors we use for the really big loads, if you can believe that. Thought it was a washing machine. Anyway, I'm sure the police will realize they made a mistake and let Evan go."

Lisa had just called him Evan? Maggie blinked. A woman her own age had just referred to her father as Evan, not Mr. Kelly? Said it just as though they were friends? Wow.

"He's not in jail, Lisa," Maggie corrected. "He's free on bail."

"Oh. Well, good. That's good, isn't it? He's out on bail, and soon they'll drop the charges. They have to."

"Again, thank you, that's really sweet of you. Lisa—what the hell happened?"

Saint Just shot a look at Maggie, gave her a slight, warning shake of the head, not that he expected Maggie to be anything more than Maggie—inquisitive, caring, and sadly lacking in finesse.

Lisa laughed, but it wasn't a happy sound. "You always said what was on your mind, didn't you, Maggie? What the hell happened? I don't know. But it sure did happen, didn't it? To both of us. I'm the dreary housewife, and you're the famous author. I always envied you, you know, back in high school."

"Me?" Maggie said, sipping her coffee. "I didn't think you even knew who I was. Well, not until the day that I—that was stupid of me, Lisa. Juvenile. I'm sorry I did it."

"I wasn't. I stayed out of a lot of backseats in those days, so that no guy would find out what I was doing. The stuffing, you know? False advertising? Oh, sure, some kids laughed at me when they found out, but that didn't last long. I was the head cheerleader, lead choir soloist, vice president of the senior class, and all sorts of other stuff, after all. And, hey," she said, shrugging, "I finally made it to the backseat and let a guy get to second base, found out what I'd been missing—sorry, Alex. Are we embarrassing you?"

"The word mortified comes to mind, yes," he told her with a smile. "But carry on, please. I am nothing if not adaptable, and I understand the modern American woman is often frank in discussions of such things."

"And he watches television, Lisa," Maggie said, holding her cup to her lips. "Even cable movies. Don't you, Alex?"

"Yes, thank you for sharing that, Maggie," Saint Just said, taking up his place at the mantel, lifting down the photograph of a large and smiling and happily filthy young man dressed in a football uniform, the number five on the muddied jersey, his helmet tucked under his forearm. "I noticed this photograph beside yours, earlier. And this would be Mr. Butts? Mr. Barry Butts?"

"Yeah, that's Barry, right after we won the state title our senior year. That was his big moment. The high point of his life."

Saint Just replaced the photograph. "Surely not," he said, looking at Lisa. "After all, his wedding day must have ranked much higher."

"See any pictures of the happy couple sitting around in here, Alex?" Lisa said, her voice bitter. "I know I don't."

Maggie and Saint Just exchanged looks, and he could see the pain in her eyes. This time he didn't bother to try to warn her off as, still looking at him, she asked Lisa, "When did you and Barry get married, anyway? I guess I'd already left for the city, huh?"

"Yes, you left town. You left, and you didn't come back, did you? That's why I envy you, Maggie. You did it. You got out. You had a dream, to be a writer, and you went after it. That's the one thing I could never do—write. Sing, dance, yell loud, but not write. Not the way you did, for the high school newspaper and yearbook. You were really good."

"I . . . um, well, I—you had a dream, Lisa?"

Lisa pushed her hair out of her eyes, smiled. "Sure, didn't all of us have dreams? I was going to be on Broadway. Singing, dancing. But Barry came first, you know? Just like Brenda's Frankie came first, and Jeanette's Bruce came first, and—marriage seemed so much . . . so much safer, you know? Easier?"

Saint Just stepped away from the mantel. "And is it, Lisa?" he asked her. "Easier, that is."

Chapter 25

Maggie strapped herself into the seat belt as Alex closed the door on the passenger side. "And you say *I'm* too blunt? *I* ask too many questions? *I* push too hard? *Is it, Lisa? Is it easier?* Cripes, talk about pushing the button and turning on the water-works. What the hell happened to her, Alex?"

"I would say that her husband happened to her. The man should be horsewhipped."

"Well, I agree on that one. All that crap she told us? How she can't leave the house unless he's with her? Not even to go pick up a carton of milk at the grocery store? Not even to work at that Laundromat unless he's right next store at his bike shop? That's abuse, Alex. Barry Butts is one sick ticket."

"Overly possessive, I agree. One has to wonder how such a cowed and frightened woman was able to sneak away, have an affair with our late, unlamented Mr. Bodkin."

Maggie put the car in gear and headed for the corner, turned left onto Wesley. "Good point, Alex. If Barry watches her every move, controls the purse strings, all her comings and goings, what she wears, what she eats—can you believe he tells her what she can eat?—then how could she possibly have an affair behind his back?"

"Yet she belongs to W.B.B."

"Lisa *belongs* to that select club, yes," she said, chewing on her bottom lip, her brain on perculate. "But Lisa belonged to every-thing. You name the club, the activity, and Lisa belonged to it. Maybe she thought she had to belong to W.B.B, too. Without, you know, *really* belonging? Her friends do, Brenda and Joyce, at least. I mean, it might be one way to get out of the house without Barry throwing a fit, since she was only meeting with other women?"

"An interesting if unappealing thought."

"Agreed. I remember Barry. Tall, pretty muscular, too. I wouldn't want to get on the wrong side of that guy. Do you think he hits her? Oh, cripes, Alex, that would be awful. Why doesn't she just leave him? Get up, get out, you know?"

They pulled in to the curb in front of her father's bachelor apartment and Maggie turned off the ignition.

"I mean, I know he could come after her, stalk her, maybe try to hurt her. But there are shelters for abused women now, even if he doesn't hit her. It's still abuse. Lisa is an abused woman."

"I agree, Maggie. But I think it might be more than that. She's a frightened woman."

"Well, sure. She let a man in the house. From the way she says he watches her, distrusts her, she had to be scared spitless he'd find out she had a man—*you*—in the house."

"Again, I think it's more than that," Alex said as he helped her from the car. "Think about this, Maggie, if you will. What did you say to Lisa when she put forth her belief that your father is innocent?"

"What did I say? I don't know. That she's the only one who thinks so? Of course, Carol thinks so, too, but Carol's a friend, where Lisa is just an acquaintance, you know, with that Laundromat business she told us about."

"Yet she was adamant. Almost, one might say, as though she *knew* your father to be innocent."

"She calls him Evan. Old enough to be her father, yet she calls him Evan. And Bodkin was old enough to be her father." Maggie felt her eyes going wide. "You think Barry Butts killed Walter Bodkin? And you think Lisa *knows* he killed Walter Bodkin?"

"It would be very simple, very neat, wouldn't it? A fanatically jealous man believes his wife has become a member of the We Bopped Bodkin club, or whatever it's called. Who is to say what such a man, when he felt betrayed, would do?"

"Yeah, but that's no more motive than any other guy whose wife belongs to W.B.B. Okay, sure, Barry's a bastard, but that doesn't make him a killer—and you'd think he'd kill Lisa, too, if he thought she'd been sleeping with Bodkin. We need a lot more than a hunch, Alex. And there's still that business Carol brought up—about how maybe Dad has an enemy, remember?"

"And your friend Lisa calls your father Evan. Just as if he's her bosom beau. If Butts wanted to eliminate the rivals in his life, he could possibly believe he'd kill two birds with one bowling ball."

"Using that reasoning, if Dad were to get off, Butts would just go after him again. A man like that? He'd think it was his right to eliminate anyone who even looked crooked at Lisa. *If* you're right. We might just not like Butts, that's all, and want him to be guily. That's what Steve would tell us."

She pushed her hands through her hair, and then leaned back against the headrest, exhausted, her eyes closed. "Oh, I can't think straight anymore, Alex. The only thing worse than no suspects is so many suspects. We're probably just jumping on the first one who looks good. Because we don't like Barry Butts for the way he treats Lisa, and because we're so tired. And if I'm the only one who's tired, let me remind you that you aren't dragging a hulking heavy cast with you everywhere you go day and night, and bearing down on a walker with each step. I should be getting a medal here, I'm being so good."

"How true. And all without uttering a single complaint. What a brave little soldier."

"Right. Another few days of this, and you can nominate me for sainthood. And don't think I don't know you're being facetious."

Then she opened her eyes, sat front, her heart pounding, as someone banged hard on the driver's side window.

"Well, well, look who's here," Alex said, opening the car door. "Shall we escort J.P. upstairs, or would you rather we speak to her privately before she sees your father?"

"I don't know. You choose." Maggie was still busy trying to slow her heart rate as she looked out at J.P. Boxer, who was leaning down to put her face all but against the window, and grinning as if she knew full well how much she'd startled her friend. "Back off, J.P.," she said, motioning for the lawyer to step away, and then she opened the door, swung her legs out of the car.

"Well, girl, would you look at you," J.P. said, her hands on her hips as she eyed Maggie up and down. "What did you do to yourself?"

"I broke my foot," Maggie told her as Alex unfolded the walker yet again and assisted her to her feet. "Tripping over a doorstop."

"Oh, sunshine, you have to do better than that. Make up a lie, make up a whopper. Tripped over a doorstop? That's so *ordinary*."

"Good thought, J.P., I'll consider it," Maggie said as they all moved to the sidewalk. "When did you get back from your vacation?"

"Last night, and I've been running myself up and down the county ever since, doing that voodoo I do so well, which you'd know if you'd turn on your cell phone, sweetcakes, or talked to your dad once in a while, because I cleared it all with him first—and Sterling, of course. He introduced us. God, I love Sterling, he's such a sweetie. You buy him the beanie hat? With the earflaps? I'll bet you did, that thing has Little Mary Sunshine written all over it. Hated to leave all that warmth for all this damp and cold, but friendship called, and I'm such an old softie," J.P. told them as she wrapped her coat more tightly about herself.

The coat was huge, bright red, cushioned more than just padded, and fell all the way to the tops of the lawyer's bright green high-top sneakers. J.P. was also huge, tall, the sort of overpowering figure that usually had the ability to intimidate the hell out of Maggie. And had, at least at first. Except that, for all her outward aggressiveness, J.P. had the proverbial heart of gold. And the worst clothes sense and choice in lovers of any woman in the history of the world.

"So you've been here, talked to Dad, seen Sterling, and then gone to the cops?"

"Not the cops. Never the cops, not after they've picked their man, put the collar on him. Had to go up the chain of command, all the way to the top. Never start at the bottom, it takes too long. Worked fast, because I like to work fast, and because I'm good, damn good. After all, how can I let my friend's daddy walk around with a murder charge over his head, huh? Which is gone, by the way, as of about fifteen minutes ago. You can thank me now. Even hug me. It might warm me up. Damn it's cold."

Maggie didn't know what to think, what to say. She turned to Alex. "Are we happy about this?"

J.P. dropped her arms, that she had opened so that Maggie could hug her, and looked from Maggie to Alex and back again.

"Okay. Somebody want to tell me what's going on here? I cut my vacation short, rush home to winter, drag myself down here to the hinterlands, tell Ms. Spade-Whitaker to take a hike—never saw a woman so happy to lose a client—take myself up to the D.A.'s office, present myself as the new attorney of record, read the evidence they have to show me, do a little dance, make a little love, get down to—well, they didn't have anything. All circumstantial, except for the bowling ball. That was pretty substantial. And your daddy has an airtight alibi in his mistress, so—"

"Carol's not his mistress, J.P.," Maggie explained nervously. "They're just very good friends."

"Never interrupt me when I'm blowing my own horn, sugar. Now, where was I? Oh, yeah. I threatened to paper the D.A.'s office with motions to dismiss, Miranda violations—more paper than the man could handle if he had a staff of twenty in Manhattan rather than sitting here in the boonies of Jersey. And he caved. Such a pretty thing to see, a man caving that way. So the charges have all been dropped, at least until they get more evidence. Which they ain't getting, right, because Sterling told me you and English here are doing your ride-to-the-rescue thing, and finding the real murderer. So, English? Did you find him yet?"

"Possibly, J.P.," Alex told her. "However, if one of our current hypotheses is correct, removing Evan as a suspect may have just put his life in danger."

Maggie sagged against the side of the car. "Go upstairs, please, Alex, and get Dad and Sterling. I'd feel better if we took Dad to Mom's house, had everyone in one spot."

"An excellent suggestion. We might arrive in time to wave fond farewells to Attorney Spade-Whitaker and her Realtor husband."

"And Tate. I'll bet he's going to bail at any moment. We have to finish this, Alex, we have to finish it today."

"Because you need to get back to the city and have me run the title search on that building Sterling told me you bought, and go over the sales contract that you're now going to tell me you didn't sign without letting me look at it, right?"

"Uh, well . . . oops?"

"You signed a sales agreement without checking with me, your personal lawyer?"

"You reneged on the free legal service for life, J.P.," Maggie reminded her weakly.

"And a good thing I did, if you didn't have someone vet that sales contract, run a decent title search. You know, Sunshine, between tripping over murders and tripping over yourself the way you do, I could end up a very rich woman."

He-e-e's ba-a-a-ck . . .

They let him go?
How could they let him go!
What did I do wrong? I didn't do anything wrong. I did it right.
Didn't I?
Now what?
Now nothing, that's what. I do nothing. I just sit tight.
I've got what I want now. Everything I want.
Unless they try to screw me.
Then they'll be sorry. Boy, will they be sorry.
I took out one for sure. I can take out another one . . .

Well, isn't he a real fun guy? But who is he? What's his major problem, other than the fact that he's an eggroll short of a combination plate.

All the clues are there, though. Promised, and delivered.

So who killed Walter Bodkin?

Better yet, if you think you're so smart, and you already know the "who" of it—*why* did this person kill him?

Bet you don't know that (and, if you do, go write your own book; why are you reading this one?).

Maggie and Saint Just sure don't know why Bodkin is dead. As a matter-of-fact, they aren't even close.

Which, unhappily for our bad guy, never stopped them before when they uncovered a murderer for all the wrong reasons. . . .

Chapter 26

"*What's he* doing here? *I* didn't invite him here. Who invited him here? Margaret, is this your doing? Why would I want him here?" Alicia Kelly asked rapid-fire, pointing at her husband as the gang, one by one, emerged at the top of the staircase leading to the main floor of the condo.

"Think I'll go get a bowl of puffed rice," Evan muttered, his chin on his chest as he scuttled past his wife on his way to the kitchen. "Sterling? You want a bowl of puffed rice?"

Saint Just motioned with his head that Sterling should accompany Evan to the kitchen—and out of the line of fire.

"I suppose so," Sterling said, hurrying after Evan. "How many calories do you think are in a bowl of puffed rice, Evan? Do you have any skim milk?"

"Since when does Sterling worry about skim milk?" Maggie asked, but then just shook her head. "Never mind, it's not important. Mom, look, it's like this. We think maybe Dad's in danger."

Alicia sat down all at once. Thankfully she had been standing directly in front of the couch. "Evan? Somebody is after Evan? Is that what you're saying? Why? Because of Walter?"

"Alex?" Maggie said, looking at him for help.

Which he gladly supplied. After all, he might not know exactly what was going on, but he knew his impeccable English accent often concealed that fact from his American listeners.

"Yes, allow me, please. First, Alicia, I'd like to introduce to you J.P. Boxer, Maggie's and my very good friend and your husband's new attorney."

Alicia smiled rather weakly as J.P. bounded across the room and stuck out her hand to the woman.

"English over there will take an hour getting to the point, Mrs. Kelly," J.P. said, "so I'll just lay it out for you. The D.A. has dropped the charges against your husband for lack of evidence. My doing, because I'm very good at what I do. Which, for some reason, English and sunshine over there seem to think makes everything worse, not better. Alex, back to you."

"Yes, thank you, J.P." Saint Just looked about the room, Tate's absence noticeable. "Your son, Mrs. Kelly?"

"Upstairs, packing. Cynthia and Sean have already left."

"Ah, shucks," Maggie said happily. "Did she take the Crock-Pot of meatballs with her? Nah, I guess not."

"I have no idea, Margaret. They called themselves a cab and went sneaking off without so much as a 'thank you for having us.' And Tate and I . . . well, we aren't speaking, so I have no idea what he's doing or where he's going. This entire family is falling apart."

"Not that it had far to fall," Maggie said quietly before joining her mother on the couch. "Do you want me to talk to him?"

"Would you, Margaret? I don't want him leaving in a huff. And I think," she added, attempting a whisper that failed badly, "I think he may have, you know, *money problems*? And I thought he was doing so well with his new business venture."

"A three-state tanning bed franchise might not have been the way to go right now, Mom, what with all the skin cancer scares. He should just stick to mechanical engineering—that he supposedly knows how to do. What did you two argue about anyway?"

"This place," Alicia said, spreading her arms to encompass the entirety of the condo. "He wants to sell it, and I said, no, I can't do that. Not without speaking to your father. And since I'm not speaking to him, I suppose the condo won't be going on the market anytime soon."

"Logical," Maggie said, grinning up at Saint Just. "Kelly-logical, anyway."

"Can't you ever be serious, Margaret? And now you say your father has been exonerated?"

"The charges were dropped, Mrs. Kelly," J.P. said. "That doesn't mean they can't be brought again, if the police find new evidence. But, yes, for now, your husband is no longer a suspect."

"But he's in danger? Didn't someone say he's in danger? You said it, didn't you, Margaret? In danger of what, for pity's sake?"

"Danger? Who's in danger?" Tate Kelly asked, entering the living room, his suitcase in his hand. "Hello," he said to J.P., holding out his hand. "I'm Tate Kelly, and you would be . . . ?"

"Wondering what the hell I'm doing here," J.P. said, shaking his hand, her firm grip, Saint Just noticed with some amusement, causing Tate to flinch. "I hear you might need a good bankruptcy lawyer? I don't do bankruptcies as a rule, but I could make an exception for a friend of Sunshine's here."

"Mom!" Tate exploded. "What did you do—rent a billboard, for crying out loud."

"Don't you yell at Mom!"

"Don't you tell me what to do!"

"Stop that this minute, you're both an embarrassment! Margaret, sit down, and tell your brother to do the same! Don't you yell at each other. You weren't raised by wolves, you know!"

"Alicia? Children? What's going on in here? Sterling and I could hear you all the way out in the kitchen."

"What do you care, Evan? I raised these children, not you. Four children, and I raised them on my own. Not you, working all the time, bowling all the rest of the time, watching television all the rest of the time."

"That's a lot of *rest of the times*, Mom," Maggie broke in, looking at Saint Just, her expression now more embarrassed than angry.

"I'm sorry you feel that earning a living, keeping a roof over my family's head wasn't enough for you, Alicia," Evan said, showing a remarkable amount of backbone, Saint Just thought. It was probably a shame he hadn't shown it earlier, as in for the last forty or more years.

"Hi, everybody, I saw Daddy's car outside and figured you were here, Maggie, and might have some news?" Maureen said from the head of the staircase, smiling as she walked into the room, her winter coat hanging open over a nondescript blue dress and her ever-present apron. "*Daddy*? You're here? What's going on?" Then she must have sensed the tension in the room. Her smile began to slip and she backed up a few paces even as she began digging in the pocket of her apron. "Ex . . . er . . . excuse me. I need to go get a drink of water."

"And there she goes, off to swallow one of her little pink pills," Alicia said, collapsing onto the couch once more. "What have I done, Evan? What did I do wrong? Erin's as good as gone, Tate's trying to sell our house from under us, Maureen's a . . . a pill-popper, and Margaret—" She stopped, blinked, and looked at Maggie. "I don't know anymore, Margaret. Sometimes you seem so *normal*."

"If she's normal, I'm Donald Trump," Tate declared hotly.

"Oh, I don't know, Tate," Maggie said sweetly. "You might not have his money, but you might want to consider trying his comb-over soon. And now that the subject's out in the open—how dare you try to sell Mom and Dad's house out from under them?"

"Maggie," Evan said, "we'll handle this, your mother and I."

"How are we going to do that, Evan? I'm not talking to you, you philandering old fart."

"Me? *I* philandered? What about you, Alicia? If I philandered, it was only because you philandered first."

"*Mom* had an affair, too? Why did I think it was just Dad?" Tate finally found his way to a chair and sat down. "Oh, I love this. I just love this."

"You would," Maggie growled at him. "You'd love anything that gets them to split up so they let you sell the house."

"They were already splitting up. Mom kicked him out, remember? And I can sell this house anytime I want to sell this house. It's *my* house!"

"Oh, yeah?"

"Oh, *yeah*!"

"Over my dead body, sport!"

"And speaking of dead bodies, Maggie . . . ?" Saint Just wasn't easily discommoded, but the idea that a family war might be about to break out in front of him was decidedly discomforting. In case everyone else had forgotten, they had a murderer to unmask. "If we could just get back to the point . . . ?"

Maggie, who was pointing a finger within an inch of her brother's jutted-out jaw, dropped her arm to her side and sighed deeply. "Well, that was fun, wasn't it? Like a flashback, or something. You're right, Alex. Back to the problem at hand. This is an old problem, and we've embarrassed ourselves enough in front of you and J.P. Sorry, Alex, sorry, J.P."

"Don't worry about it," J.P. said with a dismissive wave of her hand. "It's not really a family fight until somebody throws something. My mom's favorite was always the TV remote. She had a real hate for my dad's TV remote."

Evan, intelligent enough to know that retreat was sometimes not only the best but the only option, crossed the room to stand beside Saint Just. "I think she's weakening, Alex," he said quietly as Maggie and her mother engaged in a low conversation on the couch. "Maybe if I bought her a gift or something? Jewelry? Jewelry would be nice, don't you think?"

"Ah, no, not jewelry, Evan. Not in this case."

"But Carol could probably get me her store discount on—oh. Right. Flowers?"

"A good thought, yes."

Maggie waved to him from the other side of the room. "Alex? Mom says she's ready to hear about Dad being in danger. Our theory on it, anyway."

"Excuse me, Evan," Saint Just said before crossing the room to take up a chair only in time to rise politely from it again as Maureen reentered the room, carrying a bowl of puffed rice and followed by Sterling, whose ears were quite red, obviously a result of overhearing the Kelly Family At War.

Saint Just was more than willing to explain his and Maggie's theory, even as he knew that theory had more than a few gaping holes in it that had to be filled in only by rather large leaps in logic.

When he was done, Evan Kelly was shaking his head. "Barry Butts? But I barely even know him. Why would he want to frame me for Walter's murder?"

"Because you were handy, Dad," Maggie explained. "You and Bodkin had that fight in the parking lot. Everyone saw it. You pretty much set yourself up to be a logical choice when Butts wanted to point the finger of suspicion—trite as that sounds— away from himself."

By now, Maggie had joined Saint Just as he stood in front of the gas fireplace. Evan, wonder of wonders, had taken his place on the couch, beside his wife.

"So this is all my fault," Alicia said, her spine straight, her chin raised. "It figures. One way or another, a woman always takes the blame."

"Now, now, Alicia," Evan said, patting her hands as they lay clenched together in her lap. "I did a stupid thing. I . . . I let my outrage get the better of me. And Walter was so . . . so *smug*. So happy with himself about what he'd done."

Maureen, sitting on the piano bench, lifted her apron to her face, hiding behind it.

"No, Evan, it's my fault. I never should have told you what I'd done. What Walter did to me, to . . . well, you know."

Maureen's shoulders began to shake, and Maggie went to sit beside her, put her arm around her shoulders. "It's okay, Reenie."

"What's *okay, Reenie*?" Tate asked, and then smiled. Okay, leered. "Don't tell me Maureen—cripes, what is this, an outtake from *Desperate Housewives*?"

"Tate, I believe you owe your mother and sister an apology," Saint Just said smoothly.

"The hell I do. I'm not the one who was catting around. My God, my own mother?"

"That's it, big mouth. We've heard enough from you. Come with me. And I mean *now*, buster!" Maggie said, using her walker to all but herd him toward the kitchen. Saint Just filed away the thought that he might want to point out to his beloved one day that she might have more of her mother in her than she would suppose. But he would probably point that out from a distance.

This departure left Saint Just to answer J.P.'s next question. "Okay, I think I've got this now. Barry Butts—what a stupid name—wanted Walter Bodkin dead because his wife was having an affair with him, or pretending to have an affair with him. Because Maggie's mom and sister had also been . . . victims of this guy. Evan and Bodkin were seen fighting, Butts figured the best way to keep suspicion off him would be to put it on Evan. How am I doing so far?"

"Well enough," Saint Just said, smiling. "Now ask the question you're burning to ask."

"I was just getting to that, English. I got the charges dropped against Evan. A good thing, or at least ninety-nine-point-nine percent of the population would see it that way. But you and sunshine think I've just put the man in danger. Drumroll please, here's the question—*why*?"

"We can't be completely sure, but it's possible that Mr. Butts believed that his wife had . . . tender feelings for Evan."

"For me?" Evan looked at his wife. "Alicia, I *swear*—"

"Don't you talk to me, Evan. Don't you dare try to talk to me. Not ever again."

"You were kind to the woman, Evan," Saint Just explained quickly, "when you frequented the Laundromat where she was employed. For a man like Barry Butts, being kind to a woman he denied any male companionship could be misconstrued. Especially if Lisa Butts told her husband the sort of thing she told us—that you're a very nice man."

"I don't know if I swallow that. Isn't that pushing things, Alex?" J.P. asked him. "I know the type. They're mean, irrational. But to see Evan over there as a threat to his marriage?"

"Not to his marriage, J.P., not at the bottom of it. But as a threat to his fanatical control over his wife? He'd already believed that she'd strayed with Mr. Bodkin. To have her now saying nice things about another man? Mr. Butts would have felt he was losing his position of absolute power. Mrs. Butts is convinced, or so she says, that Evan is innocent. I think she has reason to *know* that Evan is innocent. Innocent, but still another man Mr. Butts's wife turned to, in defiance to him. After all, Bodkin was about your age, Evan, so Lisa turning from one man of a certain age to another of a certain age wouldn't be so unusual. What do they call it on *Dr. Phil*—a father figure?"

"I'll say it once more, Evan. Don't you ever speak to me again! That girl is our Margaret's age. Young enough to be your daughter!"

Evan all but leapt to his feet, to look down at his wife. "Alicia . . . shut . . . up!"

Alicia opened and closed her mouth a few times, rather like a beached fish, and finally managed, "What?"

"I said, shut . . . up. You talk too much, do you know that? *Way* too much. That's why I don't talk—I haven't been able to get a word in edgewise in about forty years. And you only ever hear yourself, only listen to yourself. Yes, we've got problems. Our kids have problems. We have problems with our kids. The whole world's got problems. The good thing is, we can fix ours, if we stop jumping off cliffs every time things don't go our way."

He turned to look at Saint Just. "Sterling told me that, told me some story about lemmings or something like that," he said, smiling weakly. "And you showed me I'm to keep my head up, be a warrior, not a victim. I *like* being a warrior." He sat down next to his wife once more, looking her straight in the eye. "This is my house. You are my wife. And that's the way it's going to be. You got that, Alicia? The kids? They're grown—let them do what they want. We started together, Ally, and we're going to finish together, the two of us. No more ultimatums, and no more cliffs."

Saint Just was tempted to close his eyes and block his ears before Alicia Kelly found her voice. He may be a hero, but any man of any sense is careful to stand very clear of marital discord.

But then he opened his eyes as Alicia said, "Oh, Evan. Where have you *been* all these years? I don't want to do it all by myself, I really don't."

"It sure looked like you did," Evan said, losing some of his bravado. "But that's all right. We'll work it out, won't we? We'll talk. We'll go to that counselor you want me to go to, all of us."

"Yes, Evan. We'll work it out. You can say anything you want, and I'll listen. I promise."

"And I'll listen to you, I promise." Evan smiled at his wife and then looked up at Saint Just. "I brought Lisa Butts a pizza from Mack and Manco's one Saturday, because she wasn't allowed to leave the Laundromat," Evan said as Alicia rubbed his back. "And I helped her fold some king-size sheets she washed for one of her customers. You know how big those are? I helped her fold them. I remember now . . . Barry came in, and just stood there, *looking* at her. She sort of stood there, too, shaking a little, and then he turned and walked out. Didn't even say hi, you know? We'd been laughing, because I kept folding to the left when Lisa was folding to the right, and the sheet was getting all tangled and— he'd kill for that?"

"We don't know, Evan," Saint Just told him as Maggie and Tate reentered the room—Maggie looking satisfied, Tate looking like a man who'd moments earlier lost the family estate in a reckless game of faro. "But, for now, we'd like you to stay here with Sterling and Alicia. And you, Tate, if you will."

"Ah, that's too bad, but Tate has to leave," Maggie said brightly. "Don't you, Tate? But he'll be back next weekend, to help you fix that piece of siding that came off the side of the house in the last nor'easter that you've been worried about, okay, Dad? And he'll be back the week after that to do anything else you need done. Mom, you'll make a list?"

"I've had a list for two years," Alicia said, sighing. "And I'll believe this when I see it, Margaret."

"Oh, you'll see it, you'll believe it. Won't she, Tate?"

Twenty minutes later, after waving good-bye to J.P., who was more than ready to climb into her rented Mercedes and head back to the city, Maggie and Saint Just stood outside the Wesley Street condo and looked at each other. Smiled.

"I rent a Taurus, J.P. rents a Mercedes, and my spendthrift brother rents a freaking limo. It's transportation, right? Getting from point A to point B? One of these days I'm going to figure out if I'm an idiot or the rest of the world is nuts," Maggie said as the taillights disappeared in the early dusk. "Or maybe I'll just buy a Mercedes for myself, now that we've got a garage of our own. You know, more than the roof terrace, the enclosed garden, it's that garage. You know how unheard of garages are in Manhattan?"

"Maggie, you're avoiding the inevitable," Saint Just told her. "What happened with Tate?"

"You know what happened, Alex. I loaned him the money he needs. At no interest, unless he screws up. Like, if he doesn't visit Mom and Dad once a week, help them with anything they need help with, like that piece of missing siding, and the leak in the guest bathroom. Tate's really good with his hands, when he wants to be. Anyway, he breaks the rules, bam, I start charging interest. And like I told him—there's bank rates, and then there's loan-shark rates." She grinned. "You can just call me Jaws. Now tell me what happened back there. I heard voices for a while, and then I didn't. And Mom's looking at Dad a little funny."

"Maggie, you wouldn't believe me if I told you," Saint Just said as he helped her into the driver's seat of her father's car. "For now, I believe it's time you and I reconnoitered this bowling establishment where Bodkin was last observed alive. We'll be obvious to anyone who remembers you from your childhood, but the time has come to do our own detecting. And then later this evening, as I've already discussed with Evan, he and Sterling will join us there."

"Daddy? Why? If he's in danger—"

"We'll protect him, Maggie. But Evan tells me that the Majestics will be practicing their bowling maneuvers every night this week, in preparation for something called the New Year's Tournament. As Barry Butts is now a Majestic, gathering everyone in one spot seems a workable solution."

"You mean you want to do a classic Saint Just Mysteries' we-gather-all-together denouement, right? But we don't have enough evidence for that, Alex."

"Which is why, my dear, I'm asking you to drive us to the bowling establishment, so that we might hopefully locate more clues."

Maggie put her father's car in gear. "All right, all right. As long as you stop calling it a bowling *establishment*. It's a bowling alley, or bowling lane. Got it?"

"And those two terms make sense to you?" Saint Just asked, facing front, as they headed up the street as dusk faded into yet another early winter darkness. "I don't think you Americans really listen to yourselves when you speak. A building can be neither an alley or a lane."

"Well, pardon us," Maggie said, clicking on her left turn signal. "Now tell me what happened with Mom and Dad while I was gone. The way they were looking at each other when we left? It sort of gave me the creeps . . ."

Chapter 27

"He called her *Ally*? Really? And she rubbed his back? Omigod, that's almost creepy."

"You have such a fascination with that word—creep. Creepy. I must say that I was myself at *point-non-plus* for a few moments, but signs of affection between a man and woman do not, to my mind, extend to *creepy*."

"That's only because they're not your parents," Maggie told him as she used the walker to clomp her way laboriously up the two-level handicap ramp that led to the front door of the bowling ally . . . lane . . . *establishment*. "Damn, they couldn't find an easier way to do this? There must be fifty feet of ramp here, and all the sections of cement pavement are at different heights. I can't imagine trying to push a wheelchair over those bumps, going uphill. You know, I have a whole new perspective on what so many people laughingly call 'handicap access.' I say we make the jerks that design these things try to go up and down or in and out on walkers, on crutches, in wheelchairs. Because somebody's doing this all wrong."

"Yes, my dear, point taken, unless you wish for me to procure a soapbox for you to stand on as you continue your tirade," Alex said as he reached over to push the metal plate meant to open the glass doors to the bowling lane.

"See? I can't reach that thing from here, can I? They think I have nine-foot arms? By the time I press the plate, get myself back over to where I can go through the doors, the doors would be closing. Stupid! Yeah, well, I'm going to write somebody a real lollapalooza of a letter when this is over. Now tell me again what we're going to do here, while I tell you that we do none of it until we've sampled their snack bar. I'm thinking pizza."

"Which we will not consume using a knife and fork," Alex informed her as he held open the door for her (the push-plate didn't seem to be working), and she pushed her way into the noise and heat and disinfected-shoes smell of one of the least-favorite haunts of her youth. That was probably because the only bowling trophy she had ever won was as Most Improved Bowler. Which wouldn't have been so bad if she hadn't improved from a score of thirty-one to finally, for one game of the whole season, breaking one hundred and fifty.

Erin was the bowler of the Kelly family. She'd copped more than a dozen trophies, twice as many ribbons, and their father's undivided time two nights a week and Saturdays.

Maggie figured she probably should forgive her sister for that. Forgive, and move on. Yes, definitely she had to write to Erin about what was happening on the home front, that it might even soon be *safe* to come home. Maybe even call her, and not just write to her. *Eeeww*, that thought hurt . . .

"Maggie, did you hear me?"

"Hmm? Oh, right. Not with a knife and fork. I've only been telling you that for months. It tastes better when you just pick it up and shove it in your mouth. Now try it with some french fries rolled up inside. Trust me—pure gourmet. Snack bar's to our right."

"Perhaps we might try the bar, instead," Alex suggested, pointing to a flashing sign that blinked red and blue, not too inventively, The Eleventh Frame. "That's where Henry Novack encountered the members of the Majestics, remember?"

"Drinking beer before they get their practice games in? I don't think so. These are dedicated athletes, or whatever you call bowlers. We'd have a better chance of seeing one of them in the snack bar. Ah, smell that? Thank God garlic can overcome any smell, even that of rented bowling shoes."

They settled in at the counter, all the plastic booth seats already occupied, and Maggie quickly ordered two slices for herself and two more for Alex. And two fountain Cokes. She loved fountain

Cokes, and since the snack bar hadn't seemed to have changed in fifteen years, she hoped the Cokes hadn't, either.

"Maggie Kelly, right?" the woman behind the counter asked as she put down the sodas and pulled a pair of straws from her apron pocket. "Heard about your dad. Cops let him go?"

Maggie smiled weakly at one of the many nemeses of her youth. "Hi, Mrs. McGert. Yeah, they figured out he didn't do it."

"Not the way I heard it. I heard they just didn't have enough to go to trial with, like that, you know? Probably pick him up again in a week or two, that's what my Jerome says. Is he going to show up here? I wouldn't, if I was him."

"Mrs. McGert, Dad's bowled here for as long as I can remember, and I never heard him say one bad word about you. You've worked behind this snack bar for as long as I can remember, and you've been bad-mouthing him to everyone who comes in this place ever since Christmas Eve, haven't you? Sure, you have. But that's okay, because I've learned something these past few days—forgive your past, and move on. So I'm going to forgive you, Mrs. McGert, and move on."

"Uh . . . yeah . . . you do that," the woman said and looked at Alex, shrugged. "She was always a weird kid," she told him and then turned her back to go get their pizza.

At which time Maggie quickly but carefully pulled off the paper at the top of her straw, eased the paper down the straw a good two-thirds of the way (she'd experimented, and two-thirds of the way gave her optimum control), put the exposed end of the straw to her mouth, took careful aim . . . and blew the paper sleeve directly at Mrs. McGert's broad backside.

"I've still got it. Direct hit."

"Hardly a challenge, with apologies to Mrs. McGert's massive posterior. I thought I heard you say you were going to forgive your past and move on."

"Not without a parting shot, I wasn't," Maggie said, prudently losing her smile as Mrs. McGert slid paper plates in front of them. "You know, crazy as this is, what with Dad still not out of the woods, I'm really enjoying myself. Maybe I ought to come home more often? Nah, that'd be pushing it, huh?"

"As you seem to revert to near childhood on such occasions—

and keeping in mind your own admission that you were not an easy child—yes, I would concur. Ah, and here comes my friend of the other day, Mr. Joseph Panelli, and look who is with him, sweetings—the footballing hero himself."

Maggie turned on her stool, her mouth still filled with the pizza she'd yet to bite through entirely. "Barry Butts," she said around the slice, and then bit down hard, the hot tomato sauce quickly burning the roof of her mouth. "Ow-ow-ow," she said, holding her mouth open as she swiveled toward the counter once more. "Coke. Ah need Coke," she said, grabbing her glass and sucking hard on the straw.

"Congratulations, sweetings. I do believe you've caught Mr. Panelli's attention." Alex stood up, extending his hand to the captain of the Majestics. "Joe, m'man, good to see you again!"

"*M'man*?" Maggie muttered. "Cripes, I have to get the man out of Jersey. Fast."

She turned around again in time to see Alex and a redheaded man about her dad's age shaking hands while Barry Butts looked on from a few feet away.

"Maggie? Maggie Kelly?" Barry said in that aw-shucks voice she remembered from high school. At the time, she'd thought he was the modest sports hero. Now she thought he was as fake as a three-dollar bill. "Lisa told me you'd been by to see her. And your friend, too, right?"

Ah. There may have been a little bit of an *edge* to his last statement, Maggie thought as she wiped her hands on a paper napkin and then shook hands with the one-time captain of the football team. The man had a grip like an iron vise. "Yeah, we did. God, it was good to see her. Sorry we missed you, but Lisa said you were at work?"

"Right. Not a lot of call for bikes in the wintertime, but I have to do repairs, stuff like that. You remember my dad's bike rental shop? Bikes, trikes, two- and four-seater surreys? *Put your butt in a Butts*? We do Rollerblades and skateboards now, too, and body boards. But the bikes are still the Number One rental."

"Do I remember? Like anyone could ever forget that fantastic slogan, huh? Still down at the north end of the Boardwalk, right, in the older part of town?" Maggie said, her cheeks starting to hurt because she had to fight to keep the smile on her face. After all, if Alex was right, Barry Butts had recently killed a man. And framed her father for the murder. And might want to kill her father. And was a bastard to her good friend, Lisa.

Well, she could think of Lisa as her good friend if she wanted to, damn it!

"Yeah, still in the same spot. Forty-two years now. Mom's been gone a long while, and Dad died a couple of years back, and it's mine now. The business, the house. I thought about moving away, years ago, after high school. But you know the saying—I'd rather be the big fish in a small pond, *heh-heh*. I have it good here."

In the back of her mind, Maggie was humming that Bruce Springsteen song, *Glory Days*. Barry and Lisa could have done walk-ons in the video . . .

"You and Lisa have it good," Maggie corrected smoothly, pulling herself back to attention. "Your mom? Gosh, I remember your dad, but I don't think I remember your mom."

"Like I said, she left a long time ago," Barry said, a tic beginning to work in his cheek.

Maggie took the words, and the tic, as evidence that she and Alex were on the right track. Barry's mom had run off, so Barry was extrapossessive of Lisa, making sure she didn't do to him what his mother had done to him. Wow. Maggie's parents may have screwed her up some, but Barry had her in that department, hands down.

But he was still a murderer, and would get no sympathy from her.

"Why don't you sit down a while, Barry," she said, patting the stool beside her invitingly just as Mr. Panelli sat down on the stool on the other side of Alex, the two of them still deep in conversation. "You're getting ready for the big New Year's tournament?"

"Yeah. It's going to be a tough one. You know, what with half the team only coming on board this week. Frankie Kelso's a good guy, but I don't know that he can plug the two-hole. I'll be . . . well, I'll be bowling in the four-hole, taking your dad's place."

"It's the most important slot, isn't it?" Maggie asked, only an effort of will keeping her from batting her eyelashes at the man. But she couldn't play that dumb, not when she'd been listening to bowling stories for nearly half her life.

"It can be, if we go down to the wire. If the match is out of reach, then it means nothing, and everybody's already walked away to watch another match. But, to my mind, the two-hole is the big one, if you want to pull away, pull away fast, you know? Lead-off strong, follow in the two-hole strong, and you're already halfway there, you know? But like I said, Frankie's number two."

"Even so, the four, um, *hole*, is a big responsibility. But, then, maybe not for the captain of the football team the year we went to states, huh?"

"The year we *won* states," Barry said, grabbing Maggie's second slice of pizza and shoving half of it into his mouth. "I'm used to pressure. I do my best, under pressure. You should have tried me out, Maggie, back in high school."

"You didn't know who I was, back in high school," Maggie said, this time losing her smile. But she recovered quickly. "You and Lisa and the others—you were the in-crowd. I was the . . . I don't know what I was. Maybe the square peg in the round hole?"

Barry leaned closer to her, to whisper his next words in her ear. "That's the round peg in the round hole, Maggie. You don't know what you missed."

Then, before Maggie could say anything—or slap his stupid, grinning face—Barry got to his feet, smoothed down his shirt, and told Joe Panelli he'd meet him back at the lane. "Gotta hit the head first."

"I'd like to hit the head—*his* head—with something really, really hard," Maggie said, swiveling to grab onto Alex's arm.

Joe Panelli leaned forward and turned his head to look at her. "Like they say your daddy did?"

Suddenly Maggie couldn't wait to get out of the bowling alley, out of Ocean City, out of the past that hadn't changed all that much in the present.

"They dropped the charges against my dad, Mr. Panelli. Didn't Mrs. McGert tell you when she was making her general announcement?"

"I know, I was just joking. Tell your dad to come by later on tonight if he can, okay? I owe him an apology. A big one."

Maggie softened, nodded. "I'll do that, Mr. Panelli. I know my dad would appreciate it. The past few days haven't been easy."

"Tell me about it. No, it hasn't been easy, not for any of us," Joe Panelli said, and Maggie saw his gaze shift to his left, as if he could see Barry Butts walking away from him. "And it's not going to get any easier when I have to tell Barry he's off the team. If your dad wants to come back, that is. But don't say anything, okay? I want to ask him myself, when I apologize."

He then stood up, slapped Alex on the shoulder. "Good seeing you again. And don't forget to come watch a while when you're done eating. Lane twenty-seven. We'll be here until ten or so. Oh, and be careful to be good to Evan's daughter. I hear he's a real killer. Just kidding!" he added quickly, laughing as he headed out of the snack bar.

Maggie and Alex watched him go, watched as another man came up to him and the two stopped to talk.

"You know who that is, Alex? Another trip down Memory Lane, that's who that is, well, minus that beer belly he's carrying around with him now, and the hair he's missing on the top of his head. That's Frankie Kelso. He graduated two or three years ahead of the rest of us—Lisa, Brenda, Joyce, and me. I remember Brenda walking the halls our senior year, though, with his class ring hanging around her neck on a chain—you know, like your quizzing glass? I was *so* jealous."

"If you wish to have my quizzing glass to hang about your neck, sweetings, you have only to ask. You were enamored of Mr. Kelso?"

"No. I was enamored of the way Brenda wore his ring around her neck. She looked so . . . so self-satisfied, I guess. Now Brenda is a housewife—not that there's anything wrong with that—and her Frankie has just become a Majestic. Which means he'll be bowling three, maybe four nights a week until he's too old to lift the ball. Just like my Mom and Dad. History repeating itself."

"I promise never to take up bowling, sweetings," Alex told her as he helped her to her feet, positioned the walker for her.

"No, you wouldn't. *Your* hobby is sticking your nose in where it doesn't belong. Not that I'm sorry, because you've been great so far. But this *Samaritan* thing, Alex? You still want to do that?"

"There are many things I want to do, Maggie," Alex told her as they made their way to the last row of seats directly behind lane twenty-seven. "First and foremost, I want to get this over with and return to the city. I begin to believe I was not fashioned for the hinterlands. Joe Panelli inquired as to whether or not I'd be interested in purchasing two tickets to the pork-and-sauerkraut dinner on New Year's Day at the local firehouse auxiliary building. And I found myself very nearly saying yes. Adding to that, I have no idea what a firehouse might be, let alone its auxiliary. Firehouse, bowling lane—I now have to assume both are buildings, don't I? And just when I had become used to partaking of breakfast in a *house of pancakes*. Sometimes I can say I truly feel Sterling's pain."

Maggie laughed out loud, causing Barry Butts to look their way as he took his ball from the return rack. "As you've probably already guessed, Alex, a firehouse is where they keep the fire trucks, and the auxiliary is the wives of the men who are the volunteer firemen—or, saying it another way, the women who run the socials and pork-and-sauerkraut dinners. And, speaking of sauerkraut, if I remember my history at all correctly, the First George ate sauerkraut or cabbage all the time. Couldn't speak a word of English, he made the Royal residences all stink like boiled cabbage all the time."

"Before my time, I fear," Alex told her quietly.

"Yeah, I know. Your George is still regent, isn't even the fourth George yet, not in our books. But I did a lot of research before deciding which era I wanted to write in, you know? I'm still looking for a way to slip it in that the household of the first George had only a little less than one hundred people living together—and employed only one laundress. I have a friend who sets her books in those times, and she once told me she makes sure her heroine and hero end up going swimming in a clear stream or get caught in the rain at least once a book, because those guys weren't exactly known for their personal hygiene habits."

"And you're digressing for what reason?"

Maggie slumped down on the uncomfortable plastic seat. "I don't know. I guess it's because Dad is going to show up soon, and then you're going to do your thing, and it's probably going to get messy."

"Hi, folks!"

"And speaking of things getting messy . . ." Maggie said,

slumping even lower in her chair. "Hi, Henry. What are you doing here?"

"Same as you, I guess," he said as he carefully juggled a plate of nachos and a vanilla milk shake. "Hey, move down two, will you? One seat doesn't do it for me. Wanna nacho?"

"Thanks, but no. Henry, I thought we discussed this. Your mother isn't overfeeding you now—*you're* overfeeding you."

"Maggie . . ."

"Sorry, Henry," she said, noticing how his smile had slipped away. "So, what have you been doing today, since I saw you, that is?"

"Nothing much. I drove home to see the body shop guy about my go-cart. Gonna cost me a penny or two I don't have. But Gabe, he's my friend, and a real genius, he told me the guy who hit me drives a black car. He could see the transfer—that's what he called it. He said I should have called the police, and I guess I should have, huh? But that's my information for tonight. The guy who hit me drives a black car. How much is that worth to you?"

Maggie sighed. "Considering the fact that every other car out there that isn't silver is black? But I think different car companies use different black paints, so maybe we should look at your paint as extra evidence the cops can use once we turn the killer over to them."

Henry looked at Alex. "The killer? You got him figured out? Naw, no way. Not this fast."

"We have made a few assumptions, Henry," Alex told the man. "We believe it was a crime of jealousy, even of passion."

"But premeditated," Maggie put in quickly. "Because the killer was trying to kill two birds with one bowling ball."

"You're weird," Henry said, popping another nacho into his mouth. "So is he here? The killer, I mean?"

Maggie leaned closer, lowering her voice. "Yeah, he's right up there, sitting on the front bench in that ugly yellow shirt."

"There's three guys sitting there in ugly shirts, Maggie. Which one is he?"

Maggie was about to point to the guy in the middle, Barry Butts, when she felt hands on her shoulders and turned her head to see her father standing behind her. "Hi, Dad. Where's Sterling? You didn't come alone, did you?"

"Sterling's at the snack bar," Evan Kelly told them, his wistful gaze on the Majestics. "And there they are. My team. My friends." He shook his head. "Never take anything for granted, Maggie. It can all be gone in an instant. *Poof.*"

Maggie felt Alex put his hand over hers and she closed her eyes, all the old nervousness back. Alex was here now, but for how long? "I'll . . . I'll try to remember that, Daddy. Oh, look, Mr. Panelli has seen you and he's waving to you. No, wait, don't go, Dad, here he comes."

"Evan, good to see you, buddy," the captain of the Majestics said, extending his hand.

Evan Kelly pulled himself up to his full height, looked straight into Joe Panelli's eyes, then raked his gaze down the man's figure and back up again, blinked, and said, "Excuse me? For a moment, I mistook you for—"

"I've got a big mouth, Evan, and I went off the handle like a jerk. I'm sorry, I'm really, really sorry. We want you back, Evan. The Majestics need you."

"—Someone I once admir—*what*?"

"I said, I'm sorry, Evan. And we want you back."

Alex squeezed Maggie's hand again as she blinked back sudden tears. Bowling with the Majestics might not be her idea of nirvana, but for her dad, being on the team meant everything to him. "Oh, Daddy, isn't that wonderful?"

"Well, yes . . . I suppose it is," Evan said, looking confused. "So who's off, Joe? Barry, right? Frankie was number one on the list, Barry number two. So Barry goes?"

"Easy, Dad . . ." Maggie warned quietly.

"Yes, Evan, now's not the time to worry about such things," Alex said, getting to his feet and reaching out his hand to Maggie's father. "Allow me to congratulate you, sir."

"Thanks, Alex," Evan said. "But I don't think I want to be here, Joe, when you tell Barry. If that's all right with you?"

"Sure, Evan," Joe said, looking over his shoulder to where Barry Butts was now standing on the lane, looking good in his ugly yellow Majestics shirt, staring down the pins at the end of the alley. "This isn't gonna be fun . . . ."

"You don't know the half of it, Joe," Evan said, and this time

Maggie reached up and grabbed his wrist, squeezing it to warn him off. God, she hated confrontations. And yet, Alex seemed to live for them.

Except maybe not tonight.

"Alex? You're being awfully quiet."

"Probably because a fool should keep his mouth shut and allow people to suppose he is a fool, rather than to open that mouth and prove it fact," Alex said, helping her to her feet. "Henry? If you'd step out of the row and hand Maggie her walker, please? We need to speak privately. Oh, and there you are, Sterling, just in the nick of time. Allow Evan to take you back to his house, if you please?"

"Alex, what's wrong?" Maggie asked once Sterling and her father were on their way out of the bowling lanes . . . bowling establishment. God, Alex was ruining her for American English. "And why are you a fool?"

"Can you guys talk louder? I'm missing most of this," Henry said as the three of them stood close to the wall, beneath the sign for The Eleventh Frame.

"In a moment, Henry," Alex said, nodding toward the lanes.

Maggie watched as Joe Panelli spoke to Barry Butts, Barry's face getting redder and redder by the moment.

Joe kept speaking, gesturing, and Barry started to breathe so heavily that Maggie actually could see his chest going up and down from where she stood.

"Can you imagine how Lisa must feel if he looks at her the way he's looking at Mr. Panelli?" she asked Alex, feeling a shiver go down her spine. "I'd be scared spitless. I think I already am, to tell you the truth."

Alex stepped in front of her as Barry Butts shouted a word that would have gotten Maggie's mouth washed out with soap if she'd said it within her mother's hearing. He grabbed his bowling ball, shoved it in his leather bag, picked up his street shoes, and took the steps up to where they were standing two at a time.

"Where is he?" he demanded, his eyes wide and wild. "Where's your murdering father?"

"I suggest, sir, that you step back," Alex said quietly, his hands positioned on his sword cane, ready for action.

"Yeah? And who the hell are you? *Where's your father, Maggie?*"

Maggie put a hand on Alex's arm, wishing he'd move away from her, and pushed her walker forward. "You're through, Barry. We know what you did."

Barry opened his mouth to say something—Maggie didn't think it was to blurt out a confession—and then turned on his heel and stomped toward the exit, still in his bowling shoes.

"He didn't change his shoes," Henry said unnecessarily. "Man, I wouldn't want to meet that guy in a dark alley."

"Or on a deserted beach," Alex said, holding onto Maggie's walker until Barry Butts was no longer visible. "And that's the piece that's missing, isn't it? How Barry Butts lured Walter Bodkin to a deserted beach at midnight, in December. All right, I believe we can go now."

"Go where?" Maggie asked, clomping her walker and wishing it, and her cast, on that deserted beach, no longer necessary. "And why are you a fool?"

"Because we were wrong, sweetings," Alex said as he pushed open the door leading to the steps and the handicap ramp.

"Wrong? Barry didn't kill Bodkin?"

"Oh, no, he killed him," Alex told her. "We don't have much time, if I'm right. Lisa could be in danger."

"Lisa? Not Dad? Why is everybody always in danger? You're getting to be like that robot, Alex. 'Danger! Danger Will Robinson!' Jeez."

"*Lost in Space.* I loved that show. Who's Lisa?" Henry asked from behind them.

Maggie looked at him over her shoulder. "Henry, go home."

"The hell I will. This is starting to be fun. Now, who's Lisa?"

Alex picked up Maggie and carried her down the steps and to the car, Henry still huffing and puffing along behind them, still asking questions.

"That's it, don't tell me. Just leave me here," Henry said as Maggie slid into the driver's seat. "Everybody always leaves me, sooner or later. Yeah, well, you know what? Not this time, folks. I don't know where you're going, but Henry Novack is going there with you."

He headed for his van, parked nearby, nearly at a run.

"Poor Henry. We could have taken him with us," Maggie said

as Alex closed the door on the passenger side and buckled his seat belt.

"He'll follow. We're going to Lisa's, Maggie. And hurry. I was wrong, wrong from the beginning. Barry Butts didn't kill Walter Bodkin or frame your father for Bodkin's murder because he was jealous of the association—real or imagined—with his wife."

"He didn't? Is that what you were being so quiet about earlier? You were thinking? And you ended up thinking you thought wrong?"

"I'll parse those sentences later," Alex said, holding onto the dashboard as Maggie turned onto Wesley. "Think, Maggie. We saw the Majestics tonight, watched them for some length of time."

"Maybe you did. I was just looking around, being bored."

"Honest to a fault. All right, *I* was watching them. Observing them. The Majestics are quite the team, aren't they?"

"You know they are, Alex. Don't drag this out with the obvious. Mae Petersen told Henry, who told me, that you just about have to have someone die to get a place on the team. There's a waiting list and everything, so they say, and—omigod, *Alex!*"

"Exactly. When Bodkin was killed, an opening was created on the Majestics. One Frankie Kelso, first on the list, took Bodkin's place. And, when your father was arrested, shamed, and dismissed from the team, the man second on the list, Barry Butts, took his place."

Maggie stopped at the red light, which gave her time to gawk at Alex. "Don't sit there and try to tell me that Walter Bodkin was killed for his place on a *bowling team.*"

"Think back to watching the team tonight, Maggie. Think back to the moment Henry asked you to point out Barry Butts to him."

The light turned green. "Alex! Just say it, okay? No guessing games. We're only a few blocks from Lisa's house now."

"All right. I suppose I'm still so angry with myself for attempting to find some deep, psychological reason for the murder that I'm embarrassed to realize that greed is the motive in at least half the murders in this or any other country. I really must stop watching *Dr. Phil.*"

"And The Learning Channel," Maggie said, turning onto Second Street. "Now spill it!"

"Joe—Mr. Panelli was sitting on one side of Barry Butts when

286 / *Kasey Michaels*

you were attempting to point him out to Henry. Miss Petersen on his other side. All three of them wearing those atrocious yellow shirts, correct? And what was Mr. Frankie Kelso wearing, hmm?"

"I don't know. Was it green? Yeah, it was green. With a Jets logo on the back. Now tell me what that means."

"It means, Maggie, that Frankie Kelso had no idea he was soon to become a Majestic, and he does not own one of those *ugly* shirts."

"But Barry, who was number two on the waiting list—he already has a shirt. Alex! He already has a shirt, because he knew he was going to kill Walter Bodkin!"

"Except," Alex said as Maggie pulled to the curb two doors down from the Buttses' house, "removing Walter Bodkin would not assure Barry Butts of a place on the team. He needed to be rid of *two* players."

"Dad," Maggie said, cutting the engine. "Don't tell me, I think I've got it. When Dad and Bodkin fought, it lit a lightbulb in Barry's brain. If he killed Bodkin and framed Dad for the murder, then he'd get his spot on the Majestics without having to wait for someone else to grow old and croak on their own." She banged her fist on the steering wheel. "The man killed to get on a bowling team!"

"Ludicrous as it seems, yes, I think we finally have the correct motive. But there's still the matter of just how Barry was able to lure Bodkin onto the beach at midnight on Christmas Eve."

"And that's where Lisa comes in?" Maggie asked, feeling a knot beginning to form in the pit of her stomach. "Oh, please, Alex, please don't tell me Lisa was involved."

"How else would you lure a man like Bodkin to the beach, Maggie? Willingly or unwillingly, I believe Lisa made an assignation with the man. Except, of course, instead of Lisa, it was Barry who made an appearance on the beach. After stealing your father's bowling ball from his bag while he, your father, was not quite having an assignation of his own, but close enough as to make this entire thing a dance of supposed lovers, and send us guessing in all the wrong directions."

"If she did it, she was forced into it, Alex. Lisa is a scared woman. She looked scared when we saw her. And, okay, maybe a little guilty, now that I think back on it, so she probably knew, at least after the fact, that her husband killed Bodkin. And that's also why she was so very sure Daddy wasn't the murderer . . ."

"We'll sort it all out later, Maggie. For now, I want you to stay here while I go pay a visit to the Butts family."

"Because you're worried about Lisa. Barry was pretty mad, wasn't he?"

"Yes. The wheels, as I've heard you say, are coming off his world. He wanted to know where your father is but, lacking Evan as a target, I believe Lisa will be the one to receive the brunt of his anger."

"Then I'm coming with you," Maggie said, unbuckling her own seat belt, just as the front door of the Buttses' house burst open and Barry came running out, heading down the street the short distance to the Boardwalk, and the building containing the Butts Bicycle Rental Shop.

"He's running! We can't let him get away!" Maggie said— shouted in the closed car. "And there's Lisa, standing at the door. Ah, man, look at her, Alex. She's holding a knife! *Good for you, Lisa!*"

But Alex was already gone, trotting after Barry, and Maggie turned the key in the ignition, not willing to be left behind. She wanted to be in on the kill, er, that is, the capture.

One hundred yards later, she slammed on the brakes, threw the gear shift into Park, and stumbled out of the car, already reaching for the backdoor and her walker, one eye on Alex, who was banging on the doors, calling Barry's name, doing both even as he was looking for a way to get inside the bicycle shop.

"Wait for me!" she yelled, hopping toward Alex, reaching him just as one side of the wide double doors flew open and Barry Butts raced by them on one of the rental bikes. Up the ramp he went, onto the Boardwalk, turning south.

"I told you to stay here."

"And I didn't listen," Maggie said, looking inside the bicycle shop. "Quick, Alex, one of those surreys. See that red one? It's a two-seater."

"And what do you propose I do with it?" he asked, even as he pulled the contraption forward.

"Simple. You pedal with both feet, I pedal with one foot, and we catch up to the bastard, take him down. Or do you know how to ride a bike? I never had you ride a bike in any of our books."

"Point taken," Alex said, lifting her onto the seat, and trotting around to climb into the other side. "Show me."

Maggie did a quick tutorial on how to work the pedals, and they were off, climbing the ramp onto the Boardwalk and heading after Barry Butts in the dark.

"How long is this Boardwalk, Maggie?"

"I don't know. Twenty-six, twenty-eight long blocks? But he'll go down one of the ramps and back onto the street at some point, don't you think?"

"Yes, I do. Keep pedaling."

There was no one else on the Boardwalk and the streetlights on the ocean side of the thing were the only illumination. But Barry wasn't that far ahead of them.

"He should be out of sight by now," Maggie said, holding onto Alex's cane as he steered the surrey and they both pedaled for all they were worth.

"He's bleeding, Maggie," Alex told her. "I saw blood on his shirt when he burst past us."

"Lisa! That took guts, didn't it? Or maybe she'd just plain had enough. Pedal faster, Alex!"

"You'll never catch him, you know."

Maggie sliced her eyes to the right, to see Henry Novack and his go-cart riding neck-and-neck with them. "Stop following us, Henry!"

He ignored her. "I can take him, you know. You've never seen me put the pedal to the metal. My pal Gabe souped it up for me. Extra battery power, or something. How much?"

"How much what?" Maggie called out in the cold wind that was slamming at them from the ocean. "How fast can you go, you mean?"

"No, Maggie," Henry shouted back. "How much is it worth to you for me to catch him for you?"

"He's a murderer, Henry. He's already killed one man, and he tried to run you down, remember?"

"I remember. Still not going to do it for free! How much!"

"Five hundred dollars, Henry," Alex said, still pedaling, even though Maggie had sort of forgotten to keep up her end.

"Oh, hell," Maggie said, leaning against the back of the seat. "Go get him, Henry. We'll catch up."

"Right," Henry said, and then surprised Maggie by pulling the sword cane out of her hands. He waved it once, above his head, pointed it out straight in front of him, yelled, "Charge!" and was gone, pulling away from the surrey as if it was standing still.

"Go, Henry, go!" Maggie shouted, leaning forward now, pedaling for all she was worth with her one good foot.

She saw Henry pulling closer to Barry, who seemed to be running out of gas—well, figuratively.

Closer.

Closer.

"Sic him, Henry!"

Closer.

Henry drew abreast of the bike and lowered the cane, sticking it between the spokes of the back wheel of the bicycle.

There was a noise. Not a nice noise. Sort of a *twanging* noise, probably caused by the metal inside the cane colliding with the metal spokes.

"My cane!" Alex shouted, and then added more quietly. "My beautiful cane."

But, as brakes went, you didn't really get much better than sticking a sword through bicycle spokes.

Barry Butts flew over the handlebars, doing a remarkable somersault, and landed, well, on his butt. That way he didn't have too far to fall when he fainted.

Alex slowed and then stopped the surrey and hopped out of it in time to see Henry holding the cane, bent into nearly a ninety degree angle, over Barry, daring him to try to get up.

"Got him!" Henry crowed.

"But my cane . . ."

"Oh, get over it, Alex," Maggie told him as she pulled her cell phone from her pocket and dialed 9-1-1.

"My cane . . ." Alex said again, and Maggie began to giggle. She'd never seen Alex so flustered. "Was that entirely necessary, Henry?"

"Seemed so to me," he said, handing the cane to Alex. "And I did it, didn't I? I'm a hero now. A five-hundred-dollars-richer hero, that is."

"Yes, you are," Alex said dully, still looking at his cherished, bent possession. "But my cane . . ."

Once upon a time . . .

. . . there was a girl named Margaret Kelly, who longed to grow up, leave her New Jersey home, and become a Famous Author in New York.

That all pretty much worked out for her.

But, as Maggie found out, some things go with you wherever you go, even as they are also waiting for you when you get back.

Like, you know, a two-fer?

Or, as Maggie's Irish great-grandmother had been heard to comment from time to time: "Ain't that a pisser?"

Did her perfect hero creation actually favor a quizzing glass because Maggie was once impressed with Frankie Kelso's class ring hanging around her classmate Brenda's neck?

Had she actually patterned the lovable Sterling Balder after her father?

And—returning to her parents' condo to tell them Barry Butts had not only been captured but had confessed, to find her parents getting more than chummy in front of the living room fireplace— would she ever get out of therapy?

Not that Maggie felt much like lingering in Ocean City, attempting to find answers for all these questions.

No, she wanted to get back to the city, longed to get back to the city.

She said her good-byes to Lisa Butts, who was almost giddy now that she could go to the grocery store without her husband as escort, not to mention ecstatic that she'd finally mustered the courage to strike back at the man (the police were terming the shallow but bloody knife wound an act of self-defense and weren't going to prosecute). In fact, Lisa now believed the whole world was opening up to her and her delayed dreams, and was only disappointed that she was now too old to be eligible to audition for *American Idol*.

When the full story had come out, Maggie learned that Barry Butts had been the one who had phoned Walter Bodkin about the free Christmas Eve bowling, and told Bodkin to call the rest of the team members. It had been Barry who had scratched the lock on Evan Kelly's car door before he'd realized that Evan hadn't locked the car at all, and then removed the bowling ball. It had been Barry who had twisted his wife's arm (literally) until she'd phoned Bodkin and asked him to meet her on the beach at midnight.

Barry Butts, who was going to go away for a long, long time, "to be somebody's bitch," as Alicia Kelly kept saying with depressing regularity as well as considerable glee.

And then there was Henry. Henry Novack, the larger-than-life hero (again, literally), interviewed by nearly every media person in New Jersey, and chauffeured to Manhattan for five full minutes of airtime with Holly Spivak.

Now, though, Henry was starving in the fat farm Doctor Bob had recommended to Maggie, at Maggie's expense (but she wasn't adopting the man, damn it, no matter how much Alex teased her). Henry had bought a computer with his "earnings," and now e-mailed Sterling once a day to tell him of his progress. Henry had a goal: To lose two hundred pounds, say good-bye to his go-cart, and set himself up as a private detective.

Maggie worried about that. Mostly she worried that Henry would show up at her new house and Alex would take him on as an associate. Because Alex still felt a tad guilty about his mini-collapse at the sight of his bent sword cane.

There was so much a woman could read into the idea of a supposedly unflappable man coming apart over a bent sword . . .

They were back in Manhattan now, and had just completed their "final walk-through" of the new house, with closing on the property scheduled for the next day.

Maggie had chosen the room she would make her office, the first time she would ever have a dedicated office, and Alex had paced off the footage in what was to become his *Samaritan* head-quarters even as Socks and Jay-Jayne had been locked in discussion as to where to place the pizza ovens on their side of the ground floor.

Yes, the New Year promised to be interesting, at the least. Along with writing her next Saint Just mystery, Maggie had already decided to try her hand at researching the history of her new home. Maybe just to prove J.P. wrong when the lawyer had said that performing more than was necessary in a title search often dragged out skeletons best left buried.

Sterling appeared flustered, anxious about packing up his and Alex's belongings, but Maggie was more relaxed. As she'd told Sterling, packing to go somewhere was hard. You had to figure out what to take. But packing to leave was easy. You just took everything.

So while Sterling was wrapping his favorite pans and worrying that his pet mouse might be traumatized by the move, Maggie was more than comfortable in her bed, Alex as her cushion.

"There's going to be an echo in the house for a while, Alex, until we buy a lot more furniture," she told him, at last pushing herself up against the pillows, so that he could use her as a pillow for a while, as she stroked his thick black hair. "I never thought I'd say so, but that ought to be a lot of fun."

"You've become domestic, sweetings," Alex told her. "It may be the female in you, desiring a nest."

"Yeah, right. I'm living with my own imaginary hero, and I'm looking for a nest? I don't think so. I mean, I try, I really do, but you weren't here one day, Alex, and then the next you were. How can any of us know where you'll be tomorrow?"

"I, Sterling and I, are doing our best to evolve, you'll remember. Become more our own persons, rather than your . . . well, your characters."

"So you can stay. I know, I remember. But what if it doesn't work, Alex? What if I wake up one morning in that big house and you and Sterling are—Alex?"

"Hmm?"

Maggie pushed him off her and reached for the bedside lamp. "No, don't sit up. Stay there," she ordered, and then pulled his

head onto her lap as she ruffled his hair with both hands. "I think
I . . . I really think I—I did! Alex, you have *a gray hair*! I didn't
write you with gray hair! You're . . . you're *evolving*!"

The Viscount Saint Just, ruffled hair and all, sat up, took a shaking Maggie in his arms, breathed against her ear: "Yes, sweetings,
I know. And as you always say, don't you love it when a plan
comes together . . . ?"